THE DEADMAN'S TRIBE  BOOK 1

good ENOUGH

NICOLE CRAIG

To My One, Ron.

Holy hell, horseshoes, and hand grenades!

When I was 30, you said, "Write it!" It took me a while, but I finally wrote it. My apologies for all of the computer keys clacking in the dark in the middle of the night, the muttering at fictional characters when you thought I was talking to you, and for just in general being obsessed with this "project." I hope it's all worthwhile. Here it is, with all of my love.

1

FEBRUARY 8TH

Kai

Kai removed her Ray-Bans as she followed Cherry into the empty conference room.

Who names their child "Cherry"? Hope it's a nickname. Must be with that red hair.

"Please, have a seat, Ms. Serrano. Can I get you something to drink? Coffee? Water? Something else?"

Kai sat in the chair closest to the head of the table and removed her Dodgers cap, placing it atop her overloaded backpack on the chair next to her. "No, thank you."

The red-haired woman smiled. "If you change your mind, just let Waters know." She laid an accordion file at the seat across from Kai and pulled the starfish-shaped speaker from the center of the table down to between Kai and the opposite seat. "Sorry to keep you waiting. It should only be a moment."

As Cherry reassured her, Kai heard the door open and close, and a figure appeared in her peripheral vision. She looked up, and her breath stopped for just a second. Scalp-cropped, dark blond hair, muscles that filled a tight navy blue Henley with sleeves pushed just above his wrists, and tan cargo pants with more pockets than any man could ever need.

Holy hell, horseshoes, and hand grenades! G.I. Joe in the flesh.

Realizing she was probably looking like a deer caught in the headlights, she exhaled. Standing up to greet him, she extended her hand across the conference table, trying to smile like a normal human being.

Hazel eyes! A corona of green around the pupil, the flames spread out into blue irises. Eyes so laser-focused, they appeared to pierce her in place. She froze again when their hands connected across the table as Cherry made introductions. "Ms. Serrano, this is Waters. He will be your liaison today."

Silence. It wasn't so much a handshake as a melding of energy. Neither of them dropped the other's hand.

A gentle throat clearing from Cherry seemed to wake them both from the trance. Their hands dropped to their sides.

He found his voice first. "Ma'am." His expression was blank, but he gave her a nod. The only show of emotion was that his irises appeared to flare.

She mentally shook herself and cleared her throat. "Mr. Waters."

"Just Waters, ma'am."

"The men use nicknames here," Cherry explained. There was a pregnant pause. "Well, I'll leave you to it. I'll patch God in shortly." The last part was directed to Waters, and she looked as if she was trying to hold back a grin. She exited.

They remained standing for another moment, just staring over the table. Kai shifted her weight from one foot to the other. Waters seemed to reset himself and gestured for her to sit. He had barely pulled himself up to the table when Cherry's voice came through the starfish. "God online."

"Ms. Serrano." A strong, raspy voice came over the speaker. He might as well have been in the room, the quality was so crystalline.

"God? Seriously?" she whispered to Waters. He just looked back at her stone-faced. "Well, I must admit I do feel a bit as if I'm talking to a nonphysical entity. But this room's a bit large for a confessional."

The voice over the speaker gave a "hmph," and she heard the crinkle of what sounded like a candy wrapper being ripped open. "Let's get to business, shall we?" he began.

Okay, no nonsense. Got it.

"Certainly. Do you want paper copies of my proposal or digital ones?" she asked.

"Both," God answered. "We'll do digital now, and you can leave the paper with us to discuss."

Anticipating her, Waters reached into one of his cargo pockets and handed her what looked like a small USB stick.

Kai raised an eyebrow.

"It will connect you to our Wi-Fi. All it does is project your material on the screen, like if you were presenting through a Zoom call," he reassured her.

Riiiiiiight. Apparently, I have the word "naive" stamped across my forehead.

She gave a muffled, unladylike snort. "I so believe that to be true."

Kai hauled her backpack up onto the conference table with a loud thunk, pulled her laptop out of the bag, opened it, plugged in the stick, and proceeded to pull up her files.

As she was rustling through her backpack for the proposal document, she looked up to see Waters staring at her bag. Handing him the flexi-binder with the treatment, she glanced at it again, trying to view it as he probably did. "Yeah. I call it the 'Backpack of Death.' If it doesn't break my back, it will take out someone or something else." Shrugging with a lack of concern, she focused back on her screen, clicked on the folder labeled *Stormfront,* and proceeded to open several files so that she could flip from tab to tab as needed.

Waters used a remote to pull up her desktop on the large telescreen behind the head of the table.

"*Stormfront.* Is that the name of the film?" God asked. His speech lost a little of its clarity as he worked around something in his mouth.

"It's a working title. We never save files on computers or refer to films by the actual title to protect it from paparazzi."

"In other words, the film has its own alias," God surmised.

Kai shrugged, then remembered he couldn't see her.

At least, I don't think he can. Perhaps there are cameras?

She surveyed the room, and when he spoke, she swore she could hear a smirk in his voice. "Yes, I can see you, Ms. Serrano."

"Okay, that's not at all creepy," she muttered under her breath.

"So, tell me what my company can do for you," God pushed.

She glanced up at Waters, but his face was blank as he intently watched her.

If he's this gorgeous while on automaton mode, a smile would probably be licensed to kill.

She turned her face back to her computer screen. "I'm looking for a Navy SEAL consultant for a film I'm directing. I had someone lined up, Kent 'Ka-Bar' Leech, but apparently, he will unexpectedly be in the field longer than planned. He suggested Tribe as a place to find a suitable replacement."

There was silence from the man over the speaker and G.I. Joe across from her. She noticed the latter was staring at a point just over her shoulder, but as soon as he caught her glance, he refocused on her.

God prompted, "And you know I have SEALs working for me because..."

"Kent wouldn't waste my time suggesting I contact you if you couldn't help me. Is there a problem here?" she asked.

"We don't do movie consults," Waters replied.

"So I gathered from Kent, but he said it was worth trying since I'm now in a bind time-wise."

She heard crunching over the speaker as God pulverized whatever he had in his mouth.

"Why do you need a *consultant?*" he asked. The last word sounded like it was in air quotes.

Gathering herself, Kai put back on her director persona. "*Stormfront* is an action film depicting a team of Navy SEALs who are sent on a mission into Central America to rescue an ambassador and his daughter from a hostage situation in El Salvador. Cliché, I know, but that's why I need assistance. I need someone with actual SEAL training skills and knowledge so that I can turn this testosterone-heavy, error-filled writing into award-winning entertainment."

"You have issues with testosterone?" God barked.

"If I were filming some sort of black leather, homoerotic, motorcycle mafia feature, no," she snarked back.

"SEAL missions are highly classified," Waters injected. "As are the means by which they do their jobs."

She nodded. "Being a SEAL himself, Kent was going to help me with what we could and could not have, while still making the story ring true by helping us work around something the Navy wouldn't want shown to the world. I won't settle for 'mostly true.'" She interlaced her fingers in front of her and leaned on the tabletop with her forearms. "Now I'm forced to find an alternative since he's on assignment."

"Trying to avoid the critics' scathing reviews on accuracy?" She could hear the sneer in God's voice.

Motherfucker is baiting me! Okay. I'll play, asshat.

Narrowing her eyes and scrunching her nose, she glared at the starfish. "What I care about, Mr. I-Named-Myself-After-A-Deity, is actual SEALs and other Navy servicewomen and men complaining about yet another Hollywood director trying to make a fuck-ton of money by using romanticized, inaccurate portrayals of who they are and what they do. What I don't give a flying fuck about is what the critics say."

Silence on the other end of the speaker stretched for several moments. She tried to focus on the starfish rather than looking up at Waters, but despite her better judgment, she felt drawn to whatever his reaction would be to her little tirade. She risked a look up at the man. He still had no expression on his face as he stared her down.

Fuck a duck! Hope I'm not drooling. So intense!

The disembodied voice interrupted her thoughts. "Exactly what are your expectations of this consultant if we agree to take on this task? And it's a big 'if.'"

This is starting to feel like an interrogation.

Her naughty brain poked at her with an evil laugh.

Let G.I. Joe interrogate me. Slap the cuffs on. I'll tell him anything he wants to know.

But then the naughty brain was given a bitch-slap by her nice brain.

It's such a funsucker sometimes.

"Why did you agree to see me if you wouldn't consider taking the job? I didn't make my intentions a secret when I called for the appointment."

"You are here, Ms. Serrano, because Kent Leech called in a favor from one of my men." The disembodied voice, which had been cold with her before, was now at frostbite level. "He used that favor to ask me to listen to your request, and that's all I guaranteed I would do. So, I ask you again, Ms. Hollywood-Princess-Think-I'm-Stanley-Kubrick-Director, what do you expect of us if we agree to take on this task?"

Her eyebrow arched at the fact that she'd managed to provoke him.

Hollywood Princess? What a fucktool!

Calmly, she replied, "First, I want training for the actors. Obviously, it would be impossible to put the actors through actual SEAL training. I'm into realism, but I'm also practical and know that type of training is overkill. But as much as possible, I require my actors to film on location and do their own stunts. This is far more expensive, but again, it means more realism. I prefer to spend my budget on hiring someone to train the actors to do the actual work rather than stressing out about CG-ing a bunch of ones and zeros into submission. Not only is computer work a pain in the ass, but it also slows down the editing process.

"Second, I want a consultant on-site overseeing the execution of training, adjusting, or retraining as needed.

"Third, I want that consultant to shape my actors into a synchronized team, or at least as close as possible."

She flipped her screen to a series of location shots depicting sets that were rendered and scouted for the film. "As part of this plan, the entire film is being shot on Roatán, one of the Bay Islands of Honduras. Inside Coxen Hole, its largest city, we've secured living space for the various crews and rented several warehouses for storage and the building of interior sets. However, the actors will be living in a house we've rented about ten miles outside the city limits. I want the actors to actually live together in that house, eat together, and bond just like a SEAL team would, without external interference from crew or locals, and all outside contact is restricted as well until filming is complete, just like it would be on a mission."

Again, there was silence, and it was even longer than before. Kai focused on the starfish; expression unflinching as she waited for God to respond. However, it was Waters' low voice that broke the silence. "What you're asking for is a rather tall order, Ms. Serrano, and to be honest, impractical. SEAL teams train for over a year, and even some of the very best end up ringing the bell. Besides that, the type of bonding and cohesiveness you're looking to create in a simulated environment takes a very long time to develop in reality."

Kai focused on the quiet soldier now, unable to avoid it since he'd finally chosen to speak.

Ohmygod. He needs to talk more often. Every time he speaks, his voice reminds me of hot fudge sliding down vanilla ice cream.

She tried telling her libido to shut up, but she didn't think it would listen.

Keep your tongue in your mouth and your butt in the chair. Otherwise, next thing you know, you'll be crawling over this table and licking him like he's the spoon with the last dregs of a sundae on it.

Rather than argue with his attempt to convince her that what she wanted was unreasonable, Kai clicked open six dossiers evenly spread across the screen that showed pictures of the five men and the actress who would play the leading roles, along with a brief synopsis of each character's configuration within the film. She then yanked six different colored folders out of her backpack and tossed them across the table to Waters.

Another long stretch of silence ensued as Waters picked up the folders and leafed through each of them for a minute or two apiece. After finishing the brief overview, he placed the folders in a neat, completely symmetrical pile on the table, then turned to look at the telescreen. One elbow rested on the table, his hand propping up the side of his face as he assessed, again with no expression on his face. She briefly wondered what it would be like to be under that scrutiny in private.

Baby Jesus on a skateboard, this guy is way too intense.

Kai refocused on her computer screen, afraid that if she watched him think in silence any longer, she'd cave and beg him to speak to her. Hell, he could read the serial numbers from computer equipment for all she cared. And to add to that nonsense, she was feeling herself salivate as she stared at his muscles underneath the shirt sleeve on the arm propping up his head.

What the hell is wrong with me? Men do not affect me like this.

Minutes later, Waters swung his body back around and opened the flexi-binder she'd given him, scanning several of the pages. Finally, he closed the folder and raised his blank face to Kai. "There are issues here without even reading the script, starting with its calling for an incorrect number of elements. Platoons are sixteen in number, or two squads of eight, or four elements of four."

"One of those men plays the villain, but his character is a former teammate, so he also needs the training."

"There are no female SEALs."

"Well, that is technically incorrect. One has qualified, and three more are currently training. So while there might not be one on a team at this time, it would not be inaccurate to portray a woman as a SEAL. However, that's a moot point because the female isn't a SEAL. She's a CIA operative. Is there going to be an actual question in here somewhere?"

He continued on, expressionless, as if he hadn't heard her responses to his concerns. "You also have some duties mislabeled and divided out."

Seriously? Oh, it's on like Donkey Kong now.

She stared at him. "Look, G.I. Joe." He blinked slowly, raising his eyebrows and lowering his chin. "I'm very aware of what my strengths and my faults are. I'm not stupid. I didn't write the script. If I had, I would have been talking to someone months ago, and all the proper research would have been done right the first time around. Instead, I was smart enough to realize that there was fabulous potential but a shit-ton of errors, and some pretty huge ones at that. It would be irresponsible of me to assume I know it all because I've done some basic internet searches. And while I know I'm damn good at what I do, I'm also aware enough to understand that allowing my ego to drive me would be a mistake. I refuse to be a detriment to the project, or worse, endanger my actors and crew. I need it done right, or I'm not doing it at all. So... here I am, searching for a consultant. An expert to fix the bullshit before we start filming."

2

———————

FEBRUARY 8TH

Waters

THE WOMAN'S EYES WERE SPARKLING, AND HER breathing was elevated after her little tirade. Waters felt like he was back in underwater training, his lungs being crushed and burnt at the same time, as he watched her chest rise and fall, her eyes crackling with irritation. Of all of Tribe Corporations' members, he was the one most collected with clients, so why was he changing his operating style with her?

Damn, she's saucy. If it were just the two of us right now, I would throw her down on this table and—

"What do you think, Waters?" God asked.

He looked at the starfish.

What do I think about what?

He blinked. Then he tried to jumpstart his brain and remember what they'd been talking about because he

12

certainly knew it wasn't about his unwanted, inappropriate thoughts regarding Kai Serrano. Ever since he'd stood across the conference table from her, he'd been willing his face into a state of expressionlessness, his body to be casual, and his dick to stand down. Also things that were unusual for him. Those shiny pink lips and that Monroe beauty mark had him riveted. He wondered if it was real or a Hollywood affectation. He wanted to touch it and find out.

Sweet Christ, what is the matter with me?

Or the long blonde ponytail he wanted to wrap around his fist—

Luckily, at that moment, he remembered that he was being asked if her request was realistic. "I suppose it's possible." He shrugged, unconvinced. "But I need more information. I don't know much about the actors, just recognize a couple of the names." He raised his gaze to Kai. "This would be extremely rough on them. Are they aware, at least somewhat, of what you'll be asking of them?"

She nodded then shifted her focus back to the actor profiles; a light pink tinge crept up her neck and face.

I bet that blush spreads over the rest of her.

She cleared her throat. "Except for our female star, all have extensive action film resumes, and all are in supreme athletic condition. Even though Sookie is new to the business, she used to be a gymnast so she understands demanding training."

God spoke up. "We need to see a script before making a final decision."

"Not a problem."

"Waters will be doing the initial assessment. How long, Waters?"

He shrugged again. "Three days."

"Will that work for you, Ms. Serrano?"

Waters watched her slide a phone out of the front pocket of her backpack and click through to a calendar app. "As long as I know by the eleventh, I'm good. I have a meeting with the producers on the fourteenth and would need to give them confirmation then."

Waters spoke up. "It's going to be a minimum of four weeks of nothing but preparation and training. Six would be better."

"Filming begins April first," Kai said, still sliding through her schedule. "All of the actors are scheduled to arrive for training on February sixteenth if we can obtain your services." She opened an email and attached the folder for *Stormfront* to it. "What email should I send the files to?"

Waters gave her his direct business account; she entered it and clicked *Send*. A muffled phone ping came from his back pocket, and he checked the screen to make sure the file came through and that it opened for him.

"Got it."

Kai pulled another flexi-binder out of her backpack, this one considerably thicker, and pushed it across the table to Waters, then began to close up her computer and stuff it back into her backpack amongst what looked like haphazard pieces of paper. Once everything was inside, she donned her ball cap. As she hauled the bag over her shoulder and stood, it swung wide, hitting her back with a thud, causing her to jerk from the pressure.

That bag is bigger than her. She's not wrong when she says it's going to hurt somebody.

"Thank you for your time." She reached to shake Waters' hand, nodded at the starfish, and headed toward the door.

Silently and quickly, Waters was there to open it for

her. She snapped her head to look at him, not hearing him come up right next to her. Her eyes were wide and startled, her nostrils flaring just slightly, and a clear pulse point pounded in her neck.

She smelled like lilacs.

Do. Not. Inhale.

Instead, he decided to get in one more tiny prod. "SEAL training, ma'am," he offered quietly in explanation. "Situational awareness is sometimes the difference between living and dying. Always know what's around you."

Her eyes narrowed in challenge. Slowly, she turned so that she faced him eye to eye without wavering. "Camera one is in the upper right-hand corner of the framed Jackson Pollack on the left-hand wall, which I admired when I first came in here. Camera two is the fake lock on the cabinet behind where I sat, where I saw you looking over my shoulder earlier. Camera three is on the center bar of the telescreen so that it looks like a power button. When something is on, it's a blue or green light; when it's off, it's blank, so the red light was a dead giveaway. Camera four is in the digital clock face, hiding as a third dot in the colon between numbers. Colons have two dots, not three. Camera five is the USB stick you had me use to hack into my system. Yeah, plug something foreign into my laptop, and it's *not* going to look at anything else on my computer. Please. And camera six"—she flicked the lowest button on his Henley—"is in this button right here. The one that's set too closely compared to the others."

She returned her cool gaze to Waters' focused stare. "I think my situational awareness is in a good place. Good day, gentlemen." She turned without a backward glance, exiting toward Cherry's desk.

Waters moved out into the hallway and watched her

walk away, the long tails of her belted, oversized blouse covering what was probably a wicked ass to go with the athletic legs in the sexiest boots to ever clack down the hallway away from him.

What. The. Fuck! How the hell...?! She... This is gonna be—

He shook his head. Well, he didn't know what this was going to be. What he did know was that it wouldn't be his problem, which, from his dick's perspective, was a shame, but from his brain's perspective, it was a relief. He was back on full duty in three weeks, so there was no reason to put him on a job that would be anywhere from twelve to fourteen weeks.

Deep in thought, he reentered the conference room, closing the door behind him. Crossing over to the wall of windows, he reached up with his left arm, laying his palm flat against the glass to stretch out the kink that was developing in his shoulder from holding himself so rigidly. He watched her exit the building.

"Did I really hear her call you 'G.I. Joe'?"

Waters rolled his eyes. "Shut the fuck up."

There was a pause before God said, "You tried to check out her ass in the hallway, didn't you? You've always been an ass man."

Quit baiting me, motherfucker. I'm not gonna fall for it.

"Well, if you're not interested"—God hummed to himself—"Nemo would probably love a chance at that. On the plus side, he's a movie buff—"

"Double shut the fuck up," Waters murmured.

He hung his head, forehead against the glass.

Annnnd you got baited, dumbass.

God started laughing uproariously at his snipe. "Think you can handle her?"

"Not interested."

Liar.

After a moment, Waters turned and looked at the camera in the telescreen bar with a frown of suspicion. "Why would you be worried about me being able to handle her?"

"She needs a consultant. Tag—you're it."

Oh, no, I do not want that drama or the distraction.

"We don't do movie consults. Why the fuck did you even meet with her?"

"Ka-Bar called in Steel's marker."

"I don't care if he called in every favor ever owed to him by anyone. That's not my issue."

"Then what is your issue, Waters?" God growled.

"The issue is I shouldn't have to do this grunt work that any former SEAL could do. I should have my medical clearance in three weeks. I'm needed back in the field."

Was that whining? That sounded like whining.

"Quit your whining." Waters winced. "This will make for a nice, easy transition back into fieldwork. Physical without being under pressure."

There was crinkling in the background as God spoke. Waters shook his head. One of those damn caramel apple suckers. Those things were shit, but God had a two-bag-a-day habit. Cherry ordered them by the thousands.

"You think I can't take the pressure?"

"No, I said this would be a transition without it."

"Forget it. Send Nemo," Waters grumbled at the disembodied voice. But for some reason, it burned him to think it, let alone say it, and he absentmindedly rubbed his chest.

"Even if I wanted to, I couldn't. He's still in Cuba with Steel collecting that baseball player and won't be back before this job starts. Even if he were here, he would be available for full field duty in the case of an emergency. You are not."

"You're seriously going to assign me to babysit her and her celebrity minions?"

God's slightly altered speech came out again as he worked around the sticky candy. "Look at it this way. You get to be outside of this damn office, running roughshod over a half-dozen A-listers who probably don't know their left from their right. Work 'em hard, make 'em cry like little girls, and enjoy it, for fuck's sake. Even better, get laid by the sassy director." Waters rolled his eyes at the suggestion. "Hey. You're like Betty White without a Snickers when you aren't getting any."

"What the fuck are you talking about?"

"Are you kidding? You've been as celibate as a monk ever since we brought you back from Egypt two years ago and just as cranky, despite all the pretty nurses offering you some extra physical therapy." Waters shrugged, but he remained quiet. God changed tactics. "Besides, watching you eye-fuck Kai Serrano is the best entertainment I've had in months."

Waters sighed in exasperation. "I was not eye-fucking her." God barked out a single-syllable laugh. "I wasn't. You're just making shit up to try and get in my head."

"And it's working, isn't it?"

Waters just shook his head as if to say *whatever you think,* then clicked the zoom button on the remote and watched Kai on the public parking lot security camera footage as she sat in her car checking her phone. He perched his ass on the edge of the conference room table, one booted foot crossed over the other, his arms crossed in front of his chest, one thumb and forefinger pulling on his bottom lip.

Okay, I was totally eye-fucking her. But so what? He's right that it's been a while. Is it the boots? Because I gotta admit, I really dig the boots.

What intrigued him about Kai Serrano was a weird set of juxtapositions that he could not resolve. Approachable, but prickly. Confident, but defensive. Take charge, but willing to concede. She was a puzzle, and he couldn't resist solving puzzles.

He frowned and tilted his head to the side. Without warning, the corner pieces of a brain jigsaw puzzle laid in place. He straightened his arms and gripped the edge of the conference table. "While convenient, this has nothing to do with a movie consult."

God snorted. "And the man wins a prize. My shit meter was just outside the danger zone before she even walked in the door."

There was crunching as he pulverized the sucker in his mouth and immediate crinkling as he unwrapped the next sucker while speaking. Immediately unwrapping more of the disgustingly plastic suckers was Waters' clue that his boss was unhappy. And nothing made God more unhappy than not knowing exactly what the hell someone was plotting.

How sad is it that I know his state of mind from his candy-eating habits?

"Did Ka-Bar call in the marker to you or to Steel?"

"Midas forwarded me a video clip Ka-Bar emailed to Steel around thirty-six hours ago, requesting that we take on the job she asked me for. Said to charge her for the work, but he wanted to make sure she had the best." He snorted. "He's asking us to 'be the best' consulting service on a movie in exchange for a marker he earned? Not fucking likely. And the request comes in as a recording, with no opportunity to ask questions? Why couldn't he call and talk to someone directly? Hell, no, he clearly didn't have time to wait for the office to open, so something else is going on here. Now my shit meter is reading beyond the danger zone."

A sucker stick pinged into the garbage can on the other end of the connection. "What do you know about Ka-Bar?" God asked.

"He was Steel's friend while in Team 5, so he'd be the better one to ask. My knowledge is by reputation only."

"Well, I can't ask Steel now, can I? So tell me what you do know."

Waters sighed.

Now we've reached 'Jerky with a chance of scattered irritation' status.

"The scuttlebutt goes that some shit went down in South America, and suddenly both Steel and Ka-Bar were exfil targets with Ka-Bar shot so full of holes he could have been a sponge."

"They shouldn't have been anywhere near South America. That's Team 4."

"Exactly. But there they were, claiming they were on leave and got caught in the crossfire of some cartel shootout. However, there were no records of liberty requests for either man. Ka-Bar recovered, was reprimanded, and then was reassigned to Team 8. Steel vanished off the face of the fucking planet until I found his ass crawling out of a sewer drain from a Black Site in Nicaragua. Now Ka-Bar shows up calling in a marker from Steel. I'd bet you my left testicle that the South America incident is why Steel owes Ka-Bar."

"Somehow or other, Ka-Bar wants our eyes on this woman because he can't do it himself."

"That would be my assumption as well."

The telescreen changed over to a series of emails layered one on top of the other. "You should also know that while you were eye-fucking our client"—Waters ignored God's jab and started sorting through the emails by sliding them around the screen with his fingers, placing them into a linear line by date, oldest to most recent— "Our golden-fingered hacker back-channeled his way into her work emails and followed a very interesting thread with her executive producer. It was because no matter the cost, a portion of the budget would be allocated to a rather large consulting fee. They've been fighting over it for several weeks, among other issues. Asshole is verbally, emotionally, and psychologically abusive, and he's holding the funding hostage. And trust me when I say that what's going on here in these emails is not even close to a civil argument. I can't imagine what it's like in person."

Waters switched his focus to the CCTV footage and watched Kai's Corvette finally pull out of the parking lot. "So whatever it is that's going on, you think Ka-Bar's asking us to watch over her."

"I'll see your left testicle and raise you my right testicle on that one. Question is, watch over her from what? His communication was very short and left a whole lot unsaid."

"Maybe the producer's the threat? Maybe Ka-Bar's worried she's in danger due to the animosity between them and thinks the guy will harm her? He sounds like a real douchebag." Waters leaned in closer to read one of the emails in front of him. "I stand corrected. Guy sounds like a real 'assclown.' I'm stealing that one."

"Shit, our Kubrick wannabe swears like a sailor, and creatively to boot. I curse nonstop, and I've never heard of half the things she's called him. There's another email where she calls him a 'jizzmop.' Kinda makes my dick hard just how unfiltered and unafraid she is."

"Keep your 'kinda' hard dick in your pants," Waters warned.

"Warning me off, are we?" God made a tsking noise. "Umm, yeah, 'not interested,' my ass." He grunted. "But to return to the problem at hand, would he really be concerned about protecting her from a movie producer whom she could expose to the world with a #MeToo tweet? Fuck, no. She seems like a woman who can handle her shit just fine. She'd probably be more likely to kick him in the balls, leave him rolling on the ground for someone else to find, and call the EMTs to take him to the hospital."

"So you're thinking she just works for an asshole, and Ka-Bar feels she needs protection from something else. Since he can't come home now to help her, he's asking us to step in." Waters considered that angle. "Or possibly he's not coming home and hiding because something he's doing is bringing danger to her door, so he's calling us to step in." Both seemed far-fetched to him, but then stranger things had happened. "What's her connection to Ka-Bar?" This was probably the most puzzling question of them all. The two individuals couldn't be farther apart—Future Hollywood Powerhouse Director and Military Golden Boy working special operations.

His woman, maybe? Lucky bastard.

The ping of yet another dead sucker stick hit the garbage can rim and bounced to the bottom. Another wrapper began to be peeled off another sucker. "No fucking clue. King Midas didn't find anything on the first go around. He's working on a deeper dossier dive on both of them. He should have something by this time tomorrow.

"In the meantime, take that script, go through it, and make the corrections she needs. Do it tonight. Get it to Cherry first thing in the morning and tell her to put together the contract for triple the pay of what she's offering. Need to make it look good, at least. According to the emails, they easily have that amount in her budget proposal. Even though she'll think she's hiring us, we're doing this as a favor to Ka-Bar.

"Once the paperwork is complete, call our director girl, Kubrick, and set up another meeting. Let's get her under our surveillance right away. I don't care what you have to do or how you do it, but we need eyes on her fast. This is a priority for you. You stay with Kubrick twenty-four seven. And while you're working with her, you can keep an eye on this slimeball producer, but I'm telling you, something about this Ka-Bar connection is making my gut roll."

"Stop eating all that sugar, then."

God laughed. "Watch it, dickhead. Between her snark and whatever smolder is going on between you two—and yes, I saw her reactions to you, too—I think our Kubrick is going to be a handful. Despite my overloading shit meter, I think I'm really going to enjoy watching you try to handle her."

There was a distinct click and silence.

Assclown. The name works for him, too.

Waters pulled up a still from the CCTV in the parking lot on the telescreen. He zoomed in on a shot from when she was getting out of her car to come into the office and locked it in place. His pointer finger traced down the right side of her face, which was turned to check for traffic before crossing the lot to the door.

I can handle her.

He straightened his shoulders, giving himself a mental

shake. Nope. No handling. Per the rules, she was off-limits. Sex? Yes. More than that? No. He wasn't allowed to attach himself to someone, making that person vulnerable. And even if he were allowed to do so, he wouldn't because he couldn't take on any more guilt.

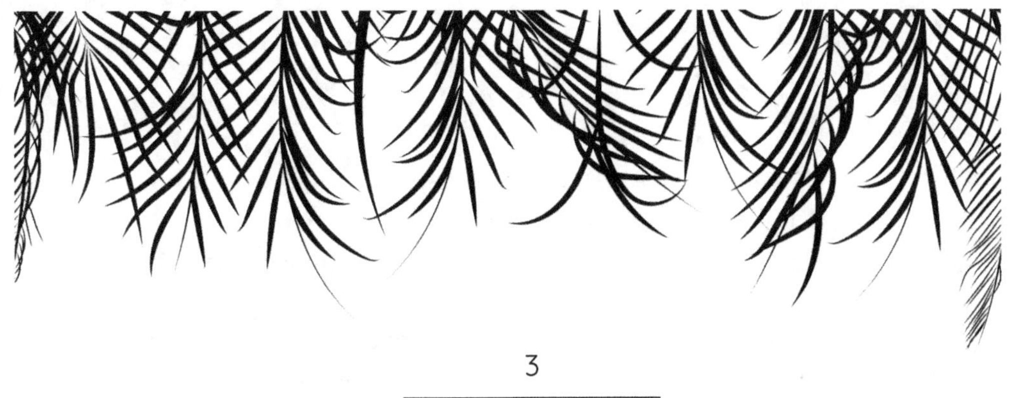

3

FEBRUARY 9TH

Kai

THE DEFAULT RINGTONE BLARED, AND KAI STARTLED. She frowned. *Unknown caller.* Shaking her head and mumbling about Russian bots, she focused back on her laptop, clicking through the renderings of the obstacle course she was designing for daily workouts on the set. Eventually, the phone stopped ringing.

As she scratched a note to her six-page list, the phone began ringing the default tone again. The frown turned to a scowl. Insistent bastards. She ignored it.

A few seconds after it stopped, it began again. She hit the *Block Caller* button.

No luck. The same number popped up on her screen within thirty seconds of blocking them. Now, she was pissed off. She threw her pen down, swiped the answer icon, and hit the speaker button.

25

"Whomever the fuck this is, I am not selling you my timeshare, voting for your candidate, or sending ransom for some random woman screaming you're threatening to chop off her hand."

Silence. Then, after a beat, a voice came over the line. "I don't need a timeshare, the elections aren't for another year and a half, and I'm not Russian. I also promise not to chop anything off anybody." After a split second, he amended, "At least, not today. Although it is still early in the day, so I guess I shouldn't make that promise."

"Shit." Kai shivered and cleared her throat. "My apologies, Waters. The number was listed as unknown, and I don't answer numbers I don't know. I assumed you were a telemarketer."

There was another brief pause. "Do telemarketers often threaten to chop off appendages if you don't purchase what they're selling? Because if they do, I need to look at what lists you're on."

She snorted, but she also wasn't quite sure if he was making a joke or not. "Well, I doubt this is a phone call to ask me on a date, so what can I do for you?" As soon as she finished speaking, she hung her head with a wince.

Shit.

There was yet another pause before he replied, "Did you want it to be?"

"Well, it has been a while." Kai smacked herself on the forehead.

Way to double down, dumbass!

"I'm sorry to hear you're short of plus ones. Now I need to know what lists you're not on."

"Yeah, yeah, yeah. Blah, blah, blah. Yet here I am, still dateless."

Stop! Stop talking! You're making it worse! Filter that shit!

"Hmm. You know they have apps for that, right?"

"Ick." She shuddered. "I'm pretty sure each and every one of those people is a serial killer or in training to be a serial killer."

"I have no experience there to judge."

"Pfft. Of course not. Looking like you do, I highly doubt you need a dating app. Women probably have an app that finds you." As soon as she said it, she slapped a hand over her mouth.

Well, open mouth, insert foot up to the knee cap. Time to just lock the trailer door, crawl under the covers, and never come out, even if California falls off the rest of the country and into the ocean. What is the fucking matter with me?

There was extended silence on the other end of the phone this time. She couldn't even hear breathing. Eventually, he asked, "What would they call it?"

"Wh-what?" Her heart was pounding, the blood rushing to her face.

"The app. What would they call it?"

All she could do was sputter random letter sounds.

"I'm guessing it would have the G.I. Joe logo for its avatar."

She groaned and cleared her throat. "Shit. I have severe filter issues."

"You can't have filter issues if you have no filter."

"Truth. My mouth runs constantly and nearly always inappropriately. I'm just going to blame it on the fact that I didn't expect to hear back from you so soon, which makes me worried your boss is saying 'no,' which means I'm fucked, so now my self-destruct mechanism is attempting to take control of my universe."

"Can't have that now, can we?"

Confused and again unfiltered, Kai asked, "Which one? Can't have me fucked, or can't have my self-destruct mechanism taking over my universe?" She lowered her head until her forehead was on the tabletop, softly banging against the surface three times. "Never mind. I'm running away from home. Please pretend I didn't ask that question."

She swore she heard a smile in his voice, but it could have been her imagination. "The first one sounds like a tragedy. The second one sounds like one hell of a superhero movie. Can't wait to hear what your character name would be. So"—he switched topics—"let me guess. Yesterday, what we saw was the 'irritated' filter imploding. This must be the 'nervous' filter imploding."

Kai winced. "I didn't fuck myself, did I?"

"Relax," he reassured her. "God was amused by it, actually. And I doubt you could offend me."

"Give me time," she mumbled.

"Mmm." Another short dead space came over the phone before he cleared his throat. "I'm calling to let you know that God has given the go-ahead as long as the modifications we're suggesting are implemented. I was going to forward you the file, but"—there was a slight pause—"he suggested that we meet so that you could ask questions in real time."

Well, he sounds less than excited about that.

Kai looked at her watch. "When did you have in mind?"

"My schedule is open. We could meet at the office whenever you're free."

She sighed, rubbing her forehead. "Much as I could use a break from the studio right now, I have a meeting with the executive producer in thirty minutes. Depending on how dickish he's being today, that meeting could be between thirty minutes and six days." She mumbled, "Shithead," under her breath. "After that, there will be people traipsing in and out of my trailer for the rest of the day. I really can't get away. Could you come to the lot around three o'clock?"

Another pause followed. "I can do that. Where do I report to?"

She snorted. "I'm guessing you know where the studios are, although thank you for the courtesy of letting me think that you're not looking at a computer screen right now with a red dot pinging my exact location. Or even better, have some satellite training its eagle eye on me and reading my heat signature."

"Mmm," was all he said.

Her eyes widened, and she pulled the phone from her ear to look at the screen. "Oh my God. I was joking, but you're pinging me, aren't you?"

He said nothing.

"Shit." She put the phone back up to her ear, huddling in on herself. "You're seriously not using an actual fucking satellite. Are you?" she whisper-squeaked.

She heard a click on the other side of the phone, like he'd tapped a keyboard. When he spoke, his voice sounded to her as if it had dropped slightly in octave. "You're looking awfully red, Serrano. But I'm betting shades of red look good on you." He clicked off before she could even say goodbye.

Oh. Fuck. Me.

Three hours later, Kai was striding from the front offices back to her trailer at Studio Lot 4, mumbling about pencil-pushing, pencil-jockey, pencil-dick, money-grubbers when her cell phone rang. This time, the ringtone was dogs barking. She stopped in her tracks, dead center in the middle of the roadway, nearly getting taken out by a golf cart as she took a deep breath and swiped the answer icon. "Hello, Gerald. Sorry! My visitor is here, isn't he?"

"Good afternoon, Ms. Serrano. There's a man here who says his name is Waters. Just calling ya to confirm he's expected."

Kai smiled. "Yes, Gerald, I can vouch for him. I'll come to collect my guest."

"Thank you, ma'am."

She could feel her body heating up and resisted the urge to duck into the nearest ladies' room to check her appearance. Not normally a vain woman, somehow Waters seemed to bring out some sort of primitive female insecurity within her that worried if she was presentable. She gave an unnecessary tug to her blue chambray tunic so that it smoothed out under her wide-waisted western-style belt, then snorted at her behavior.

Who cares if I'm presentable? He's here to set up a job. I'll probably never see him after today. Which, while disappointing from my libido's perspective, is probably for the best from a timing perspective.

Resigning herself to a smidgen of disappointment, she neared the west gate. He was standing in the middle of the driveway just outside the center bars in the open sun. Immediately, the disappointment teetered on the edge of despair.

Can't we play with him just a little bit? He's so yummy.
Nope. No, we can't. Work to do.

The gates pulled open, revealing him without obstruction. His arms were crossed over his chest, his legs spread shoulder-width apart. Wearing a tight dark-red T-shirt, another pair of tan cargos, and hiker-style boots, he screamed former military even without the uniform. Mirrored aviators covered his eyes, but the same as yesterday, his expression was blank. Despite that, his presence was not going unnoticed. It was safe to say that every pretty young thing's head—both female and several male— swiveled in his direction, and curiosity was rampant.

However, Kai did allow herself a dose of possessive glee. He was here to see her. While it might be strictly business, no one else necessarily knew that. And her insides could riot away with all the erotic fantasies it wanted as long as she kept it cool on the outside.

Kai grabbed a visitor's badge out of the guard shack and then walked toward Waters, who also took several steps in her direction. They met face-to-face, staring at each other for a few moments. She saw herself mirrored in his glasses as she handed over the badge, which he promptly clipped to his belt loop. "Red looks good on you as well."

"Mmm." His expression didn't change.

Attempting to gloss over the uncomfortable attempt at a joke, she offered an abrupt, non sequitur apology with a shy grin. "Sorry about our overprotective guard dog. I was planning to tell them about the visitor coming, and then the executive producer was screaming about my 'exorbitant spending habits.' Next thing I knew, the dogs were barking, and you were here. Gerald treats his gate as if it were Area 51."

"Dogs barking?"

She laughed sheepishly. "Ringtone on my phone."

"Ah." He nodded in understanding. "Dogs. Guards. Got it."

Despite the heat, he appeared unaffected by standing out in the sun. Not a drop of sweat broke his brow. "This way." She gestured and began walking toward her trailer.

Out of the corner of her eye, she noticed slight turns of his head as he took in all the chaos. Golf carts whizzed by with harassed-looking drivers, even more harassed assistants, and actors or suits busy on their cell phones.

Ah, the joy of self-importance. The I'm-too-busy-and-important-to-walk-anywhere with the proletariats.

She saw his jaw tick, as if he wanted to smile but was trying to hold it back. She stopped. "What?"

He shrugged. Then it hit her.

"I said that out loud, didn't I?"

He nodded.

With a sigh, she started walking again. "Told you I have filter issues."

"Filters are overrated," he said with another shrug.

"I agree. Just time-suckers. I try to filter my mouth because otherwise, I run the risk of 'offending' the snowflakes whose egos pass out the money and grace the big screen. I can smooth ruffled feathers and even complete angry bird moltings, but the past couple of weeks have been difficult, so my filter is for shit. In fact, I think it's successfully one hundred percent nonexistent after the last three hours of my life that I'm not getting back."

"I take it you were unsuccessful at unruffling Stapleton's feathers."

She turned her head to frown at him. "How did you know his name?"

His eyes stayed focused on scanning the surroundings. "Research. Never go into a situation without knowing the players. You mentioned a meeting with an executive producer, and that meeting's length would depend on temper tantrums. Your paperwork lists Craig Stapleton as the executive producer, ergo, you unruffled Stapleton's feathers."

"Mmm," she murmured his signature response. "And how did you know his feathers were in a bundle?"

"Isn't that a mixed metaphor? Wouldn't that be *ruffled feathers* or *undies in a bundle*?"

She waved her hand in front of her face. "He was between 'ruffled' and 'molting,' so it was an alternative. And I doubt the man wears underwear. It would mean he can't get his dick out fast enough to measure it or stick it in someone's mouth."

It was at least three steps before she realized he was no longer next to her. Turning back to face him, she saw that his jaw was clenched, and there was just a hint of pink coloring in his cheeks.

"He didn't try that with you, did he?" His voice sounded near strangled.

She chuckled. "I don't exactly have a dick to measure against."

"Don't get cute with me."

"You mean I wasn't cute before?" she mocked.

Nice one, dipshit. He's going to think I'm flirting with him. Am I? Feels a bit like flirting.

He made a guttural nonverbal noise.

She blinked. "Did you just growl at me?"

"Stop trying to redirect. It won't work with me. No woman should have to put up with that crap from any man. So I'm asking again. Did he try that with you?"

Her grin had a touch of you-got-me in it. "No, he hasn't done that to me, so ease down, G.I. Joe, or you'll burst a blood vessel. He tried early on to romance me, if that's what he wanted to call it, but I shut that down very quickly. But I appreciate your concern."

She turned and began walking again. She wasn't positive, but she thought she heard Waters mumble, "He better not try it, or I'll cut it off and shove it in his own mouth."

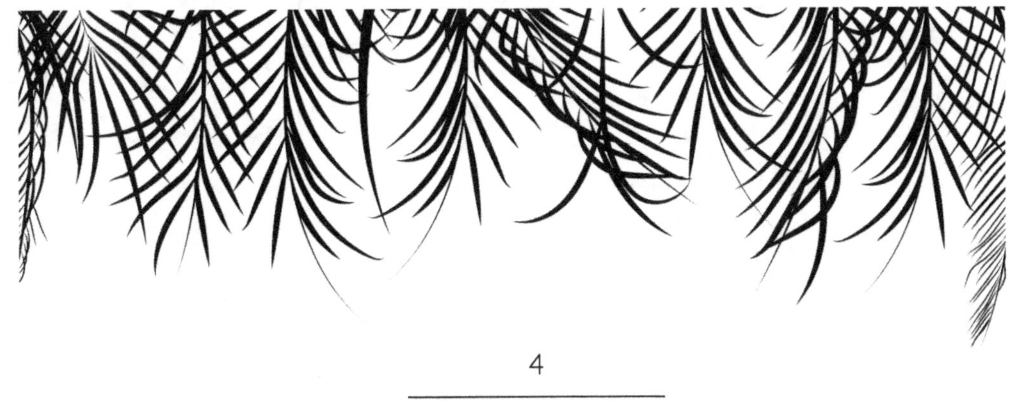

4

———————

FEBRUARY 9TH

Waters

OVER THE NEXT TWO HOURS, WATERS FOLLOWED Kubrick, God's nickname for her, around the studio lot. She was stopped at least once at every location they visited. He watched how each person interacted with her and how those who passed by reacted to her. Nothing was outwardly out of place, but his skin was crawling.

Something isn't right.

Finally, they arrived at Kubrick's office, a trailer on a side street between sound stages and visible to the inner parking lot. She handed him a bottle of water from her refrigerator. Cracking her own open and downing half of it, she slid into the round booth-like table littered with papers, pens, highlighters, notepads, photos, blueprints, and renderings. She began unpacking her backpack of death. It was clear that she used the table as her desk. She motioned for Waters to have a seat across from her.

35

"So, what do you think?" she asked.

"I think you need a bigger workspace," he commented as he sat.

Blushing, she stood as best she could between the bench seat and the table edge and started to pick up piles of items, attempting to put them into some semblance of a neat stack. "Sorry."

He reached over and placed his hands on top of the pile she was trying to pick up and held them down. Their eyes met.

Her skin is burning me.

He drew back his hands. "No need to be sorry. Everyone works differently. I'm just used to clear space, in and out boxes, and folders," he replied. She sat down, brushing her hair back, trying to tame it into her signature ponytail. She was embarrassed, and that hadn't been his intent.

She smiled, looking up at him through her eyelashes. "Yeah, I'm a bit obsessive about having everything on paper. And it looks like a bomb went off, I know, but I can lay my hands on anything at any moment."

"Nothing wrong with it. You should see our conference room table when planning a job. Tablets are popular, but I still love paper planning." He sat. "As for OPT, I always have contingencies for contingencies."

"OPT?" she asked.

"Obsessive Planning Tendencies. I do nothing without extensive plotting and planning."

She bit her lip as if she were wondering if she should say something more, then clearly decided against it by sitting up straight and looking at him directly. "What I meant," she said, getting back to her original question, "was what do you think about what you saw on the walkabout?

"I saw a lot of things, so you'll need to be a little more specific."

She shrugged. "I don't know." A soft sigh came through her lips, and she began rolling a pencil back and forth on the table, focusing all her attention on it. "Between that and the mess of a script I handed you, it seemed like the perfect setup for an opening salvo. I figured I would meet that head-on."

He studied her suddenly downtrodden expression. He was puzzled. "You're expecting me to take shots at you?"

This woman is an emotional whirlwind. Keeping up with her is definitely going to require me to pay extra attention.

"Well, yes, to be honest." Her eyes turned to the window that was to her left. As she peered through the slats of the half-closed blinds, he heard a wistfulness in her voice that he'd not heard from her before. Like she was resigned. "It's been a theme for today. I'm never very high on my producer's list, never good enough for his expectations. I'm unclear as to why he hired me if he hates me so much. But today, he was being extra dickish. It's getting tiresome fighting him for each and every budget line item. Next thing I know, I'll be forced to count every single paperclip I use." She snorted. "It took everything in me today not to beat him to death with a stapler. Ironic since the man is such a tool himself."

He tilted his head a little as he studied her.

Curious. Another juxtaposition. Confident in her abilities but vulnerable when under the microscope.

"No love lost between the two of you."

A sardonic bark of laughter came forward from her.

"That bad, huh?"

She shrugged, then blew air out of her lips and up

toward her forehead while turning her gaze back to the pencil in her fingertips. "You're a former Navy SEAL. If I paid you extra, could you tie him up to a chair with some zip ties, put a black hood over his head, and leave him in a deserted shack until May sometime?"

He quirked an eyebrow at her.

"I guess that means helping me with doing away with him and hiding the body is definitely off the table."

Both eyebrows raised this time.

"Well, fuck. There goes doing this the easy way."

This woman was ridiculous in an amazing way. "I realize you're not serious with those questions, but are you always so open with what you want?"

"Pretty much. I find that playing games takes too long and too much effort. Most women seem to excel at that kind of thing. I've never been able to master that particular XX chromosome characteristic."

Thank fuck for that.

She looked up at him through her eyelashes again to gauge his reactions, but he knew his face would be blank. There was a slight grimace on her face as she continued. "I have patience problems, I guess. But, honestly, being direct gets me where I want to be faster, and there are fewer communication disasters. It's something I'm known for around here," she admitted.

"Noted—accuracy, no bullshit, and no filter."

She nodded. "For the most part, it gets me results. But there are always those who don't appreciate my tactics."

"Stapleton."

"Stapleton," she confirmed with a head tilt to the left.

"Is he a problem for you? Other than the obvious."

Laughing lightly, Kubrick shook her head. "The last few

weeks, he's been King of the Assnozzles. No idea what's crawled up his butt further than usual."

"Is he like that with everyone, or just you?"

"Oh, it's everyone. But I've been keeping watch over my crew, especially the women, so that any problems are dealt with immediately."

"What about you directly?"

"When I first took this job, he was annoying, like a mosquito. Handsy. Smarmy." She held up her hand when she noticed his jaw clench. "I told you, I took care of that bullshit real quick. Unfortunately, since he's the lead moneyman, all that jacked-up behavior often goes with the job. I kept putting him in his place, and he eventually stopped. Now, I just have the desire to throat-punch him on a nearly constant basis. But, if this film is a success, I won't need people like him anymore. I plan to finance my own projects with my residuals from this one." Her face lit up with excitement and anticipation at her last comment.

Confidence returns. That's hot.

"An action movie about Navy SEALs will be that much in demand?"

"If done right, I think this could be the biggest action film of the year. I have a friend who writes historical paranormal romance novels. She says that contemporary protector romances, especially those featuring former military men, are the hottest thing in the book market these days, so I'm going to capture a corner of the market that action films haven't taken full advantage of. Definitely better than any comic book draw starring an Australian-accented male playing a Norwegian god," she grumbled. The look in her eyes went fierce. "I even hired some of Hollywood's allegedly most handsome eye candy and highest box office draws, so maybe it will even be the highest box office take of all time." She grinned sheepishly. "Cocky, huh?"

Challenges herself but is self-aware. Double damn, why does she have to be all the things I love in a woman?

"My co-workers would call it 'determined.' I can certainly respect that. It's probably part of why God agreed to do this."

"Because I was a bitch to him?" she asked incredulously.

"No. You were firm. You knew what you wanted, and you had a clear vision. You didn't come in wanting us to solve all the problems, just the ones we're the experts at. And you obviously care. You clearly want to do this right. He can see honesty a mile away, even if he's not in the room."

And you've got some potentially serious shit going on that you don't even know about.

"I expect everyone's best, and in return, they know they get mine."

"So I noticed."

Frowning, she asked, "What do you mean?"

He leaned forward, his forearms on the table with hands clasped. He watched her hungry eyes travel from the string bracelet on his tanned wrist, up his muscled arm, to his face.

Yeah, guess God is right. She's not immune to me.

"I watched how you handled people all afternoon. You do it so well, they never know they're being handled. You pay attention to them, you look them in the eye, you know personal things about them, and ask about their lives. Hell, you even knew that the two-days-on-the-job makeup girl's dog had surgery and asked how it was doing. You do those kinds of things, and later, I bet that when you ask these people to do things you want or need, they break down doors to make them happen. They probably work twice as hard as they want to, or intend to, just to earn your praise."

She bristled. "It's not my intention to incur favors or make people feel like they owe me something. I try to treat people with respect and reward them for good work. Help people when they need it."

"I don't think of it as being manipulative." He tried to correct her misunderstanding. "They genuinely like you and work harder because you see them. They're not just paid employees. You include them."

"Hmmm. You saw all of that from two hours around the lot?"

It was his turn to shrug. "It's what I do." She tilted her head with a look of disbelief on her face. He raised his hands in mock surrender. "I may have also spent some time on the internet last night researching you."

"Former Navy SEAL, burgeoning psychologist, and internet stalker. Killer combination. Tell me, do you sleep?"

"Come again?"

"If only," she muttered, not realizing she was speaking aloud.

Comments like that may make our time working together either super awkward or very interesting.

"You just got this script late yesterday, so you've reviewed the script, made notes, discussed with God, analyzed, and researched me all in a very short time. I'm wondering how that all gets done if you sleep."

No way in hell am I going to tell her that Midas did the bulk of the research as soon as Ka-Bar called in his favor.

"Again. It's what I do, Kubrick."

"Kubrick?"

His mouth quirked up at the corner. It wasn't a smile,

but it wasn't a non-smile either. "It's what God nicknamed you." He shrugged. "You're stuck with it, I'm afraid."

"Ugh. Great. I don't suppose you could call me Kai? Or at least just Serrano?"

"Nope." He popped the p when he said it. "Once you've been named, it stays. Military regulations."

"What bullshit. That is not written in any military manual. And even if it was, I'm not military."

"However, I was, and at Tribe, we use nicknames for safety when on a job. You hired us. Our rules trump yours. Besides, if you want an in-sync team, using their character names, not real names, will help create that effect on set. They'll start to become those people instead of being themselves."

Kubrick began grumbling to herself. Somewhere in the quiet ranting and raving, he heard "assclown," which he hoped was directed at God and not him. Then he heard "G.I. Joe," which truth be told, he was starting not to hate as long as she was the one saying it.

Waters took pity on her and changed the subject to safer topics. "I suggest we start by going over what your proposed schedule is. Then we can start going over the largest alterations I'm suggesting and work our way through to the smallest."

"We? You're going to be directly involved with this?"

"God assigned me to your job, yes. Problem?"

He watched her swallow. "N-no. I just thought you were the middleman, so to speak. Isn't it a bit below your pay grade?"

"I'm on medical leave. I won't be cleared for a few more weeks. So, I'm your man."

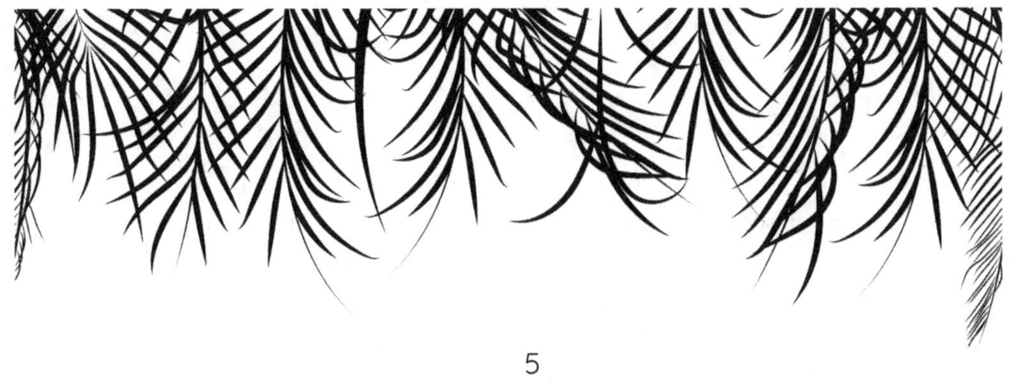

5

———————

FEBRUARY 9TH

Kai

"So, I'm your man."

There had been a pregnant pause after he said that.

How do I read that? Does he mean it to be a double entendre? It sounded like a double entendre.

To cover how the comment had thrown her, she began to dig through the haphazard piles she'd started when he sat down. The problem was, now she no longer knew where anything was. Organized chaos was her modus operandi. The fumbling probably wasn't helping make her look professional.

Or is that because he's watching you as intensely as a sniper watches a target?

After a few false starts and some quick paperwork solitaire, everything was relatively back where it had been, and she was clicking along on all cylinders. He explained how he set up his notes in the script, letting her know that he trusted her to read them rather than be patronizing and go through them one by one. While reviewing some of her ideas, he offered suggestions when they were asked for, asked intelligent questions for clarification, and never once interrupted her. Instead, he waited until she finished a thought, making sure that she was done speaking.

It was not the Hollywood way. Everyone here was always in a hurry; their way was the only way, and everything was a power play. Initially, she found herself outside her tornado mode, ending her sentences with question marks. When he didn't show signs of correcting her, she eventually dropped the questioning and paused when she normally wouldn't, again waiting for him to correct her, scoff at her ideas, or something. But he never did. And it didn't take long before she became comfortable with working alongside him to where she was steamrolling through at her normal pace of a thousand miles an hour.

His response? He had cleared a small space, dug one of her legal pads out of her chaos, swept up a Disney villainess pen, and began making notes. He should have looked ridiculous. He didn't. He looked focused. Contemplative.

Hot.

Like Kai, he was a lister. She internally laughed at the symmetry of a SEAL using bullet points. His printing was precise, block, capital letters. If he made a mistake, he used a clear, single strike-through line. His work on the page was much like him: solid, strong. However, unlike him, it was readable.

When the hell did he swing around next to me in the booth? I distinctly remember at one point turning things in his direction and looking at everything upside down.

She'd been so focused that the change in their proximity hadn't even registered.

While they were working, people were constantly knocking on her door: signatures needed for the casting director to restructure a contract, renderings needed for the costume designer to correct decorations on the Navy uniforms, and approvals needed for various expenditures. Whenever someone came in, he sat quietly. Patiently. She could feel him watching and knew he was listening closely. He never spoke to those who entered other than to return the greetings and partings, handshakes on both ends.

The sun had gone down before Kai realized how much time had passed. Currently, they were looking over elements of the obstacle course she wanted to build, and Waters was making sketches on his notepad, annotating for the construction crew what would be needed for the various elements. Suddenly, her door whipped open. No polite knock. Not even a cursory knock. The door slammed behind the man entering.

She knew it was Stapleton, but she refused to look up and acknowledge his rude entry, which she knew would make him crazy. Interestingly enough, Waters also ignored him and kept writing while she was talking to him, and she had a sneaking suspicion he was more than aware of everything about the new presence in the room.

"Serrano, who the hell is this?" She continued speaking to Waters, looking at him, then at the screen where she was pointing with her stylus. "Serrano!"

Fuck a duck, here we go.

Kai finished her sentence to Waters before looking up. "Craig. I didn't hear you knock." The jab was light, but she knew he recognized it. Waters was now looking directly at Stapleton. His face was neutral, but she was certain that he was running an assessment of the situation similar to when the Terminator came through to modern-day Earth. "What can I do for you?"

"I asked, who the hell is this?" He jerked his head in Waters' direction.

Stapleton was Hollywood handsome with black hair, blue eyes, a wide smile, and tan skin. When he smiled for the cameras and people he met for the first time, he gave the impression of confident, successful, and friendly. Once you got to know him? The hair screamed dye job, the blue eyes were clearly colored contact enhanced, the tan sprayed on, and his pearly white teeth often conjured images of a shark just before it tore into its prey. Always dressed to the nines and always an ass.

"This? This is Waters, from Tribe. They've agreed to do the consulting for the film. I reminded you about them this morning."

Stapleton glared at Waters, not offering a hand in greeting. "I didn't approve that expenditure yet. His being here is a little premature, don't you think?"

"His presence is an approved portion of the budget."

"Well, I don't have a contract with details, nor do I have the appropriate work releases, NDAs, and employment forms on file, and until I do, he's not getting paid."

"He's not an employee, Craig. He's a consultant. His firm pays him out of their fee, which I know you remember. As for NDAs, he's a former Navy SEAL, so I'm guessing he knows how to keep a secret."

Stapleton grunted. "I still think this is an unnecessary expense."

She bristled at the pronoun relegating Waters to a thing rather than a person. "He," she emphasized, "has already clarified several huge mistakes in the script that would stand out to anyone with experience in military service, so yes, we do need him. We discussed all of this, for what feels like the ten millionth time, at our meeting this morning, so I refuse to discuss it any further. Now, was there something new you wanted, or can we get back to work?"

A muscle tic in Stapleton's cheek showed the level of anger he was holding back. "Invoices," he ground out.

"What?" Kai was confused.

"Invoices. For your purchases. I want to look at the invoices."

"Why?"

"Because, as you recall from this morning's meeting, I have concerns regarding your spending. Therefore, as executive director, it's my prerogative to view them. I am in charge of the money, after all."

She rolled her eyes. "You get a copy of every invoice as soon as it arrives. Why would you need mine?"

"Just give them to me, Serrano."

"Oh, for fuck's sake, keep your pantyhose on." Kai slid out of her seat and went toward the back of the trailer. "It's going to be a minute. Waters, don't poke him. I doubt he's had his rabies shots."

When she returned a few minutes later with a file box, Stapleton stood as tall and imposing as he could, arms folded over his chest as he stared down his nose at Waters. Waters was sitting just as she'd left him, staring back at Stapleton with no expression whatsoever. Neither seemed aware of her presence, but she would bet her next residuals check that Waters was more than aware. She slammed the box down on the table, but neither man flinched, their eyes still locked on each other. Kai rolled her own in disgust and sat back down.

"All my copies are in that box, organized by budget item

line and then by date. Try not to fuck up my system, please, so that I don't have to waste my time refiling everything."

"That's what an assistant is for," Stapleton growled.

"No," she muttered back, "an assistant is to assist with duties that need assistance. I don't need an assistant to file pieces of paper I'm perfectly capable of filing. Now. Are we done?"

Stapleton's eyes cut to hers, and his molars were grinding again. "For now."

"Well, Waters and I have a lot of work to do, so I'll see you at our meeting on Monday at one o'clock." And with that, she turned her attention back to her computer screen, picking up her conversation with Waters right where she left off. Waters held Stapleton's gaze for just a moment before devoting what appeared to be his full attention back to her. When it became clear that the pair would completely ignore his presence, Stapleton muttered an expletive and stormed back out of the trailer.

With the banging of the door, Kai looked up and was going to apologize to Waters, but he put a finger to his lips, giving a minuscule shake of his head. He then pointed at the obstacle course drawings and made a circular motion with his hand. Instantly, she understood his message. Stapleton may have blown out of the trailer like a hurricane, but he was likely standing just outside that same door, hoping to overhear their discussion. She took his cue and kept rattling about the obstacle course wall.

Waters slid around and out of the opposite end of the booth, and he silently stepped to the hinged side of the door, flattening himself along the wall and sneaking a look out the porthole. "He's gone."

Just as silently as he'd left, Waters came back to the table, but instead of returning to the inside seat next to her, he motioned Kai to slide inside and perched on the outside edge of the bench, effectively boxing her in. Kai stopped speaking and grabbed her water bottle, finishing it in several swallows. Her heart beat a bit faster. In this position, his hip, thigh, knee, calf, and foot were just barely touching hers, making her blood run like lava. When they'd been immersed in working, she'd been able to suppress her physical attraction to him. Now, it was like her insides were doing the red alert Klaxon.

"What's going on? Why are you in protector mode?" she hissed.

He looked at her quizzically.

"You've put yourself between me and the door." She shook her head. "I highly doubt Stapleton knows how to hurt someone unless it's by cutting off their funding. And dick he may be, but he's got no reason to physically come at me." Her eyes narrowed again. "What's going on, Waters?"

"Nothing."

She snorted. "I'm not dumb. And I don't need protection from the shitweasel."

"It's ingrained. I always put myself between a target and a threat. He may not be a physical threat to you, but he definitely has you as a target." His tone softened in explanation. "I don't like his method of approaching you. You should lock your door so he can't come barging in whenever he wants."

"While I appreciate the alpha male concern as much as the next female, if I lock that door, no one will be able to get in, and I will get zilch accomplished. Do you understand just how many people need access to me on a daily basis? Easily over a hundred, sometimes more. There's no way appointments can be made for that, and you can't be with me every second of the day."

"I will if I have to be."

All the time? Did that mean all workday or twenty-four hours a day, seven days a week?

She could tell he didn't like that her practical explanation was accurate, but he did concede a bit. "If the circumstances don't fit my recommendations, then we change the circumstances. Your trailer is off limits to that douchebag."

"You can't be serious?" Stunned, she looked at his completely stone-cold expression. "You are serious."

Waters put his left arm around the back of the booth seat behind her and his right forearm on the tabletop, basically hemming her in. "As a terrorist attack."

Kai threw her hands up, and they fell on the tabletop. "Waters, what the fuck? He's an executive producer. I haven't met one who isn't a dick yet, so it must be a requirement in the job description. He'll never agree to that."

"He either works under those parameters, or he doesn't see you."

"You act like he's going to barricade the door and demand my virtue in payment for letting me do my job."

"He doesn't exactly seem like the type that wouldn't."

"Well, I hate to inform you, Sir Galahad, but my virtue was officially handed over a long time ago. And not to some fucknut that thinks his cock controls every woman's world."

"Glad to hear it."

She shifted arguments. "Look"—she smiled, shaking her head—"it's really sweet that you want to defend my honor, or... whatever the hell you want to call this," she admitted with a wave of her hand, "but I've been handling him for weeks now. He doesn't scare me, and he can't hurt me. Other than running my mouth, I haven't done anything even remotely close to being fired for, which is the only power he has over me. And doing that hurts him more than it does me."

"And I repeat, I don't care. This way or no consult."

What the hell is going on?

"This is a bit over-the-top for consulting on Navy SEAL procedures."

His pupils flared minutely, the green flames surrounding them seeming to spike in the blue of his irises. Had she not been paying extremely close attention, she might have missed it.

He's thinking about what to say.

"The hairs on the back of my neck are standing up. Like someone is watching. They have been since we met at the gate."

She laughed. "Waters, this is Hollywood. Someone is always watching." While she was speaking, she had placed a hand on his forearm that rested on the table, and she felt a zap followed by a sting of sharp heat from her fingertips throughout her entire body. Kai sucked in a breath and retracted her hand immediately, barely repressing the need to put her burnt fingers in her mouth to soothe the burn.

Wow! What the hell was that? An electric shock?

Both of them froze. Time might have stood still for a few moments, but she wasn't positive she was even breathing right now. It was as if she had sucked in all the oxygen in the room on her gasp and then held it, fearful if she let it out, she'd never get air again.

Is it possible for someone's heart to stop beating due to static electricity?

When she regained her power of speech, she stuttered, "I'm s-sorry. I shouldn't have touched you." She rubbed the affected fingers. "That was inappropriate of me."

His eyes went to where she had touched him.

"Must be dry here from the heat. Hopefully, the zap I got didn't zap you too hard in return," she offered up in feeble explanation.

Way to go, Serrano. Electrocute the guy the first day on the job.

Then she noticed his pulse in his neck and saw his chest deflate just a fraction with a controlled exhale.

Finally, he spoke. "No," he said quietly. "You didn't zap me too hard."

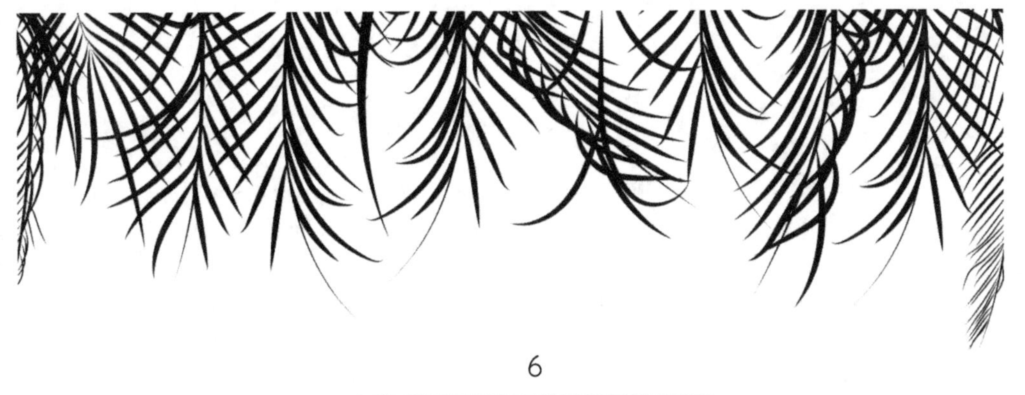

6

———————

FEBRUARY 9TH-10TH

Waters

WHAT. THE. ACTUAL. FUCK?

"Zap" didn't even begin to cover what he'd just felt. Waters had been tasered as part of his training. He'd been given electrical charges as part of his torture during his captivity.

That was a fucking lightning strike.

While technically his brain understood it was static electricity, the primal portion of his brain felt the jolt as an earth-shattering bolt. Yet, the aftershock was a pleasant hum throughout his bloodstream, warm and pulsing, traveling at quicksilver speed. The points of contact from her hand still felt heated. By the expression on her face, Kubrick was experiencing the same thing.

He watched her try to put her focus back on the computer screen, trying to pretend whatever just happened hadn't happened. But the truth was, it had happened, and

53

clearly, they were not going to get any more work done tonight because of it. He needed to leave... but it was also the last thing he wanted to do. Physically, he wanted to gather her into his lap, strip her down just enough, and fuck her until she couldn't speak. However, he needed to get the hell out of Dodge before she upset his equilibrium any further.

Becoming attached to her makes her vulnerable, and I've already made that mistake once. I cannot afford this distraction. I really can't make a play for her, no matter how much I'd like to. Now I'm so fucked up, I'm too paranoid to even think seriously about having sex with someone.

But if he didn't use sex to stay, coming up with another reason would be more challenging. And he for damn sure didn't want to leave her alone without anyone watching over her. God said to stick to her, but how was he supposed to do that? Once Steel and the others returned from their projects, it would be easier to watch from afar. With just him? Not so much. At one time, it wouldn't have fazed him to sleep with her just to be able to watch over her. But not anymore.

Yeah. It would be just because I need to watch her.

"It's late." He slid out of the booth seat and stood at the table edge. "I'll be back in the morning, and we can review what we went over today. I'll also bring you a signed copy of the contract for Big Bird."

She smiled up at him, a genuine uptilt of her mouth at his obvious nickname for Stapleton. "Thanks. I'll be here tomorrow around eight. Keep your badge. I'll let the guard shack know to expect you so you can come and go as needed."

He walked to the door, opened it, and stepped outside.

He turned back to look at her, one hand on the door jamb, the other on the door handle. "Kubrick."

"Yeah?"

"Come here."

Her eyes went wide, and she sat frozen. He let go of the door handle and crooked his finger at her. Mesmerized, she slid out of the booth and walked trance-like the few steps to the door. He looked down at her. "Lock the door after me."

She swallowed. Nodded. A flicker of disappointment, perhaps? He stepped back and shut the door, waiting to hear the click of the lock. Then he jogged down the steps.

I'm definitely going with disappointed.

THREE HOURS LATER, HE WAS STILL CAMPED OUT IN the shadows of the nearest soundstage across from her trailer. Luckily there was a twelve-foot-tall crate and several smaller ones sitting outside the huge bay door to hide him. He could blend into shadows without shelter, but this certainly made it easier. The lot was quiet. About every half hour, a security guard rode through on the golf cart. There must have been three of them at least because he saw the same guard every other time, and he heard both report to a third voice over their radios.

Dumbasses. You can almost set your watch to their patrols. If anyone wanted to get to her, it would be easy.

He snorted. He'd broken back in, hadn't he? And he didn't even have to try.

Suddenly, he felt his butt vibrate. He pulled his phone out of his back pocket. "Yep."

"Struck out, huh?"

"You're a persistent fuck, aren't you?"

"I figured for sure you'd have charmed your way into her La Perla panties hours ago, and I'd have to call at least twice before you fumbled in the dark to answer."

"I'm not charming my way into anything, dickhead. Now, what do you want?"

God grunted. "Midas looked into Kubrick. Squeaky clean. She owns a house on Ivywood Lane. Mother was connected somehow to the British aristocracy, but it's really far down the line—about seventeen people. Fifth daughter of a baron or some shit. However..."—he paused for dramatic effect—"she has a brother."

Waters exhaled. "Ka-Bar."

God agreed. "Fuckin' Ka-Bar."

"Why didn't she say something? It's not like he didn't come up. For fuck's sake, why didn't he say something when he contacted Steel?"

"Steel might have already known, so the information would have been redundant. As for her, I'm not even going to hazard a guess. But why Midas didn't find it the first time around is beyond me. He does not miss shit."

Not Ka-Bar's woman. She was technically no longer off-limits. If he was interested. Which he wasn't.

"I guess it's not like we didn't know there was a connection somewhere. I mean, he's not going to call in a favor for a stranger." Waters thought for a moment. "Did you talk to Steel yet?"

"He's still dark. He should be emerging soon, but until then, we're running blind. Unless Midas can work his voodoo. Stay frosty, Waters. If Ka-Bar's asking us to watch a family member, then he's scared. And scared military men are usually scared for a reason. Especially Spec Ops members. We probably should be bringing her into the Tribe right now, but... I'm gonna hold off on that temporarily."

Why the hell wouldn't God grant her absolute protection? There's certainly the bond of brotherhood to Ka-Bar, and they were ninety-nine percent sure she was in danger, so what was the holdup?

God broke the silence. "What did you learn today? Anything of value?"

Yeah. I learned she makes me wish I were a different man.

"She's popular. People seem to want to please her. Lots of positive relationships with people. She's good at what she does, at least so far. To be honest, I didn't spot anyone or anything out of place, but my spidey senses told me she's being watched. No guarded looks, no suspicious behavior, no masked expressions. Nothing overt except for Big Bird. He's going to be an issue. He's got a severe hard-on for Kubrick. She can handle herself, which is hot as hell, but something's off about him, and I don't trust him. Midas should run a check on him if he hasn't already."

There was a pause. "So. She's hot as hell?"

Fuck. Of course he'd latch onto that. Her lack of filter is rubbing off on you.

Waters heard the taunt behind God's question and could have kicked himself for the slip-up. He let the silence stretch. No use trying to deny he said it. It would only make it worse.

His boss let it go. "Who's Big Bird?"

"Stapleton, the executive producer. Ruffled feathers. Molting. Lots of screeching. Long story. Seemed better than 'assclown' for a nickname."

"Okay. Trust your instincts and watch the fucker. I'll

have Midas run a report. He's probably high on the list for him anyway, but I'll put a rush on that one."

After a long silence, completely serious, God added, "Waters?"

"Yeah?"

"Do not let her out of your sight. Unless you want to sit out in the cold every night and get no sleep, you better find a reason to get inside with her. And I still think inside of her might not be a bad idea either."

"Now who's the assclown?"

God laughed on the other end of the line and clicked off. Waters had to admit, the man wasn't wrong. It would be a lot easier if he could be inside her living space with her or at her side all of the time, but that just wasn't possible right now. He needed Steel and Nemo to get home from Cuba soon. He could go for several days without sleep, but it was dangerous and could make him sloppy. And he would not be sloppy about protecting Kubrick from whatever shit-storm was coming.

He chose not to think about why he was so concerned.

She had left just after one o'clock this morning. He'd followed her to her house—a pink, turn-of-the-century, three-story house complete with a closed-in wraparound porch that formed octagonal gazebo shapes at the corners. Victorian streetlamps led up the walkway to her door as it was set back slightly from the street and bordered on a wooded area with a path.

There were neighbors, but there were easily several

acres of wooded land in between the houses, which were on large plots, so there was minimal street traffic. He would have to find somewhere to park his truck, so it went unnoticed, and then it would be a long night in the woods, watching.

Damn. Can't catch a break, apparently.

Using the car's customized navigation system, he found a pond about a half mile from the back of the house. Again, not optimal, but there was a dirt track leading into the woods back there, so he pulled the truck inside the trees. He changed into a pair of black cargo pants, made sure his jacket was zipped tight, then hopped out of the truck and jogged onto her property, doing a circuit of her yard. He sent a quick text back to the office, then watched from the tree line on the side of the building through her office window as he waited for a reply. A few minutes later, his watch beeped. Checking the time, he noticed it had been about ninety minutes from when she left the lot, and now she was finally turning out the light and going to bed. His watch beeped again. Completing the sweep of the property, he made his way back to his truck.

He locked the doors and engaged the window tinting, then turned on the truck's navigation screen. After pressing an unlabeled button by the radio volume control, the navigation screen changed to a black background. A glowing red frame appeared around the terminal, and he spoke three separate codes—his identification number, a sixteen-digit alphanumeric string, and then the day's passphrase. A young man's face—scalp-cropped dark hair, soulful brown eyes—gazed back at him. His mouth was smiling and chewing at the same time, a hum of enjoyment at the chocolate, peanuts, and nougat. He waved the candy bar, label clearly framed, at his teammate and winked.

And the bastard is eating a Snickers. Goddammit, I'm gonna have to throat-punch my boss for starting this nonsense. Betty White, my ass.

"You're a lot more clothed than I expected, Boss," he mumbled around the candy in his mouth. The Afrikaans-tinged accent didn't help with articulation, either.

Waters glared at Midas. "Don't talk with your mouth full. What do you have?"

Midas grinned his Cheshire smile and chuckled. "You mean other than a major sugar rush and probably twelve instant cavities from this piece of shit candy bar? They're so awful, they're fantastic. How did I not know about these?"

"You're not going to have to worry about cavities because the next time I see you in person, you won't have any teeth. You'll be sucking your food through a straw."

Midas tsked him from his side of the call. "I will not be sucking anything. I think that's something she should be doing."

For the love of...

"Quit pissing me off. Are you going to fill me in on what you've got, or am I going to kick your ass all the way back to Johannesburg before I get the update?"

"You are very confused this evening, brother. I'm not filling anything. That is your job," he corrected with a point of the candy bar toward the screen. The dark-haired man turned his head to his left and perused another screen. "However, I gotta admit. She's pretty hot. I could probably be persuaded to 'fill in' if you feel you're not 'up' to the task."

Oh, hell no!

"Go anywhere near her, and I will break those golden fingers of yours, Midas. You're not irreplaceable, you know. Computer experts are a dime a dozen."

Still grinning wide, Midas shook his head. "You're way too easy, mate. Collect yourself." The grin disappeared. "Seriously, though, she's totally into you. You should go after her."

Waters took a deep breath and pinched the bridge of his nose. He was in such trouble. His Tribe were worse than the stereotypical coffee klatch. Midas had been watching the meeting with Kubrick, which meant by now, the entire team had, too.

"I can see your gears grinding. Relax, Boss."

"Spare me, Midas. You telling me you didn't make a copy of the initial meeting with Kubrick and send it to everyone?"

"What do you take me for?" he asked innocently.

Waters sighed with relief.

"Of course I did!" Midas joked. "Don't be an idiot. That's the best entertainment we've had since Nemo got caught with that waitress and her ass on the salad bar."

Water exhaled and resisted the urge to growl, which would just make the whole situation worse.

Midas continued, "I meant relax because I also made everyone a hard copy for posterity. Don't ya wanna be able to show your grandchildren where it all started?"

Midas needs to die. That's all there is to it. Then I'm going to have to hide a body.

"As stimulating as this conversation is, do you have anything useful to tell me?"

Midas went all business. "Check your email."

Waters grunted as he scanned through the documents. Midas had enclosed property maps of Kubrick's house, the studio, and the shoot locations, including the house the actors would be living in beginning February sixteenth.

Waters began spitting out orders. "I want eyes inside

her house and trailer. You'll have to get in during the day tomorrow. She said she'd be at the studio starting at eight a.m. I'll try to lure her out earlier to breakfast. What's the ETA for the rest of the team?"

"Dumb and Dumber are en route. Just doing an overnight stop to drop off the defector with his new baseball team. TB got back an hour ago from his little side job."

That left just one player out of the mix. "And Demon?"

Midas looked at him and shrugged, his face noncommittal. "His week off. Not a fucking clue. Somewhere with a vat of Sex Wax, I'm guessing."

Great. Demon's out "hanging ten," and I need help with recon. Perfect.

"Okay, so I need a few more things."

"Deep dives on Kubrick, Ka-Bar, and Big Bird." Midas started clicking away on one of his many keyboards. "Already started. You should have final reports on all three by morning, but I'll continue digging even after that."

"Why didn't we know about the Kubrick/Ka-Bar connection?"

Midas huffed in frustration. "Because they're both adopted." Head shaking, he continued, "Basically, it's because they aren't blood-related. And both have their real parents on their documents, so the relationship, or lack of it officially, was not obvious."

"How the hell does that happen?"

"Their 'adopted' parents are their godparents. Both sets of biological parents were killed when Kubrick and Ka-Bar were young, and the third couple were the named godparents for both kids, so when the kids were orphaned, the third couple took them in. Not atypical adoptions, but no one ever bothered to make it legal, hence why I didn't find it."

"Got it. Anything there look like it might be related to the marker being called in?"

With a shake of his head, Midas turned his attention back to Waters. "No. Both sets of parents were killed in separate accidents, but there's no link between the deaths, and there's never been anything threatening to either of the kids. Ka-Bar's family were some kind of archaeological ambassadors—mother was a British national; father was American, both professors with expertise in ancient Egypt —killed in a car crash by a drunk driver in Cairo." Midas cleared his throat as he snuck a look at his boss. "Sorry, Boss."

Waters waved off the apology. Yeah, definitely a place to forget. His own fault as to why, but the guys had to stop getting twitchy like they were bringing up an ex-wife someone on the team was sleeping with. "Continue."

"Kubrick's family were British born but lived in the U.S. most of their lives other than Oxford schooling, which is how the three couples—Ka-Bar's parents, Kubrick's parents, and the godparents—met. Mother was a socialite with a minor royal connection. Her father worked at the embassy in Washington, D.C. They were killed in a personal seaplane crash just off the coast of Athens while on vacation. Four years between deaths, six years difference between the two kids, and they look nothing alike, so while I shouldn't have overlooked the relationship, it's not all that surprising. I'm used to digging for information, not having it in plain sight."

"No worries, Midas. Only connection seems to be the Egyptian Embassy, but in your abundant free time, keep looking." Midas winked and took another bite of his candy bar with the label still clearly in view. Waters shifted in his seat. "Anything immediate on Big Bird?"

"Other than he has some serious issues with women, no."

"Do tell."

"In summary, he's a douchebag overall and a real pain in the ass to any woman who's trying to make it through the glass ceiling. Kubrick seems to handle him much better than most. A couple of formal complaints against him, but mostly just for being..." Midas scrutinized a screen to his right, squinting. "'A number-crunching Neanderthal who can't read his own spreadsheet with the help of a shit-flinging monkey.' Huh. Not sure where the monkey comes in, but it certainly creates an image." Midas laughed. "Fuck, Boss. Your girl is unfiltered." He flipped a screen or two. "I've been keeping a list. Asshat, Assclown, Assnozzle—I think she shares your ass fetish, you lucky bastard." Waters grunted. "Fucktwat—very British, must get that from Mom —I like it; Ruptured Douchebag—ewww; Man Whoring Sycophant, and God's personal favorite, Jizzmop." Midas started laughing hard. "But this is the best: 'Try that douchebaggery again, and I will kick your ass so hard that your vertebrae will spit out of your mouth one-by-one like a Pez dispenser.'" He looked at his boss with a shit-eating grin. "Whatever you do, don't piss her off."

Waters rolled his eyes and scrubbed his face with his hands. "I don't think I want to know what provoked that comment."

Midas' face went serious. "Let's just say, the threat fits the cause. She can clearly take care of herself, which rumor has it, is hot." Midas winked.

Waters shook his head in disgust.

"I have to admit I'm surprised she still has a job after some of what she's put in print to him, but... I'm thinking he's a masochist and figures that it's all foreplay."

Waters went stone cold. "Has he threatened her physically?"

"Easy, tiger. No, you know I would have led with any sort of threat, physical or otherwise. It's more demeaning her gender and verbally harassing her staff. Not physical. But the guy is clearly a Fucktwat," Midas agreed with one of Kubrick's assessments.

"Definitely not going to be alone with him again."

"What's that, Boss?"

"Nothing, Midas. Just proved my instincts were right about the man." Waters leaned his outside elbow on the window frame, his index finger running back and forth on his lip, his eyes staring out into the night. "Get some sleep now while things are quiet. My brain is saying that this will get twitchy at some point, and then no one will be sleeping."

"Copy that, Boss. I'll get you some coverage ASAP so that you can stock up on sleep yourself. Never know when you might need the reserves." Midas gave one final smirk, taking another chunk off his candy bar.

Waters blacked out his screen.

7

———————

FEBRUARY 10TH

Kai

Fingers of sunlight streamed through the slats of the wooden shutters, and the air seemed to sparkle inside the rays created.

Waters, shirtless, tan camo pants up around his waist but undone, stood with his back to the window, arms crossed over his pecs, aviators on, and no expression on his face.

She stood at the foot of the bed, facing him.

Her insides twisted with want, and she squirmed.

"Take off your boots," he ordered.

She leaned down and unzipped her left boot, pulled it clear, and dropped it off further to her left.

She repeated the same process with the right.

"Now, the leggings."

Her thumbs hooked into the waist of her pants, and she

66

slid them down her legs, stepping out of them as they pooled at her ankles.

"Unbutton your shirt," he ordered.

Her hands went to the placket, shakily slipping buttons through holes.

"Don't take it off," he ordered.

All of the buttons were undone, and she had no idea what to do with her hands, so she let them drop to her sides.

Her eyes felt trapped under his stare even though she couldn't see his eyes behind the aviators.

"Sit down on the edge of the bed."

That order came softer, but it held no less demand.

"Lie back."

"I can't—"

"Don't refuse me."

She felt herself slowly descend back to the mattress, her legs still bent over the edge of the bed.

"Good girl."

"Waters... please."

"'Please,' what?"

"I... I don't know."

He smiled.

It was a devilish smile.

"You can have whatever you want, Kubrick, but you're going to have to ask me for it."

She whimpered.

"Ask," he softly commanded.

"Touch me."

"That's not a question, sweetheart."

"Will you touch me?"

The devilish smile deepened as he responded, "Oh, I will most definitely touch you."

The three steps he took to her were the slowest steps ever taken.

He knelt at her feet, placing his palms on her knees, his thumbs softly caressing the inside of the joints.

She moaned.

"You like my hands on you."

It wasn't a question.

His hands slid up the tops of her thighs and reached under the tails of her shirt.

"You want me to kiss you."

"Yes," she breathed.

Feather-light touches of his lips began at one knee and worked up to her pelvic bone.

He retreated and repeated the process up the other leg.

She watched as his face, aviators still on, turned up to her as he placed his final kiss.

He rose between her thighs like an ocean god from the surface of the water.

His hands reached for the shirt and pulled the panels away from her skin to fully view her beneath him in a bright red lace bra and matching panties.

One of his fingers reached out, touched her lips, then dragged itself down to her chin, the hollow of her throat, the valley of her breasts, her navel, and finally stopped at the small bow at the top of her panties.

His sunglasses returned from following the journey of his finger to her gaze.

"So beautiful."

Taking in air became difficult, as if the atmosphere in the room were slowly squeezing her lungs.

"I want you, Kubrick."

"Then have me, Waters."

The smile disappeared.

His gaze returned to the bow.

Both hands slid to the thread of material at her hips, holding the lacy material in place.

His index fingers curled under the threads, and she felt every moment the material dragged down her thighs, past her knees, down her calves, around her ankles, and over her feet.

She didn't see what he did with them because her eyes were paralyzed at the expression on his face.

Even though she couldn't see his eyes, he appeared dazed.

Mesmerized by the sight of what he had uncovered.

His lips pursed, and as she felt cool air blow onto her center, she closed her eyes, she arched her back—

Suddenly, Justin Timberlake and Timbaland burst into her world.

With a groan, Kai groped blindly for her phone to stop the blaring music. Not for the last time, she vowed to change her alarm to something much more soothing. She pulled the pillow from under her head to cover it instead and drifted almost immediately back to sleep.

Moments later, the ringtone began again. Her brain muzzily connected that it wasn't the alarm but instead the phone ringing. With a groan, she fumbled for the phone, bringing it under the pillow to her ear as she answered.

"That was a really good dream you woke me up from, so whoever this is, there better be a good reason for waking me up."

"Why is your voice so muffled?"

"Because my head's under my pillow, where any normal human being's should be at this ungodly hour of the day."

"Somebody's cranky." There was a pause. "A really

good dream, huh?" The voice turned curious and sugges-tive. "Care to share?"

Underneath the pillow, her eyes flew open to register that just under its edge, she could see the bright sunlight coming in through the slats of her shutters. Kai jackknifed into a sitting position, the pillow flying across the room, knocking several photo frames and who knew what else from the dresser onto the floor.

Holy fuck, it's him! That ringtone was a warning so you could act cool and collected when he called. Obviously, that didn't work. Fuck, fuck, mother-mother-fuck.

"Wa-Waters?"

"No sharing? Damn. Can't have been that good then." He paused again. "Or maybe it was so—"

"What do you want, Waters?" she interrupted him. "And it better be good or, although you could probably kill me six hundred ways with a napkin, I'll go Angry Birds on your ass the next time I see you."

"Well, 'chirp chirp' to you, too, Mama Bird. I'm not sure what constitutes 'good,' but you were the one who told me that you'd be in by eight, so I thought—"

"Oh my god, what time is it?!" Kai struggled to untangle herself from the bedding, nearly falling out of bed trying to exit it.

"Kubrick, relax! It's six o'clock."

Her hand to her heart, her breath soughing in and out in panic strokes, she closed her eyes and tried to calm herself. "What the hell, Waters?"

She heard him chuckle on the other end of the line. "Well, if I can tear you away from your really good dream, I thought we could have breakfast."

"Breakfast."

"Breakfast," he confirmed. "You know, the first meal of

the day. Usually involves coffee, orange juice, eggs, cereal, pancakes, and bacon. Some combination of those items."

"You want to have breakfast."

"Yep."

"With me?"

"Yep."

"I won't be tearing you away from anyone you'd rather be doing? AnyTHING!" she corrected quickly. "Any-THING you'd rather be doing."

Just kill me now. Maybe I can blame that slip of the lip on the fact that he woke me up? He doesn't need to know he was the central star of the best sex dream of all time. Or that it was a sex dream. Yeah. Best he doesn't know that either. In fact, forget about it yourself.

"Mmm... nope. Only pussy out here is Zoe, and she's probably not looking for the same type of breakfast I had in mind."

"Excuse me?!"

"Zoe. That's what her tag says. Real friendly calico cat that is currently weaving in between my legs."

Kai's eyes narrowed in confusion. "Where the hell are you?" A sudden realization made Kai's eyes open wide, her mouth drop open, and her feet carry her over to her bedroom window. Opening the slats on one of the shutters of her turret bedroom window, she saw Waters' truck parked at the curb of her house below in the street. He was standing in front of the passenger door of his truck, in his normal feet shoulder-width apart stance, and sure as shit, the neighbor's calico cat, Zoe, was weaving figure eights with her sinewy body around his gorgeous legs.

Lucky fucking cat. I hate her.

His face tipped up, signature aviators reflecting the early morning sun, and unerringly found her peeking at him through the slats. "Mornin'. You gonna come down and go to breakfast with me, or are you gonna hide up there in your ivory tower?"

"Umm... breakfast... yeah. Gimme fifteen minutes."

"Make it ten, and I'll buy."

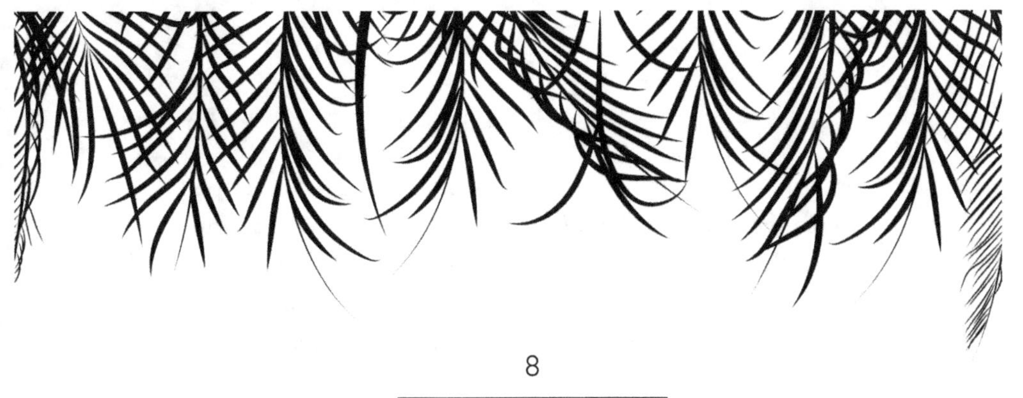

8

———————————

FEBRUARY 10TH

Waters

She and her *Backpack of Death* were down and out the door in seven. He watched her bound down the steps, the outer door of the enclosed porch banging shut behind her. Today she was in a bright blue Dodgers jersey over white leggings, the jersey so large it dropped almost to her knees.

Still no view of the potentially wicked ass. Damn.

Dodgers cap back in place, and her blonde ponytail pulled through the hole in the back of the cap. No boots today. Mentally, he groaned. This was kind of worse.

When the fuck did heeled Chucks become sexy?

He snagged her backpack. "Jesus Christ, what do you have in here?"

"Oh, quit your whining. You could probably lift that with your little finger."

He closed her inside the truck, then came around the

73

front. Stowing her bag in the cab behind his seat, he hopped up into the truck. "The fact that I can is beside the point." He watched her struggle with a twisting seat belt for a few moments before he leaned across her and untangled it. With a quick, assertive flick of the strap, he pulled it across and buckled her in.

"Nice, Captain Caveman." She began to bat her eyes at him and simpered. "Thank you, Waters. That seat belt was so confusing."

Do not laugh. Do not encourage her.

He shrugged as he started the truck, focusing out his windshield. "It rarely gets used, so it can be unruly when someone tries to pull it."

"No one rides in your truck?" she asked incredulously.

"Not usually."

"Typical military alpha."

"What the hell does that mean?"

"You're clearly a 'rules' guy. My truck–no one drives it but me, no one rides in it because they'll mess it up, and if someone does get to ride in it, no touching the tunes. And I bet it especially applies to the opposite sex. Obviously, you have a no-chicks-in-the-truck rule.

"So, let me guess what other rules there are. Never take a girl back to your own bed, definitely never spend the full night, and hell-to-the-no on kissing or cuddling. I'm guessing you only pick up women in bars or maybe at some function, and you likely prefer hotels. Five-star ones. That way, when she wakes up alone, room service is waiting for her with a 'Thanks for the fun' note."

He huffed. "No note." Snapping her head in his direction, her eyes were wide when they met his. "Letting her know it was fun only engenders hope the event might recur."

She sat up ramrod straight and turned full forward, refusing to look him in the eyes. "So, um... to what do I owe the invitation to ride in your truck and go to breakfast?"

Hmm. Little uncomfortable, are we?

He shrugged. "It's morning. We both need to eat. We're both going to be at the studio working together. Figured we could eat together. Now, I'm very curious about this dream I woke you from. Define 'good.'"

"I know a great diner just outside the studio gates where you came in yesterday. Alice's. Best chocolate chip pancakes in L.A. Coupled with hot chocolate and peppermint extract, it's heaven."

He lay one wrist on the top of the steering wheel, his fingers hanging loosely. The other hand rested on the gear shift. "Don't care. Dream. 'Good.' Spill it." Schooling his expression into its usual blankness, hiding his eyes behind his aviators, he stared at her, waiting her out.

Finally, she sighed. "Great gravy! You woke me out of a dead sleep, Waters. I don't even remember what I said to you. It was probably garbage."

"Um, no. You said, and I quote, 'That was a really good dream you woke me up from,' and you were not happy about being woken up."

"Not a morning person," she grumbled.

"I'm like a virgin sailor on his first shore leave looking to get laid, so you might as well give it up." Pulling out from the curb, he watched her out of the corner of his eye as he drove. He knew he was baiting her, but a twisted part of him found it fun to rile her up. And she was fidgeting. A lot.

Interesting. Must have been really good.

"It was nothing," she lied.

"Uh-uh. Try again."

"I was dreaming about the movie."

"Doubtful."

"Oh, fuck me, Henry! Fine! I was having a really sexy dream about... about my leading actor. There! Happy?"

His smile was huge as he chuckled. "Liar," he murmured. He glanced at her for a moment as he got ready to switch lanes. Noticing the weird look on her face, he questioned it. "What?"

"You laughed."

"And?"

"You're smiling."

"So?"

"It's the first time I've heard or seen a genuine version of either of those from you."

He kept his focus out the front window. "I am human. Humans do those things. G.I. Joe's not allowed to do that?"

"No, it's just... unexpected, I guess. You should do both more often. Suits you."

He cleared his throat. "Thank you."

Abruptly, she turned and stared out the front window. "Yeah. So. Yeah."

Yeah. That about sums it up.

"So," Kubrick began, "has there ever been an *almost* Mrs. Waters? Or even someone who went beyond one night?"

He glanced up to see her shovel a huge bite of chocolate chip pancakes with extra chips and extra chocolate sauce into her mouth, very pointedly not looking at him. "A few girlfriends in high school. No near misses at the altar."

He set his coffee cup down and watched her continue to eat.

This woman is serious about her pancakes. Or is it just the chocolate? Either way, it's sexy as shit.

"I'd ask if there's ever been an *almost* Mr. Kubrick, but I don't think there's room for one in your life based on your unhealthy obsession for chocolate."

She rolled her eyes and ticked off her reasons on her fingers. "A) No time for a 'Mr. Kubrick.' B) There is no point in not enjoying the fifth food group when it's better than an orgasm."

He blinked.

Okay. Wow, she just throws everything right out there, doesn't she?

He shifted in the booth and attempted to adjust himself without drawing any attention to the fact that she'd just made sitting very uncomfortable. He wiped his mouth with his napkin, hopefully catching any overflowing saliva that seemed to have gathered in his mouth. "You are not dating the right men."

"Volunteering?" she teased, her eyes crinkling with laugh lines as she sucked the chocolate sauce from her fork.

He dropped a hand into his lap to try and calm his dick down again. Watching her eat was deadly. "I don't date. Remember?"

"Ah, but you are having breakfast with me," she joked, waving her fork in the air.

"Yes, but I didn't spend all night fucking you so hard you couldn't walk prior to this breakfast, so it doesn't count."

She dropped her fork with a clatter on the table.

Wow. Okay. Her unfiltered mouth is contagious.

Eyes wide again for just a moment, she quickly refocused her attention on picking up her fork, putting it to her plate, and scraping the last of the chocolate sauce from its surface, licking the tines, then closing her lips around them and pulling it through her lips. Her uncomfortable moment was quickly forgotten as her eyes closed with a hum, and he made a note that she likely had a serious chocolate fetish.

Not that I need that information... but I like trivia as much as the next man.

"Pity. Bet that G.I. Joe app would make a lot of money with you as the beta test." She opened one eye and looked at his blank expression. "Why?"

"Why what?"

Both eyes were now open. "Why don't you date? I would think there's a line around the block for you."

"Volunteering?" he shot back her word with a cocky grin.

She shook her head and started drawing abstract designs in the dregs of the chocolate sauce on her plate. "Relationships are too much work to maintain. It's exhausting trying to make connections, then finding time to fit people into the schedule of life, not to mention all the drama of the physical aspects. For whatever reason, relationships have never been on my list of things to do. Other things always seemed more important. There have been a few plus-one types over the years, but nothing that amounted to anything. As for you"—she sighed—"you're yummy to look at, but let's be honest. We're a bit mismatched."

Yummy? Oh my.

He refocused and looked at her, puzzled. "What do you mean 'mismatched'?" When she shrugged and kept drawing, he reached across the table to stop her hand. "No avoidance. Why would you think we're mismatched?"

You just couldn't let it go, could you? Idiot!

She sighed. "We are not exactly in the same league. Even if I wanted to get involved with someone, I'm not the type of girl a man spends fucking to the point she can't walk the next morning." She pulled her hand back from his and put her fork down carefully on the table. "This is a pointless conversation." She put her hands in her lap as the waitress arrived to clear the table.

Once the woman left, the charge in the air had changed. He watched her try to reset into work mode.

"Where do you want to start today?" she asked, trying to get them back into a work-mode relationship.

I want to start by finding the nearest five-star hotel and proving to you just how wrong you are.

He cleared his throat. "With some rules." The waitress brought the check, which Kubrick tried to grab, but he grabbed it and pointed a finger at her. "I asked you to breakfast, so I'm paying. You want to pay, you can ask me to breakfast." She gave a huff of exasperation. He raised his eyebrow at her in challenge. "So. Rules."

"I don't like rules." Her arms crossed over her chest, and her lips pursed.

"You're cute when you pout." She stuck her tongue out at him and blew a raspberry. "Nice. Okay. For the second time. Rules." She sighed and looked out the window.

"One. I need a copy of your schedule a week at a time so I can plan accordingly. Your assistant, or whoever, can get that to me by email.

"I don't have an assistant."

He looked at her in question. "What director doesn't have an assistant?"

"Me. Like I told Stapleton, assistants assist you with things you need assistance with. I can keep and manage my own schedule and other clerical tasks. I don't need an assistant to do that. Besides that, they're annoying." He stared at her, trying to process that she did all this work on her own with no help. And he'd witnessed firsthand that it was a lot more work than he'd ever imagined.

Partly explains the paper explosion of hers.

"I tried it," she attempted to defend herself. "But it was too invasive. It was like having a babysitter, and I don't like people touching my stuff. It may look like chaos, but I honestly know where everything is in the chaos." She started tapping on her phone. "I'll mail it to you on Sunday nights."

"Two. At the top of every day, I need an updated daily schedule. There will be no deviations from said schedule."

Glaring at him, she explained as she made another note, "Filming doesn't work that way, Waters. Sometimes there's weather. Sometimes there are delays, or things go faster than expected. It's an unpredictable business, and time is money. Literally. I always have to have contingency plans and adjust on the fly."

"Then, as soon as you know there may be a problem, you tell me. I need to have my own contingencies in place.

"Three. Whenever we're doing something that's a SEAL-type maneuver, my word goes. If I say something is too dangerous for the actors, or it's wrong, whatever, it's my call.

"Four. And this is nonnegotiable. There will be no meetings with Big Bird without me present. None, Kubrick."

"It's a miracle I could function before you came along. However did I survive?" She batted her eyes melodramatically, snark oozing with every word.

"Sauce gets you nowhere, babe. Those are the rules. Take it or leave it."

"Oh, for fuck's sake," she muttered under her breath. "I've managed all this time without anyone helping me out. Now, suddenly, because you're here, I need protection. Give me a fucking break."

"I'm not joking, Kubrick, the guy is bad news. Never when I'm not around. I don't care if there are twenty other people in the room with you, if I'm not there and he is, you're not there."

"I hired you as a consultant. If I don't need an assistant, I sure as shit don't need a babysitter."

"No, you don't. But it would be remiss of me if I, as your consultant, didn't look out for you. My job is to make sure you can do yours accurately and properly. He is working in the exact opposite direction, trying to make it as difficult for you as possible. And his behavior is anything but appropriate."

Fine," she pouted. "But I can take care of myself. Let me handle him."

"As long as he makes no threat toward you, I'll stay out of it. Last but not least, rule five. You go nowhere without me. I pick you up in the morning, I escort you wherever you need to go, and I drop you off at night. Also nonnegotiable. I trust that fucker only as far as I can see him."

"Jesus Christ on a crutch. Anything else, *Dad*," she barked.

That should not make me harder. I better get hazard pay for this job because my dick is going to be damn near broken.

Leaning across the table and dropping his voice so only she could hear, he warned, "Extra sauce will get you a spanking, sweetheart, and I'll bill you extra for special services. Not really into age or role play, but if it keeps you out of trouble with him, call me whatever turns you on."

He watched the color drain from her face, but she rallied quickly. "You're tying my hands, Waters."

"I swear on my trident pin, I'll tie more than your hands, woman. I'm not fucking kidding around with you."

She stuck out her tongue at him again.

"I lied. One more rule. Rule six," he grumbled under his breath. "Keep that tongue in your mouth unless you plan to use it on me."

Her eyes widened, and her mouth opened, but no sound came out.

Oops. Said that out loud.

"Close your mouth, Kubrick. I don't want to be tempted to shove something in it." And with that final oops statement, he slid out of the booth, extending his hand to help her out of her side, then led her up to the register to pay the bill.

It was a very quiet ride to the studio.

9

———————

FEBRUARY 14TH

Kai

It was Monday morning, and things had been weird, for lack of a better word. There was a supercharge in the air since breakfast the other day, but oddly, it wasn't uncomfortable.

Unsettling. That's the best word I can use to describe it.

Right now, she was supervising Waters and the construction crew as they assembled the obstacle course materials for shipping to the set location when she noticed him take a limping step and wince. She waited until the other men walked over to another set of materials before approaching him. "What's with the leg?" she asked.

He turned his head, aviators reflecting her in their lenses. She noticed fine lines at the corner of his eyes by the frames. At first, she wasn't sure he would answer her, figuring her G.I. Joe wouldn't admit weakness of any kind.

"Old injury," he grunted, then walked over to correct an error in the builders' knot on the support.

Head tilted, she watched him closer. He straddled the band of wooden planks, lifting them up so that one of the crew could slide a belt underneath them and then cinch them together. His muscles bunched and flexed, but he appeared to be barely exerting much force. She shivered. When he walked back her way, she pursued. "Do you need to take a break?"

He looked over the top of his aviators at her.

"Okay, be a macho asshole, G.I. Joe. Heaven forbid you're as human as the rest of us."

"You need another hot chocolate? You weren't all sunshine and light this morning yourself. And here I went all out on Valentine's Day."

Wow, what a grouch.

"Pardon me if I was expecting flowers," she shot back.

She heard him mumble something about the impossibility of lilacs in California.

Hands on her hips, she reminded him, "I warned you I'm not a morning person. If hot chocolate and peppermint cure it, who am I to complain?" Noticing the tightness of his jaw she asked, "Are you not sleeping? This is going to get way more tiring as we go. Maybe you should find someone to split time with."

He grunted. "Your job was unexpected, and I've had to pull some extra duties. The guy I've been covering for will be back on duty tonight. I'll be fine."

Shrugging, she checked her watch. A sigh escaped her. "Well, as stimulating as this argument is, it's time to get ready for Big Bird and the rest of the Sesame Street gang. You don't have to go with me. I sincerely doubt the producers will attack en masse." She turned her back and began to walk toward her trailer.

"Rules four and five," he called out.

"Stubborn jackass."

"That's redundant, as is my reminder." He caught up to be in step with her. "Originally, I thought I needed a swear jar with you. Now I think I need a Rule Reminder jar."

"Argh!" She stopped and whirled to face him. "Some days you are so... frustrating!"

He put his hands on her shoulders and turned her toward her trailer. "C'mon, Grumpy, let's get this over with. We've got more important shit to do today."

They headed back to her trailer, his hand going to her lower back as she stepped from the curb to the street. It was eighty-some degrees today, but suddenly, the temperature seemed to get significantly hotter. He needed to stop with the touching. None of it was overt or even close to sexual. Helping her out of the truck. Hand to the back as he guided her toward a table or somewhere else he wanted her to go. Yesterday, he'd tucked a tag into the back of her workout gear before they went for her daily run.

Gah! Perfect boyfriend material.

And yeah, he'd meant it when he said she went nowhere without him. That meant he was working out with her, eating meals with her, and going to meetings with her that had nothing to do with SEAL stuff. He kept reiterating he didn't want Big Bird to have any opening to get at her unawares, and when she started poking at him about that, he just argued that everything on the film was related to SEALs; therefore, he was doing his job to make sure she got it right. Finally, she yelled at him that he might as well just move into her house with her as it was the only place he didn't go. He mumbled, "That would be a big help," so she just threw her hands up in the air, stomped off, and muttered about "crazy, overprotective military types."

AFTER SHE COLLECTED HER LAPTOP AND STUFFED IT into the Backpack of Death, Waters grabbed her bag and followed her to the corporate offices and her last meeting with Stapleton before heading out to location. Entering the offices, she didn't break pace as she passed security, flashing her badge.

In the elevator, she stood facing forward, watching the elevator numbers go up. "Now, pencil-dick is going to be extra pricky with you there, so don't go all caveman on me in the meeting. I can handle him."

"He behaves, I behave."

"Hmph. Are you always this pushy with your clients?"

"Probably worse," he admitted, "because I've seen you at work, and I know you can handle yourself verbally. But Kubrick, I do have lines he will not cross, and I will not apologize for my actions if he does."

Gah! It should not make me tingle that he thinks I can push Big Bird around.

The doors opened, and Kubrick pushed forward, Waters' barely present touch at her lower back leading her out of the elevator. She was coming to think of that as her hot spot.

Instead of my G-spot, it'll be my h-spot.

God forbid he ever put actual pressure there.

She waved to Big Bird's assistant and grabbed her backpack from Waters. She loved that he was willing to do nice things for her that were unnecessary, like carrying the Back-pack of Death. But he also understood that inside Big Bird's office, the backpack was a piece of weaponry meant to intimidate. To show how strong she was physically, implying she was not a woman to be trampled or ignored.

She barreled through the conference room doors without bothering to knock, effectively stopping whatever conversation had been going on prior to her arrival. Swinging the bag onto the polished table, it landed with a thunk, making one bean-cruncher jump in his seat. Internally, she gloated that she frightened at least one of these men. However, she would never show her enjoyment outwardly. That would be a power play.

She surveyed the table. The only empty seat was at the foot of the table, along the side, and closest to the door.

Really? He's going to try this power play with me? Not going to work. Time to level the playing field.

She removed her laptop from the bag, opened it, and powered it up. Pointedly, she moved the chair from the placement designed to make her weak and rolled it to the end of the table opposite Big Bird. Now, instead of being the least important guest at the table, she was "hostess" to his "host," leveling the power between them. She sat, and with a smile that did not reach her eyes, she asked, "Shall we begin?"

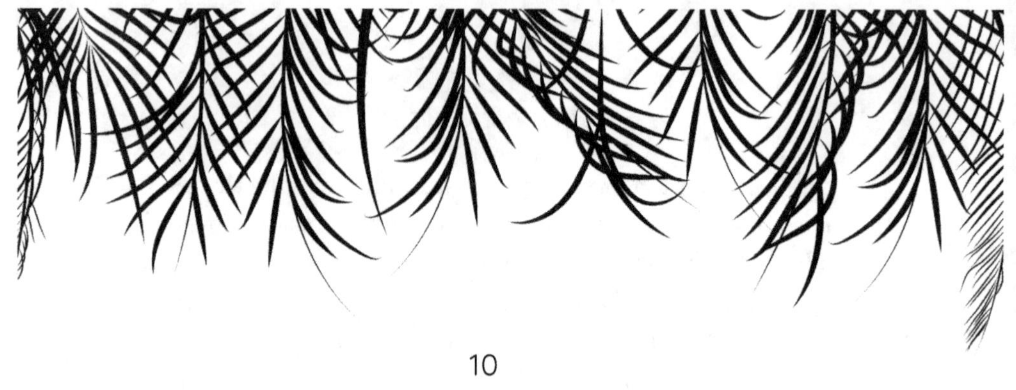

FEBRUARY 14TH

Waters

NICELY PLAYED, KUBRICK.

Big Bird wanted to show her he was in control, and Waters would take the sure bet that the positioning of the suits, starting with Big Bird at the head of the table, then going back and forth from his right to his left and down the table would signify the amount of money each man put into the pot. Clearly, this was a boys' club since Kubrick was the only woman at the table, let alone in the room.

There was no vacant chair for him, so Waters put his own power play into motion. Kubrick didn't need him standing behind her like a muscleman to protect her, so instead he leaned on the wall next to the door, arms crossed over his chest, one ankle crossed over the other in fake nonchalance. And if he purposely flexed and locked his arms in place, showcasing his muscles in his tight gray T-shirt... oops.

Knock 'em out, baby. You got this.

"Why is he here?" Big Bird growled.

"I'm sorry, which 'he' are you referring to? I'm the only 'she' in the room, so it's rather vague."

Kubrick one, Big Bird zero.

"You know who I'm talking about, Serrano."

"His name is Waters. You can stop talking about him as if he's a thing rather than a person."

"He's unnecessary at this meeting."

"I want him here, so that makes him necessary. Waters is the consultant on the film; therefore, any discussion of items related to SEAL factors is pertinent to him."

Big Bird stared her down for at least a minute. When it was clear she was only going to stare back, he spoke. "Gentlemen, page twenty, please, line two hundred and thirty-five."

Return shot across the bow. Big Bird ties up the score.

He only addressed the men in the room. He also noticed that a paper copy of the budget had not been provided to Kubrick. She seemed unperturbed by it, pulling a binder out of her backpack.

"My page twenty of the budget stops at line two hundred and twenty-four, Stapleton," Kubrick said loud and clear over the turning pages.

"It appears you haven't downloaded the recent changes, Serrano," he replied dismissively.

She pulled her laptop out of the backpack, and after a few clicks in her email, she responded, "I can't download what I'm not given."

"That's not my problem. It was sent to my administrative assistant and ordered to be sent out. I don't have the time to double-check her work."

Big Bird takes the lead.

"Don't you dare blame this on Felicity. I'm willing to bet your residuals she wasn't given my name to send it to. Shall we check with her?" Kubrick gestured to the door, and Waters, without missing his cue, began to reach for the door handle.

"We don't have time for your childish temper tantrums, Serrano. Banks, give her your copy."

The seat-jumper tentatively pushed his packet down the table to Kubrick as if afraid she'd bite him. To her credit, she flashed him a smile, but Waters noticed that while her lips turned up, it was all teeth. And it was not a pleasant smile. He willed his cock to stand down.

Swing for the seats, woman.

She reviewed the line, then he watched her flick back a page and scan the list. Her eyes narrowed further and further with each line she reviewed. He knew the exact moment she went from irritated to furious.

Bottom of the ninth. Here we go.

She closed the packet and shoved it several inches in front of her. "Who authorized the removal of Tribe as the consultant and added the U.S. Army in its place?"

"I did," Big Bird replied smoothly.

"Aside from the fact that the contracts were already agreed upon by a majority vote Friday, in what universe would you think it was appropriate to have the Army consult on the procedures of Navy SEALs?"

Waters noticed that the gentleman one down from Stapleton's left was trying to hide a smile.

Okay, so she's not completely unsupported. Good to know.

"Tribe costs too much. The Army can give us military consultation at a much cheaper rate and keep us under budget."

"So, you'll sacrifice accuracy for dollars?"

The suit at the far right of the table dared to speak up. "We discussed it, Ms. Serrano, and a majority of us agreed that the average person won't know the difference. It will appear accurate enough. It's a necessary sacrifice to ensure we have room in the budget."

"You discussed it?" She looked around the room. "I believe that's a violation of contract, gentlemen." She flipped to a page with a yellow flag.

Uh-oh. Mistake. Nuclear bomb in three... two... one.

"I direct your attention to page forty-two, section nine of the contract: 'All discussions regarding budgeting and film direction will be held with the director, Kai Serrano, in attendance.'"

She flipped a few pages further to an orange flag. "Page fifty. Section four: 'Once a budget line has been voted into acceptance, no changes may be made without a unanimous vote of all parties, including the director. Item B under that section states that if a previous consultant has been approved and signed a contract prior to that unanimous vote, then removed without physical evidence of negligence, the consultant will be paid the agreed-upon fee plus a ten percent bonus for inconvenience.'"

She flipped a few more pages to a red flag. "Page fifty-nine. Section one: 'In the event that this contract is violated, the director will be free to remove herself from the project and collect her full fee, as well as retain her residuals from future film revenues.'"

Oh, baby, three-two and two outs. Get ready for the fallout, gentlemen.

She closed the binder, then primly folded her hands on top of it, leaning on her forearms. "So. What will it be? Will you accept your new, unapproved budget that violates the contract—thereby effectively firing both Tribe and myself, which, I'm no mathematician, but I'd say that costs you a fuck-ton more money than you're already agreeing to spend with the previous budget—or will you stop allowing this dickhead to bully you into his misogynist antics and let me make the best goddamn movie this studio has ever produced?"

Score is tied. So hot. Mine. Mine. Mine.

It took every ounce of Waters' control not to grab her, drag her out of the room, and then find the nearest supply closet or abandoned office to fuck her silly.

There was a cough in the ensuing silence, then Big Bird attempted to double down on his stupidity. "Kai," he began patronizingly, "I don't think you're capable of interpreting that contract with any sort of—"

"Enough, Stapleton."

Waters' head moved to the voice that had spoken up to see the smiler stand up behind his place at the table and button his suit coat. There was no smile on his face now. "I warned you this was a dick move, one that I did not support, and I'm guessing that several cowards at this table also do not support but are too chickenshit to say so and that she'd nail you on it. I've been proven correct, which only solidifies my support of Ms. Serrano." He closed the budget packet. "If she is removed from the project, whether by you or herself, my money is out of the project and this studio. And I believe you can find that this is a legal move based on page ten, section one."

And there's the walk-off from a pinch hitter. Game to Kubrick.

With that, the suit put his sunglasses on, turned, and left the table, not bothering to push in his chair. When he reached the door, he gave Kubrick a nod, which she returned, and without looking back, he threw the budget packet in the trash as he exited out the door Waters had opened for him.

Her gaze had turned back to the gentlemen at the table. "I would also remind you that none of my pictures have ever come in over budget. Not even close. I find it extremely offensive that you would suggest that this picture would be any different, no matter what you may have heard from a third party." Her glare at Stapleton did not go unnoticed. "My methods and style of running a production have not changed."

There was no response from anyone. In fact, the only one looking at her was Big Bird, and he was beyond pissed. Now, she'd have to look over her shoulder for him, and Waters would have to be on extreme alert.

"Well, I guess that's it." She smacked her hands on the table surface and stood. She began packing her bag back up. "I'll be leaving tomorrow for the set location. I believe all further communication can be handled electronically, don't you, gentlemen?" She flashed a deceptively cheerful smile at them. A smile that she even included the head of the table in. "Have a nice day."

SHE MOVED WITH PURPOSE BACK TO HER TRAILER, HER ponytail bouncing violently with each step. She was pissed. He followed behind, recognizing she was not in the mood to talk, watching everything around her. She opened her door at her trailer, walked inside, dumped her backpack in the middle of the floor, and went straight to the cupboard.

Waters picked up her backpack and set it on the booth seat at her table, his eyes never leaving her. The smile was gone. She had pulled a bottle of Santo tequila and a tumbler down from the shelf, poured herself a liberal shot, and slammed it. She leaned on her locked arms on the counter edge.

"Exhale, Kubrick."

Her body actually shuddered as she let all the air out of her lungs. Shaking her head, she poured another shot. "I'm taking a shower."

Throwing her ball cap on the counter and taking the tumbler with her, she pulled the hair tie out of her ponytail and headed back to the bedroom portion of the trailer. He waited until he heard the water start, then he exited the trailer and sat on the front step to make his call. There was no way he could stay inside knowing where she was, what she was doing.

Nemo answered on the first ring in an old lady falsetto. "Lonely Hearts Club, how may I assist you today?" Waters could hear the cheeky grin on the other end of the phone.

"Welcome home. Any problems?"

"Nah. Didn't even need to fire a round. Bo-ring."

Good. At least the defection went smoothly.

"I do have to admit, though," Nemo drawled, "the in-flight entertainment was highly amusing. I especially liked her camera spotting. Smokin' hot, that."

Fuck. Here we go.

"Yes, well, it doesn't take much to amuse a toddler, does it?"

"Awwww. Still in the consultant zone, huh? When do I get to meet her?"

Waters shook his head in frustration. "Never, fucker. Stay away."

The sound of gum cracking over the line caused Waters to roll his eyes. Nemo was such a kid. "Ah, that's okay. I'll just wait until you get shot down."

"She'd put you down within thirty seconds, easy."

"Hey, I don't mind topping from the bottom."

"Shut the fuck up. Where's your brother?"

The gum cracked again. "I'm coverin' while he catches some zees for an hour or two. God's got him trying to locate Ka-Bar and told him he's not allowed to come out of the tech cave without results. I'm paraphrasing, of course. His actual words were not appropriate for a toddler, such as myself."

"Whatever. Any luck?"

"Crickets."

Waters was silent for a moment. "Isn't that impossible?"

"For the almighty Midas touch? Yep. God's about to blow his wad. He actually ran out of suckers and sent Cherry to Costco. I think Midas has slept as little as you. He's so pissed off he can't find the man." The clacking of keys could be heard briefly in the background. "Speaking of which, Steel has the watch tonight. He'll be there shortly. He said he had an errand to run first."

A sigh of relief came from Waters, and he ran a hand over his head and clutched the back of his neck. "Yeah. I've about hit my limit. Everyone's going to have to be vigilant on this right now."

"I read your report. That dickwad giving her trouble?"

Waters barked a short laugh. "She didn't just poke the bear today, she flayed him alive. Then she filleted a room of eight suits. I don't think any of those idiots even knew what hit 'em. But Big Bird is going to be a problem. I want someone on him, too."

"You think this guy is our objective?"

"Normally, I would say no. But I haven't gotten a legitimate sniff of anything else weird, so what else could it be?" He looked out over the studio grounds he could see. "This doesn't make sense, Nemo. We're missing something major. And the fact that there isn't even a whisper of Ka-Bar for Midas to find? That's screaming at me."

"Well, Steel will be out there soon, and I can go find the big-beaked one and follow him a little bit tonight. We shouldn't need to stretch too thin on the schedule. TB, Demon, and I are all back in the office working on prep for tomorrow. God pulled us off everything else for the time being, so you concentrate on your girl, and we'll handle the rest."

"She's not my girl," Waters sighed.

There was silence on the other end of the phone. "Dude. You were salivating. And I'd be willing to bet my next paycheck you've spent the last four days trying to rearrange your dick so that you don't have to go to the hospital."

Waters' cheek developed a tic.

There was another second of silence, and then Nemo got serious. "We got ya covered, Boss. I'll let you know what I learn about Big Bird."

Nemo clicked off. Waters put his phone away, then hung his head and clasped both hands behind his neck.

And I'm fucked.

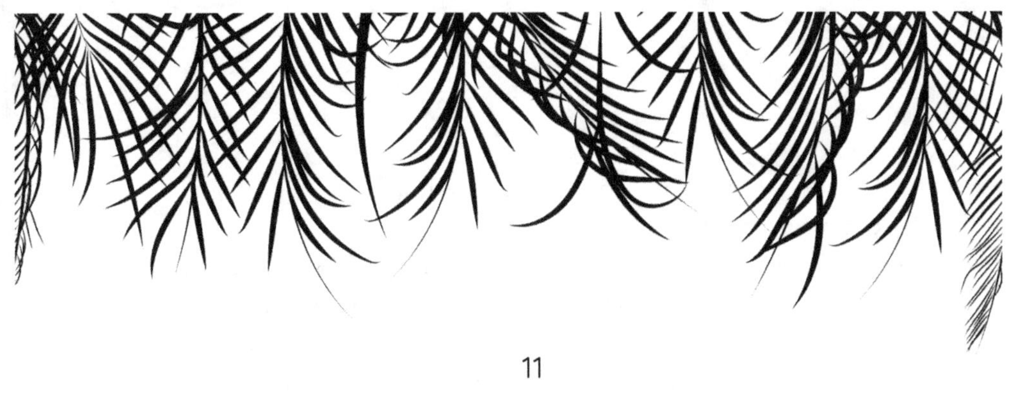

FEBRUARY 14TH

Kai

THE SHOWER WASHED AWAY THE PERSPIRATION SHE'D developed facing off against her boss, but it did nothing to wash away the exhaustion she was experiencing. To this day, she still did not know what she had done to piss that man off, although it seemed like if you had a vagina, that was good enough.

Well, you've always wanted to be "good enough" to someone, somehow. Be careful what you wish for.

Every meeting with that man was a fight. And even when she won, which she always did, her psyche came away battered and bruised. She almost had herself convinced that he provoked her on purpose just so that occurred. That he didn't care if he won or lost the skirmish of the moment with her, even when it made him look like a raging asshole, because if it tore down her defenses just a little bit every time, he would eventually win the final climactic battle.

Toweling off, Kai caught a glance of herself in the vanity mirror. Hollywood was still very much a man's world, no matter what field you specialized in, and women directors had it the worst. Yes, actresses were susceptible to being taken advantage of, although that was less of a buried industry secret now with the #MeToo movement. Even the girls who worked on the crews were vulnerable. It was one of the reasons that she worked with female-heavy crews whenever possible and did her best to protect them. But female directors? The business was brutal. If someone wasn't harassing you through sex, they were beating you down verbally and emotionally. You weren't smart enough, capable enough, or connected enough. It was never good enough.

Am I wrong for wanting to be good enough for a worthy reason? Is that the eighth deadly sin no one talks about?

And now there was the hottest of hot men in her trailer, a man who had only to look at her, and she became a puddle of goo inside. A man she wanted to lick like her fork after chocolate-covered pancakes at Alice's Diner. A man she wanted to drag into her bed, tie him down, and fuck him like a total sex goddess would. But she couldn't. She was nowhere near good enough for that, let alone for him. Waters was so out of her league that he might as well be in another universe.

Get over it, Kai. You're not the one-and-done type, anyway. You're not even a commitment type. Who the hell knows what type you are?

Sighing, she slipped on a white gauze sundress that slipped off one shoulder. It was times like this when she couldn't bear being confined by her typical battle armor.

She felt suffocated—hugged by the leggings, buttoned up by the tunics and oversized blouses, and forced upward by the heeled boots. Mindlessly running her fingers through her long hair, she began to braid it into a single plait over her shoulder. It was going to be a long night of last-minute details—likely a sleepless one—and she just didn't have the energy to dry it.

Another glance in the mirror, and she cringed at what Waters had witnessed this afternoon.

Time to face the music and apologize for my temper tantrum. Could I be lucky enough that he's already gone so that tomorrow I can pretend it never happened?

Kai emerged from the bathroom and entered the kitchen area. The blinds had been closed against the sun that would have been shining directly through the window, and the single light over her worktable was on with Waters sitting in his typical place, shuffling through her papers, putting everything into logical groupings, and lined up neatly in the top left corner. He must think she was a total slob.

Something brought her presence to his attention. It was a little spooky that he knew when she entered a room without making a sound, but she supposed that was part of the situational awareness he was always preaching. No one could ever accuse him of being oblivious to his surroundings.

He looked up, his face expressionless, and their eyes locked. His stare was so intense that she had to look down at the floor.

"I'm sorry about that," her voice just above a whisper and apologetic.

"Sorry for what, Kubrick?" he asked quizzically.

"I didn't want you to see that today."

"What shouldn't I have seen?"

"I was ugly. A bitch."

As if he were approaching a frightened animal, he slid out of the booth seat and crossed over to her. The tumbler was taken from her hand and placed on the counter.

Hands spanned her waist, and she felt herself being lifted into the air. Gently, he placed her on the counter so that he had to look slightly up at her. Under her lashes, she saw him pour a generous shot of tequila into the glass, and she followed his tanned hand, picking it up and handing it to her. Holding it in both hands, watching his face, she swallowed about half of it, allowing her neck to tilt back an extra bit as she felt the smooth burn down her throat.

Then he took the glass from her hand. As he shot the remaining clear liquid out of her glass, her gaze was drawn to his slow intake of the fiery liquid, his deliberate swallow, and then she locked eyes with him again as he set the glass down on the counter, pushing it and the bottle just out of her reach.

The back of his hand slid over her cheek. For just a moment, she allowed herself the guilty pleasure of closing her eyes and leaning her face into the stroke of his hand. When she opened her eyes, she confided to him, "I just can't seem to keep my mouth shut. I've been told repeatedly throughout my life that it's not a very attractive side of my personality."

Cupping her cheek, his thumb brushing gently back and forth, he spoke softly to her. "Depends on who's looking at you. Perhaps those people who find it so unattractive are envious they don't have the ease you do in speaking your mind. As for what I think? I think you were on fire."

"I pay you. Of course you're going to tell me that."

Confusion flared in his eyes. "I know we haven't known

each other long, but what the hell, Kubrick? Does it strike you as my style to mouth platitudes at anyone?" His hands framed her face. "What is this really about?"

Biting her lip, she dropped her gaze, but he wasn't allowing her to hide from him. He tilted her face up so that her eyes instinctively went to his own. She could feel tears stinging. She could not cry in front of him. That would be the final blow to her ego. She whispered, "When will I no longer need to fight for every inch of what I've already proven I can do?" A deep, ragged inhale and exhale escaped her. "I've made eleven movies, all box office successes, each bigger than the last. I've made careful choices and diversified across genres so that I can't be pigeonholed. I've had to fight tooth and claw for each one of those jobs, all because I have tits instead of a dick. I'm not afraid of working hard, so I've pushed and pushed and pushed. But it never seems to be enough. When am I good enough, Waters, just as I am?"

His hands left her face, lowering to gather her skirt in his hands, dragging the material to just above her knees. Gently pressing them away from each other, he stepped in tight to the counter to be closer to her. Brushing back the already drying wisps of hair escaping her braid, he begged her, "Don't doubt yourself. You were fierce today. I have never witnessed a woman wield power as you did. It was the most phenomenal thing I've ever seen in my life."

His smile was sad. "The problem is, you're so used to fighting your own battles you assume no one will stand beside you. But I've watched everyone around you, and I see a very different story. The people who work for you... they love you. You build them up instead of tearing them down. You show them they're important and that what they do matters to you and, by extension, others. You protect them by putting yourself in the line of fire for them, and you keep getting up each time you're shot at, too stubborn to lie down and take it.

"But you're not bulletproof, Kubrick. You can only take so much punishment before, eventually, the damage will become too great to rally. When that day comes, you'll need to lean on those people. You have an army you aren't even aware of. They'll heal the wounds you suffer, and they'll do it gladly, without question."

"You sound like you've been there."

His eyes seemed to go far away for a brief moment so that he wasn't really looking at her but at something past. "That's because I have. I have my tribe to hold me up when things seem darkest." Then, he was back to the present moment. "Learning to accept the help of others is one of the most difficult things to learn. Asking for that help is the only thing more humbling."

His forehead to hers, he reassured her, "You are good enough. More than good enough. A force to be reckoned with. I'm proud to work at your side."

Smiling with gratitude, she asked, "Why are you so fucking perfect? It's not fair."

"Not even close to perfect," he admitted. "But thank you for stroking my ego."

His irises seemed to flare, and then ever so gently, his forehead was replaced by a soft touch of his lips, where they lingered for just a second too long. He followed with a nuzzle of his nose tip to hers, then, as if realizing he might have crossed a line, he stepped back two steps from her.

Clearing his throat, he said, "I should go." His voice was only a step above a whisper. "Be careful not to micromanage here tonight. Just put all those papers in the file folders I laid out and into the Backpack of Death. I'll see you in the morning. Go home," he emphasized the last two words. "Pack. Get some sleep."

He walked to the door, but after he opened it, he looked back at her. "Don't forget. Fierce. A force. So much more than good enough." Then he left, reluctantly it seemed, shutting the door behind him.

Well, what the hell do I do with that?

She slid off the counter and crossed over to the table he had vacated, a smile on her lips at the neatness and order he left behind. Her face froze in thought.

He left behind... He left.

Waters broke one of his own rules. Rule five. One of his nonnegotiable rules.

"Huh. Interesting."

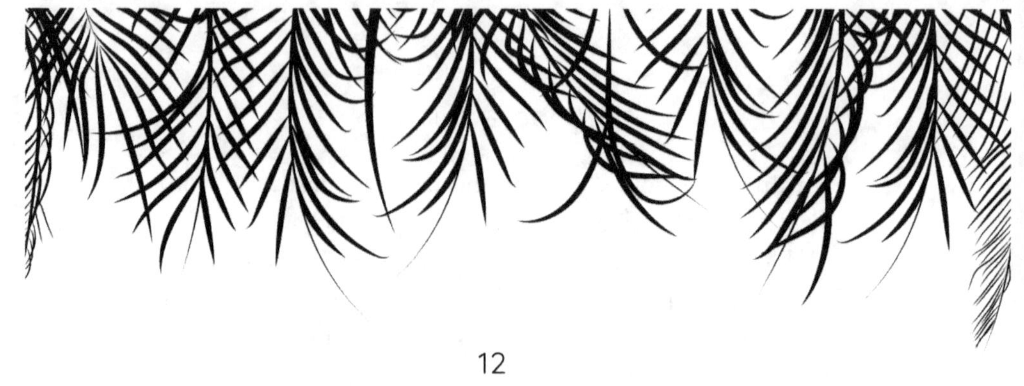

12

———————

FEBRUARY 14TH

Waters

WELL, WHAT THE HELL DO I DO WITH THAT?

It was currently just after four. He had to leave Kubrick's trailer before he made an even bigger mistake than the comforting kiss, but now he had to worry about her getting home since his dumb ass broke one of his own rules. What the hell was wrong with him? He didn't break rules. Ever.

First things first. Find a place to watch from until Steel arrives.

The studio was way too busy for him to use his normal space, and his truck was too recognizable even if he moved it, so he needed to come up with something else. The semi-trucks were gearing up to pull out and head to the airport with all of the freight for the cargo planes, along with crew leads and their builders. The actors were arriving throughout the day, starting the day after tomorrow, from

104

their various locations around the globe, with an orientation the day after that and training beginning the day after. The rest of the crew would be heading to Roatán in waves over the next four weeks, depending on what they did and when their services were about a week out from being needed. There wasn't anything for Waters to do other than help Kubrick to keep herself from micromanaging all the paperwork on the table.

She's probably totally confused right now about what you just did, and that paperwork will now be her coping mechanism to ignore the issue. Smooth move.

He stood at the bottom of the steps from her trailer door, rubbing the back of his neck with a hand that desperately wanted to smack himself upside the head. As he contemplated the merits of turning around and walking back into the trailer, his watch alarm went off with a double chime. Steel was checking in.

Please be here. Save me from myself.

Waters jogged lightly to his truck in the lot, a vantage point from where he could still see Kubrick's trailer. Once inside his truck, he engaged the ignition and activated the communications system. When it came online, he entered all his codes and dialed Steel's cell.

Steel picked up before the first ring had even finished. "Hola, Jefe."

"Welcome home, Steel. Get any sun?"

His teammate grunted. "I hate sun. And heat. And humidity. The Caribbean sucks. You ready to be relieved?" Steel asked.

You have no idea.

"On your way?" Waters asked.

There was a double tap on the passenger window.

Waters disconnected from the comm system and

punched the unlock feature on his doors. Barely opening the door, Steel slipped inside, tossing him a plain white bag. "God sent it for you." Waters reengaged the locks, then looked inside the bag.

Snickers bars.

"I hate that man," he groaned.

Steel just smirked and helped himself to one. When he noticed Waters' *really?* expression, Steel shrugged. "I'm hungry." He took a bite of the candy bar. As he adjusted his Raiders baseball cap over his black spiky hair, his ice-gray eyes were assessing his boss. "You look like shit."

"Thanks, honey."

Steel gave a small smile. "Update?"

Slipping on his aviators, Waters snuck a quick look at Kubrick's trailer. "She had a tough afternoon on multiple fronts." He shook his head before collecting himself. "She's busy gathering all her paperwork and last-minute files. On top of that, she hasn't packed yet, and we take off from LAX at seven-fifteen tomorrow. She'll probably pull an all-nighter, despite orders not to, so I guess at least you won't be watching dark windows all night."

"Cool. A home movie." It was the closest to a joke that Steel would probably make.

"You've seen the house?"

"Stopped there on the way here. Did a sweep. Tripped all eyes, outside and inside, to make sure everything's working."

"You went inside?"

Shrugging, Steel confessed, "I'm thorough. I'm watching one of my team's women."

"She's not my woman," Waters sighed. He felt like he did that a lot lately.

"Yeah, because you put every woman up on a counter, share a glass of tequila, and then kiss her on the forehead."

Waters bowed his head. "Fuck."

"Live feed at all times. Your orders, even. Hermano, you've got to stop giving them so much material to work with."

Some days, I hate my team.

"She was having a vulnerable moment. It's not going to happen again."

Steel said nothing.

"I did create a problem, though, which is I need to get her home safe."

"You could just barrel back in there, take her home, and let nature continue to take its course."

"I thought we were friends."

"I'm just sayin'." Steel shook his head in disgust. "Plan B, then. Still have my Uber sticker and app from that job last year. Tell her you have an old Navy buddy who's an Uber driver and that you arranged a ride."

Waters took out his phone and began to text Kubrick. "Brilliant. Plus it will force her to go home at a decent hour. I owe you."

"I'll add it to the list."

Waters abruptly switched gears. "You've seen Big Bird?" Steel nodded. "You see him approach, call me. I don't care what time it is. And you need to get into the room with them. I don't care if it breaks your cover. She is not to be around that man without protection."

"You still suspect him?"

"Yes and no. He's definitely got it out for Kubrick, but he may not be the reason we were contacted."

"She's a strong woman who clearly handles him just fine. Why the hypervigilance with him?"

"The guy's a prick."

Steel tilted his head at Waters' response.

Waters confessed. "I don't trust him with her."

Steel sat silent.

"He's vicious to her, Steel. Tries to undermine her every way possible, not to mention he just plain hates women. And besides all that, the way he goes after her, it's personal. I don't know what he's got against her, but she is unsafe around him."

"None of this is a reason to be so overprotective of someone who's 'not your woman,'" Steel reminded him, putting the last part in air quotes.

Scrubbing his face with his hands, Waters attempted to redirect the conversation again. "Tell me about Ka-Bar."

Steel shifted his gaze out the windshield. He took another bite of the candy bar and waited to speak until he swallowed, which Waters knew was a stalling technique to put together what he wanted to share. "Not much to tell. We were friends while we were in the teams."

"And you gave him your marker?"

Steel nodded. "There was a bar fight in South America that I needed some assistance with. Ka-Bar was nice enough to oblige."

"That tells me nothing."

"I know you've read my file. Hell, you gathered most of it."

"I know about the fight. I don't need a recap of the event because I'm looking for what's not in the file. What I don't know is why a Middle Eastern operative and a worldwide operative were in South America on their liberty, one of whom apparently took a barrage of shots to the chest and almost died. Get a little lost?"

Looking out the front window, Steel answered in a low

voice. "He helped me ship a package I couldn't get out of the country by myself. I owe him far more than a single favor. He has unlimited markers from me."

Waters shook his head and drummed his fingers on the steering wheel in exasperation. "Ka-Bar wouldn't need protection for her from a verbally abusive boss. She shreds him on a regular basis, so whatever's going on, God and I are relatively certain it's connected to Ka-Bar."

"And now Midas can't find him."

"It's like he's been erased."

"Yes, Midas has been agitated. That one does not suffer failure well."

Waters snorted. "That's because he's never failed. He's worried about his perfect record."

Nodding, Steel added, "That and I think he's developed a tendre for Kubrick. He has created a whiteboard worthy of a shrine to the woman. Very obsessed with her language skills." He grinned. "And he's developed a taste for these candy bars, so he is under a constant sugar rush. Cherry's already under orders to supply the office with God's disgusting suckers and Nemo's bubblegum. Now she's been told to supply the office with Snickers as well."

"Kill me now," Waters groaned. "Why is everyone so concerned about my lack of a sex life? I am NOT that grumpy over being celibate that I need candy like Betty White in that stupid commercial."

Steel grinned. "They never get to tease you, man. You've turned so straitlaced. Let them enjoy it a little."

"They're all making way too much out of this."

"Are they?" Steel's tone was serious now instead of teasing, and Waters knew that he would be unable to pass it off as nothing.

"She's... dangerous."

Shaking his head, Steel reminded him, "She's not Sarah, amigo."

"Not going there," Waters growled.

"But until you do, whatever this is with Kubrick will continue to confuse you."

"Did you hear what I just said? I'm not going there."

"Avoiding the problem is not going to make it go away."

"Fine. You wanna go there? Let's go there. If I couldn't protect Sarah, my own flesh and blood, my sister, for Christ's sake, I'm not going to be able to protect Kubrick."

"And this is where your problem is."

"Really? Exactly what is my problem?"

Steel shook his head in frustration. "Stop comparing the two women and their situations. Sarah was an operator. Kubrick is not. The situations aren't even close to the same."

"Exactly. It's worse."

"How so? Explain it to me because I don't see how."

"I cared about Sarah; my job made her vulnerable, and she died because of the choices I made. Don't mistake me; I'd make those same choices again. They were the right choices at the time. But I'll be damned if I put another woman in that position again. Just being seen with me puts her at risk."

"Then the same could be said for your entire team. You're putting all of us at risk, but that doesn't seem to bother you."

Waters opened his mouth as if to contradict Steel.

Steel cut him off before he could even utter a sound. "Your sister knew what she was getting into when she came to work for Tribe, same as you. Her *job* put her at risk, not you. What happened to her is a tragedy, and I wish it hadn't happened. We all do. Her death changed us all, but for you, it has a stranglehold on your heart. Those traffickers took Sarah. They're at fault. You didn't hand her over.

"You used to be impulsive, confident to the point of arrogance. I was always the one to keep you in line. Since Cairo? You've been quiet. Reserved. Oh, you make jokes here and there, try to make it look good. It's like you know what needs doing, yet you hold back, hesitant to commit to any action without overthinking. Sometimes, it feels like you are expecting the worst from us when you should be relying on what you know we are all capable of because you taught us to be who we are. It is not the Waters we knew before Cairo."

There was silence in the truck as Waters digested Steel's words.

Steel broke the silence. "Since taking on this job, Midas says you've been much less..."—he searched for the word he wanted—"restless. Oh, you piss and moan over the Snickers bar thing, and you threaten when everyone teases you, but you're... lighter. He said you've even smiled once or twice. It's not lost on us that there's an obvious reason why. All it took was one handshake over a conference table, and we all knew. You've been caught."

Waters sighed in exasperation. "Even if I was interested in pursuing something, I couldn't. God decreed that if we wanted to work for Tribe, then we forfeited our real-world lives to prevent the kind of shit we went through over Sarah. And even if God did decide, for some reason, to lift that restriction, it wouldn't change the risk to Kubrick.

"Besides that, how the hell would my world even begin to mesh with hers? She's a celebrity on the cusp of becoming a megastar. Hard to be dead when you're walking a red carpet with a major film director. And we'd never be together. She'd be off filming somewhere, and I'd be halfway around the globe in some hellhole, putting myself at risk. She'd have to give up her whole life to be with me, and she'd never know if I was coming back every time I went out the door. I would never ask that of her."

"You could give up Tribe for her."

Waters tilted his head toward Steel and looked over his sunglasses at the man.

"Okay, fine. Ridiculous option. But you're looking at this the wrong way round. You cannot quantify relationships in absolutes. It's never a 'her' or 'me' mentality. That's why it's called 'being a couple.' And even if her giving up this life was the route chosen, or you giving up this life, that's not your choice alone to make. You do that together. As for God? Let's just say his rule about relationships is probably as realistic as Nemo ever growing up to be a real boy."

They both chuckled at the unlikelihood of that.

Steel went to open the door. "Go home. Get some sleep. I'll watch over her. TB, Demon, and Nemo will be on the plane with you. Midas and I will cover things here and keep working on locating Ka-Bar and watching Big Bird."

With that, Steel slunk out of the truck as quickly as he had appeared.

Waters gave one last look at Kubrick's trailer.

What he wouldn't give to storm back in, throw her over his shoulder, and take her home until it was time to leave tomorrow morning. To show her just how "good enough" she was. But he couldn't. While, in theory, Steel might have logical points, it didn't change the fact she'd be the perfect target. She could be used as leverage, and he couldn't go through what happened with Sarah again. A second time would kill him for sure.

And yet, it took everything within him to put the truck

in reverse and head home to sleep for a few hours rather than act upon what he wanted.

Sleep. He needed sleep and then tomorrow, things would reset. Everything would go back to normal. He was just tired. Not enough sleep was making him think crazy thoughts.

Yup. There ya go. Lie to yourself some more.

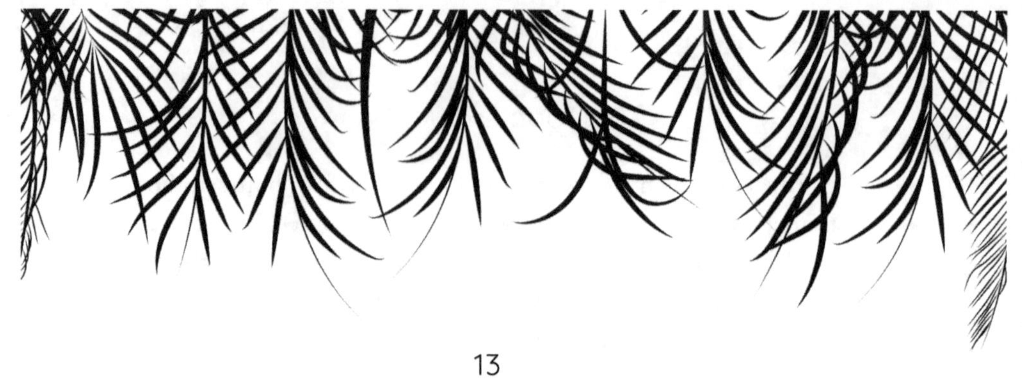

13

FEBRUARY 15TH

Waters

PULLING UP TO HER HOUSE THE NEXT MORNING, HE perused the street and noticed its isolation at this hour of the morning, so early that it was still dark. Getting out of the truck, he saw Kubrick exiting her front door with a duffle bag and her Backpack of Death. He jogged up the walk as she was locking the door. "Good morning, Sunshine!"

She scowled at him.

He looked at her two bags. "This is it?"

She blinked at him grumpily. "I travel light. Leggings and a few shirts don't take up a lot of room. Don't need boots where I'm going, so two pairs of running shoes, a light jacket, a hoodie, and my Dodgers hat. Add bug repellant, sunscreen, deodorant, body wash, toothbrush, toothpaste, and a brush; what else would I need? Plus, it's not like I'm going out clubbing while in Roatán."

Clubbing? Ugh. Did not need that image in my head. I'd be beating up guys left and right.

He cleared his throat. "Just figured you'd have a lot more bags since you'll be gone for almost three months." He looked at the duffle bag. "No designer luggage?"

She rolled her eyes. "Not my style. Not a big designer girl. Shit just gets damaged, and then it costs thousands to replace. Swiss Army"—she patted her backpack—"works just fine."

He shook his head as he grabbed her bags. "You sure don't fit the Hollywood mode, Kubrick."

"Nope. And damn glad. Way too fake." She yawned. "Way too damn early for this bullshit."

He opened the passenger side door for her. "C'mon, Cranky. Hop in." She flipped him off, to which he responded with a big grin of amusement. "There's a present for you in the truck," he offered, as if he were trying to lure her into the vehicle.

Opening his own door, he placed her bags behind his seat. When he slid in, he saw her looking at the extra-large thermal coffee cup in the holder of her seat like it was a mirage. "Two days in a row? I might get ideas."

"Seriously? Just drink it, Kubrick."

She sighed in resignation and popped the lid. "Is this from Alice's?"

"Not only is it from Alice's, but it's three of them. She saw me pull up and let me in to get it for you. I told her you needed your Crankiness Bomb, nuclear style. Thought she was going to hurt herself from laughing. Said that she was going to put them on the new menu with that size name just for you. So start drinking. Can't have you tongue-lashing the crew and other passengers with your awful morning personality."

Her tongue pushed through her lips at him, eyes scrunching up.

Staring at her lips, he huskily reminded her, "Rule six."

He swore she lost color at his words.

That'll shut her up.

He watched her out of the corner of his eye as he pulled the truck away from the curb. Lips pursed, blowing air on the liquid through the top hole, she sipped the hot chocolate laced with peppermint extract, and her eyes, honest to God, rolled back into her head. She even moaned. Awkwardly, he shifted in his seat, trying to adjust himself.

Shit. I'll buy her ten a day if that's the reaction she's going to have.

"Thank you. This was nice of you."

"You're welcome. You thought yesterday's Valentine's Day surprise was an aberration?"

Shrugging, she took another sip. "I figured one of the runners got it and passed it to you for me. They're always looking for reasons to talk to you. Perfect opening."

"No other women, Kubrick."

She side-eyed him. "Could have been Christoff and not one of the women."

He groaned, and then she was giggling.

"I love watching your face when he comes up to you with something. He's got it bad."

"Don't remind me."

"He told me since you're retired military, he wanted to see your gun.'"

"What did I just say to you? Am I talking to myself in this truck?"

Now she was full-out laughing. "I wonder what God would say about the harem plus one you've got on the lot.

And you've only been here a week. Imagine the damage you'd do if you hung around longer."

"Kubrick," he warned.

"We'd have to put you on retainer to take care of all the women's needs. And Christoff." Tears were leaking out of the corner of her eyes.

"No Christoff. No other women. I'm only interested in taking care of one woman's needs."

Kubrick stopped laughing.

Well, that came out wrong. Not a lie, but it came out wrong.

The rest of the ride was quiet. When they got to the airport, he swung his bag, hers, and her backpack onto his shoulders, then proceeded to secure the truck.

He did, however, get held up checking in due to his weapon.

"What was that all about?" Kubrick asked him at security.

"Must have been her first time checking in a weapon."

She stared at him blankly. "Excuse me, but did you say 'weapon'?"

"Yep."

"Umm..."

"Kubrick, I've had it every time I've been around you, and to be honest, since age eighteen, I haven't been anywhere without it. It's all legal; it's in a locked case in the cargo hold with the baggage, so everything is copacetic."

"We're on a movie shoot. Why would you need a weapon?"

He looked at her over his sunglasses.

"Oh, great gravy, okay!" Her voice went deep and growly, doing a Tarzan imitation. "Me big badass SEAL. Must have gun. Pew! Pew!" She made the universal gun shape with her thumb and forefinger as she pretended to shoot villains.

"No 'big badass SEAL' has a gun that goes 'Pew! Pew!' And I don't know that I'd make that gesture or talk about firing guns in an airport, or you'll get yourself on the No Fly List."

She waved her hand in front of her face as if to say *whatever*.

He leaned forward to whisper in her ear. "You know you sounded a lot like Cookie Monster, right?"

"You suck, Waters."

"I have about five smartass replies for that."

She rolled her eyes. "And all so original, I'm sure. C'mon, G.I. Joe. I want to make sure I get a decent chair in the Flight Club since some jerkface made me get here three fucking hours early."

Just short of the TSA screener in the precheck line, she tossed over her shoulder, "That wasn't your only weapon, was it?"

"What do you think?"

"Fuck me. What if you get caught?"

"Really?"

"How?" she hissed.

"Industry secret."

"Fuck me."

That comment he left alone.

Two hours later as he was walking along the concourse to the gate, he was shoulder-jacked by a giant of a man with dark spiky hair, a tan, and mirrored glasses over his eyes. "Sorry, mate," the man apologized in a New Zealand accent and with a slap on the front of his shoulder.

"No problem," Waters replied.

He took his sunglasses off the top of his head as he watched the man continue down the concourse. Placing the glasses in his inside jacket pocket, he felt an envelope tucked into it.

Alternate passports and cash in case of emergency. Check.

When he and Kubrick were boarding, a blond male flight attendant stopped her for a random bag search. "So sorry, ma'am. I need to search your carry-on."

Waters watched her shoulders go down the slightest bit in exasperation, but she handed it over without comment. The attendant put on latex gloves, opened the backpack, pulled out her computer, a mass of folders, and swept the inside for the check. He neatly placed everything back in the bag, then opened each of the pockets, sliding his hand inside and sweeping the sides. Zipping the last pocket to a closed position, he handed it back to her. "Thank you, ma'am." He scanned her ticket, and Kubrick passed onto the jetway. As the man scanned Waters' ticket, he gave him a slight chin lift and a smile. "You're all set, sir. Have a nice flight."

Trackers placed. Check.

Waters' chin lifted in return. "Thank you."

Inside the plane, Waters helped Kubrick extract her laptop from her backpack, then put the bag in the overhead compartment for her. He made sure she was settled in the window seat of the first row, then sat on the aisle seat, watching the people continue to board.

About five minutes later, a man with shoulder-length

dark hair, wire-rimmed glasses, and dressed all in black came aboard. His eyes went straight to Waters, and he stopped for a moment at his chair. "I'm glad I found you. You left this at Security." His Irish lilt and smile were nothing but friendly as he handed a small tablet over. "Looked for you everywhere on the concourse, so I guess it's the luck of the Irish I found you."

Waters took the tablet from the man and thanked him; then the other passenger went down the aisle.

Last-minute directives and secure messaging. Check.

He glanced over at Kubrick. Totally oblivious to what was going on around her. She was already clacking away at emails on the plane's Wi-Fi. Did the woman ever stop working? However, despite the three Crankiness Bombs, she was still yawning.

Enough is enough.

Waters flipped up the arm between their reclining seats, then reached over and closed the computer.

"Sleep, Kubrick. There's plenty of time for that when you've napped or while we're waiting in Houston."

She huffed at him, but the exasperation wasn't very energetic. In fact, she drifted off before the safety spiel even started, and by the time they were next in line to go airborne, she had curled up sideways in her perfectly comfortable seat, leaning her head on Waters' shoulder.

When the seatbelt sign went off, the male flight attendant was at his side, smiling, a blanket in his hand. "I noticed she looked exhausted. Thought she might want this." With that, he unfolded the thin blanket, which was large enough to technically cover them both, and spread it over Kubrick, folding the half that could go over Waters back on top of her again. He winked. "Just in case you get cold as well and want to cover up."

"Fucker," Waters murmured to the attendant's retreating back.

Without thinking, he turned his head and placed a soft kiss on the crown of her head. Settling into his seat, he opened the tablet and entered his codes only to find a group chat going on.

–TB, Demon, Nemo already in chat

– Waters now online

NEMO: You owe me $100.

TB: Not without confirmation.

NEMO: I had visual confirmation, Tuberculosis.

TB: Where?

NEMO: Top of her head. So cute!

DEMON: i hate coach cant c missing all the gud stuf

DEMON: u guys suk

DEMON: y cant i b in biz

TB: Because I'm 6'7 and 240, jackass. There's no way I'm going to fit in Coach. Someone has to be in the back of the plane. You barely weigh 200 lbs, so quit bellyaching.

NEMO: You had the chance to be the flight attendant, Demon. You said you didn't want to have to "work" on the flight. And Godzilla over there definitely can't be the flight attendant.

TB: RAWR

DEMON: f u

TB: You know, it's difficult sometimes to believe you have a Harvard education. Can't

spell. Can't punctuate. Can't write a literate sentence.
DEMON: f u 2 hate txtn

—God now online
—Midas now online

MIDAS: What did we miss?
NEMO: Ok, to sum up. TB owes me $100 for a kiss to the head. I'm proposing double or nothing Waters gets her off under the blanket during the flight. Triple if he does it on the LAX to IATA leg.
TB: I'll take that bet.
MIDAS: I will, too!
GOD: Get back to work, Midas. You're in the shithouse. You don't locate that package fast, I'm gonna fire your ass and you're going to need that $100.
MIDAS: I can multitask, bosshole.
GOD: Quit quoting your new girlfriend and get back to work.
WATERS: NOBODY IS GETTING ANYBODY OFF ON THIS FLIGHT OR ANY OTHER FLIGHT!!!!!
DEMON: i have 100 you strike out keep thinking that way
WATERS: WHAT IS WRONG WITH YOU PEOPLE?
DEMON: u want reel anser 2 that

MIDAS: Definitely need to get him a Snickers during the snack run.
WATERS: I QUIT. RIGHT NOW. YOUR MOTHERS SHOULD HAVE EATEN YOU ALL AT BIRTH.
NEMO: Wow.
NEMO: Guess I better give him 2 Snickers.
MIDAS: You can take down the caps, Betty. You're yelling.
WATERS: BECAUSE I'M PISSED!
NEMO: Better have more than 2 ready. Might have to toss them at him like marshmallows to bears in the zoo.

—Steel now online

NEMO: Hmmmmmmm
NEMO: I just had a thought.
TB: Don't hurt yourself.
NEMO: Here's a question.
DEMON: No!
TB: Who allowed Nitwit on the tablet? Control your genetic disaster Midas.
MIDAS: Hey I tried to absorb him in the womb.
WATERS: NEMO DON'T YOU DARE!!!!!
NEMO: You hurt my feelings. 😭
TB: I'm gonna hurt more than your feelings if you start that stupid game.
NEMO: How, Godzilla? Flight marshall will taser your ass.

NEMO: The creature is eating the plane from the inside out! Ahhhhhhhhhhh!

TB: I swear I'm going to shove that tablet down your throat when we set up base camp.

NEMO: Ok, so…

NEMO: Would you rather…

TB: Have me shove the tablet down your throat or up your ass?

NEMO: Get caught in the middle of the Big O while joining the Mile High Club…

NEMO: OR…

NEMO: Have the airplane toilet overflow with you locked inside?

WATERS: Mission name for this job: Shitshow.

MIDAS: Shitstorm maybe?

TB: More like shitstain.

STEEL: Well, this conversation went to the ninth level of hell fast.

DEMON: 😲

DEMON: so dun w/ u all

MIDAS: Is it even possible for the toilet to overflow in an airplane?

TB: We could send Numbnuts in to play with the blue water and find out.

MIDAS: Query. How long is the flight?

TB: Why would that matter?

MIDAS: Well, is the flight long enough to join the Mile High Club decently? I mean, I hate short timing that kind of thing.

MIDAS: Or is it a short enough flight that I

wouldn't be in the bathroom long enough to drown in shit?

DEMON: Really??????

MIDAS: It's a serious question.

MIDAS: You haven't seen some of the ways Nemo got in and out of places on a job.

STEEL: Amen, bro.

MIDAS: Oh, yeah. Nicaragua. Ewww. Sorry.

TB: Wow. You really upset the Harvard reject. He actually used punctuation.

DEMON: Fuck you, you twat. Number 2 in my class.

TB: Number 2 is right.

GOD: I pay you idiots too much money. Is ANYONE doing any damn work?

TB: Neither of those would happen to me because I don't fit in an airplane bathroom.

NEMO: Hell, I didn't realize emotional support dinosaurs were even allowed in the main cabin.

DEMON: this convo is unhygenic

STEEL: Mile High Club not romantic. And I've already traveled through a near-full sewer before and survived, so guess I'm locked in.

MIDAS: I'm all about Mile High Club.

NEMO: Waters?

NEMO: Waters?

NEMO: I know you're online, boss. It doesn't say you left.

WATERS: I'm wondering what possessed me to hire you people. I want to lock all of you in the same bathroom and let it fill up so you drown in shit together.

STEEL: No one but yourself to blame for hiring us.

WATERS: I hate you all right now.

NEMO: Great! So what's your answer?

NEMO: Come on, boss. You know the rules. You have to answer.

MIDAS: Of course he's going for the Mile High Club. He's on the plane with Kubrick.

WATERS: You're fired, Nemo.

GOD: No, he's not. Only I can fire him.

WATERS: Christ. Locked in.

NEMO: Liar. God's going to take away your Christmas bonus.

GOD: All of you get off this goddamn chat and back to work or I'm firing all of you.

—God now offline

NEMO: What a funsucker.

TB: I think you're grounded.

MIDAS: Which then means I'm grounded because I'm stuck here with the bosshole as well as related to your sorry ass. Way to go, fuckstick.

WATERS: Ok, guys, fun time is over. You all have shit to do. Move along.

WATERS: Midas, let me know as soon as you find even a single breadcrumb.

MIDAS: Roger that.

MIDAS: Have fun boss! I'll make sure Nemo throws away the key if you can get her in the bathroom.

—Midas now offline

WATERS: You're not just grounded. You're dead.
NEMO: 🙂
NEMO: On that note, I have to go start drink service.
NEMO: And find the Snickers stash.

—Nemo now offline

DEMON: Sleep boss we got ya covered

—Demon now offline

TB: Ditto.

—TB now offline
—TB now online

TB: BTW
TB: She's mouthy. My kind of girl.
TB: Don't fuck it up.

—TB now offline

STEEL: You ok?
WATERS: Yeah.

STEEL: I'll try to get them to ease up.
WATERS: Don't bother. It'll just make it worse.
STEEL: They'll give up if they get bored when you don't react to it.
STEEL: Probably.
STEEL: Maybe.
WATERS: Do you believe your own bullshit?
STEEL: I have an active fantasy life.

—Steel now offline.

"Fuckers," Waters mumbled under his breath. "They'll be the death of me."

To his left, Kubrick sighed and snuggled further into him in her sleep. He kissed the top of her head again and then shut his eyes. It was going to be a very long three months.

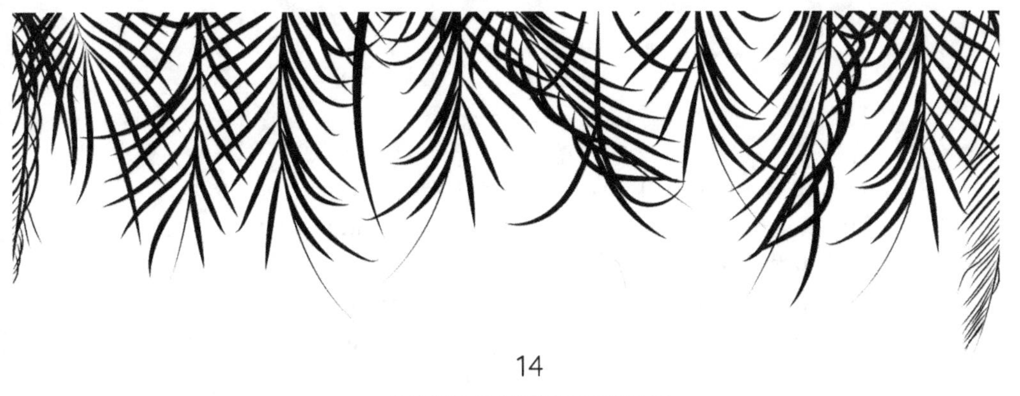

14

———————————

FEBRUARY 23RD

Waters

THE HOUSE THE EIGHT OF THEM WERE LIVING IN WAS A security nightmare.

It had the capability of modern conveniences, but they were not entirely dependable since the nearest town, Coxen Hole, which was also the capital city of the island, was ten miles away. There was the town, and then suddenly there wasn't, so things went from primitive to archaic quickly. This meant there was electricity, but other than the kitchen, it was relegated to fireplaces downstairs, one table lamp per room, and a single naked bulb ceiling light in the bathrooms. There was a possibility for hot water, but usually only in the downstairs sinks and tubs. And the internet was available, but service could be spotty.

On the second floor, the actress had a room to herself, and the five men were bunked as a double and a triple while

129

sharing a single full bathroom between the six of them. There were no curtains on any of the windows and only floor rugs on any of the floors.

Downstairs was only slightly better conditions-wise.

On the first floor was a large farmer's style kitchen, with a huge picture window above the sink and a mud room between it and the so-called backyard. While there were electrical outlets, most of the appliances they attached to were ancient. Waters noticed that the stove was gas and there was no coffee maker, so cooking would be simple, and they'd be making coffee and hot chocolate the old-fashioned way.

The front of the house was split between two main rooms: an old-fashioned parlor room and a library.

He had taken the old-fashioned parlor, which had somewhat recently been turned into a bedroom for someone who had been unable to climb the stairs of the house. A bathroom existed between the parlor and the kitchen, but it was so tiny he barely fit in it along with the toilet, sink, and claw-foot tub.

Across the hall from the parlor was what Kubrick dubbed the War Room, which was basically an old-fashioned library. Double doors opened into a large space with bookcases on three walls that went to the ceiling, two tall windows looking out into the so-called front yard from the fourth wall, a fireplace, a massive handmade antique desk with a high-backed leather chair behind it, a long leather sofa with a matching loveseat and armchair, a long rectangular coffee table, plus her workstation, which was basically a stand-up drafting table.

Weirdly enough, the room did have an older flat-screen television that could get a few local channels, including baseball for Kubrick. Secretly, it also gave Waters a source for Midas to hack into for security cameras. Thank goodness the man was a genius at seeing and hearing in places where most people could barely get cell service. During their first day of training, TB, Nemo, and Demon were going to be rushing to install short-term cameras and microphones for surveillance.

The one saving grace was that Kubrick's bedroom suite was only accessible through the War Room.

After the first four hours in the house alone, he'd tried to reason with her about locking up rooms and safeguarding personal items, as well as personal safety. She'd shot him down.

Then he tried playing the "prevention of curious locals from poking around" card and emphasized the potential invasions of their privacy, let alone their personal safety, especially when they would be out of the building for long periods of time with no security staff to watch over the building. She'd thrown back her head and laughed in his face.

When it was clear she wasn't going to see things his way, Waters had to give Kubrick an unconditional rule seven, which was that, at the very least, the War Room was to remain locked at all times. She'd gotten all ruffled and stomped off, muttering "Christ on a crutch" and something about military men with an obsession for bad guys around every corner, but she hadn't actually argued with him about it, so it was a huge victory in his mind.

As far as the film project itself, despite himself, he was encouraged by the actors' commitment and impressed that they weren't the prima donnas he had feared they would be. It gave him pause, too, because he hadn't expected to like them as much as he did. There was very little ego amongst them when they were together, and they balanced the work with the fun. Not the stereotypical idea of Hollywood stars at all.

But then again, is that a surprise? Would Kubrick willfully work with people who were difficult? Not likely.

Benjamin, nicknamed Lazarus, was playing the part of a former SEAL gone rogue, making him the villain in the film. He appeared to have some Native American ancestry in him that made all the women on the crew lose their ever-loving minds.

Maddox, nicknamed Dawg, was the perfect male lead: tall, blond, ripped, and as Sookie described him, "sex on a stick." Without question, his real-life persona and his nickname fit together all too well. Waters had a feeling it would be a very bad idea to introduce him to Nemo, Tribe's resident bad boy. He could only imagine them keeping scorecards on the scandalous things they'd done and where they'd done them.

Luca, nicknamed Jumper, came from a small rural town in Wisconsin and had been a three-sport athlete who could have signed to play quarterback at several major universities but chose instead to follow his heart to Hollywood. When Jumper arrived, he was dressed all Ken-doll chic with perfect blond hair and blue eyes. The next morning, he'd shown up with a self-shaved head, missing the blue-colored contacts, and ready to run.

Caleb, nicknamed Brick, lived up to the name. Of African ancestry, he was built like a rugby player—short, compact, and all muscle. His mouth was constantly going to the point that Kubrick kept telling him he had diarrhea of the mouth—it just kept running. Waters had a very difficult time keeping a straight face on that one and had to pretend he'd swallowed wrong to cough and suppress the laughter.

Cameron, nicknamed Enigma, was a dark horse. Tall, dark, and handsome, he was muscled and tattooed to the point of being the movie cliché SEAL. All the stereotypical vices had been a part of his life: the uppers to keep him focused, the benzos to get him to come down, blackout drinking, hangers-on supplying every narcotic known to man, a new woman on his arm every time he was photographed, and arrests for the destruction of property and assaulting a paparazzi. But this Enigma that Waters saw seemed to have things under control and was allegedly going on five years sober.

The last piece of the puzzle was Sookie, nicknamed Vixen. Tiny to the point of ridiculousness, long brown hair, and exotic green eyes, she was a walking dynamo and reminded him of a World War II pin-up girl. She was a blindingly beautiful girl, sugar sweet, and sincerely kind. However, she was a terrible flirt with all of the guys, including him, which was something he was finding uncomfortable for the first time in his life.

Overall, he was pleased with the group's efforts. It was easy to see that they would be good for the parts Kubrick had cast them in as they were already playing with personality traits when they trained—another insistence Kubrick made of them in order to try and get the foundation work for their characters to be natural, so they didn't have to also work on that when it came time to film. Things that she liked, they finessed into their process. Things that didn't work, they tossed and didn't return to. She was efficient at layering the job, like the character development on top of the training. At meals, she had them develop and share backstories for the characters, or she would have them improvise scenes the characters might find themselves in during everyday life. One of the things he had noticed about the script was that she often reworked scenes around action —eating meals, cleaning guns, packing parachutes—so that everything felt like it moved. Like people always multi-tasking in real life, nothing was static.

After the evening meals, they met in the War Room and continued the work, doing read-throughs, discussing scenes, and running lines. But they also used the time to get to know how each other worked or hang out. They genuinely liked each other, and it took almost no time to develop. Just last night, they had found a closet filled with board games, and a near-violent game of Team Battleship erupted with the stakes of laundry, garbage, and dish duty for a week on the line. Dawg and Brick lost spectacularly, which caused Jumper to go outside and roll around in the mud just so the laundry became more interesting.

And heaven forbid they caught anything baseball-related on the local TV, even a rerun from thirty years ago. The actors would heckle Kubrick and whatever team she rooted for as if they were fans of the opposing team, drink warm beer, make popcorn in the fireplace, and then throw said popcorn at Kubrick. All this while she tried to watch the game, answer emails, storyboard scenes, do rewrites, and discuss ideas with him. But she got distracted often. Mostly by food.

Cute. As. Fuck.

Currently, they were going over the week's schedule and trying to come up with contingency plans because there was potential weather coming in the next few days due to a tropical storm. Jumper had been channeling his high school baseball days, imitating batting stances all night long, and once he'd made it through the batting order, then he started to imitate the pitchers. Now the actors were singing a horrifically bad rendition of "Take Me Out to the Ball Game." At moments like this, it felt a bit like running an insane daycare.

Waters was sitting on the floor, his back against the couch, trying to concentrate. It wasn't working, but it wasn't because of the actors. Kubrick was sitting cross-legged behind him, and she kept leaning over his shoulder to steal potato chips out of his bag. When she wasn't stealing his food, she was shoving papers under his nose for him to review.

"Did you eat a ton of sugar before coming in here? Christ, woman, slow down. I can't keep up."

"That's because you're an old man," she teased.

"Umm... you're older than me."

"Pfft. Two months. Barely."

She laughed at him, then lunged for the potato chip bag, which he successfully thwarted despite the dizzying cloud of lilac scent he'd come to recognize as all Kubrick.

"Get your own," he groused.

"Mine are gone."

"Well, eat yours more slowly next time. Don't just dump them into your mouth directly from the bag. It's like your own damn version of Pudgy Bunny."

"Are you calling me a pig?"

Waters began to make pig snorting noises.

"You cheeky fucker! I'm going to give you such a pinch!" That, of course, was another epic fail, and he had to save her from falling off the couch two separate times. The second time, he got a handful of her breast, but other than a solid inhale from him, the fake fight just kept going with her trying to go at him from the other side.

"Do you have any fat on your body anywhere? Shit on a shingle, there's nowhere to grab any skin."

"Pretty much zero body fat." He slapped his abs with both hands.

"But you eat junk food," she marveled. "I've seen you shove a whole donut in your mouth. More than once."

"And work out way more than I should have to, especially since I'm herding cats here for you."

She laughed. "They're not that bad."

"No," he agreed, "they're pretty good. Dawg needs some corralling at times, and Brick needs a gag, but they focus well when they need to."

"Hmmm. I wonder if Jumper has a ball gag with him," Kubrick mused.

He turned almost entirely backward. "What?!"

She shrugged with an impish grin. "As for their focus, I put this group together very much by design. I don't hire problem children. No time or patience for it."

"You work with Big Bird." He turned back to face front, more than a bit disturbed by the throwaway comment from her about Jumper.

"Ah, but I didn't hire him. He hired me. And while I had major reservations and still wonder at my sanity for saying yes, as well as wonder why he wanted me since he detests me so much, I wanted this job almost more than I love chocolate. This could really solidify my career."

"You don't need solidifying. Your other work is excellent."

"You've seen it?"

He nodded while reviewing the cover shot storyboards she'd handed him.

"Which ones?"

He frowned, turning some pages so they were the right way round and shuffling them into chronological order. "All of them, I think."

"Wh-when? Why?"

"Before we left L.A. For research."

"Oh."

Will she ask?

He figured she would want to know which movie he liked best. The question she asked was unexpected.

"Did you believe what you were seeing? I mean, did you feel like it was real when you were watching them?"

Looking over his shoulder at her, something clicked. She had kept pushing with him and God that truth was what she worked toward in her work. It wasn't technical accuracy that she meant, although she did strive for that as much as possible. She wanted Truth. The capital T version. She wanted people to live in the world she created and be a part of the experience. "Yes. Even the wolf shifter romance, and I'm not fond of those kinds of movies. I can't buy into all the creatures. But when I watched that one, I just saw people who couldn't get along because they believed in different life philosophies." He turned his head back to the drawings and began adjusting one of her sketches with his pencil. "It reminded me of Afghanistan, actually."

"I'm not sure if I should be sorry about that or flattered."

She reached over his shoulder with her own pencil and made some adjustments to a storyboard frame on the far left. He breathed deeply, as quietly and unobtrusively as he could.

I will never smell lilacs and not think of her.

He cleared his throat to settle himself. "The people in the Middle East, most of them are pawns on a chessboard.

It's not their fault what's going on. Most of them don't want it any more than we do. But they're just as powerless to stop it as the average American. The kindness I saw while there for our soldiers, especially with the wounded, was sometimes even greater than what we experienced back home. We tried not to trade on that because villages got punished for helping the Infidel. But we always tried to do what we could. The kids were the best. We'd get our asses handed to us on a regular basis by them. Their soccer skills were insane."

He reached into his thigh cargo pocket and pulled out a thin credit card sleeve, sliding out a folded photo of himself and an Afghani teen. Handing it to her, he watched her reaction. The photo was beat up, as he'd been carrying it around for over a decade.

She was smiling softly before looking up at him. "You're such a baby there."

"It was my first tour. Nineteen. His name was Hesam."

She handed the photo back to him. "Was?"

"At one point, there was a reporter with us for a while, and he sent me this after he came home from doing his story. He was there when Hesam died shortly after our unit moved on. He thought I'd want to know." He slid the photo back into the sleeve and put it back into his cargo pocket. "One of those innocent victims. I carry the picture to remind me that good people exist everywhere. Corny. But sometimes, in my line of work, you need a reminder."

Lilacs wrapped around him comfortingly as she placed a hand on his shoulder and whispered in his ear, "You're a wonderful human being, Waters. Fucking perfect." Her lips barely pressed against the side of his head.

Without thinking about it, he reached a hand up to grasp hers as she lifted it from his shoulder. He tilted his head to brush his cheek against the back of it. "You're pretty damn perfect yourself, Kubrick."

It was late. The actors had all drifted off to bed. Kubrick and Waters barely even noticed that everyone was gone. She was lying on the floor, shoveling more junk food into her mouth, a paper script in pieces in front of her —which were clearly out of order now, given the grumbling and page flipping that was going on—and there were a number of pencils she had worn down to blunt tips scattered around her. Waters sat on the couch, feet propped on the coffee table, tablet in his lap. He was trying to concentrate on the email in front of him, but between her constant whispered swearing and the contents of the email, he couldn't stay focused.

Doesn't help that she's ass up on the floor, either. Knew it would be wicked.

He watched her unwrap another Zinger and start shoving it in her mouth.

Grinning and shaking his head, he went back to his computer screen.

Hey, Boss.
Midas still has no new information on our missing sailor.

Boss is so pissed and ate so many suckers he broke two teeth. Cherry took away his stash.

Now everybody in that office is cranky. Glad I'm here with you.

Cyclopes is up and watching all entrances and exits, plus the main rooms and hallways, live 24/7. Bedrooms are also recording but are not live to view. If you need him to turn off the feed for any reason (wink, wink, nudge, nudge), just use "Stanley" as a code, and the system will shut down until you tell him to turn it back on.

Fun story. We sent Nerdboy on a field trip around the property. Dumbass got bit by a snake, so Demon had to play doctor. Apparently, it was the poisonous kind, so Nerdboy is limited for a day or two. By the way, Demon got his contract of employment today, so he'll be officially in place on set tomorrow.

— TB

It was concerning that there were still no leads on Ka-Bar, there'd been no attempts of anything hinky in connection to Kubrick, and that meant they were still at Ground Zero. That, in itself, was proof enough to Waters that something wasn't right, and obviously, God thought so as well if he was breaking perfectly good teeth.

"I give up." The groan from the floor was tortured as well as muffled. Kubrick was softly banging her forehead on the floor since she was face first on the carpet, arms and legs splayed like she was floating dead in the water.

"Never give up," Waters admonished. "There are still Zingers left in the box."

Without looking up from the floor, Kubrick grabbed the box and shook it. No sound came. "Nope. I ate them all."

Waters blinked. "There are twelve in a box."

"Yup." She threw the box across the room and huffed into the carpet.

"You ate twelve Zingers."

"Yup."

"Am I going to have to hold your hair while you puke them all up later?"

"Doubtful."

He shook his head in disbelief. "You're a human garbage can, you know that, don't you?"

"Yes, you've already established that you think I'm a pig."

"I do not think you're a pig. I do, however, worry your stomach is rotting from the inside out." He closed out his screen, shut down his tablet, and then slid to the floor, lying down next to her propped up on his elbows. He sorted through the pages strewn about. "Are you playing paper-work solitaire again?"

"Bite me," she snapped.

He glanced back over his shoulder at her ass. His mouth actually watered.

Oh, sweetheart... don't tease.

"Seriously, what are you trying to do here besides create a mess?" he wondered.

Kubrick rolled over onto her back, staring at the ceiling. "I thought I was making notes for blocking the first set of scenes, but I've got myself so turned around I can't even figure it out anymore."

"You do know you have over four weeks before cameras start rolling, right?"

"I know, but I'm a serial killer when it comes to planning."

He stopped sorting through the pages, glancing over at her with raised eyebrows. "Excuse me?"

She blew air out of her mouth up toward her forehead, and stray hairs blew out of her eyes. "Serial killers plan the work and then work the plan. I do the same with my scripts." She turned her head to face him. "Not a very pleasant analogy, is it?"

"No, it isn't. You need to stop watching all those crime procedurals."

Her gaze went back to the ceiling. "Mmm. Maybe that's why I can't get a date."

Waters swallowed tightly, then turned his attention back to the scattered pages on the floor. "Likening yourself to a serial killer could dampen someone's interest."

Hasn't dampened mine, but I'm pretty sure I'm certifiable when it comes to you.

"I wish it were that simple. I just don't think I inspire that sort of interest from men. Hell, I'd take interest from a woman right now."

Thank God I'm on my stomach on the floor right now. Awkward!

Clearing his throat, Waters reminded her, "You once told me that men are a nuisance."

"Oh, they are. But they have their uses. Particularly when things are frustrating." She looked back over at him. "The problem is, I don't even know why I'm frustrated with this right now. Things are going well. It's not like Big Bird is here throwing crap in my way, or the actors are creating drama. Maybe that's the issue. There are no problems for me to solve, and I'm used to there always being problems to solve."

"Hang in there. I'm sure problems will arise."

I certainly have a problem that has arisen.

A soft caress, barely there, whispered across his right shoulder. He turned his head to see Kubrick's index finger following his ink over his bare shoulder from front to back, where his tank top revealed a piece of his tattoo.

"It's driving me crazy. What is it? It's got to be a huge tattoo because I can see more ink on the back of your neck, and the design on the left side is similar in style."

"It's a Kraken."

"Not an octopus?"

"A Kraken is an octopus," he clarified.

"The Kraken is a Titan," she corrected, "not a simple octopus."

"Actually, technically, it's a giant squid, and extra technically, it's Norse, not Greek."

It was clear from the look on her face that his tone had been sharper than he intended. The tattoo was not something he was comfortable talking about with her. That message was obviously received because she retracted her hand quickly from her tracing.

He apologized. "Sorry. That came out a bit grumpy."

"Just a little. But that's okay. I was prying. I shouldn't have, and I'm sorry for crossing the line."

"No, it's okay. If it were that much of a dead zone for me, I wouldn't let the ink show for people to see. I just"—he ran a hand over his hair—"I guess I'm not ready to talk about it. At least not tonight."

"Understood." She rolled over and gathered the sheets of paper from her side of the floor, making a haphazard pile of them. "Maybe someday you'll share. But it's okay if you don't." She took the orderly pile of papers he'd collected and added them to her stack, then stood up from the floor. "I'm heading to bed. I don't want to be tired and cranky, or my trainer will make me run extra tomorrow." She winked at him, then took the stack of papers over to the desk. "Night, Waters," she called without looking back at him.

The door to her suite closed behind her.

"Night, Kubrick. Good dreams."

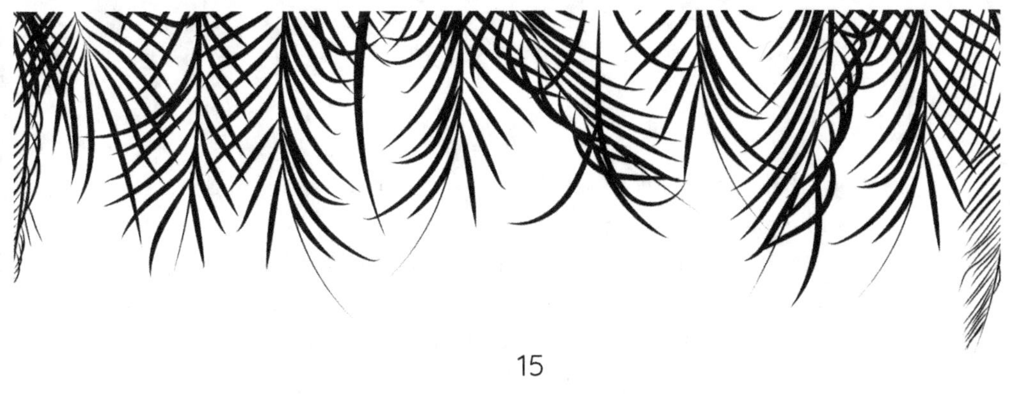

15
———————

MARCH 6TH

Waters

Things had settled into a comfortable pattern with Waters and the actors. And on the surface, things with Kubrick were smooth, too. But there were signs that some slight tension was present and felt by everyone when the two of them were together. Conversations would stop momentarily when one walked into a room where the other one was. If they were talking to each other, no one else talked but suddenly made themselves very focused on whatever they were doing. And even between the two of them, there was a subtle sense of wariness. Not painful, but clearly present.

Today, the actors and Kubrick had been training since seven a.m. It was now 10 a.m., and the rain that had been threatening for days had begun. Normally, February was when the rainy weather socked in, but today, the radar showed that they were on the edge of a late storm, and it was likely to be miserable today and possibly tomorrow.

After thirty minutes, the rain had picked up to "vigorous" and the temperature "bracing," per Dawg. Lazarus, the grouch, but also the most focused one of the bunch, was grumbling something about "I'll show you vigorous," to which Dawg just laughed. Brick and Jumper were trying to outdo each other, pushing and shoving each other as they ran like two five-year-olds, and Enigma was keeping pace with Vixen. Kubrick was running by herself. Waters would speed up and slow down as needed, watching form primarily but also helping with the obstacles. Lately, no help was needed.

He was at the wall and turned to see the actors' placement. His gaze automatically sought out Kubrick. She was just behind the leaders, Dawg and Lazarus. When they had started the course, she had been in a black Adidas running jacket, leggings, and sneakers, her Dodgers cap pulled low over her eyes, and sunglasses on despite the overcast day. He noticed that somewhere along the line, the jacket and glasses had been dumped. Now she was left in her sports bra, and the ball cap was turned backward with all of her hair piled up inside of it. They had just crawled through the mud pit under the barbed wire, and she was covered in the muck, almost looking like it was a spa treatment.

Mud, wet running gear, backward hat. Good goddamn, she's gorgeous.

He had purposefully not paced with her despite how much he wanted to. He didn't trust himself. It was hard enough standing beside her most of the day, listening to her direction, watching her reenact things for the actors. Filming wasn't due to start for three weeks yet, but that didn't stop her from using moments of training to do more foundational work that would be reenacted on film. She was not one to waste a chance to set and practice things early. The worst moment for him had been yesterday when she was showing Vixen exactly how to get into the proper body position she should create for the kissing scene with Dawg that happened directly after a fight scene they had just been practicing.

He didn't know how he was going to be on set for the sex scene when that came up later in the filming process. If she was going to demonstrate any of that positioning, he'd lose his shit. Technically, there would be no reason for him to be there, but since she couldn't go anywhere without him still, he obviously would need to be present. It was his job.

Keep telling yourself that, buddy. And while you're at it, how many more places and ways can you think of to hide the bodies if those guys keep looking at her?

He knew his thoughts were irrational. They had to look at her when talking or listening to her. But he couldn't help thinking stupid shit.

But now, the rain had become nearly torrential even though there was no thunder and lightning. Vixen was flagging, and they were approaching the last obstacle before the final quarter mile of straight-out running.

Suddenly, Brick and Jumper poured on the speed, bypassing Lazarus and Dawg, and hit the base of the wall, but they didn't shoot to the top. He was about to yell at them for stopping but pulled himself back just in time. His jaw may have even dropped open. They turned to face each other and made a basket with their hands.

Within seconds, Lazarus and Dawg were on them using the guys' hand baskets as springboards to the top of the wall.

When they had the top of the wall in hand, they pulled themselves the rest of the way and sat astride the wall. Kubrick had turned on her speed as Brick and Jumper had passed her, and she had it perfectly timed to be at the height of her stride, jumping to put one foot in the basket Jumper still held. He flew her to the top of the wall so she could grab on, where Lazarus and Dawg grabbed her forearms to pull her to the top.

Dawg then slid over the opposite side of the wall, and once fully extended, hanging by his fingertips, he dropped to the ground. Kubrick followed, but when she let go, she fell into the waiting arms of Dawg. In the meantime, Jumper formed a lunge position against the wall so that Brick could scurry over him. As the smaller, stockier man stepped on Jumper's shoulder, he was lifted like a circus acrobat, where Lazarus grabbed him by the forearms and hauled him to the top. Together, the two men sat astride the top, waiting to help the rest of their team.

When Enigma and Vixen arrived at the wall, Jumper formed the basket for Vixen's foot, and she was up where the two men at the top each grabbed a hand, working together to secure her to the top of the wall so that she could crawl over, then slide down into Dawg's waiting arms. When she hit the ground, Dawg grunted, "Go," and the two women took off.

In the meantime, Enigma had backed up for a running start, and with Jumper's help, he flew up to the top and over. Jumper backed up, then took a running leap for Lazarus' and Brick's forearms. Once atop the wall, all three men slid down the opposite side, and no sooner did their feet touch the ground, they were all off and running.

They never said a word during the process other than Dawg's order to the women. No instructions. No encouragement. They had used situational awareness and worked together as if they'd choreographed the maneuver and practiced it a million times.

Well, fuck me running.

Waters took off after them, not sure he'd actually seen what he'd just seen. He couldn't help but be impressed. They were looking like a team and a damn competent one at that. He knew they were miserable, frozen, and tired. But not a single one of them asked about quitting, even as a joke. They were all in, just like Kubrick had said they would be.

Then he saw Vixen stumble, and it looked like she turned her ankle. Kubrick didn't miss a beat. She helped Vixen up, put an arm around the injured girl's waist, and kept her moving.

My golden girl. Never leaves anyone behind.

And there was the tension. He was starting to think of her as all sorts of things with "my" in front of them. He couldn't help it. The attraction was too strong. He liked her. He damn sure wanted her. But pursuing anything would likely cause one or both of them to be hurt when he left, and he didn't want it to be her. So, he did his best to ignore what his body wanted.

He began to increase his own speed, but the guys had already seen what had happened and pushed their limits to get to the women. Enigma got there first and swept Vixen off her feet, passing her onto him piggyback style to get to the finish line. The rest of the team formed a circle of protection around them.

Well, double fuck me running.

He caught up to the group at the lean-to that sat at the start/finish line of the obstacle course. Enigma had Vixen on the bench, shoe and sock off, examining her already swelling ankle. "Way to go, woman. You know there are easier ways to get us out of running in the rain, Vix," Dawg teased.

"Shove off, Dawg. I didn't do it on purpose."

"All right, ladies, break it up," Waters barked. "Chafes me to say it, but this rain is getting too heavy. Head inside today. Make sure to stretch out. Take a long, hot shower. Get some rest."

What are you doing? There's other training you all could do.

Enigma stood and presented his back to Vixen. "C'mon, Flash. Let's go get that ankle looked at."

He began to walk off, happening to catch Waters' eye. Waters gave him a miniscule nod; Enigma's chin lift was just as small, and then he took off with Vixen at a jog.

"Dammit, I'd have carried her," Dawg grumbled. "He's so getting laid this afternoon."

Jumper smacked the back of his head. "Aww, it's okay Dawg. You're getting laid, too. Just by your right hand."

"Maybe it'll be a ménage," Brick piped in. "I hear Dawg is ambidextrous."

Dawg clenched his jaw and then grumbled. "You're just jealous I get some variety to my strokin'." The guys continued to jab at each other as they took off for the house. Lazarus and Waters stood watching the three goofballs as

Brick smacked Dawg's ass, stole Jumper's hat, and tore off down the trail.

Lazarus grinned and shook his head. He looked at Waters. "I'm guessing she didn't tell you that you'd be babysitting late-twenties grown men going on five?"

"Nope. That wasn't quite how the job was described," he admitted.

Lazarus' eyes wandered over to Kubrick, who was collecting her jacket and glasses, and Waters' molars began grinding. He could see the heat in Lazarus' eyes.

"You know," Lazarus began quietly, his eyes drifting back to the three amigos who were now just specks in the distance, "she's special. I envy you."

Waters went still.

"Kubrick," Lazarus continued as if they both didn't know whom he was talking about. "She's special."

Fuck, fuck, fuck. I knew it. They have a thing.

Lazarus carried on. "I thought about approaching her once, but I took a film project and was gone for four months. When I came back, she was on location for two months, and our schedules just never seemed to match up after that. The next time I see her is in February for this shoot, but... her heart is already engaged elsewhere. I thought maybe she'd met someone in Egypt, but it turns out the guy was much closer to home."

Brain whirling on which guy Kubrick seemed to be focusing on more than the others, he forced that to the back and let his mouth ask the more pressing question. "Kubrick was in Egypt? When?"

Lazarus thought back. "Middle of November, she went to Europe, so maybe in the middle of December? Something like that. I know she met with a director friend to research and scout somewhere on another possible project. That was just before Thanksgiving, and she came home by New Year's." He glanced behind him. "Anyway... don't screw up like I did." And with that, Lazarus flipped up the hood of his short-sleeved running shirt and took off in the rain for the house.

Can't screw up what doesn't happen.

As he walked over to her, Kubrick spoke up from behind the bench. "We're stuck for the time being. If the rain stops, we can start back up, but the radar shows it getting worse."

She was tapping on her smartwatch, looking at the forecast, totally unaware he was studying her. Her skin was flushed from the exercise and pebbled from the cold, but her breathing had finally normalized. Most of the mud had come off her skin in the rain, but her clothes were caked with it. Strands of her hair escaped from under her mud-stained hat.

She looked fucking amazing.

He unzipped his windbreaker, removed it, put it over her shoulders, encouraged her arms into it, then zipped her up tight. He smoothed it down her form, noticing that it fell long past her ass, just like one of her signature blouses.

Thank Christ, because I knew her ass would be wicked in those leggings, and it sure as hell is.

Her face was scrunched up in confusion at his actions.

"Your jacket is soaked, and you're freezing," he explained.

"What about you? Won't you be cold?"

He just looked at her with his eyebrow arched.

"Right," she whispered.

After a minute or so, he cleared his throat. "You all did well. Great, truth be told. Some strong teamwork. They're starting to develop what you wanted."

She beamed. "Yeah, they are. Thank you for that. It's all your doing. They respect you."

He shrugged. "They do it for you because they like you. Me? I'm mean to them. If I'm soft on them, they won't push themselves. I doubt it's respect."

"Yes, you're tough on them. When they're in a group, you're downright scary when you push them. But when you work with them one-on-one, you're different. More encouraging. They respond to that. And while Vixen's still a bit afraid of you, the attraction is starting to overrun that. Enigma's not going to like the competition. Pretty soon you can probably expect her to be looking for even more excuses to get close to you," she teased.

Well, she was trying to tease him. He could tell her comments were tasting a bit sour in her mouth. Could that someone Lazarus mentioned be him? He knew he was attracted to her, and he knew she wasn't disinterested in him based on prior conversations. There'd been this weird feeling between them since the tattoo discussion, and he wasn't quite sure what to do with it.

Oh, you know exactly what to do with it, dipshit.

He could have just ignored her words, but something inside couldn't let it slide. "She's a nice girl but... not really my type," he admitted. He stepped into her personal space, pulling the collar of his windbreaker out from where it was stuck inside of itself, then unnecessarily smoothed it over her shoulders. "She's certainly attractive, and she's not as spoiled as I thought she would be, but she's much too docile, as well." He gently took Kubrick's chin in hand and used his thumb to swipe a trace of mud off. He heard his voice drop to almost a whisper. "I'm much more attracted to fearless women who want to be equals with their partner."

Now you've done it. You know what happens when you touch her.

"I see." He could tell she didn't, though.

The rain pinged off the metal roof of the lean-to. She was staring at him with no expression, but he couldn't help feeling that something had just changed forever. Again, they stood quietly watching each other. Finally, Kubrick said, "I'm gonna tell everyone to take the rest of the day off."

Think of something quick, idiot. You're going to lose this... whatever it is... with her.

He told himself he needed to find a way to keep her with him the rest of the day. The operator in him was justifying that he could use the time to work the conversation into her trip to Egypt. He had a sneaking suspicion Ka-Bar's favor might have to do with that time period. The country was officially coming up way too often in their digging.

However, the man in him figured maybe he could dig a little and sound her out about Lazarus. Was she interested in the man? This second-guessing wasn't his way. Normally, he'd bulldoze his way through for the information. But the two seemed to be nice and easy together, and he did feel like he couldn't compete with a Hollywood icon. After all, if it wasn't Lazarus, could she really be into him? Or was it one of the others?

The thought caused his gut to roll. It sucked. He liked Lazarus and the guys. He wanted them to be shallow pricks so he could hate them. Unfortunately, no such luck. It sucked wanting to put the hurt on someone you liked only because he kept touching the woman you wanted to claim but couldn't. Or shouldn't. Or didn't.

"I'm going to go dry off and then work in the War Room. You, um, wanna get a head start on the rest of the week with me?" she asked.

Bad idea. Don't do it. Too much time that close to her is a terrible idea. The War Room is too sequestered. Too cozy. It won't end well.

He swallowed hard. "Sure."

The operator in him puffed up with satisfaction. Problem solved. She made it easy for him to question her without even knowing it. Now, he could distract himself from the magnetic pull he felt to her by doing his job.

Yeah... lying to himself was becoming a terrible habit.

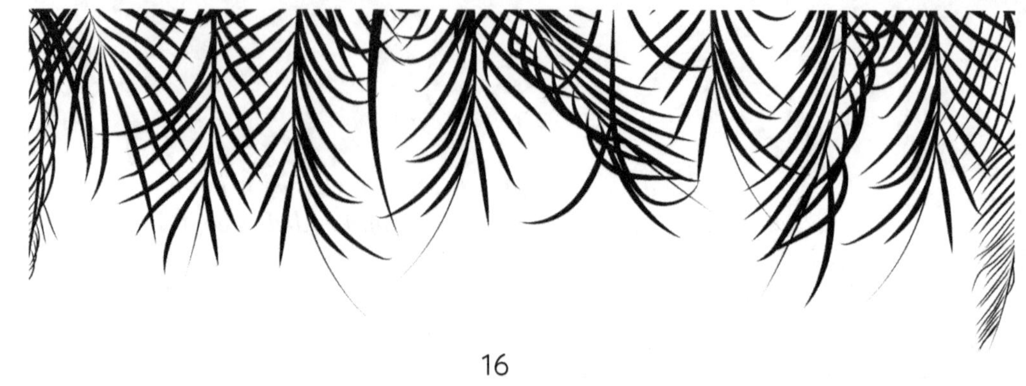

16

———————

MARCH 6TH

Kai

KAI STEPPED OUT OF THE SHOWER, WRAPPED A TOWEL around herself, and proceeded to finger-comb through her hair. The overall temperature might be in the seventies, but the storm and mud had left her with quite a chill, and the house always felt a little bit damp. With everyone showering right now, she was lucky the water was warm enough to take away the chill. Quickly, she applied lotion to her arms and legs, moisturizer to her face to help take out some of the sting from the wind burn, and then slid into her bra, panties, Dodgers hoodie, gray joggers, and a pair of matching Dodgers ankle socks.

Tossing her towels over the tub's edge, she exited the bathroom, passed through her bedroom, and moved into the War Room, stopping just short of gasping. Waters was already there. He, too, was fresh from his shower. He wore a dark-gray tee and black track pants. Around his neck, he had a white hand towel, and his feet were bare. He had a coffee cup in one hand that he sipped from as he flipped through the storyboard renderings on her easel table.

So not fair. No man should look so edible.

He looked up at her and handed her another coffee cup. "Hope it's right." His gaze went back to the boards.

Kai cradled the ceramic mug between her hands, soaking up its warmth and inhaling the rich chocolate scent wafting up from the content's surface. Cautiously, she sipped the heated liquid and couldn't contain the moan of enjoyment.

Holy shit, he made me a Crankiness Bomb?

Through half-raised lids, she saw him intently watching her, a soft smile on his lips. "I'm guessing it's right. Never seen a woman enjoy chocolate like that. I've heard for some of you it's a sexual experience, but damn."

Blushing, she moved to stand next to him at the table, dropping her eyes to what was on the papers. "We've already discussed my intense relationship with chocolate." She lightly hip-checked him. "And yes, it's perfect." She took another sip. "What are you looking for?"

"I had a thought when I was in the shower." He looked at her and saw the smirk. Now it was his turn to hip-check her, which he did a little harder than her effort had been. "Stop it. About the movie."

"Uh-huh." She sipped more of the minty sweetness from her cup. "Was it a 'good' thought?"

He snorted at her throwing their first breakfast morning in his face. "Not that good, I'm afraid. Was only a five-minute shower."

"Wow. With your strong sense of control? Here I thought you would make it at least seven."

"Saucy. Don't tease. I'll put you over my knee."

"Pshh. Try it, and I'll break you. I know a big, bad, former Navy SEAL who's taught me some pretty freaky shit to put the hurt on men like you."

He chuckled. "That's my girl. Seriously, though. I was thinking about the wall. I think you should use that in the film. Use some of that with the cliff climb you had planned." He had put his coffee mug down to the side and was flipping through pages, looking for what he was picturing. He found it and pulled the rendering clear. "Here. What you all did today was seamless. Natural. Especially afterward when Vixen turned her ankle. It would show their teamwork much better."

Kai grabbed a clean sheet of sketching paper and a pencil. Noticing it was dulled down to a nub, she started looking around for a sharpener.

"Gimme." He took the pencil from her and sharpened it. After he handed her the fresh pencil, he worked on sharpening several more as she stood and sketched.

Frame after frame poured out of the pencil tips. He disappeared at one point with her cup, came back with a fresh mug, and helped switch out the pages as she needed new ones. She was so focused that an hour of silence passed other than the grinding of the sharpener, the flipping of pages of storyboards, and the scratching of the pencil on paper. When she was done, she set the pencil down, reaching high to stretch out her back from being hunched over the table. A cramp moved through her knuckles, and she shook out her hand.

"Come here." Waters grabbed her hand and pulled her over to the leather sofa in front of the fireplace. At some point, he must have gotten it going as she finally noticed that the room had lost some of its chill. He sat on the couch back, pulling her to sit on the cushion in front of him. Bundling her hair into a single ponytail, he moved it over her shoulder, then proceeded to work the knots out of her neck and shoulders from being hunched over the table.

"Oh, God. Don't ever stop," she begged.

Wow. That didn't sound desperate at all.

There was a slight stutter to the rotations of his thumbs. He didn't say anything, but he also didn't stop. She wondered if she should be embarrassed by her near sex-moan over the massaging fingers on her body. Luckily, her face was turned away from him. Hopefully, only her face was burning scarlet and not her neck and ears, which he could see from his perch behind her.

He slid down behind her, his thighs now hugging hers on the cushion. "Hand," he ordered. She tried to move from between his legs, but she was stalled by his knees squeezing her thighs and his repeated command of "hand." She lifted her right hand from her lap. Two veiny forearms came around her from the back, hugging her close as he began massaging the palm, back, joints, and fingers. It was impossible to stop the moan that issued forward.

"Saucy," he warned.

"Hey, it's your fault, not mine. I can't help it that you have magic hands."

"Magic, huh?" His question was a bit muffled by the forced proximity to her hair over her shoulder. She swore she heard him whisper into her hair, "If you only knew."

He was hell on her equilibrium, and she would fall for him headfirst if he didn't stop being so damn good at everything. She shivered, but it wasn't because she was cold. At her movement, he slid out from behind her and grabbed the blanket that was at the end of the couch. "Under."

She scooted to the corner of the couch, leaning into the oversized pillow there, and he spread the blanket over her. "Do you talk to all women in single-word commands?"

He grunted. "No." She quirked an eyebrow at him and tilted her head to the side. He looked away from her teasing gaze and intently focused his eyes on where he was, ensuring she was tucked in under the blanket. Then he shrugged. "Just with you. Otherwise, I'm known for being much more... verbal."

"Ooh, do tell," she drawled.

"Only if I get to hear the truth about that good dream that you have deftly sidestepped telling me about for almost a month."

"Absolutely not."

He shook his head as he explained, "Well, then I guess you're going to be disappointed."

She sighed. "Damn. And here I was, hoping for a sexy bedtime story."

He grunted again and grabbed the remote. "Behave and watch your boys." He turned on the television and clicked some buttons to connect it by Wi-Fi to his tablet.

"You recorded the game for me?"

Shrugging like it was no big deal, he answered, "You missed last night's preseason game because you were arguing with Big Bird."

Before the second inning, sleepiness started to overtake her. She was curled up under the blanket pretending to watch the game, and he was sitting just out of reach of her feet, his legs stretched out with his heels crossed on the coffee table, checking emails on his laptop and scowling at whatever he was reading. He was terribly sexy when he was irritated.

And when he's smiling. And when he's working out. And when he's talking to the actors. And when he's watching TV. Don't think he's ever not terribly sexy.

For a tough guy, he definitely was thoughtful. He gave her his jacket to keep off the rain and chill. He made sure she had her Crankiness Bombs, and when she couldn't make it herself, he attempted to make one and worried if it was right. He saw to her aches from standing at the worktable. He tucked her in. He recorded her damn baseball game when he saw she had to deal with her batshit boss.

He truly is fucking perfect.

Recognizing the torture she was putting herself through, she turned her attention back to the game. Between the warmth from the fireplace, the constant pelting of the rain on the outside of the house, the comfort of the couch, the exhaustion from the morning's workout, and the ease of Waters' company, she nodded off into a peaceful nap.

A soft rumble of thunder woke her. She felt firm, gentle circles being rubbed into the arch of her foot. Holding her breath and trying not to telegraph that she was awake, she looked through her half-closed eyes down the length of the couch. The soft amber light from the fireplace and the glow from the TV screen lit Waters' face as he watched the game. His laptop was on the coffee table, closed up, and her feet were in his lap where he was massaging one without watching what he was doing.

"Have a good nap?" he asked, still not looking at her.

Embarrassed at being caught awake, she tried to pull her foot back, but he gripped it tightly in his hands. She stopped struggling, unable to relax at him touching her now that he knew she was awake. He said nothing, just kept massaging her arch. Eventually, it was easier to let the tension go than to worry about what he was doing or why he was doing it.

She couldn't tear her eyes away from his profile. He truly was beautiful. So beautiful, it hurt to look at him. In a few short weeks, he'd be gone, and she wasn't sure how she would recover from him. How had that happened?

The volume of the game was so low she couldn't hear more than a muted undertone. Looking down at her foot, he swallowed, seeming to come to some sort of decision. Something that was weighing on him. Then he slid ninety degrees on the couch to recline against the opposite arm, one foot flat on the floor, the other folded underneath him. "Tell me something about you."

"What?" she asked, rolling completely onto her back, the pillow propping her up halfway.

He shrugged. "Anything. Something I don't know. Something that's not in your file. Something... insignificant."

Should I be offended that he's dug into my background?

"I like massages."

"I said something I don't know. I already know you like those." At her blank look, he winked and gave her that sexy grin. "You moan on the up swipe."

She gasped. Her tone was petulant when she denied, "I do not moan."

"Oh, yeah," he taunted. "You moan. It's quiet, and it's breathy, but...You. Moan." Blushing, she tried again to pull her foot away, but he wasn't having it. "It's cute," he admitted. "C'mon. Give me a Kubrick factoid."

"Umm..." Her brain whirled and was coming up with nothing until she blurted out, "I can't wear mismatching socks."

He blinked. "You can't wear mismatching socks?"

"Yeah. When I was a teenager, it was a thing. You didn't wear matching socks. So, like one would be green, and one would be orange, or two different patterns like one would have dogs on it and another one bananas or something."

"Why in the world would people wear mismatching socks?"

She giggled at the horror on his face. "It was a stupid girly trend. Not everyone is OCD regarding matching like you military types. You probably iron yours, everything's always so neat."

"I promise. I do not iron my socks." He considered. "So, why no mismatching socks?"

She contemplated her response. Finally, she replied, "I think it's a control thing. I did try. I closed my eyes and tried to pull two different colors out of the drawer and put them on, but I couldn't even stand up and walk across the room in them. Made me feel like the world was tilting on its axis. I'm that way about everything. Everything always matches. I'm even more fanatical about my bras and underwear."

His hands froze, placing pressure in the arch.

What the hell, woman? For once, can you please filter your thoughts from your tongue?

All she could hear again were the muted announcers, the fire popping, and a distant rumble of thunder.

Then she heard, "So, what color are they?

"What?" she squeaked.

"I can see you're wearing matching Dodger-blue socks. So, what color are your bra and underwear?"

"Umm... pink?"

"You're not sure?"

"Why are we talking about this?" She squirmed.

"You brought it up."

"Yeah, but it was an oops. And I didn't think you'd latch onto that and wanna discuss it. A gentleman would ignore it."

"I'm not a gentleman, Kubrick," he warned. "You can't put that out there and leave a warm-blooded man wondering about that information. Besides, 'oops' comments of yours are my favorite. Keeps me on my toes. Soooo???" He circled one hand in the air, suggesting she get on with it. "And please tell me they're sexier than your socks."

"What is wrong with you?"

He chuckled. "Depends on whom you ask." His hands stopped moving on her foot. "They're not Dodger themed, are they? For the love of all things good in this world, tell me no."

"They only make boxer shorts," she grumbled.

"Good grief. You've actually researched that, haven't you?"

"What if I have?" she defended herself. "A girl's gotta support her boys."

"I'm thinking a bra is supposed to support her girls, but that's a whole other conversation. So. Pink." His fingers had crept up her legs and were working out the knots in the base of her calves. "Just pink?"

She rolled her eyes. "Seriously, why can't you let this go?"

He stopped his massage but kept pressing into the muscles.

"Ow! Fine! Be a dick. They're pink with black polka dots."

He began massaging her calves again. "I like pink."

She huffed. "I bet you do." She picked up a throw pillow from underneath her and tossed it at his head. "Just for that, I'm not telling you if they're sexy or not. You'll just have to let your imagination run wild."

"Mmm." He closed his eyes and engaged in a pleasure-filled smile.

"Oh my God! Get your dirty mind off my underwear!"

He started laughing and tossed the pillow back at her. "You're so easy."

"You wish. Okay. Turnabout's fair play. Tell me something I wouldn't find in the file of Super-Secret Badass Waters."

"Badass, huh? I'll take that. Hmm..." She could see the gears turning as he thought about what to share. "When I'm at home, I sleep with a night light."

She stared. "I don't even know how to begin to process that."

He chuckled. "No, I'm not afraid of the dark. And I don't do it anywhere else. Just at home."

"Dare I ask why?"

"Because when I was in the military, the light could be dangerous, so we kept everything pitch black. Besides, if I ever decide to have company at home, I'm guessing I'd like to see what's in front of me." He winked again.

Holy hell, horseshoes, and hand grenades!

He changed the subject. "Why the Dodgers? You're not originally from L.A."

"For as far back as I can remember, I always wanted to

live in L.A., so anything that centered around the city was what I loved. But you want to know a secret?"

"Always wanna know your secrets, Kubrick."

Bet you don't want to know the Big Secret. The one where I can't stop thinking about kissing you.

Hugging the throw pillow to her stomach, she shoved that secret to the side. "My favorite player isn't a Dodger. I mean, Kershaw is a god greater than Thor, but my secret crush is actually Yasmani Grandal."

"That's serious treason," he teased.

"Shh. You have to protect me from the Dodger spy network." She giggled. "My turn. I know you can't tell me your real name, but why do they call you Waters? Is that your Navy nickname or Tribe?"

"Navy and Tribe."

"Is it because you were a SEAL?"

"No. It's because I never used to talk."

"When I met you, I wouldn't exactly have called you a chatterbox, so I'm guessing not much changed. But what does that have to do with your name?"

"My team said that they never knew what I was thinking, and then when I did talk, it was always 'sensitive' or some shit, so they took it from the phrase 'still waters run deep.'"

"Ah. Makes sense. Do you ever wish it was something different? Like Zeus? Or Maverick?"

He laughed. "No. I've never really thought about my name. You get called a lot of different things until a nickname somehow sticks. It's not like anyone gets to pick their own. And you get used to responding to it. Better than Petty Officer Miller, or whatever."

"It suits you. The nickname."

"G.I. Joe isn't better?"

"Too much of a mouthful to yell in a firefight, and just Joe is too generic."

His eyes drifted from her face to his hands on her calves. "Do you want to know it?"

Her forehead crinkled in confusion. "Know what?"

"My real name."

17

———

MARCH 6TH

Waters

This is so not a good idea. Any of it. Touching her. Trading personal information. Telling her my name. And I'm still gonna do it. What the hell is wrong with me?

He couldn't stop himself from doing any of it. He was breaking the ultimate rule. His "real" self was a dead man. But, here, in this room, just the two of them cocooned away from the rain and the rest of the cast and crew, it was easy to conveniently forget they weren't really alone. Just to prove how much he'd lost his mind, his fingertips slipped up above the elastic at her ankles, softly massaging the bare skin of her calves now.

"If you tell me, do you have to kill me?" She was trying to lightly tease, but it came out more like a breathy whisper.

He smiled; his eyes still focused on where he was touching her. "Taylor. Taylor Miller." He paused. "My sister..." His voice broke. He cleared his throat. "My sister called me Taj for short. So until I went into the Navy, that's what my family called me."

"Taj. I like it." She glanced down at the pillow in her grip, playing with the fringe.

Fuck it. Might as well just screw it all up at this point.

He cast a quick glance at the television, which he knew had a webcam link for Midas to watch through. Quickly, he mouthed "Stanley" at the camera, knowing whoever was on duty would turn off the camera with the prescribed code word until he signaled to turn it back on.

When he saw the black dot in the upper corner disappear, which looked like a bad pixel to anyone else, he grabbed her ankles firmly and pulled her across the leather couch until her feet were over his legs and flat on the couch next to his hips. She squawked at the surprise movement but just lay where he left her in front of him. The pulse point in her neck began to beat a little more rapidly, and he desperately wanted to cover it with his mouth. He wanted to feel her hummingbird heartbeat, knowing that he made her breathless. Mark her skin to claim her.

"Are you interested in Lazarus?"

"God, no," she laughed. Noticing his serious expression, she frowned. "I certainly like him as a person, but I'm not 'interested' in him. Did he say I was?"

"He mentioned being interested in you, but the timing didn't work out."

"Well, I've made it a policy never to date any Hollywood types." She thought about it for a moment. "I guess maybe he had an interest not too long ago, but then I took a trip to Cairo."

He inhaled. "Cairo?"

She gave me an in. I didn't even need to come up with a line of questioning.

She nodded. "Yeah. Kent, sorry... Ka-Bar, emailed me when I was in Europe for work and asked if I could stop by the consulate and pick up a package he left behind before leaving for a mission."

He heard a clicking sound in his brain, like an edge piece was locking into place in a jigsaw puzzle that came with no picture.

And so it begins. Now, we may be getting somewhere.

He watched her closely. "Why didn't you mention to us that Ka-Bar was your brother?"

She blushed. "Well, we're both adopted, so technically, he isn't, although we might as well be siblings. I guess at the time, it didn't seem relevant. Does it matter?"

Tread carefully. Don't spook her.

"To me, personally? No. I was just curious. It came up during our workup on you, and in my line of work, people are usually quick to try and trade on relationships."

She nodded. "In hindsight, I probably should have mentioned it. I figured you all would know him somehow since he recommended you, but who I was to him wasn't all that important. Is that why you took the job? Because he's my brother?"

"I'd be lying if I said it wasn't a consideration. But if God didn't want to take the job, he wouldn't have taken it, regardless of who you were. And neither he nor I knew your brother personally."

His hands stopped their movement, palming her calves beneath her pant legs.

He switched back to the line of questioning regarding the package and her trip to the embassy. "Seems odd, though. He couldn't just have someone where he was stationed mail it wherever? You had to physically go to

Egypt to pick up a package? And not from his base? Sounds presumptuous, even for a brother to ask."

"Stopping in Cairo wasn't a terrible hardship. It's where I spent a good part of my childhood, so I visited some friends while I was there. I don't get back often."

"So what was so all-fire important?"

"No idea," she admitted with a shake of her head. "I went to the consulate to pick up the package, but when I got there, the guy whom I was supposed to pick it up from wasn't there. The clerk didn't seem to know anything about it, either. By the time I had to return home, the clerk had said the guy still wasn't at the embassy, so I left my address, and he said they'd pass along the information and ship whatever it was to me when he arrived." Her expression turned thoughtful. "Thinking about it, I still hadn't gotten it by the time we came here. Guess I better email the consulate later to double-check."

"I'm sure it will turn up. I mean, Ka-Bar obviously wasn't in a panic about it, was he?"

"No." She had stretched out the word a little. She looked thoughtful at his question, though. "I'll have to email him and make sure. I mean, it must have been somewhat important to him, or he would have just waited until he got back from wherever he was to take care of it himself. Of course, who knows how soon I'll hear back from him." She nudged him with a foot. "He's like you. Can't tell anybody anything."

His fingers slid a few inches up her legs. "I told you my name."

"Yeah," she whispered. "Why?"

"Maybe I thought it would get me one step closer to seeing your sexy pink underwear," he teased.

Hands extended out to give him a shove in the chest in

fake exasperation, but instead, they ended up in his grasp, and with a sudden pull, she was straddling his lap, hands held tight to his chest, looking down into his eyes. There was no way she could miss how hard he was. He searched her face, watching carefully for signs that she wanted him to stop.

"So..." he asked quietly, "if I kissed you, I wouldn't be interfering in a plan to get together with Lazarus?"

Her pupils dilated, and then she slowly shook her head.

"Or any of the other guys, either?"

She shook her head again.

Letting go of her wrists, he scrunched his hands into fists and covered his eyes. "This is a bad idea, Kubrick, but I just can't seem to stop."

"Good ideas are often overrated," she whispered, her hands sliding to clutch his shoulders.

Unclenching his fists, he reached up and gently stroked the back of his fingers along her cheek. "I don't want to hurt you. This thing between us can never be more than the moment, Kubrick. It's a rule," he confessed. "No relationships, clients or otherwise. I'm a ghost. I'm technically dead."

He let her absorb that for a few moments.

"Even if I were allowed to, I wouldn't be able to promise anyone the possibility of being permanent. Every time I get sent somewhere, it's fifty-fifty I'm coming back, probably less, and I can only ride that lightning for so long. Attachment is too dangerous. For me. For a woman or a family. Piss off the wrong person, and suddenly, someone I care about could be used against me. I can't risk it. And despite the danger and the solitary life, I love what I do. I can't change who I am, and I don't want to. Tribe always wins."

He raised his hands back in a position of surrender and

looked up at her. "So tell me no. Take the decision out of my hands. Get up and walk away. Pretend this afternoon never happened," he begged.

Her eyes were glassy, but no tears fell. Instead, she reached for the hem of her hoodie and pulled it over her head, dropping it to the floor next to them. "I can't pretend this isn't here." With that, she cupped his face in her hands and brought her lips to his.

He didn't know who opened to whom, but their tongues were tangling, stroking, and she tasted so good. Like chocolate and peppermint. Mouth breaking away with a heaving breath, he held her a scant inch away, his eyes searching hers. "Are you sure? Knowing this is all it can be? While the film is going, and then it's done?"

She nodded twice.

Internally, he groaned. At least, he thought he did. Maybe it was out loud. He didn't care. He gave up.

Growling at her, he sat up and ordered, "Wrap your arms around my neck and your legs around my waist, baby."

His hands gripped the backs of her thighs to help her as she complied immediately, almost frantically, clutching him so hard he wondered if he'd have bruises on his hips later.

She was already mewling in frustration. "Look at me," he commanded.

Rotating his hard cock against the cradle between her legs, he watched as her brown eyes dilated. "That's it, baby. Hang on, and don't you take your eyes off me. I want to watch you as I grind into that sweet pussy and make you come before I even touch you."

She gasped at the sudden and unexpected dirty words from him.

"Don't look away."

He felt her lock up.

He pressed up hard into her again, twisting against her at the last moment. Once. Twice.

He watched her suck in air, preparing for the explosion, her eyes glued to his.

She began to tighten and shake, coming undone for him. "Fuck, yeah, baby, let it go. Give it all to me, Kubrick."

Collapsing onto his chest and into his arms, head on his shoulder, panting and boneless, she wailed, "Oh my God, Waters!"

"So fucking beautiful," he whispered.

As she recovered, he allowed his hands to smooth the skin of her back. He pressed soft, openmouthed kisses to her exposed neck.

And now I'm totally screwed. I started something I can't one hundred percent finish. Idiot.

Normally, he would be happy to take her to bed and make her lose all sense of time and space, but there were some things he needed to clarify before he could allow this to go further.

"I hate to ruin the moment, baby, but we need to talk."

He felt her breath freeze inside her. "What is it?"

"Relax." Pushing her off of his chest to bring their faces together, nuzzling the tip of her nose with his. "I see panic welling in those beautiful brown eyes. I'm not changing my mind. Exhale, okay?"

"Okay," she agreed. He felt her exhale, purposefully trying to relax. And failing miserably.

Brushing the hair out of her face, Waters made sure she was looking at him and completely aware of him. "Neither one of us is new to sex, but we've obviously not discussed certain factors. It wasn't like either of us woke up this morning thinking we'd be where we are right now. I just want you to know you're safe. I cleared all my physicals after my injuries two years ago, and I haven't been with anyone since then. But—"

"Before that, you were leading a parade?"

Her words stung a little bit. "That wasn't where I was going with this, but I don't know that I would have called it a 'parade,'" he groused.

She leaned down to kiss him on the forehead, then brushed a fingertip across one eyebrow. "That's okay. I didn't expect anything different. I've been with two other men, the most recent being six years ago."

Waters took a moment to process.

What the fuck? How the hell has this woman not had a string of lovers? Definitely should have had more than two.

Not the issue. Need to tackle the real issue.

"What I was about to say was, I'm not physically prepared for this to happen. I figured if I didn't bring anything along, I wouldn't be tempted."

"Oh." She was trying not to show her disappointment.

So fucking adorable.

"No worries, baby. Tonight, we can play. But I don't want to run any risks for you, so we'll just have to wait for the really good stuff until I can run into Coxen Hole."

"That city really should have a different name, all things considered," she mumbled and blushed.

He thought about what he'd just said and started chuckling. "Yeah, it probably should."

Both were grinning as he pressed a light kiss on her beauty mark.

"I'm on birth control, but... I get it. Safer all around to both be protected."

"I promise I'll make it worth the wait."

He lowered his hands to grip underneath her ass, then turned off the couch so both feet were flat on the floor.

Standing with her still wrapped around him, he headed toward her suite. "In the meantime," he growled, "no more talking except to tell me how good it feels when I make you come." His mouth crashed into hers, teeth immediately nipping her bottom lip to have her open her lips and let his tongue in to wage war on the inside of her mouth.

Once inside her room, he set her on the edge of the bed, flicking a finger and telling her to move toward the center. He made sure she complied, then he turned and closed the double doors to the War Room, flipping the lock. Returning to the bed, he followed her down onto the rumpled sheets. Kai's legs slid to dangle off the side of the bed.

Kai's neck arched as Waters lowered his mouth to her pulse point. His warm breath pressed openmouthed kisses along the column of her neck, his hands gently squeezing her breasts. He was murmuring something to her, but he was so overwhelmed he didn't know what he had said. All he knew was that the words felt as if they were affirmations, as if he were telling her all the ways she pleased him.

He went up on one knee between her legs. "Waters," she moaned as he moved off of her.

"Shh, baby. I'm still here." He moved his arms behind his head and pulled his T-shirt up and over, chest and arm muscles rippling with the action, then flexing as he folded it and lightly tossed it toward the chair in the corner of the room.

Her eyes glittered up at him, and she exhaled a soft moan. "Why is that so fucking sexy?"

Looking down at her, he asked, "What's that?"

"When men take their shirts off like that. Just grab it from behind their shoulders and whip it off."

One hand reached up to trace his ab contours, but he captured her exploring hand in both of his, gently kneading the palm with his expert thumbs. "Don't know, baby." He kissed the pads of each finger. "I don't think about guys taking off their clothes, so it's never been on my radar." He sucked the tip of her thumb into his mouth, laving the pad with his tongue, his eyes never leaving her face.

"I need to touch you. Please," she pleaded.

"Well, I guess I have to agree to that since it's way too early for you to be begging," he teased as he let go of her hand and shifted his legs to straddle her thighs. Now her hands were free to smooth over his abs, his pecs, then slide over his shoulders as he leaned down to touch his forehead to hers, her nails lightly scoring the skin she touched. His hands were also busy, gently caging her waist and softly stroking small circles with his thumbs. "So beautiful," he whispered.

She blushed at his praise, and her hips involuntarily bucked up trying to make contact with his own. "Waters," she whispered.

"What, baby?"

"More kissing, less talking."

His whole body felt like it was on fire as he kissed her forehead, both of her eyelids, and the tip of her nose, then finally settled butterfly-light on that Monroe beauty mark that drove him to distraction. From there, it was an easy reach to touch the tip of his tongue to the seam of her lips. She opened on a sigh, and he slipped inside, taking a full tour of her mouth. He stroked her tongue like he planned to stroke the inside of her channel with his fingers, and eventually his cock.

He continued to lay a trail of kisses down her body. Her chin, the underside of her jaw, the hollow of her throat, the valley between her breasts, her stomach, and finally, just above her belly button before dipping the tip of his tongue in her navel.

Watching him, she giggled at the tickling sensation as he rimmed her. "That tickles."

Slowly, he crawled part way back up her body and dropped sweet, chaste kiss after kiss across the top of her bra cups, fingertips lightly drawing random patterns on the material covering her breasts. His eyes held hers captured. "I definitely like pink." He dipped his mouth back between her breasts and gave a soft lap with his tongue to the side of one breast, then turned his attention to the other. Sliding his hands to the straps of her bra, he asked, "Yes?"

She nodded.

He slid her bra straps down her arms, using them to pull the entire garment down to her waist without unhooking it. Her nipples popped the moment he bared them to the air in the room. "Fuck me," he groaned. He framed both breasts with the palms of his hands, his mouth devouring one nipple and then the other, nipping, sucking, until Kai was thrashing underneath him. "So sweet, baby. You taste like cotton candy. Can't wait to get to the sticky-sweet parts."

"Waters, I... I..."

"What, baby?" he whispered. His tongue granted mercy to her nipple and moved away from the sensitive peak. But it wasn't really a mercy move because a moment later, he blew air across the distended tip and brought on a whole new form of torture as her skin pebbled in gooseflesh.

And when his teeth lightly grasped the bud, she gasped, her eyes going wide in surprise. Her back arched, and Waters watched in awe as another orgasm washed over her body.

"Goddamn, Kubrick," he marveled. "That was... incredible. You come so pretty."

"Please," she begged between pants.

"Please, what?"

Now he truly understood what a "hot mess" looked like. Her breath was coming out in rapid pants, her hair was a tangled halo around her head, her heart was racing, and her skin was flushed and burning beneath his touch. "I... I... oh my God, I don't know. I can't even think clearly."

"Tell me what you need," he demanded.

Her face contorted in something that looked like a mixture of pain and embarrassment.

"Kubrick, if I'm going to learn to please you, I need to know what you need. Some of it I'll learn by doing. I'll be paying attention, trust me. But if you want something specific, you have to tell me."

Her expression struggled a bit more, and then she clearly gave up with a groan. "Do that again."

Now, the smile became one of the cat who got into the cream.

"Is that all? My pleasure." And her other nipple was captured by his talented tongue.

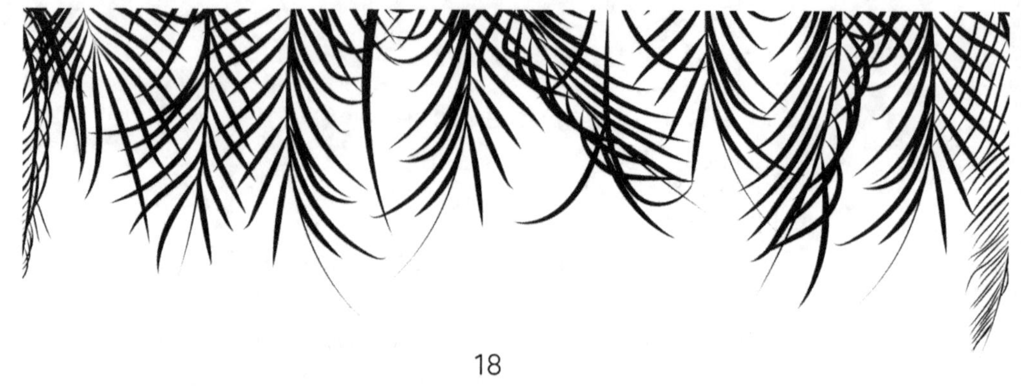

18

———————

MARCH 6TH

Kai

Fuck, fuck, fuck!

A third orgasm rolled over Kai's body, Waters' promise fulfilled from her request of a repeat. Was there something wrong with her that her body flipped for him like this?

I think he broke me.

For a brief moment, she recalled Waters' comment at the diner when he joked that she'd been dating the wrong men. Had she just managed to pick partners poorly? Or maybe she'd just been killing time until this one came along? Either way, it was worth it for her body to have waited for this man.

At thirty-five, Kai had never felt like she'd missed out before. Occasionally, she wondered if something was wrong with her because sex just never seemed to be on her radar. Then Waters walked into her life, and she became a hormonal mess and couldn't stop thinking about it.

180

The misfires in her brain stopped, and her senses slowly began to return. "Mmm, that was better than chocolate. Thank you."

He slid up next to her in the bed and turned on his side, his head propped up by one hand. His other hand was drawing lazy patterns on her stomach. "I'll take that as the highest form of praise, but did you just thank me for orgasms?"

"Yes, please."

He chuckled deeply. "Babe, that answer to the question didn't make sense, but... I understood."

Turning herself on her side to look at him, she wrinkled her nose. "You've learned to speak 'Kubrick'?"

"Mmhmm." He kissed her shoulder. "It's not that difficult if you pay attention."

"Really?"

"Yup," he nodded. "There's only four key words and phrases you have to know."

"And those would be...?"

He threaded the fingers of his free hand with one of hers and kissed the back of her hand. "Chocolate." A kiss to her fingertips. "G.I. Joe." He dragged the tip of his tongue from the thumb to the heel of her hand. "Fuck, in assorted formats and contexts." A touch of his lips to the palm of her hand. "And a wide variety of derogatory words that are created by putting 'ass' in front of or behind them." He gently sucked the pulse point in her wrist while looking up at her with a devilish grin. "And a propensity for sticking your tongue out. So I guess it's four verbals and a visual."

Tentatively, her other hand went to reach for his bare chest and stopped part way before dropping to the bed. Should she touch him? Would that make him uncomfortable if she reached out without an invitation? Did it make her look needy?

"Why did you stop, Kubrick? I think we're past needing permission."

"How did you know that's what I was wondering?"

"Babe. Your face is telegraphing everything you're thinking and feeling right now. Believe it or not, you suck at lying." She blushed and hung her head, so he ducked his head to see her face. "Why are you hesitant to touch me?"

She blew a strand of hair off her face and turned it to the ceiling to prevent him from seeing her directly. "I'm not good at this. Ask me to direct a movie, even a love scene, for God's sake, and I'm fine. But when it comes to reality, not so much." She shook her head.

He smiled at her. "Touch me all you like. I'd prefer you did, actually." She smiled shyly back at him. "There's something else, isn't there?"

She sucked in her bottom lip as she debated what to say. "What we just did, it didn't feel normal."

"What do you mean by 'normal'?"

"The orgasms. They were odd. Like, eyes roll back in my head odd."

"And that's not happened before? They didn't feel like that?" She shook her head. He chuckled, kissing the back of her hand again. "You really were dating the wrong men."

She laughed and pushed at his chest. "Maybe you're just that good." He puffed up a bit. "Oh, quit preening, you big peacock. I'm sure you know just how good you are."

"Something about the words 'big' and 'peacock' just doesn't seem to fit together."

"Don't get all smartass on me right now." She was tracing the edges of the tattoo on his chest. The subject shifted back to serious. "I've never come that hard. Or that many times that close together. And definitely not without any pressure on my clit. Have you..." she started, stopped, inhaled, and then pushed through with her question, still refusing to look him in the eye. "Have you made other women do that?" She huffed. "Sorry, that was such a 'girl' question. I don't want it to sound like I'm pumping you for information about your past because it really doesn't mat—"

"Kubrick," he interjected. "Plenty of people need significant recovery time before they can come again." He took a lock of her hair between two fingers and curled it around the digits. "You, apparently not. And that makes me a very happy man because, to be honest, I'm not a one-and-done guy. I want to make sure you feel good, and I like to go for a while. If I'm going to do something, I'm going to do it well." He gave her a cheeky wink. Then his face became serious. "As for coming without touching your clit, no. I've never made a woman come just from touching or sucking on her nipples. I've heard some women can do that, but when it happened with you, that was a first for me, too." He moved his mouth to the shell of her ear. "And it was hotter than hell. I can't wait to do it again." His tongue flicked out and traced the cartilage of her ear, his warm breath tickling and arousing her all at the same time.

"What if what I want isn't...?"

He reversed out of the crook of her neck, and his eyebrow quirked up.

"Forget it," she retracted her question. She tried to pull away from him, but he rolled over so that he caged her beneath him.

"Nope, not happening."

"It's embarrassing."

"Kubrick, I've heard your mouth run a million words per second. I've heard you say some of the raunchiest, most inappropriate, and downright evil things, all of which are a major turn-on, by the way. Suddenly, this afternoon, after what we just did, you're self-conscious. And that's concerning to me. So what has got you so hung up? Please. Tell me so I can make you feel better." A thought occurred to him. "Is this about the diner conversation and us being 'mismatched'? Are you worrying about being 'good enough' for me?"

Her fears came out in a tidal wave. "I'm thirty-five and clueless. I've wanted you from the moment I saw you. Honest to God, your voice made me think of hot fudge, and I wanted to lick every goddamn inch of you like you were a spoon. Eighty million things are running through my head that I'd like to do to you, with you, things I've never even given a second thought to before. Now I've had about thirty minutes of you, and I'm worried I'll do something dumb and make you back off because it's childish, or needy, or clingy, or freaky, or whatever. Like this stupid, unfiltered confession. You're so beautiful and I'm so, not. I don't understand why you're interested in doing this with me. I have next to no experience, and you've been with tons of women—"

He grabbed one of her hands and pressed it against his hard length, guiding her to stroke him through the material covering him.

"Fuck, what are you feeding that thing?" she whispered.

His lips slid to her jawline, then her mouth, as he mumbled, "Virgin sacrifices?" When he came up from kissing her thoroughly into oblivion, he dragged her hand below the elastic of both the track pants and his tight-fitting boxers. His voice was breathy when he pushed his hips forward into her hand and asked her, "Does this feel like I'm not turned on by you? That you're not 'good enough'?"

Slowly, she shook her head.

"Good. Because I was thoroughly stunned by you the moment I walked into that conference room, and I was totally turned on the moment you put us in place with your camera catches." His voice dropped to a pained whisper. "And, baby, I was one... hundred... percent... fucked the minute you licked that fork clean of chocolate in Alice's. All I could think about was pouring chocolate on my cock and you wrapping those pink lips around my dick and sucking it clean.

"You are the sexiest woman I've ever known, and it's going to take every bit of control within me to wait until tomorrow night to fuck you so hard and so long that you get to the point you can't move because you're exhausted and deliciously sore." He groaned, and his mouth moved to nip the lobe of her ear. "Know what else I'd do? I'd take you home, and I'd fuck you on every surface all night long. When morning came, I'd make you breakfast and feed you while you lay like a queen in my bed. And I'd be whispering in your ear how fucking great a time I had with you."

What the hell? He'd break his rules for me?

His skin was so soft to the touch but solid in her grip. He radiated intense heat from every pore, even in the slight dampness of her bedroom. Holding his cock in her hand, listening to the dirty talk coming out of his mouth, knowing that being with her made him respond this way was empowering. It was like someone had opened the doors to a cage, and she was free for the first time. He made her feel free. Free to take what she wanted and be whom she wanted. With that, her decision was made.

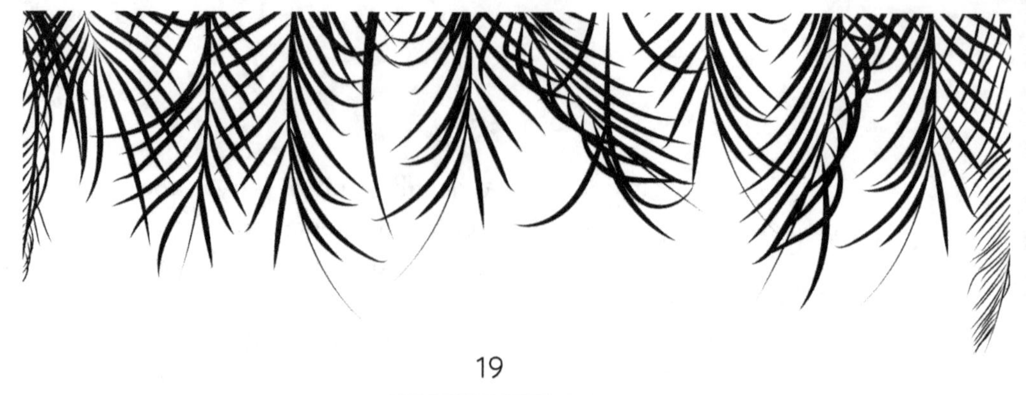

MARCH 6TH

Waters

SHE'D CAUGHT HIM BY SURPRISE WHEN SHE SAT UP IN the bed, pulling on his arms for him to sit up as well. Normally able to hide his emotions, right now, he was incapable of schooling his face into a detached mask.

What is she going to do?

She was raised up on her knees, her hands resting on top of his shoulders. Holding his breath, he watched as she leaned down and softly kissed the ends of each of the three Kraken tentacles at the top of his right pec. Her lips were burning against his already fevered skin. Slowly, she traveled around his body, crawling around him, tracing the edge of a fourth tentacle across his clavicle with her tongue, over his shoulder to the body that covered the entire expanse of his upper back. He kept trying to reach for her so he could put his mouth on her as well, but she brushed his hands away.

He gave up the fight. It just felt too damn good, especially with her bare breasts brushing against his skin. "Fuck, baby. Use that hot little mouth on me. Anywhere. Everywhere. Don't stop," he groaned.

She steadied herself by placing her hands on his shoulders, continuing to trace the new tentacles curling over his other shoulder. When she reached the end of the Kraken, the other four tentacles strangling a bleeding human heart decorated with the letter "S," he was speaking softly, nonsensically to her, finally able to anchor his hands in her hair and hold her close as she sucked at the skin. "Mark me, Kubrick." He hissed at the sting of her teeth biting down on his nipple, followed by the lapping of her tongue to remove the sting, and finally, the cool breath she blew across his wet skin. She pulled away, admiring her handiwork at the small love bite she left on his chest.

Her index finger traced the heart in the tattoo.

"The 'S' is for Sarah." She looked up at him. He wavered, but it felt like he had to tell her something. Maybe it would ease if he said it out loud. "She was—"

That same finger went to his lips. Once he was silent, her palm went flat to his chest over the letter. "You're carrying this loss and pain with you every day. Therefore, whoever it was, this person is important to you. I respect that."

It was then he saw her truly notice for the first time the other marks on his body, and confusion spread across her face. Softly, she touched each one as she investigated, her expression becoming more intense with each brush of her fingertips. He swallowed hard as she did, watching her face intently for disgust, waiting for the inevitable questions. He really didn't want to have this conversation with her. Anyone else, he'd redirect them. Any other woman, he'd simply get out of the bed, dress, and leave. But he found he couldn't do that with her. However, the situation was not pretty, and he wasn't sure how either of them would react to his answers.

She'd moved on to his back, and he heard a soft gasp, then a fluttering over his skin, not even enough to be called a touch, at where his right kidney should be. He swallowed again, looking over his right shoulder at her. The soft, warm touch of her lips dropped onto the jagged scar that reached from the base of his shoulder blade to disappear below the waist of his pants, then her arms came around his shoulders from behind, hugging him tightly. She buried her face in his neck, and he felt wetness hit his skin. His hand reached up to grab her forearm that stretched across his chest, holding it lightly, and he dropped a kiss to it. No question came.

She's giving me an out. She knows I might not want to talk about it, so she's just showing me she hurts for me. Christ, how can she possibly think she's not "good enough"?

"Afghanistan." Clearing his throat, he swallowed again, then continued to speak. "The details are pretty grim, but the short of it is, I lost a kidney. Most people have their scar in the front, but my circumstances were a little unique."

Silence followed. Just a kiss pressed behind his ear. She just held him close.

Good goddamn.

"It's why I had to leave the Navy. You can't have only one kidney and be a SEAL." His thumb stroked her forearm. "Tell me what you're thinking, baby."

"There are even more of them, aren't there?" Her voice was small from where her mouth rested against the back of his shoulder. Her fingers gently ran the length of the scar, top to bottom.

Nodding, he confessed, "Yes, but most are not from

Afghanistan. Five years ago, when I was recovering from the kidney, I was brought into Tribe. God hired me from my hospital bed. I had a bit of a reputation for my analyst skills already, as well as a reputation for authority issues, and he had apparently been watching me for a while." He brought his lips down to her forearm again as if drawing strength from her arms to say the words he needed to say. "Three years later, I was on a recovery job in Egypt. It would be too simplistic to say that it went badly. In the past, I had a very bad habit of rushing in where angels fear to tread, so to speak. I was quiet, but if there was trouble, I'd be first in line to meet it and the last one to leave it. I never thought before I acted. Just reacted. On that last project, I was captured. My rash decision forced my team to come in and get me."

"You were tortured."

In more ways than one.

"Yes."

She crawled around to the front of him. Remaining on her knees, she took his face in her hands and lightly kissed him. "Your knee? It didn't heal properly. That's why you limp sometimes."

"I honestly didn't think the limp was that noticeable anymore."

Blushing, she gave him a sad smile. "I may watch you quite a bit."

He grinned. "Quite a bit, huh?"

"Saucy," she warned, throwing back at him his favorite word for her.

He pulled her close and fell backward on the bed, gathering her close, her head under his chin, his arms wrapped tight around her. "Don't feel bad for me. It's nothing compared to what it could be, and probably far less than I deserved for being an idiot. I'm alive. At least I could walk, and I was able to come back to work. Everything else healed, but the marks will always be there to remind me of my mistakes."

She raised her face to his, placing a kiss on the side of his mouth. "At least they left this beautiful face alone."

"Mmmm. This beautiful face doesn't want to talk about it anymore. I have much better things to say to you while we're in this bed. Now shut up unless you're moaning my name."

Two hours later, Waters left Kubrick sleeping in the bed. They'd spent most of that time making out like teenagers. Eventually, they'd both ended up naked under the sheet, swapping positions, exploring each other, and Waters finding out exactly where her sweet spots were. He grinned to himself, recalling a certain area on the inside of her knees that was particularly stimulating to her.

For the first time in his life, Waters felt like sex was fun again, and he wanted to savor the time with a woman. He didn't need to experience it all in one night. In fact, if it had taken weeks to get to sex, he would have been more than fine with that. He also didn't want her to think that all he wanted was sex.

Wow. You just told her that's all you can give her, but you don't want her to think that's all you want? Way to send mixed messages, asshole.

The irony was not wasted on him that now that he'd found someone he would love to explore more than a short-term arrangement with, he couldn't.

Closing the door of her suite behind him, Waters sat in the high-backed leather chair behind the desk. He powered up his tablet and dialed the office for a video conference after punching in his security codes to scramble the service. As Midas answered, the screen split in two, showing the cyber guru on the left and a black box with a voice sound wave depicted on the right for God.

Time to get roasted for real.

"Well, hel-lo there, stud muffin. Nice hickey."

Waters flipped his middle finger. There was no hickey.

Well... not on my neck. Can't say that for other areas. My right ass cheek still smarts.

Midas made a show of checking his watch. "Only two hours and forty minutes? I'm disappointed in you. I figured we wouldn't see you until tomorrow." He grunted. "I would have thought that would be goddamn embarrassing for a former SEAL. Where's your pride? And fuck, that also means I lost the pool." Midas consulted the bets on the whiteboard behind him. "Steel won. He picked two hours and thirty-eight minutes. He know something about you we don't?"

Waters shook his head at the shit-talking. "Everyone's gotta come up for air sometime. Can you go that long without breathing?"

"Niiiiiiiiice," Midas drawled. "Almost makes me wish I was a chick."

In the background, he could hear Steel mumbling to himself in Spanish. Waters refused to translate out of fear of what he would hear. Instead, he redirected. "Updates?"

"Can I put the camera back up?" Midas asked.

Waters turned his head toward the suite door. "Leave it a bit longer. She doesn't know, and I don't want her to be embarrassed unnecessarily." He turned his gaze back to the screen. He prompted again, "So. Updates?"

"Other than Nemo getting his ass bit by a snake, Demon and TB report nothing amiss. Enigma prowls a lot at night but primarily to Vixen's room. He's not exactly spending a lot of time in his own bed."

"No surprise. Any luck with Ka-Bar?"

"No. I'm starting to get twitchy. And I don't get twitchy, so that means we've got problems. At this point, if I can't find him, I'm worried he's nowhere to be found. Or at least not without a cadaver dog."

God asked, "Do you think Kubrick might know somewhere he would go that we wouldn't think to look or be able to find?"

"I don't know. She doesn't talk about him at all except when I ask directly, so it makes me wonder how close they actually are."

"They're close," Midas affirmed. "I can find pictures galore of them together, and not just prior to his military days. She's been his plus-one at a number of military events over the years. As recent as last year. I think I see Fourth of July decorations in the corner of one picture, but I'm not one hundred percent positive. Her hair is a little different in the picture than it is now, too. And they email all the time. Granted, there are huge gaps, which coincide with when he's out in the field, but it's at minimum daily when he's not in action."

There was a crunching noise over the speakers. "Do you think she knows anything she's not telling?" God asked around the candy he was pulverizing.

"I don't think so. She's not exactly a 'subtle' kind of woman. She pretty much lays everything out there for you to see, although she can mask her emotions most of the time."

Except when it comes to you.

Waters grimaced at a particularly loud crunch. "I thought Cherry took away your suckers?"

"She did," God growled.

"Yeah, she did," Midas confirmed, "but he just went online and ordered them to be shipped directly to him in his batcave. I think they're being delivered by drone."

God grunted. "Listen, Waters, we're coming up empty, and under normal circumstances, I'd say we're spinning our wheels. But with Ka-Bar up in smoke, I'm thinking it's even worse than we imagined. I think it's time to push her for anything at all she might have, even if it seems insignificant or totally useless."

Waters sighed. "Yeah, not sure how she'll take the fact that I'm really on this job with her because we think Ka-Bar's in trouble, and somehow she's leverage."

"Worse will be when you tell her that Ka-Bar is missing," Midas added.

"Yeah, then there's that."

Running his hands over his head and to the back of his neck, Waters leaned forward on his elbows on the desktop. "I'll see what I can do. I'm gonna need a little time."

"Don't be a pussy, Waters," God warned. "The longer we go with no leads, the worse things look for Ka-Bar, and the more in the dark we are with how Kubrick is involved. Time is running out."

God wasn't just warning him about finding Ka-Bar. It was also a reminder that his time with Kubrick was also finite. "Roger that."

Waters shut down his tablet and sat back in the chair with a sigh. He was not looking forward to questioning her and wasn't even sure how to go about it. His best approach was probably just straight at it and confess everything. But he wasn't sure if she was going to be mad, scared, both, or something else altogether. And God was correct. They didn't have time for him to be overly cautious because with each minute they didn't act, if Ka-Bar was being held hostage, the more time that passed, the less likely he would be alive when they found him. If they ever found him.

Pushing up on the arms of the chair, he headed over to the doors of Kubrick's suite. Quietly, he opened the doors, and just as silently, he shut them behind him, turning the lock once more. If she tried to storm out on him, he'd at least have the extra second or two that unlocking them would give him.

She lay diagonally across the bed, the foot of one bent leg peeking out, the sheet around her hips, her bare back beckoning him. He remembered covering her with his body earlier, kissing his way up from the top of her waist to the nape of her neck. Her skin was incredibly soft to the touch, and as always, the ever-present scent of lilacs seemed to surround her. Her face was turned to the window in sleep, hair thoroughly tousled, one hand tucked into her chest, the other straight along her side.

She was perfect.

He needed more.

Walking across the room, he stripped off his T-shirt and pants that he'd pulled on in haste to go make his call, quickly folding them and placing them on the chair in the corner of the room. He turned back toward the bed and lay one hand gently on the ankle of her partially exposed leg, then slid it loosely up the calf muscle. When his hand reached her knee, he leaned down and kissed the back of her thigh, pointing his tongue and licking a stripe up to the underside of her ass. He brushed the sheet aside, exposing her naked form to the room. A quick nip to the cheek directly in front of him caused a soft noise to come from her throat, but it was the very deliberate tongue swiping between the two cheeks he gently pulled apart, from her pussy opening to the dimpled mid back that caused a sleep-hazed gasp to emerge. He smiled against her lower back, and he knew the smile was wicked.

Yeah, it isn't an ass fetish, but I am definitely an ass man. And hers is as wicked as I imagined.

Just to be greedy, he repeated the tongue swipe, a second of pressure and a swirl against her back hole, then continuing up to the lower back where he breathed an openmouthed kiss.

Bracketing her thighs with his knees, he placed both hands at her hips, sliding them up her back, then brushing the mass of blonde hair over the nape of her neck. When the space was clear, he closed the distance between them, bracing himself just above her body, his teeth taking light purchase in the skin there. He brushed aside his subconscious, making snide comments about claiming what he couldn't, before he moved his mouth to where the nape met the shoulder. One hand tunneling underneath the blonde hair and gripping firmly, he sucked hard enough to raise a bruise.

She moaned with need in her sleep.

After admiring his work, one fingertip brushing the marked skin, he slid to her left and lay on his side, the hand that had been gripping the roots of her hair brushing tendrils off her forehead. He caressed the silk skin of her breast, feathered kisses along her shoulder, touched the tip of his tongue beneath her ear, sucked the lobe briefly into his mouth, trailed his lips across her cheek to the corner of her mouth, the Monroe beauty mark, the tip of her nose and the corner of her eyebrow all in an effort to sweetly wake her up in anticipation of, hopefully, more snuggling and kissing.

You have really got it bad, dude. Snuggling? Kissing? The guys are totally going to take your Man Card and rip it into shreds.

Her hand smoothed over the mattress and up his chest to curve around his neck. "Hey," she whispered.

"Hey," he returned, foreheads touching. "Sleep well?"

"Mm-hmm." Her eyes closed with a deep inhale, and they reopened on the exhale. "I thought I woke up, and you were gone, but I must have dreamt it."

"No"—he kissed her lips—"I did leave for a couple of minutes. I needed to check in with the boss."

Kubrick leaned up, pulling the pillow tight to her chest to prop herself up. "Something wrong? You look sort of... uncomfortable."

"I am," he admitted.

She lowered her head to lie on the scrunched-up pillow but kept her eyes turned up to his. "Everything okay?"

He looked at the door over her shoulder, not really seeing it, thinking hard before he spoke. Then he decided to just rip the duct tape off in one quick swipe.

"It's about your brother." He returned his gaze to hers, drawing his index finger up and down her bicep.

"Ah. I wondered when he might come up."

"You did?"

"Yes. I'm not stupid." He opened his mouth to deny he thought so, but she beat him to the comment. "I'm not saying you think I am. I'm just saying that I know more about you and your company than you likely believe I do, and I know that he sent me to you not just because there were SEALs working at Tribe. He's an overprotective ass, and as soon as I heard he called ahead, I figured something must be going on that he wanted me under someone's watchful eye; otherwise, he would have been my consultant."

"So you're not mad?"

"About what?" He gestured between the two of them. "Did this happen as some sort of interrogation ploy because you need to ask me about whatever's going on with my dumbass brother?"

"This afternoon? No."

"Then, no, I'm not mad."

Thank fuck.

He let out a breath he hadn't known he was holding inside. "Not what I was expecting. But... I still need to ask you a couple of things."

"It's not good, is it?"

"I honestly don't know, Kubrick." He grabbed her hand closest to him and held it tight. "He's missing. Midas has been looking for him since he called in Steel's marker. There's nothing, and even if he were on a mission, for my teammate to find nothing... the odds are similar to being struck by lightning three times in one's lifetime. Is there anywhere he might go if he thought he was in trouble?"

Kubrick appeared to turn her thoughts inward, her face screwing up in concentration. After a few moments, she replied, "The last I knew, he was stationed in Egypt. He had just returned from an assignment, and he emailed me about the package. A day or two later, there was another email, but it was just a two sentence thing with Tribe's phone number."

"Think hard. What did it say?"

"Just something like 'Call Tribe. They don't normally

do consultations, but you're short on time, so they can help you with what you need.'"

"'Short on time? Help you with what you need?' Those were his words?"

"Yes. Something to that effect." He saw the exact moment she caught where he was going with his question. "You're thinking that he didn't mean the movie."

Waters swore under his breath. Kubrick was definitely in trouble. "No, baby, but he used that as your ticket in the door to us to prevent you from panicking. He used a marker from Steel, so we were pretty sure he was asking us to protect you. The fact that he didn't outright ask? That's even more concerning. That means he couldn't. He probably thought somebody was watching him."

"But I know nothing about what my brother does. He tells me nothing about his work—not even what he had for lunch that day. He's fanatical about it." She squeezed Waters' hand. "I'm dead serious. Not a smidgen of information."

"But you've visited him overseas, so you could have easily been seen with him if he were being watched. They might not know your exact relationship; they could even think you're lovers and not siblings. There's no official paper trail showing your connection, so it wouldn't have been obvious whom you were to each other without digging deep. And they wouldn't be able to be sure what you know and what you don't, so they might not be willing to take the chance."

"Who're 'they'?"

"Whomever he might have pissed off."

"So, he didn't come home to help me because he's out in the field. You think someone took him."

He grimaced. "There's no chatter, and we can't find a

digital footprint. Your brother is sort of a recognized expert on disappearing. Normally, when someone disappears, they leave at least a breadcrumb for someone to find in case it's under duress. We have several typical ways, and then we're trained to look for atypical things. But he didn't. So, we're not sure if he's really in trouble or just hiding really well."

"I'm sorry. I want to help, but I really can't. I'd do anything to help him."

"Any place he would go to be alone, some place no one but him would know. Does he have any friends in Egypt he'd go to if he were in trouble? Or maybe just over the border?"

"Again, he never spoke of knowing anyone outside of the embassy. He was close to Jacques, the French Ambassador, but I'm guessing that's not the kind of person you're looking for. You're looking for exit contacts."

He smiled with a wink and tapped the tip of her nose. "Clever girl."

She huffed. "I read, Waters. And I make movies, including an espionage thriller, remember?"

"Yeah, that one was probably my favorite." He gave her a wicked grin and several quick eyebrow raises.

"Gee, I wonder why. Was it that beautiful red-haired spy, I wonder?"

"Mmm. Very sexy. But I know someone sexier," he teased. He framed her face in his hands, looking her over, amazed that he was actually in bed with this woman.

And you're not fucking her, you moron.

"Not to beat a dead horse, but I need you to think about anyone Ka-Bar might contact, anyone he knows in Egypt, no matter how insignificant. If you think of anyone, I need you to tell me. And if you remember anything... anything at all that someone might be angry at him for or want to teach him a lesson for... I need you to tell me that, too. Even if it seems long past, petty, or not worth mentioning."

"I guess I would suggest starting with talking to anyone who was there when we lived there. I was between nine and ten back then. About nine months total, I think. I mean, the embassy was crawling with all kinds of people living there, working there, visiting there. They would have registration books, much like a hotel, recording every time anyone came in and out the doors. It'll be a shit-ton of people. Hope your tech guy is a robot. It'll take forever to comb through them all."

Waters kissed the tip of her nose. "You're so damn smart."

She rolled her eyes, shaking her head. "I don't want to talk about my brother anymore. It might ruin the next little while." Pushing him onto his back, she lay on top of him. She worked her way down his front, her nails dragging behind, causing him to groan. When she reached his navel, she looked up at him through her lashes. Then she went back to kissing him, following the cut of his hips.

The first swipe of her tongue had him groaning. "Kubrick, you don't have to—"

"Shut up and enjoy it," she mumbled.

And when she took the tip of his cock into her mouth, he was a goner. He fisted her hair gently and watched her do her magic.

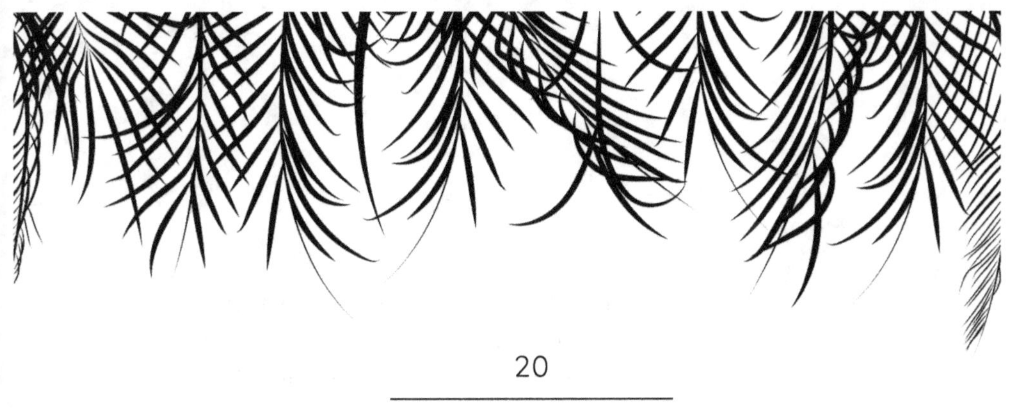

20

———————

MARCH 6TH-7TH

Kai

"Serrano. Where the hell are you? Call me. And don't screen your calls. I expect you to be available when I want you." Click.

Insufferable dick-smoker. I do not have time for you and your molting fits.

With a sigh, she leaned back in her desk chair and slouched, one elbow resting on the arm of the padded chair as she massaged her temple. Whatever he wanted was going to piss her off. Then again, everything he said, did, thought, and wanted pissed her off.

Waters walked into the War Room, thankfully clothed, and handed her a Crankiness Bomb and a plate of eggs, bacon, and toast. "Thank you. Breakfast for dinner is awesome. I'm going to need the fortification."

He perched his ass on the desk. "Brick was cooking and made you extra. What's up?"

Kai sighed. "Big Bird is molting again. He just called me."

"Did he say what he wanted?"

"No. Other than he called once, and because I didn't answer, he accused me of screening my calls and avoiding him. That man is annoying even half a continent away." She sipped her hot chocolate and then started to devour her food.

Ohmygodeggs! Yet another clue this was a unique situation—starvation after sex.

She noticed the fucker was smirking at her as she shoveled the food down. "I'll be in the room when you call him. Be sure to put him on speaker."

"It's a phone call. He's not going to be here," she grumbled as she tore into a piece of bacon.

Stealing the remaining half of a piece of bacon from her fingertips, he reminded her, "Rule four," then put the strip in his mouth.

He's even sexy when he's eating. What the hell?

"Stop chewing," she grouched and forked more eggs into her mouth.

He grinned. "Too sexy for you. I know."

Then, the jackwagon stole her toast. Unreal.

She sighed and rolled her eyes in exasperation. "You're killing me, Waters." Her fingers went to rub at her temples.

"Headache?" His voice went serious, suddenly filled with concern.

She gave a short laugh. "Yep."

"Do you have anything for it?" he asked.

Shaking her head, she closed her eyes and laid her head against the chair back.

"Hand."

Kai extended her hand to him, and he immediately

pinched and held the pressure point in the webbing between her thumb and index finger.

"Better?" he checked with her.

She nodded. "Where did you learn that?"

"Out in the field, I learned how to cure some simple stuff with reflexology. Some things work better than others."

She smiled. "So many talents," she teased.

He winked at her again, then pulled himself off the edge of the desk, leaning his lips into her ear. "I've heard I have magic hands."

She smacked his arm. "Humble much?"

"Not something I'm known for, no." He grabbed her empty plate and put it off to the side. "Call your boss." Before she could say a word, he reached back and removed his T-shirt from over his head. Pushing aside her laptop, he pulled her up out of the chair, then picked her up and sat her on the open space in the center of the desk. He lowered himself into the desk chair, pushed her legs as far apart as he could get them, and rolled all the way into the desk.

"What the fuck do you think you're doing?" she hissed.

Grabbing her legs, he placed a bare foot on either arm of the desk chair and started kneading her calf muscles. "I'm taking care of your headache."

"You're what?"

He pressed a kiss to the inside of her knee. Her foot shot out, almost kicking him in the shoulder, which made him laugh. "Glad I had my hand around your leg." His eyes looked up at hers, their green flames blazing. "Call him, Kubrick."

Mesmerized, she picked up her phone and dialed blindly. "No funny business."

"Scout's honor."

As she listened to the phone ring in the background, she looked at him through squinted eyes. "I don't trust you."

He laughed as he pressed a kiss to the other knee, both hands wrapped around her respective ankles. "Those are good instincts. I was never a scout. And there's nothing I'm about to do to you that's funny. But I am getting down to business, so move it along, or you will have serious issues."

Before she could even think of hanging up the phone or chastising him, Big Bird picked up his phone.

"Serrano! About fucking time. I tried to call you, and you didn't answer."

"Craig, I've missed you, too."

"I want a status report. What's my money getting me while you waste time soaking up the sun and surf down there for five weeks?"

Kai felt a nip on the inside of her calf. "Relax, Big..." She received another nip, which helped her catch herself. "Guy, your money is being well spent."

He grunted. "I doubt it. I have half a mind to come down there and oversee the work to make sure everything runs smoothly."

"Oh, for fuck's sake, Craig! We're training nonstop. The actors are spending fourteen-plus hours a day learning all the shit they need to do, and we haven't even gotten them onto a cliff wall or into a plane yet for rappelling. And when they're not training, they're working on character development and line memorization. With me in the room, I might add. And then they're sleeping off the exhaustion."

Warm, openmouthed kisses were trailing the inside of her calf slowly toward her knee.

"You're far too forward, Serrano," he growled.

I'm not the one who's forward. If that mouth gets any

further forward on my leg, I'll be moaning Waters' name and eventually screaming the walls down.

Instantly, she knew that she had pushed too hard. Be too aggressive with Big Bird, and he would be on the next plane just to fuck with her. The last thing she needed was him dogging her every step and getting in the way. And not just in the way of the filming. "Look," she tried another tactic, her voice softening its edge, "you want to come down and supervise, be my guest. You'll enjoy the weather. It's been nearly a hundred degrees every day. Everything is gorgeous here, including the snakes, the spiders, and I think I saw some sort of rodent the size of a small dog.

"There are some downsides, I'll admit. The house is drafty, damp, and the plumbing doesn't work well. We don't have hot water most days. Food is simple—eggs, coffee, bottled water, maybe some fresh fish, fruit, and vegetables if we're lucky. We're crowded in this derelict, but the idea of a luxury hotel in Coxen Hole is definitely going to be more Bates Motel than Ritz-Carlton."

Waters' hand gave her butt cheek a couple of gentle taps communicating "good girl" regarding her strategy for talking Big Bird out of joining them. Then he resumed sliding his palms up and down Kubrick's thighs, slowly going just a little bit higher to her hips each time.

He wouldn't dare while I'm on the phone!

His fingertips had reached her hips, hooking into the waistband of her leggings. She put the palm of her hand onto his forehead, attempting to push him back. He merely looked at her with an expression of "Don't test me!" and then began to pull the leggings down. When his hands hit the desktop, he nudged her with his shoulders pressing against her thighs. When she refused to lift her ass up off the desk so that he had a clear path to removing them completely, he just gave a violent tug that pulled them out from under her. As he dragged them down, his eyes never lost hers.

Oh my God, he does dare. Eek! That is hot, hot, hot!

"Craig," she implored, the warmth of Waters' mouth on the skin on the inside of her thigh and the caress of his hands on the outside causing her voice to rise. "I really need to get back to work." The muffled chuckle against her bare skin made it feel like her whole body was flushing. "Stop it!" she hissed, covering the speaker portion of her phone.

"Stop what?" She could feel Big Bird's suspicion all the way through the airwaves.

Shit! Missed covering the speaker.

"Nothing, Craig. One of the, ummm, farmers brought some fresh plantains over, and his, uh, his dog is trying to jump in my lap."

Waters' shoulders were shaking with laughter as he looked up at her and mouthed, "Arf." Then he leaned down and pressed his mouth to the lace gusset of her underwear, pulling at it with his teeth.

"Please, stop," she moaned. His head went back and forth, like a dog pulling on a rope toy.

"Are you all right, Serrano? You sound ill."

"No, no, not ill," she squeaked.

Holy fuck. Definitely have a fever, but I'm not ill. Unless you count an addiction to that mouth.

Big Bird gave an exasperated sigh over the line. "I want a deep accounting of your actions there. No minute can be unaccounted for or wasted. This is costing far more than it should."

"Yes, yes, you'll get your update. Hanging up now!" She clicked off her phone and threw it across the room. She heard it thunk off something, and it sounded like something cracked.

Oh, who the hell cares? If it's broken, he can't call me, and I'll only be able to talk to him through email.

She put her hands to Waters' ears and pulled his face up to look at her. He still had a portion of lace in his teeth. "If you wanted to become part of the troop and go for the sex badge, you should have also paid attention to the part of the Boy Scout motto that talks about being prepared."

His teeth let go of her underwear, but his left hand was holding them off to the side. He held up his right hand, three fingers in the Boy Scout salute. "Oh, I'm prepared enough for right now." Then his grin went wicked as he turned his fingers and slid them inside her and proceeded to show her how *helpful* and *friendly* he could be.

Needless to say, her headache was forgotten.

Sun streamed in the window of her room through the sheer white curtains when Kai woke the next morning. Waters was not in her bed, and he wasn't in the War Room. Disappointed, she showered, dressed, and wandered into the kitchen. The others were sitting around the breakfast table running lines for a scene with Vixen watching the script for accuracy.

They'd made a game of it with the poker chips they had found in the game closet. Each of the actors had one hundred dollars in poker chips. Every time someone made a mistake, she made an annoying buzzer sound. Whichever actor screwed up would then throw a dollar chip into a bucket at the center of the table, usually amidst much groaning from the payer and a lot of ribbing from the non-payers. Then, they went back to the top of the scene and started over. If you lost all of your chips, you had to buy more in five hundred dollar increments, and the money went to the local school for supplies.

"Enigma! Stop staring at Vixen's tits, or we'll never get through this stupid scene," Dawg teased. "Those kids are going to have one-to-one computers the rate you're going."

Vixen rolled her eyes and looked plaintively at Kai. "I want more money. These guys are ridiculous."

"Bullshit, sweetheart. You love us, and you know it," Dawg teased.

Ignoring the banter, Kai dropped down on one knee to the floor and checked out the wrap around her foot. "How's the ankle?"

"Better. The doctor taught Enigma how to re-wrap it in case he's not around and I need it changed." She looked at Kai with an apology in her eyes. "He said I'm not allowed to run yet, so Waters suggested I take Enigma with me to the dock and go practice some diving stuff."

"It's okay. We don't want you taking the risk of re-injuring it. Swimming shouldn't be too strenuous on it as long as you don't push too hard." She checked her watch to see that they were just shy of start time for the day. Standing up, she clapped her hands. "Okay, Lazarus, lead the rest of this motley crew out to the course. We'll start there."

Grumbling and groaning good-naturedly, the men headed out, somebody challenging the others to a race. Kai shook her head as they left. They really were overgrown teenage boys.

Vixen was still at the table, closing up her script and clearing the dishes.

Kai cleared her throat. "Waters isn't here. That's odd. Did he say where he was going?"

That sounded casual, didn't it?

"He said he had an errand to run in Coxen Hole and that he'd be back ASAP. Said he forgot something at home that he needed." Vixen was smiling but not looking at Kai. "I can't imagine what that would have been? I mean, considering the War Room was closed all afternoon and evening, and nobody could find either of you anywhere yesterday, it is a mystery." Vixen looked up at her director with overly innocent eyes and batted her eyelashes rapidly.

Both women looked at each other for a moment, then the corner of Vixen's mouth twitched. Kai couldn't keep the laughter inside, which then led to Vixen joining in. "Oh my God," Kai lamented when she was done laughing, her hands covering her cheeks in embarrassment.

"No worries, Kubrick. Everyone's thrilled you two hooked up. We've been watching him watch you ever since we got here. We were wondering when Soldier Boy was going to finish reconnaissance and head into battle. So to speak."

Kai's head tipped back to look at the ceiling. "So glad to know my actors have nothing better to do than spy on me."

"Lazarus has been trying to push him into making a move by being territorial. And I kept pushing my boobs into him. Wow, did that make him uncomfortable. He kept looking to see if you noticed. Way too much fun. Did it work?"

"I wondered why Lazarus was being overly attentive." She shrugged. "Waters did ask me to clarify what my connection was to Lazarus. I'd say my answer"—she paused

—"seemed to satisfy him. As for you, I just assumed you were trying to get his attention."

"Pfft. Waters is way too intense for me. Scares the crap out of me, actually. So." Vixen put her hands flat on the table and leaned over it so she could whisper to Kai. "Is he as awesome as he looks?"

Will she keep this between us? Can I trust her?

As if reading her mind, Vixen drew an "X" across her chest, then put a finger to her lips. "To the grave, sister. As long as I get updates."

"Will you share what's going on with you and Enigma?" Kai was sure that her eyes and voice were giving away her desperation for an outlet to share.

"I would love to share with someone. You know him well, and I'm so out of my league. But he's impossible to resist," Vixen confessed. "And it feels like he's interested in more than just during the filming run." She sighed and shook her head. "So. Deal?"

"Deal."

"I want deets. Is he skilled?"

Kai glanced down the hallway to make sure the men were long gone and that Waters hadn't returned yet. Kai mirrored her stance and whispered back, "Skills with thrills."

The women burst into a fit of giggles.

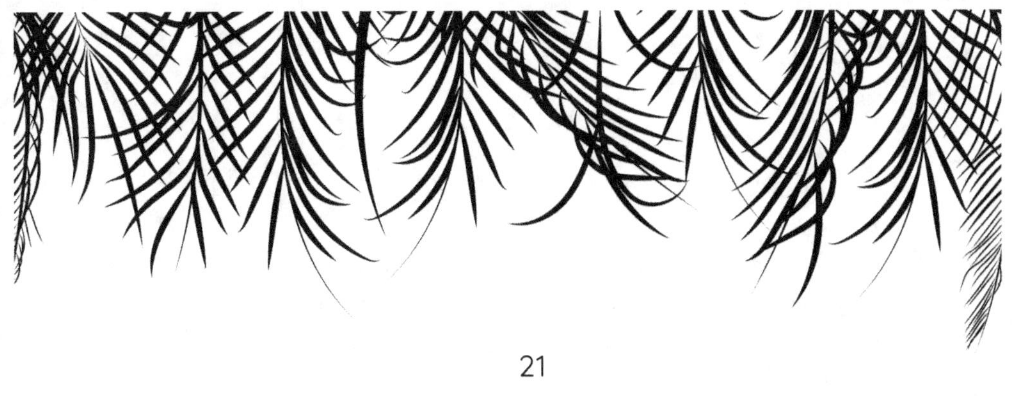

MARCH 7TH

Waters

As soon as Waters was a mile from the house, he pulled the Jeep down a dirt track turnoff and into the trees. He didn't have to wait long before the back flap opened to allow Nemo to roll into the storage compartment, and the side door opened to allow TB to cram himself into the passenger seat. Waters didn't look at them. He just sat in the driver's seat, drank his bottled water, and waited.

The car was silent for a while. Given that TB was an "information specialist" by trade, he had the silent treatment down. He would never be the first to begin a conversation unless he wanted to. Waters had withstood some of the worst interrogation and torture known to mankind, but if TB was going to use his "soft" approach, he knew that he would never win the Silent Game against his teammate. The twisted part of Waters refused to just give in, so he held out as long as he could.

TB sat and looked at him. He didn't move. He didn't blink.

After three minutes of silence where the only sound had been the crinkling of the plastic bottle that Waters drank from, he tossed the bottle in the back and refrained from smiling at hearing the soft "Hey!" from Nemo when he got hit with it.

Another minute or so went by without any noise at all. Waters just sat in the driver's seat, one wrist resting on the top of the steering wheel, staring out the windshield.

The fingers of his free hand resting on his leg were getting ready to twitch.

"Just get it over with and spit it out," Waters eventually grumbled.

Nemo piped up from the back. "Four minutes, nineteen seconds, Boss. New record. Way to go!" he praised with a congratulatory smack to the shoulder.

"Have you registered for china yet?" TB rumbled, totally straight-faced.

Here we go.

"Fuck you. I'm registering for a new Glock so that I can put you in the hospital and shut you up for a few days."

Totally deadpan, the giant informed him, "I'm just checking. Wanna make sure I'm prepared to purchase early. I don't want to be stuck as the chump who's left with the gravy boat for four hundred dollars at the end."

"Midas and I already have dibs on the gravy boat, so you're stuck with the thousand dollar place setting," Nemo offered just as deadpan.

"Okay, okay, you two have had your fun," Waters interrupted. "What do you have for me?"

Nemo reached into his pack and pulled out a brown

paper bag, stuck his head between the seats, and tossed it into Waters' lap.

"What the hell is this?" He looked inside and laid his head back on the headrest. "That's not what I meant."

"Yeah, I know. But it's what I have for ya. Cherry double-checked your kit before you left and noticed you weren't packing. And after the last couple of weeks of watching you and Kubrick dance around each other like the hippo and the alligator from *Fantasia*, I figured that you needed them."

With a look of disgust on his face, TB snarked, "I don't think she'd find that comparison flattering." Suddenly, he turned in his seat to look behind himself. "And why do you know that movie?"

"Name a movie I don't know about, Total Brontosaurus. Why do you know it? Okay. So. Anyway. We noticed you were taking an unscheduled trip into town after yesterday's blackout, so then I knew you needed them." Another congratulatory slap on the back. "Smooth, motherfucker! Of course, now I'm kinda pissed that it's imminent I'm going to lose the pool."

Waters rubbed his forehead and grimaced. "Could we please not have a betting pool on my sex life?"

"Dude," TB said, "there's not much else to talk about right now. If I have to do one more round of *Would You Rather* with Nozzle, here, I'm gonna strangle him."

"And even those games have been themed around your sex life," Nemo added.

"Kill me now," Waters moaned. "It's not about me. I can take your trash, but it's disrespectful to Kai, you dumbasses."

Silence reigned in the vehicle. Waters knew he'd made a mistake the minute he'd said her real name. He leaned his outside elbow on the windowsill and covered his mouth with his hand.

Fuck.

"Well, there it is," TB said.

"Okay, then," Nemo added.

That one slip had made it clear he was declaring that his feelings were more than casual. A catastrophic rule break. More silence invaded the Jeep until TB decided to take pity on him and not make a bigger production out of his mistake. "Midas found a breadcrumb."

Waters went into operator mode, removed his sunglasses, and turned to TB. "You couldn't have led with that?"

TB shrugged. "Thought the other might be more fun. Problem is, the bread crumb is pretty tiny and pretty stale. It could be nothing," he warned.

"Midas wouldn't have mentioned it at all if he didn't think it was something, though."

"There is that." TB's eyes continued to scan outside the car. "On the day of Ka-Bar's last email to Kubrick, the French Ambassador in Cairo—the one he's tight with, Jacques something-or-other—had an emergency. He left the embassy under the radar. No security. Now, he could have been going out to meet his mistress for all we know."

"But that's highly unlikely," Nemo followed up. "He's pretty damn devoted to his wife and kids."

"Correct," TB admitted, "but we have no record of where he went, whom he saw, or what he did. He could have been doing something as innocuous as buying a birthday present for someone. But, add to the fact that he accessed his personal safe before exiting the building, put one and one together, and you get three."

"He could have been accessing exit packages," Waters surmised.

"That's what God thought. The embassy records every time anything is accessed within its walls. This includes personal safes, locked doors, and computer logins; hell, they even keep track of how many times the water gets turned on and off and when. After doing an inventory of past usage, the man hasn't opened that particular safe in over two years. So, yes, Midas thinks he was accessing emergency exit contacts and providing someone—hopefully Ka-Bar—with a package because he couldn't get to his own stash. The problem is, Midas was only able to follow him a few blocks on CCTV, and then the guy just disappeared into thin air."

"Since that's impossible, that means we have a rough idea of where to search. Ka-Bar must have been hiding out in that vicinity. We're now left believing he would know that someone would look into the embassy, find the discrepancy, and use CCTV to trace the ambassador. Even if he's not there now, he could have left another breadcrumb wherever he was," Waters commented. His elbow propped once again on the windowsill, and he rubbed his top lip with his index finger. "Thin."

"The thinnest," Nemo agreed.

"Right now, anorexia is better than nothing," TB reminded them. "Besides, we need something soon. Our dental benefits can't handle the rate at which God is losing teeth."

Waters gave a small laugh despite the situation in front of them. "I just wish I knew if this all connected directly to Kubrick. It doesn't make sense."

TB looked back at Nemo. "Well, that's the other piece of news."

"I'm not going to like this, am I?"

"As you SEALs are always so fond of warning each other, 'brace.' We now have confirmation. Her trailer was searched."

"That's definitely what you should have led this conversation off with. Goddamnit!" Waters struck the steering wheel with the heels of both hands.

TB ignored him. "Cyclopes went off around oh-two-hundred. Someone was looking for something. They didn't trash the place, but they did break in, and they didn't hide the fact that they were there. By the time Steel got there to check it out, whoever it was had already left. No prints, either."

"And we know it wasn't Big Bird who broke in since if it was, Steel would have been there to witness it happen. Apparently, our angry bird brain was at a club all night, then went home with some internet influencer. He was there until just after three o'clock." Nemo shook his head. "How depressing. They only got to her place at about two-thirty. I should apologize to her for him when I get back."

TB smacked Nemo upside the back of the head and shook his head.

"What do you want to do, Boss?" Nemo asked.

Waters drummed his fingers on the steering wheel, thinking carefully before he answered. "Tie Kubrick up and cart her off to a safe house for starters."

"Kinky."

"Shut up, Nemo, or I'll tie you up and put you in a coffin with that snake."

"That's a low blow."

"How's your ass feeling, by the way?" Waters sniped.

"Like two fangs punctured it. And not in a good way."

TB looked at Nemo. "There's a good way for that to happen?"

Remembering a set of fangs that had punctured his right ass cheek last night, Waters shifted uncomfortably in his seat. "Everybody's got their kink."

Nemo got back on topic. "Well, we don't have a safe house here, and I highly doubt she'll agree to shutting down her film to go to one stateside."

Waters grunted at that.

"And while tying her up sounds fun," Nemo continued, "I don't want to go another round with that snake. So... what do we do?"

Sighing, Waters scrubbed his face with his hands. "It wouldn't take someone too long to figure out where she is. Right now, I can watch her just fine. It's her, me, and six actors. We're basically in each other's pockets twenty-four-seven. I can limit crew access to her with help from you guys, but more and more of them are arriving daily. Shit, once filming gears up, add extras in, plus gawkers, there'll easily be two to three hundred people running around, and I won't know who belongs and who doesn't."

"Can we lock down the shoot?" TB asked.

"Three of us can't maintain that. Hell, we're good, but even all six of us couldn't do it. We're talking total clus-terfuck."

"Well, you're not planning on leaving her side anytime soon. Not that you had been before you decided to play house. But at least now it won't look weird if you keep with her."

"Yeah, but then we have to make public that we're in a relationship."

Goddamnit.

TB smirked and looked out the passenger side window to hide the smile. Nemo just raised an eyebrow at him in the rearview mirror, a shit-eating grin on his face.

"You tell anyone what I just said, I will bury you both in a pit of vipers like Ragnar."

"Nice. Double confirmation for the betting pool. With that, I shall make my exit." Nemo clapped him on the shoulder, a little lighter this time. "She makes you smile. I don't even need binoculars to see that. Enjoy it, Boss." With that, he rolled out of the Jeep and disappeared into the cover of the jungle.

Silence hit the Jeep once more. TB showed no sign of leaving any time soon. Waters sighed. "Something on your mind, TB?"

"Just wondering if you've thought this through. Don't forget. I'm the one who hauled your ass off that meat hook in Egypt. All because someone took off with a woman close to you."

"It's not the same."

"No, Kubrick isn't your sister. She's your woman. In some ways, that's probably worse."

"She's not 'my woman.' It's not serious. It's a short-term thing, done at the end of the shoot. Besides that, no one's looking to get at me. I'm a dead man."

"You were a dead man when those fucksticks took Sarah. But you know in our line of work that attachments are dangerous. Any day, we could piss the wrong person off, and then someone we love gets put in harm's way to make us pay. That's why God delivered the message from on high to you, then us.

"Sarah was taken because you happened to piss off the wrong guy who had some crazy-smart tech guys of his own. She was God's unfortunate, expensive proof that operatives having attachments in the real world can be catastrophic. And those of us who did still have family and friends when we took the job? If we hadn't already, we forfeited them as soon as Sarah died. So now we have each other, but each of us knows the score if something goes FUBAR."

"I know." Fingers playing absently with the thread bracelet on his wrist, Waters stared at the Jeep's console, but he wasn't seeing it. "I tried to resist her. I really did."

TB shook his head. "You think I'm condemning you? Fuck, no. That's not where I'm going with this. I'm happy you've found someone who's bringing you back to life because heaven knows you, not me, have been the total bastard of the group since you came back to work. I want you to make sure she's worth the risk. Just take that into account because it doesn't have to be over when the assignment's over."

"God says no—"

"Fuck God and fuck his rules. He has no right to hold you to them."

"She's totally out in the open. I can't do my job and be with her."

TB sat in silence for a moment before going in for the kill shot. "Are you really going to keep making excuses? Whom are you trying to fool? Not me. Not any of the guys, including the boss, so you must be trying to fool yourself."

Waters let TB's words sink in and begin to digest when suddenly a surprise question came.

"Do you love fieldwork?"

Waters shrugged.

"No, you don't. You love analysis. You're the demigod. Mind like a fucking steel trap." TB smiled. "Yeah, you're great in the field. We know you've got our backs, and we've been lucky to have you with us. But none of us can do fieldwork forever."

"You make me sound old. I'm only thirty-four and younger than you."

"It's got nothing to do with age, and you know it. Did being younger than us keep us from accepting you as our team leader? Fuck, no. It's everything to do with using assets where they're best suited. You're certainly not a liability. Look, would you send Midas out as a sniper?"

"If I absolutely had to."

"Right. 'Absolutely had to.' He can shoot better than the average man, but he's best behind his screens. It's the most efficient use of him.

"Want her in your life? Then use your sexy analysis shit and figure out how to keep your ass out of the field, or at least out of the direct line of fire. Fuck, all it takes for you to do what you do in person is for us to wear comms, and you watch through the body cams, like the past year. You were out of the loop completely for a year and working remotely on projects for the past eleven months. We've been working that way just fine." He held up a hand to stave off Waters' protest. "Trust me. We would have rather had you with us. But we're okay. And you've been excellent in the office running interference with God. Believe me, we appreciate him not being up our asses all the time. Thrilled your ass has been taking it instead of ours.

"So, keep your hand in. Do the day-to-day bullshit jobs. Vet the clients. Hire some extra help, and you can take on some local work or even actually do consulting jobs to hide us better. Run the analysis. Be the eye in the sky and order us around. And there's never a shortage of shit to do that none of us like doing, but you're totally boss at.

"But hear me on this because it is most important. Be with her if that's what you want. And if it is, then it just means adjustments inside the group, which, given the year of recovery and year of office duty, doesn't really change all that much." TB looked over at him with concern. "And if

God would try to put through the final edict, you know we would help you two disappear, right?"

Waters felt that to his soul. They were willing to come between him and their boss? Just because he caught feelings?

TB broke the silence. "Does she know about Sarah?"

"No. She saw the scars. I just told her that I'd been captured on a job."

"You'll need to tell her."

"If I have to."

"Tell her. She's strong." He smiled and smacked Waters on the arm. "Take care. And don't use those all at once," he joked with a head nod to the bag. "I told him to triple what he got, but they were out of your size."

"Fuck you. How would you know what my size is?"

TB exited the jeep, leaned on the roof, and looked at him through the open door. "And Boss? She's probably more than worth it."

"She is. She's fucking perfect," he agreed, using her constant compliment to him. "But it would gut me to know that my life somehow makes hers impossible. It's just not a good idea."

"Well, you've got a number of weeks to figure that out. No need to make that decision now." He closed the door, banged two times on the roof, and with that, he was gone from the Jeep and disappearing into the jungle.

22

———————

MARCH 7TH

Kai

A HAND TOUCHED THE SMALL OF HER BACK, AND AN insulated coffee mug came from behind her as lips softly brushed the back of her shoulder. Standing on the edge of the dock, Kai allowed herself a ghost of a smile. Waters came around the side of her and squatted to stare down past the water's surface. "Good morning."

"Morning," he whispered with a glance in her direction. "Everybody good?"

Nodding, she sipped her Crankiness Bomb. "The stunt coordinator arrived and has all the guys demonstrating what you've taught them, so I thought I'd come down and supervise Vixen and Enigma."

"How are the two lovebirds?"

"Tired. Happy. They should be up soon. I made them promise to do ten-minute check-ins because of Vixen's ankle."

222

"Mmm. And what about you? Are you tired? And happy?"

"I slept well. I could be happier," she grouched.

"Salty today, are we?" Waters teased.

She winked at him.

He stood up next to her, his hands reaching around her waist to tag her hip and pull her close. "Patience," he murmured with his warm breath in her ear.

"Remember how we discussed my patience problems?"

"I remember working on those patience problems last night. Sounds like someone needs a reminder."

She gave him a hip check. "I'll give you a reminder later as to why you never make a woman wait for anything."

"Will it be a tongue-lashing?" he asked.

"Hmph." She cast a sideways look out of the corner of her eye. "Heard you were on a road trip."

"Mm-hmm."

"And was said mission successful?" she asked as she sipped her drink without looking at him.

"Mm-hmm."

Thank God!

She turned to look at him.

He was trying not to laugh.

"I said that out loud, didn't I?"

"Yes. Yes, you did." He grabbed her free hand. "You're not alone. Feels a bit like the afternoon of Christmas Eve." He kissed her cheek and pulled back about five seconds before Vixen breached the surface, followed shortly after that by Enigma.

23

———————

MARCH 7TH

Waters

Can I give Kai more than these next few weeks?

That was the million-dollar question, wasn't it? And it was distracting him from his job right now. Giving himself a shake, he tried to convince himself he'd have plenty of time to mull it over later.

Later. There's a whole other level of distraction.

His meeting with TB and Nemo took care of two things: updates and saving him from a trip into the town. He wasn't about to look a gift horse in the mouth. However, it was difficult not to think about later, not to plot and plan their time alone when he knew there wasn't anything to inhibit him now. And he wasn't sure which was more dangerous: thinking about what would happen behind closed doors or thinking about what was going to happen at the end of the filming.

All of a sudden, his watch began beeping softly and

224

rapidly. Frowning, he glanced down to see a red light flashing in time to the beeping. A couple of clicks silenced the beeping and flashed a code on the screen: C1.

Kubrick's room!

Kubrick was squatting down at the edge of the pier talking to Vixen and Enigma, checking in on her injured actress and discussing with them if they thought working an injured Vixen into the script as a moment might have value. He didn't want to leave her alone, but someone or something had tripped Cyclopes back at the house.

"Kubrick, I'm going to go check on the others. You good here?"

"Sure thing. Everything okay?"

"Just stay here with Enigma and Vixen, okay?"

Kubrick frowned but gave a single nod.

It took everything he had in him not to take off at a run for the house, but he didn't want Kubrick to panic. Plus, he knew that TB, Nemo, and Demon would all be getting the same alarm. One of them would be close by to keep an eye on Kubrick, and the others would be moving toward the house. Once he had turned the corner on the path between the lake and the house, he tapped into his watch's comm system.

"Sitrep," he barked.

An Irish brogue came over the speaker. "C1, C2, and C4 perimeters breached. On my way there now."

"No one was watching the house?"

"Nemo was."

A feeling of unease rippled through Waters. "Has he checked in?"

"Negative."

"TB?" he called out.

"Got my eyes on Kubrick. Go."

"How close are you, Demon?"

"Southern corner now."

"Wait for me. Be there in sixty."

Waters took off at a jog, swinging around to come in from the eastern side so he could coordinate with Demon. "Here."

"No sign of Nemo, but no sign of disruption, either."

"Slow and easy. I'll go in the front with a detour past her window to see if there's anything there. You take the back. Swing out to the tree line and take a quick look for Nemo."

"Already done. He's not there."

"Okay. I'll check in before we enter."

"Copy."

Walking as nonchalantly as he could, looking for all of the world like he was simply returning to the house for something, Waters continued toward the house at an angle that would allow him to scout out Kubrick's room to see if anyone was inside. The alarm on his watch was still flashing, but then again, it wouldn't stop until he reset it on-site.

As he passed the window, he used his peripheral vision to see if he could spot anything. The shutters were open, but nothing looked off from the outside, and he didn't want to get closer and tip off anyone who could still be inside. Whoever had tripped the alarm had accessed the room through the kitchen and then the War Room entrance.

As Waters arrived at the front door, he removed his gun from its place at the small of his back and moved into position on the porch. He tapped a quick text to Demon to breach on three.

Tapping the countdown on his audio, when he hit three, Waters swung through the door and quickly cleared the hallway. He listened carefully. There was no sound of

Demon entering the house, but then again, there wouldn't be. Unfortunately, there was also no sound to indicate anyone was within the walls at all. Waters trained his weapon on the War Room doors, which were cracked open. Backing up to the door of his room, he quickly tested the doorknob, and it was still locked. With both hands to his weapon, he noticed a text from Demon.

"Nemo out cold, but okay. Coming out."

Waters breathed a small sigh of relief that Nemo was still breathing, but the intruder could still be in the house. Did Nemo spot him and get caught following, or did the intruder sneak in behind him? Nemo wouldn't have had any reason to enter the house unless he was following someone. But what if there were two of them? Nemo could have followed one and then been snuck up on by a second. It would have been odd for him to miss a tail, but not impossible.

Demon came from the kitchen, giving the "all-clear" sign.

Waters motioned to the War Room doors, pointing Demon to go high. Counting down from three on his fingers, the two men burst through the door.

It was trashed. Papers were everywhere surrounding the desk. The worktable with all of the storyboards was overturned. Desk drawers were pulled out and dumped on the desk. Both his tablet and Kubrick's laptop were missing.

The doors to Kubrick's room were also cracked.

After clearing the room, Waters again motioned for Demon to go high, and he used his fingers to count down, breaching the door. If the War Room was a mess, then her room was a disaster. Everything was ripped apart. Literally. Pillows had been cut, and the filling dumped. The mattress was tipped, slashed, and clearly searched. Her backpack was dumped, and the contents were strewn across the floor. What little clothing she had brought with her was also littering the space.

When they had entered, after the cursory sweep showing clearly that no one was still in the bedroom, Demon had continued on to clear the bathroom. He now surveyed the windows, running his fingers along the frames, looking for evidence that they'd been recently opened.

"Clear," Demon informed him.

The two men proceeded to clear the rest of the house and found themselves alone, save for Nemo sprawled on the kitchen floor. Once they confirmed no intruders remained behind, they went to collect and revive their teammate. Demon did a quick pat down to check for injuries and found nothing more than a significant bump on the back of his head. While Waters made an ice pack, Demon broke an ammonia stick beneath Nemo's nose. It didn't take more than a second or two for him to wake and issue a complaint of, "I'd have rather gotten bitten by the snake again." Together, Waters and Demon hauled him up from the floor and put him in a chair.

While Demon proceeded to take vitals for Nemo, Waters used his watch to call TB. He picked up immediately. "All clear here."

Waters appreciated that TB knew exactly what his first concern would be. "Good. Here, not so much."

He looked over to where Demon was working on their teammate. "Nemo took a whack to the back of the head. No details yet, but can't rule out the possibility of two Charlies, so keep frosty."

"Roger that." TB clicked off.

Waters made a second call. Midas answered almost as swiftly as TB had. "What the holy hell is going on down there? Nemo's life alert went off, Cyclopes is going apeshit on C_1, 2, and 4, and there are two men in black systematically destroying the contents of C_1 and C_2."

"I'll have Demon reset the alarms momentarily. Someone broke into the house. Do you have any pictures for me?"

"Umm, yeah. I don't know who these guys are, but they're fast and efficient." Keys were clacking in the background. "From what I can tell, there's only two of them. Facial recognition will be no good as they're covered head-to-toe. I might be able to get some rough estimates on height and weight, but that's not super helpful. Right now, I don't see any distinguishing marks like tattoos or birthmarks, but I'll go through it frame by frame when we're done and double-check. One thing I can tell you, they're both male."

"Could they be Egyptian?" Waters asked.

"Possibly. No way to tell that, though."

Demon stood up from rechecking the knot on Nemo's head and left the room, presumably to reset the alarms. Within moments, the red lights on their watches went dark. He re-entered the room and leaned in the doorjamb.

"Midas," Waters began, "I need you to put the video up on the TV in the War Room. Both my tablet and Kubrick's laptop are MIA."

"They'll be there before you are."

"Nemo, you good?"

"Five by five, Boss." He got up from the chair with a wince, but he didn't complain or groan as they moved through the house. When they arrived, the television screen already had the video surveillance paused on the screen. Midas' face was in a small box in the upper left corner where the damaged pixels normally appeared. The timestamp in the bottom right corner showed they entered the house, searched, and were out in less than five minutes.

On screen, the entry, search, and exit were fast and smooth. Intruder One entered through the kitchen door. Nemo quickly followed, and Intruder Two took Nemo down with a tap to the head using what appeared to be a baton.

The man winced at watching himself go down. "Sorry, Boss."

With each action committed by the two men on the screen, Waters got angrier and angrier, especially when they began pawing through Kubrick's personal items.

"Fecking arseholes," Demon muttered. He looked at his team leader. "What's the play?"

"If I had Steel here, I'd track them, but that's obviously not happening. And knowing that there are two of them, there's no way I'm sending anyone out alone after them. We need to get the actors back here and under wraps, at least temporarily."

"How's she going to take it?" Nemo asked.

"Typical, Kubrick, I'm guessing. She'll be pissed but collected. Might call them a few more creative names."

"Got my list here to take inventory," Midas quipped as he gestured to the whiteboard behind him. The list was growing as every day she seemed to have a new Kubrick-ism for him to add to it. There were checkmarks next to them as a show of how often she repeated them. "Assclown" was by far the favorite.

Waters allowed a small uptick of one corner of his mouth. He was angry, but he could see how his woman's filthy mouth would be high entertainment to his teammates. He might help add some names to Midas' list as well.

"You want us visible?" Demon asked.

"Negative. I'm okay with her knowing I have some security measures in place. She already knows the bare bones about Ka-Bar and what's going on. But I refuse to cause panic amongst the actors. Let's get the War Room at least appearing normal-ish to the naked eye. We don't need to worry about disturbing evidence. Both had gloves on from moment one."

"What about the electronics?" Nemo asked.

Midas answered. "Waters and Kubrick's were both tagged. If they turn his on without the proper fingerprint on the lock being used, the drive automatically wipes itself in five seconds. They won't even get to a start-up screen."

"None of the other alarms were tripped, so they knew right where they needed to go. Or thought they did. It was a streamlined ingress and egress, but they were clearly on a timeline of some kind." Midas looked to his left and squinted. "Your tag and Kubrick's are live, but the signal is screwy. They might have them inside something that's messing with the signal. Like an iron box. Once they try to open yours, the signal will terminate, too, so then we'll only have Kubrick's to work from. I'll keep an eye on it and see if we can catch a break."

Demon looked to Waters. "How will she handle the loss of the computer?"

Waters shrugged. "As far as I can tell, she hates the fucking thing. Most of the work she did was on all of these sheets of paper. She's a bit old school that way." He shook his head. "The disaster of things being out of her organized chaos will probably be the tipping point."

He scrubbed his face, dragging his hands down his cheeks. Hands on hips, he stared at the screen. "Something's weird about this break-in. Damned if I can see what." The two men knew the look and let him process.

They began picking up the room, making piles of papers on the desk, dumping supplies into random desk drawers, righting furniture, and generally making it look good to where the actors wouldn't recognize anything being off.

Waters had watched the video footage three additional times before he spoke out loud. "Midas, she's going to have to report this to Big Bird since her computer is gone. We need to track his every move. I don't want her surprised when he shows up."

"You think he'll come all this way?" Nemo asked.

"I know he will," Waters replied. "He won't be able to resist the opportunity to come down here and read her the riot act, even though it's not something she provoked. Well, not wittingly."

He sucked in a full lung of air and let it out. "One more thing."

"What's up?"

"Her brother asked her to pick up a package in Cairo. That's why she went there in December. When she got there, no one knew anything about a package. She has no clue what it was, but maybe someone thinks she has said package, and that's what they're looking for. Because of this added link to Egypt, I want boots on site."

"Got it. I'll get Steel on a plane and out playing Hansel to Ka-Bar's Gretel, plus start tracing back all the mail going out of the embassy from that day forward. If I strike out, I'll search all packages going through the public services from the embassy outward."

"And Midas?"

"Needed yesterday. Got it?" Midas' face winked out from the screen, and there was quiet.

"She gonna be okay, Boss?" That came from Demon.

Waters nodded. "Yeah. I'll be stuck to her side whether

Big Bird comes down or not, but I'm pretty sure he'll book himself on the first flight after her call. He'll take over my space, and I'll bunk with Kubrick."

"He'll love that," Nemo quipped. "He already loves you so much."

"Don't care. She's my primary concern, not dickwad." He shook his head in frustration. A selfish part of him couldn't help thinking this might derail his plans for tonight. While it gave him the perfect excuse not to hide his relationship with her in front of the others, in truth, he wasn't exactly sure how she'd take the thought that they'd been invaded. His entire being was screaming at him to lock her down, to hell with her movie, but he knew that was never going to happen. As long as they were all vigilant, it was clear that the intruders hadn't found whatever they were looking for, and they could manage to keep her secure.

If they never got together as planned, he'd still be close to her. That was all that mattered in the long run. And frightening as that was, he couldn't find it within him to care.

24

———————

MARCH 7TH

Kai

A LITTLE OVER AN HOUR LATER, WATERS RETURNED TO her side at the dock. Slowly, over the past weeks, his face had become more open, his posture less ramrod straight, and his movements easier. Right now, he was in full operator mode and as tense as the first day she met him.

Okay, scary G.I. Joe is back. That's not good.

"What happened?"

She watched him scan the lakeshore left and right, then narrow his eyes to look to the far side of the lake. "We had a break-in," he murmured. "They trashed the War Room and your room. Your laptop is gone."

"Shit." She looked out across the water. "You had security measures up at the house. That's why you took off."

He didn't acknowledge her statement, which was confirmation enough. "They didn't touch the rest of the house, so it's very clear your belongings were the target."

234

His jaw tic was back. "I didn't want to worry you, but someone also searched your trailer back at the studio. That was a more methodical search, but then again, they knew there was little chance of being interrupted since you were already here. The security on the lots is pretty much shit, even though there are so many 'secret' things there and celebrities running around. Way too predictable and definitely not enough bodies."

"So, someone thinks I have something they want."

"Yes."

"And you still think this is connected to Ka-Bar?"

"It's our best lead."

"The package I was supposed to pick up in Cairo. Could it be that?"

"Crossed my mind."

"Then I need to call the embassy and find out if Agent Carter has come back, if he has it, and if he sent it."

Waters seemed to consider this plan. "I'm not sure that's the best idea. Someone's probably watching for that. Possibly even listening in somehow."

"What do you suggest?"

"Midas, my computer guy, found a very weak clue to suggest an area where Ka-Bar was when he disappeared. We think the ambassador he was tight with might have supplied him with exit contacts because he couldn't get to his own materials. I'm sending one of my teammates to check out the area."

"All the way to Cairo?"

Waters nodded. "This is an in-person issue. He should be there shortly. We have a general area where we think he might have been lying low. Steel might get lucky enough to find something if Ka-Bar was able to leave behind a breadcrumb to lead us to the next step of finding him. After this length of time, it's clear that whatever exit strategy he had was unsuccessful." He apologized. "Sorry. This is really the first chance I've had to fill you in on all that."

She waved him off. "Not accusing you of holding back anything. I know you'll tell me what you can when you can."

"I want to move everyone back to the house. We need to fill them in on the break-in. I will give them enough information to put up their defenses, but not so much that I scare them. I just want people to be extra aware of anyone hanging around."

"Got it. And better to address it once rather than multiple times and field any questions so everyone hears the answers."

Waters turned her to face him so he could put his hands on her biceps and look her in the eye. "Midas is already working on trying to identify the thieves, but I have to admit, it's going to be tough." He kissed her capped forehead and held her close. "I promise we'll get them, Kubrick. We'll find your brother and take care of all of this. Trust me to protect you."

Good grief. This man.

Looking up at him, she smiled sadly. "No need to ask for that trust, Waters. It's been yours for some time now." She exhaled with a tinge of irritation. "I can't avoid reporting the break-in to Big Bird since my computer's gone."

"Agreed."

"He's going to go full-on nuclear-molt."

"Atomic."

"He's going to come down here."

"Anticipated."

"He absolutely hates you."

"Mutual."

Groaning at the havoc the man was going to cause in her life, not to mention her cast's lives, she lamented, "Where are we going to put him? He'll refuse to stay in Coxen Hole."

"The perverse part of me says we pitch him a tent in the jungle. But I know we can't actually do that. He can have my room."

She looked at him suspiciously. "And where will you be? Not in that same tent you were proposing."

He brushed some errant strands of hair behind her ear and up under her cap. "There's this sexy blonde across the hall I've been wanting to shack up with. Think she might not be immune to me staying with her for a bit."

"Mmm. Presumptuous."

"Not presumptuous if it's true."

She grinned. "I warn you. I don't sleep neat."

He dropped a quick kiss on her lips. "No, you don't. But if I wrap you up tight next to me, you probably can't do too much damage. Besides that, I'm not sure there'll be a whole lot of sleeping."

She snuggled back up to his chest, and they stood in silence on the dock.

When Vixen and Enigma surfaced, Kai told them to gather their gear and meet back at the house. Waters made it very clear not to separate from each other for a moment. They would explain more after they collected the rest of the group from the rappelling station.

Everyone showered, changed, and met around the kitchen table. While they ate, Kai laid out the break-in, explained that while there didn't appear to be any danger expected, she wanted no one to go anywhere on their own as a precaution in case it was the work of a fan who had crossed the line. A potential "crazy fan" wasn't all that out of the realm of possibility to them, so there were no uncomfortable questions.

After lunch, the actors headed to the shooting range that had been set up, and Kai went to make her phone call to Big Bird before meeting them there. Waters sat on the edge of the desk while she called him.

Slightly different seating arrangements than my last call to the assclown.

She felt her face heating up as she picked up her phone and dialed. Looking up as it began ringing, she caught Waters' smirk. He knew exactly what was causing the flushed skin. He winked at her but otherwise stayed put leaning on the desk.

As expected, Big Bird went atomic. She simply sat there, rubbing her forehead, waiting for him, like a tantrum-laden toddler, to eventually burn out of energy, and then she could address the issue rationally.

Kai was paying so little attention to what he was screeching that she didn't notice Waters' tolerance level for bullshit was at an end. Suddenly the phone was out of her hand, and he was speaking.

"Stapleton, this is Waters. I'm hanging up this phone. When you've finished your bout of hysteria and can speak rationally, call back." Then he clicked off, turned the power off, and threw the phone gently on the desk.

"I was just letting him burn to the end of his wick. I wasn't even listening to anything he was saying."

"Don't care. Why does anyone work with that man?"

"Simple." She shrugged. "Behind the dickhead nature, he can sniff out a winning picture better than a crack whore in a warehouse of smack. And he's richer than the gods of Olympus, so if he's throwing money into something, that means it's a winner. Unfortunately, that's how Hollywood works. Follow the money to success."

"You are not to touch that," he ordered, pointing at the phone, "until tomorrow morning. You're skipping the range today. Get your cute little ass into my room and take a nap."

"Why?"

"First, whether you realize it or not, the adrenaline crash is coming, and I can't have you on the range with a live weapon when that happens. Brick will make one dumbass joke, and you'll shoot him.

"Second, my room because your room qualifies for national disaster relief funds from FEMA. Most of it needs a complete replacement, which I will help you figure out later.

"And third"—he grabbed her chin in his hand—"we have a date later, and you're going to need all the rest you can get." With that, he tore the cap from her head and threw it off to the side. Then his mouth was swooping down onto hers, teeth clashing with his intensity, his tongue plundering her mouth to show her exactly what energy he had stored up for her.

The kiss was hard and hot but over quickly, leaving her stunned into silence. "Get in my room and get in my bed," he ordered.

"Yes, sir," she parodied with a sarcastic salute. When she turned on her heel, she readied to take a step, and there was a massive *crack* sound, followed by a stinging sensation on her right ass cheek.

An arm snaked around her waist, and then another loosely around her front, dragging her back against his chest. His breath was hot in her ear when he threatened, "You bet that wicked ass, 'Yes, sir.' Now take your saucy attitude out of here, or I'm gonna make that ass red from the palm of my hand." Then his teeth gently nipped her earlobe before he let her go with a gentle push.

When she got to the door, she took the chance to look back. What she saw pushed her internal temperature up a couple more degrees. He was rock solid, almost statue-like in appearance, and laser-focused on her face.

"Waters?" she asked softly.

"Kubrick?"

"Wake me when you're all back from the range."

His grin was positively feral. "My pleasure, baby."

She shivered, then stepped out of the War Room, closing the door behind her. Quietly, she slipped into his room across the hall and locked the door behind her. Stripping down to her sports bra and boy shorts, she dropped her clothes on the floor where she stood and crawled between the sheets of his perfectly-made bed.

So typical! Could probably bounce a coin off of this bed. Why make a bed you're just going to get back into later that day?

Kai buried her head in his pillow and inhaled. She couldn't prevent the groan escaping from her throat. His smell was everywhere. Wanting it to imprint on her body, she pulled the sheets tight around her and snuggled deeper into the pillow. It might creep him out later that she was covered in his scent, but somehow, she doubted it. That would probably cater to some sort of natural claiming behavior he had going on that his woman smelled like he'd rubbed himself all over her, marking her so other males knew to stay away.

His woman.

Is that what she was?

Why do people have to put labels on everything?

For now, at least, it appeared he'd marked her as his. But at the end of filming, they would go their separate ways, and what was she then? His ex?

At that moment, it suddenly became too much to think about. Her bones felt like they weighed twice their normal burden, her eyes felt gritty, and exhaustion slammed into her with the speed and force of a freight train. Her eyelids closed, she burrowed deeper into the comfort of Waters' bed, and fell instantly asleep.

25
____

MARCH 7TH

Waters

WATERS TRIED HIS DOOR AND SMILED AT FINDING IT locked. Smart girl. He pulled the key from his pocket and entered his room silently, moving through the darkness without turning on the lights. The moon provided enough light through the window for him to see that Kubrick was exactly where she had been when he checked on her in the afternoon. And while TB said she hadn't exited the house, he didn't feel secure until he'd witnessed her sleeping for himself.

You've got it bad, dude.

She rolled over onto her side away from the door; however, she didn't wake. He took in how tangled the sheets were, pulled up tight to her chin up front but leaving her back side completely uncovered. They were pulled entirely free of the bed, and the bottom end of the sheets were shrouding her, knees to feet, as tightly as an Egyptian

242

mummy. He half-heartedly smiled at what would happen if she woke suddenly and tried to fly out of the bed.

Definitely does not sleep neat. It looks like she's hugging your sheets as if they were you.

He picked up her clothes from where she'd dropped them on the floor and folded them, making a pile on the bedside table. Then Waters sat on the edge of the bed to take off his boots and socks, peeled off his tee, and then stood to remove his belt and pants. He looked down at the sleeping woman.

Yep, she has her face buried in your sheets.

Clothes folded and piled on a nearby chair, clad only in his boxers, he went into the bedside drawer and pulled several condom packets off of the strip, laying them neatly on the tabletop. Then he slipped his body into a spoon behind hers in the bed, and his mouth skimmed over the skin between her neck and shoulder. Carefully, to not wake her just yet, he slipped one arm underneath her body to cup a breast, kneading it gently. His other arm slid between her arm and her waist, his fingers gliding to the soft skin of her belly, where he drew lazy patterns on its surface.

I could wake her up like this every day.

Now, where did that thought come from?

The question was wiped away from his brain as he felt Kubrick come up out of sleep. Her body stretched out to its fullest to shake off the grogginess, and he knew the moment she registered that she wasn't alone in the bed.

Languidly, she arched her back, pushing her torso out to further meet his hands. "You all spent a long time at the range."

His nose brushed the shell of her ear, taking in her flowery scent, and he pulled her tighter to him. "When we got back, you were passed out. I didn't have the heart to wake you up. So, we went and climbed some trees, some rock facing, stuff like that. I wanted everyone to be good and worn out tonight."

"What about you? Won't you be tired?" she teased.

"Hush, woman. SEALs don't get tired."

His rough fingertips slid underneath the material of her sports bra and pushed it over her breasts. Both hands cupping her, his forefingers found her nipples and brushed softly over them, causing them to pebble. The almost nonexistent touch back and forth caused Kubrick to groan low in the back of her throat with each brush, pushing her ass back against his hardening cock while pushing her breasts further into his touch.

I don't want to go back to before.

While he had enjoyed the flirting, the snark, the easy working relationship, the friendship that they'd had, he wanted more with her. Wanting and having were two different things, though, and he knew that if he proceeded to do what he'd promised tonight, there would be no going back. Kubrick's heart was involved already, at least in a hormonal way, as he remembered last night's activities. But making love to her would be a whole new ballgame, and her heart would become emotionally invested.

And let's face it, yours, too, big guy.

He did know that he loved working by her side. She was beautiful to him on a physical level, and he was not hypocritical enough to admit that her attractiveness mattered. But he truly found her to be a fantastic partner in every way for him: funny, intelligent, and confident. When she faced down people who tried to belittle her, she was on fire. It was probably what attracted him the most about her.

But working for Tribe made their relationship an impossibility. The rule was that no one could have proof they existed beyond having met them. Once a job was finished, the client might come back to headquarters, but the team members never saw that client again. The client wasn't given access beyond the lobby for any reason. All communication was cut. Once payment came through, Tribe denied all connections, then buried all payment records. Any alternate IDs used besides their nicknames were fake and burned after their project use. Up until now, he'd never even had an ounce of concern about those rules, let alone a desire to break them. Then again, they didn't spend an inordinate amount of time with clients. But his chest ached at the thought of those rules coming into play when the filming ended.

TB seemed to think he could stay, just not work in the field. Would God even entertain that thought?

And again… was that what he wanted?

Time to make a choice. Go forward and never go back? Or pull back to what this was the day you first met?

One thing was clear to him. It had to be one or the other. Inside his head, he groaned.

Is there really even a choice? Either way, there's going to be pain. If I go back on right now, we'll both be hurt. When we separate at the end of filming, we'll both be hurt. If God makes me "disappear" because I'm going to break the rule, she'll be hurt, and I'll be dead in truth. We can't win.

Truth time—there was no choice. For there to have been no pain to either of them, he should never have given in to his impulses yesterday. He would take the blame. So he might as well fuck up totally and completely.

He inhaled deeply, committed to his next action, and then exhaled.

His right arm banded tighter around her, his left hand drifting down to her hip. Feather-light, lips still on her skin behind and beneath her ear, he growled low, "Mouth." Kubrick turned her head to meet his lips over her shoulder. "Open your legs for me, baby. Let me in," he whispered against her lips.

As she started to allow space between her legs, his hand hitched her top leg and draped it over his so that she had no choice but to have her ass pressed back against his hard cock and be completely spread open for him. His hand slid inside the material of her boy shorts and glided through the slickness accumulating between her legs. Gathering her wetness on his fingertips, he pulled them free and brought his hand up to her lips, spreading her juices on their plumped surfaces. "Taste yourself, sweetheart. This is what I thought about all day when I imagined being with you. So fucking spicy."

Her tongue slipped between her lips to swipe at her taste, then captured his index finger in her mouth with a nip from her front teeth. She bit down just enough to keep it trapped, then swirled her tongue around the calloused digit before beginning to lightly suck on it. Her action reminded him of yesterday when he finally let her take his cock into her mouth because she had done the exact same thing then. With that thought, he could feel himself hardening further against her ass.

His response caused him to remember her frustration with him at the time. When he got close to his orgasm, he refused to let her finish, insisting that the first time he came inside her, it would be in her hot, wet pussy. Instead, he let her stroke him off between them, his release spraying her hand and belly. He thought perhaps she remembered as well due to the sudden increase in the pressure of her suction.

His hand slid back beneath the waistband, down into

her wetness again, but this time, two fingers pushed into her channel, stroking her inside walls. Immediately, her hips began thrusting against his hand, his fingers scraping against her G-spot, the heel of his hand grinding against her clit. She had been doing her best to be quiet to not disrupt the house, but as he felt her inner walls begin to clutch his fingers, she whispered his name in warning. His other hand slid up to cover her mouth, and with an extra twist and pressure on her sex, she exploded against his hand.

"Fuck, baby," he gasped as he felt her breath soughing deeply behind his hand. "Everything off," he growled.

In a split second, he was off the bed. Kubrick moved a little slower, recovering from her orgasm still. While she struggled to right herself, he stripped out of his boxers, placing them on his pile of worn clothing, and sheathed himself in a condom. Then he kneeled on the bed at her side, yanked the bra up and over her head, followed by giving her a firm but gentle push to lie down again. He grasped her shorts at the hips and yanked them down her legs, placed both clothing items on top of the bedside table, and settled himself between them so that they were finally hip-to-hip.

"I need you," he ground out through gritted teeth. "Gonna fuck you hard, baby, but I'll try to start slowly since you say it's been a while."

He lined up his cock with her entrance, just the very tip slipped into her opening. Then he reached for her hands and threaded their fingers together, the backs of her hands pressed to the mattress beside her ears. Certain that their eyes were locked on one another, he gave a sharp, smooth thrust as he buried himself inside her until their pelvic bones ground together.

Both registered a moment of shock as they felt her walls

immediately pulse around him so snugly inside her, after-shocks causing her hips to twitch. It was as if some invisible switch had been flipped. His nostrils flared, his eyes narrowed, his grip on her hands tightened, and the sexy grin that had been on his face disappeared. Agonizingly slow, he dragged his length out of her until only the tip of his cock remained poised in her entrance, and then even more slowly, he pushed back in. "Fuck, you're so tight." He pulled himself back to the tip. "Tip your hips up to me, Kubrick."

As she arched her hips upward, Waters slid back fully inside her and began an in-out pace that was slow and steady. He watched her eyes squeeze shut as her muscles tightened further, causing delightful friction. "Open your eyes, sweetheart." Ever so slowly, her eyelids raised. "There she is," he crooned. "There's my pretty girl." He kissed the corner of her mouth. "You ready to fly again, baby? Ready to show me how pretty you come? I can't wait to see how sexy you are when you come because my cock fills you so well. I want to watch those eyes when you fall over the edge for me."

Waters felt the temperature of his body begin to rise with each stroke inside her. At the back of his mind, he couldn't get over the fact that she'd only had two lovers other than him. It just didn't make sense. How could a woman like her—so empowered and so filled with life—go unclaimed? It just didn't make sense.

Maybe she was waiting for you.

Her breathing was a series of gasps punctuated with soft cries of pleasure. It didn't take him long to realize that she was fast approaching another orgasm, and he wanted to make sure he saw the whole thing unfold in front of him.

"That's it, Kubrick. Let go for me. Give me that sticky-sweet again. Want to feel it coat my cock. Want to be able to pull out of you and stroke my cock through your sweetness."

He circled his hips on the next up thrust, simultaneously reaching down and dragging the flat of his tongue over a distended nipple, triggering her orgasm. Quickly, he pounced by pushing even deeper and molded his mouth over hers to capture as much of the scream as possible. While everyone in the house would likely figure out quickly that they were a couple, he didn't want to announce it like this.

As she shuddered, shook, and clawed at him, he groaned at the pleasure skittering up his spine. He could come now if he wanted to, but some unused portion of his alpha self wanted to wait. Deny himself until he'd wrecked her to the point of no return. He'd always prided himself on being able to withhold his own release for long periods of time because it made the final moment more explosive for him. And while he knew he would do that with Kubrick, he also wanted to experience that feeling with her over and over again.

He left soft kisses along the side of her face, down and across her throat, then up the side of her neck beneath her ear, murmuring nonsense to her as she came down through the aftershocks. Letting go of her hands, he brushed back the strands of her damp hair from her face, watching over her. Finally, her heartbeat and breathing seemed to level out.

"Kubrick?" he murmured.

"Mmm, thank you," she replied.

A wicked smile crossed his face. "Just checking."

And then he started all over.

26

———————

MARCH 10TH

Kai

THE PEACE WAS OFFICIALLY SHATTERED, AND TENSION was high. Big Bird had arrived the day before, and everyone was miserable. From the moment he got out of the Jeep to the current moment in the War Room, he had been raving about something. The lack of a direct flight. The delays. The turbulence. The lack of "real" rental cars. The bumpy, rutted roads. The heat. The bugs. The housing accommodations.

And it was not missed by the man that Waters and Kai were sharing quarters now because of his arrival and refusal to stay in Coxen Hole. If anything, he'd truly gone atomic over that—Kai sleeping with the help. According to him, it was completely inappropriate and unprofessional.

Waters was present for all of his tirades. As promised, he never left Kai alone, which was both endearing and frustrating on her end. But to his credit, he never spoke up

250

during her conversations with Stapleton. He just stood near a door, arms crossed, leaning against the wall, waiting to "take out the trash" if it got to that point.

It had been too late today for Kai to take Big Bird on the tour he wanted, so instead, she showed him the work they'd accomplished in the War Room, informing him of some of the changes they had decided upon, all of which he vetoed, and all of those vetoes she ignored. He had no script control according to the contract. She had made sure of that. Now, he was looking over invoices. Again.

"Serrano, this is totally unacceptable," Big Bird complained.

"What is, Craig?" Kai sighed.

God, I hate this man. This is the last time I will work for someone else. Once this movie clears the box office, I'll be set for life and can make my own films.

He sat behind her desk, flipping through invoices. "This wasteful spending."

Sitting on the leather couch, Kai didn't even look up from the script that sat in her lap. She was back to reviewing blocking and camera angles that she wanted for shots when filming started in a few days. If she didn't engage him with eye contact, sometimes he backed off.

"Craig, you know very well we're actually below the projected budget for our timeline. Food is currently much cheaper here than expected. We have been using hardly any electricity since we got back from training; we are too damn tired to sit up and turn on the lights at night. And we haven't been going to town at all, so we're not using any fuel, eating out and using per diems, or enjoying any entertainment. How could we possibly be wasteful in our spending?"

"Apparently, you didn't need to be down here this early."

"Why do you say that?"

"Well, you've been doing all of this unnecessary training. We could be shooting already."

Kai resisted the urge to sigh again. "It's not unnecessary, Craig. We have been over this and over this. It may not appear so right now, but it will be worth it in the end. Trust me. I know what I'm doing."

He hmphed and threw the invoices down on the desk. "I sincerely doubt that. I still contend that this 'extra training' you're doing is a waste. And I will continue to say it so that when it proves true, I'll enjoy the opportunity of saying 'I told you so' all the more."

Counting to ten before answering, Kai laid her pencil down, closed her script, and gently set it on the coffee table.

"Well, until that day, Craig, let's just assume I'm right."

He grunted, casting a malevolent stare in Waters' direction. "Clearly, you've too much free time on your hands as well."

She felt Waters tighten up from across the room as she turned her head to look directly at Big Bird. Her face felt hot, and if it had been possible, she would have shot daggers at him from her eye sockets. "And how have you determined this from your lumbar-massaging, ergonomic, baby cow leather desk chair back in L.A.?"

"You obviously have time to shack up with this Neanderthal, which means that the time you've spent rolling around in the sheets with him is time you could have been working." Craig was involved in a stare down with Waters, which was dangerous enough in itself. But what was worse was that it took his focus off of Kai, and that was a big mistake.

"Whom I spend my nights rolling around in the sheets with is not your business, you fuckwitch," she hissed, "and never will be. You have no right to censor my behavior as long as it doesn't compromise the work I'm doing, which it clearly doesn't. You're just searching for any little reason to rattle my cage, something you've been doing since our first day working together." Her eyes were glittering so bright they could have spit venom. "I strongly suggest you go to bed and get a good night's sleep. In the morning, you should get in the Jeep with one of the crew, head straight to the airport, and go home. You are not needed here, nor are you wanted. You'll only get in the way and create the distraction and impediments to our progress that you claim you want to prevent. Hell, I'll even drive you myself and charter a private jet to get you on a direct flight if it gets you off my set."

Big Bird smiled, but it didn't reach his eyes. "I'm not going anywhere, Serrano. You need to be taken in hand here, and I'm going to see to it that that happens."

Kai took her steps toward the desk slowly and carefully. Her palms came down to lay flat on its surface, and she leaned over to get eye level with the bastard who sat there smirking at her. Her voice dropped even quieter, a sure sign that she was about to let loose if he didn't come to heel. "You couldn't even begin to take me in hand, Stapleton. I would break you into so many pieces you'd cry like a fifteen-year-old girl who got stood up for the prom. And when I was done pulverizing your soul, even the angels couldn't put your sorry, jigsawed ass back together. I doubt the demons from hell would, either. Don't you dare threaten me. Ever."

With that, she turned on her heel and headed toward the hallway door. When she pulled up even with Waters, she turned back to the producer. "I'm going to the kitchen to get some dinner. When I come back, you'd better be gone because I plan to spend the rest of the night rolling around in the sheets with my unnecessary Neanderthal. If you're not gone, I'll pay him from my own pocket to feed you to an extra large snake out in the jungle, which I will then personally chop into pieces and feed to the sharks."

She opened the door, passed through without looking at Waters, and slammed it behind her.

27

MARCH 10TH

Waters

OKAY, BIG BIRD, TIME WE HAD THIS OUT.

Waters recognized the dick move of trying to intimidate him. Did this man not understand whom he was dealing with? Did he not realize the things Waters had seen and done as a SEAL that would make this baiting seem like a five-year-old having a tantrum rather than an actual threat? He couldn't possibly be this obtuse, could he?

"I suggest you back off, soldier boy," Big Bird warned.

Apparently, the answer is yes.

Waters said nothing. There was no point. Like Kubrick, he knew when to let the man spin his wheels to exhaustion point. No sense in getting his blood pressure up over the assclown.

When Waters didn't answer, he pushed again. "Did you hear me?"

"Yes."

255

"Good. I'm glad we understand each other." The producer went back to the paperwork in front of him. After several minutes, he looked up to find Waters still standing in the exact same place and position, just watching him.

"What is it?" Stapleton snapped. "You have something to say?"

"No."

"Then why are you still here?"

"Just trying to figure out what it is you have up your ass about Ms. Serrano."

"My issues with Kai Serrano are just that—mine."

"See, that's where we disagree. My job is to make her job easier. That includes dealing with asswipes like you. You are not making it easier; therefore, it has now become my business."

"Your job," Big Bird sneered, "is to consult on SEAL operations, which it appears you are not as familiar with as you should be. SEALs take orders, and you don't follow any you're given.

"I don't answer to you."

"Oh. You answer to a woman, then?"

"If she hires me to do a job, yes. I don't have a problem with following orders from a woman. Apparently, you do."

"Kai Serrano does not tell me what to do."

"Mmm. Appears that she did a few moments ago. I can't force you onto an airplane and out of the country... yet. But I aim to see that you do as she requires."

"I won't be going anywhere."

"Wrong answer, Mr. Stapleton. You will leave this room, and you will leave now." Now, it was Waters' turn to smile without it reaching his eyes. "After all, I'm not sure you really want to see Ms. Serrano and I rolling around in her sheets."

Rising from the desk, Big Bird stalked around it like a raging bull. He pointed a finger at Waters. "Keep your hands off of her, or you'll wish we'd never met. Get out of here. Now. Take all of your shit with you, get in the Jeep, and get out. You're fired."

"You can't fire me. Only my boss can, and she's my boss while I'm working here. Plus, I believe she established what happens if you terminate the contract early."

"Just try me."

"Mr. Stapleton, did you do your homework?"

"What the fuck does that mean?"

"Do you know the company you're threatening?"

Stapleton's finger poked him in the chest. "I know exactly who I'm threatening. A sissy-ass military wannabe who's working a piece of ass that isn't worth the time."

At that, Waters raised an eyebrow. "If it's not worth it, why are you so desperate to get rid of me?"

Growling, he gave Waters a shove. "Fuck off."

Waters stood from his leaning position against the door jamb, spread his legs shoulder-width apart, and let his arms fall to his sides. "Touch me again, and I'll show you how creative I can be at breaking bones. Then, every time it rains, the arthritis that will develop will make sure you never forget me." Waters opened the door and gestured for Big Bird to leave. "You're not welcome in the War Room again. Do not attempt to talk to her or be in the same room with her if I'm not in it. You will be nothing but respectful to her, no matter how much it galls you to do so. If not, and whether she gives me instructions to do so or not, I will escort you off the set with pleasure." The bastard stood in front of Waters, chest heaving, eyes narrowed to angry slits, hostility pouring off him in waves. "Now, Stapleton. Or you'll find out just how not 'sissy-ass' nor 'wannabe' I am."

He must have heard the seriousness in Waters' monot-one. The dick actually made a show of letting all of the tension out of his shoulders by dropping them, then rotating his neck. He stepped out into the hallway but threw over his shoulder, "This isn't over, military man." Then he walked across the hall to his room, shutting the door firmly behind him.

Waters left the War Room, making sure to lock it. The actors wouldn't come down to hang out tonight as they were unwilling to chance running into Ballbuster Stapleton, as they called him. And Waters didn't trust the fucknut not to come sneaking back over to rustle through all of Kubrick's things. Quietly and quickly, he made his way to the kitchen.

He stood just outside the light that spilled from the kitchen into the hallway. Kubrick was sitting at the table, angrily stabbing her spoon into her cereal bowl, not eating. Her passions were always so close to the surface. He liked that about her. Not only did he not have to work too hard at knowing how she was feeling, but the closer her feelings were to the surface, the more she was willing to talk. And he needed answers about the problem between these two to attempt to protect her from the strong desire to undermine and sabotage.

He leaned in the doorway. "You okay?"

Kubrick didn't look up. Didn't answer. Just kept stabbing her cereal.

"You know, I don't think cereal works quite the same as a voodoo doll," he added.

She looked up at him, and he felt one corner of his mouth quirk up.

Stepping up to the table, he took the cereal bowl from her, dumped the contents, and rinsed the dish before placing it in the sink to be washed in the morning. He placed his hands on her shoulders and squeezed gently, his thumbs rotating at the base of her neck. "He's gone for the night."

Pushing back her chair with a huff, she stalked back to the War Room, only to have to wait for him to unlock it. Once inside, he relocked the door. She had pushed into the center of the room, then stopped, her shoulders rounding over, her hands covering her eyes. He came up behind her, turning her into his chest. With his arms around her shoulders, he rested his head on top of hers, brushing his chin up and down the crown of her head.

"I'm sorry," she whispered.

"Shh. No need to apologize for that fuckwitch."

She gave a soft laugh at his copying of her.

"I've dealt with way worse," he admitted. His arms slid down to hold her elbows, thumbs brushing over the skin as if soothing a frightened animal. "Kubrick, what is the deal with him? Why is he gunning so hard for you?"

She sighed and dropped her head. She turned in his arms, laying her head on his chest and wrapping her arms around his waist. "I wish I knew, but it always comes back to money with him. From day one, it is all he has ever harped about with me. I don't get it since I still have a record of coming in under budget and producing good films. It's part of why I work the actors the way I do right now."

He nodded. "The layering. I get it now. Working multiple angles creates efficiency as long as you're not doing too many things at one time."

"Right. It's something I learned in college. So I just kept doing it everywhere else as well. As a woman director, I needed every advantage to sell myself. I was studying business, not film, but I became intrigued with movies. I made some really low-budget shorts as samples of what I could do.

I mean really low budget. Several with no budget at all. My first full-length film, I basically sold my soul to get in the door." She looked up at him. "I promise. Just my soul."

He smiled at her understanding of what his concern would be. "Thank you for that."

"Anyway, when I was offered this job, I considered turning it down. Big Bird's reputation is legendary. But I desperately wanted this chance, so I figured I could manage to make it work. But he's been relentless. Every penny must be accounted for. He always seems to find shit to question me on."

"Is that why the obsession with the invoices?"

"Yep."

"Hmmm. I know he's the money guy, but is that normal? Seems weird to me."

"There are always bean counters raising questions, but not like him. I can only assume that the reason he's so rich is he's a scrooge when it comes to expenditures, wringing every single penny out of a production."

A new angle for Midas to dig into?

He reached up to smooth her hair back. "You know," he dropped his voice lower, "I think that tomorrow's another day, and someone promised a certain Neanderthal a roll in the sheets." Tilting her head to his liking, his lips found hers, a hand curving around her jaw to hold her in place, the other dropping to her hip and banding around her back to pull her closer.

When he let her come up for air, her eyes were closed, a satisfied smile on her face. "I guess I did," she whispered back.

Turning, she slipped into the bedroom, Waters following close behind. He stopped her at the side of the bed and gently stripped her clothes from her. He pulled back the sheets and urged her under them. After she was settled, he took her clothes and folded them, neatly placing them on her dresser, then pulled off his own clothes, doing the same with his own. He crawled into the bed where he laid face-to-face with her, each of them with one arm beneath the other, hands smoothing over skin as lips met in soft, short kisses.

While she wouldn't have refused him going farther, he recognized her body starting to sink into a relaxed state. Curling her into his chest, he held her tight, kissing her temple. "Sleep, baby. I'm right here."

"But—"

"Shh. Tonight sucked, and you need your strength for tomorrow. I'm not going anywhere, and right now, holding you just feels right."

He felt her relax, signaling he made the right choice. Within a few short minutes, her even breathing filled the room. Only then did he feel like he could close his eyes, but it was some time before he actually slept.

28

———————

MARCH 24TH

Waters

THE ACTORS AND CREW HAD BEEN FILMING FOR ELEVEN days. For the most part, it had gone smoothly, but Big Bird's presence on the set definitely brought continual increasing tension. In the last day or two, he had been disappearing for short intervals back to the house. Last night, he took a Jeep into Coxen Hole, refusing to have one of the locals hired to maintain vehicles drive him in. Nemo had been on "Bird-watch," but there wasn't anything to report. The producer had gone to a bar at the main hotel in town, had a few drinks, talked to no one, and returned to the house in the early morning hours.

Waters turned to look at Kubrick and saw her using a Jeep hood as a desktop, rifling through her Backpack of Death. She was struggling with it as she had a huge handful of loose papers in her left hand, allowing her only the right to go through the remaining contents.

262

Waters grabbed the stack in her hands. "What's wrong?"

"I can't find the invoices for the ammunition," she said, diving back inside the backpack. "I need to order some additional squibs and caps, but with my new laptop back at the house, I have to call to order them, and that means I need an invoice for my contact's number and the inventory numbers. I could have sworn I ordered twice the number we have, and when I spoke to the company yesterday, they claimed that amount was sent. But they're nowhere to be found." She huffed in frustration. "The last thing I need right now is to get hung up in filming because I'm out of ammunition."

Waters leafed through the papers. "I checked in those materials myself since they are connected to the weapons. Are you sure the invoices aren't here? Could they be with the crates?"

"I thought of that since we opened everything and counted to verify it was all there. But that doesn't help. The crates aren't here either."

"What do you mean they're not here?"

"I mean, they've vanished. We loaded them on the plane and unloaded them when we got here, but now they're nowhere. I sent Christoff earlier for some additional product, and that's when we discovered they were gone."

His brow furrowed. "What would someone want with squibs and caps? It's not like they're useful to anyone other than a special effects crew."

Kubrick shook her head and grabbed the invoices out of his hands, shoving them back into her bag. "Down here, anything can be worth money on the black market if you can find the right buyer. But it is damn odd. I trust my crew. I've worked with almost all of them on my past two films, and I'd swear every one of them is trustworthy. If someone were in money trouble, they'd be more likely to tell me because they know I'd help them out. There'd be no reason to steal from the inventory to sell for quick cash."

Glancing at her, his heart stuttered. "You'd help them out?"

Without looking at him, she shrugged her shoulders as if it were no big deal. "Everyone runs into trouble at some point. My crew is my family. Besides, it's just money."

"What kind of money are we talking about?"

Still rifling through her backpack, "Well... Cindy, you know, the new girl with the dog? I paid the vet bill. She's new to L.A. and is living on another crew member's couch right now." Kubrick picked up her head and stared into the distance. "Then Gerald's wife needed some special treatment for cancer last year. Their insurance is shit, and she hadn't worked in almost two years, so..."—she went back to her bag—"I helped them out with that."

"I'm guessing that's not the end of the 'help' you've offered."

"I've maybe helped with some college tuition and other medical bills." She blushed. "You take care of the people you care about."

Waters shook his head, then stepped forward. An arm wrapped around her shoulders, and a quick kiss brushed the top of her ball cap. "Yes. Yes, you do."

She's so easy to love.

And there was that word. He'd been avoiding it, trying not to even think about it to himself. Now, it was too late. If he hadn't already known who she was and how perfect she was, this would have proven it. He was lost.

She huffed in frustration. "This just chaps my ass. Where the hell is the inventory? And where are the damn invoices? I know my backpack rivals the Bermuda Triangle, but I always know where everything is in my chaos."

"Maybe Big Bird moved them when he was messing with your desk a while back?"

"Normally, I would agree that his pawing through the paperwork would mess up my pseudo-filing system, but I've seen the invoices since then, and the crates were all there two days ago. This just doesn't make any sense."

"We'll find them, even if I have to dig through the entire warehouse myself."

"I hope you're right."

THAT AFTERNOON, MORE THINGS WERE DISCOVERED TO be missing. An entire case of latex for making wounds, plus the entire shipment of fake blood. Several cases of lamps for the lighting system. Bolts of canvas and material for extra fatigues. A hundred boxes of batteries for the comm systems the actors used. And those were just the things they knew about. Kubrick was extremely frustrated, so she sent the actors with the second unit director to do some cover material while she supervised a recount of all the materials in storage.

Big Bird stood by on a catwalk, watching her like a hawk waiting on a telephone line to swoop down on unsuspecting prey.

Waters shook his head in disgust. The guy was really something. He had heeded Waters' warning about not being welcome in the War Room, but that just made him more of an asshole everywhere else. He always seemed to be five steps behind Kubrick at all times, complaining to all and sundry about the conditions as well as belittling her every decision. At one point, even Vixen lost her cool.

"Kubrick, I can't work with that man on the set! I'm sorry, I don't mean to be a bitch or create problems, but he won't stop staring at me, he's always making snide remarks, and he keeps trying to touch me."

Kubrick put an arm around the girl and pulled her off to the side. "You're not a problem, Vixen. If he's making you uncomfortable, then I'll have Waters escort him off the set. I'll tell him he's not welcome."

The starlet's eyes were full of tears. "I don't want to make trouble for you. He's such an asshole already. And don't play the party line, Kubrick. We hear how he talks to you. Enigma would have intervened for you if he hadn't known that Waters is with you every minute. I'll never work on another one of his pictures." She gently wiped her eyes, trying to keep her makeup from streaking. "That is unless you were directing," she added shyly. "We all love working for you. I've got to admit to a serious girl crush."

Waters put his arm around her from the other side. "She is pretty mesmerizing, isn't she? I've got a pretty serious crush myself." He winked at Kubrick.

She rolled her eyes, laughing, and Waters felt a burst of something come from his chest. His woman was amazing. She inspired a lot of love and loyalty from both the cast and crew. It made Big Bird's reaction to her even more perplexing. He knew the man appeared to hate women, other than as conquests, but what could she have done to provoke such venom from the man? Granted, he was a dick of the first water whether he was around her or not, but there seemed to be no motivation for his vitriol toward her.

The worst blow came the next morning. Demon, hiding

out as the film's medic, had to call in a series of sick crew members and had to escort two of them into the hospital in Coxen Hole. Somehow, the catering company became the source of a rash of food poisoning victims. Luckily, none of the actors had breakfast with the crew, as Brick usually made breakfast for everyone.

"A whole day lost filming. Goddammit!" Kubrick threw her clipboard across the room, papers scattering all over the floor. "Big Bird is going to have a stroke. He was already having a shit fit when I pulled myself from filming yesterday to inventory. Now today, we have to shut down because my entire camera crew and twenty others are puking their guts out and living in all available bathrooms."

"He can have all the fits he wants to. Your crew is down for the count. You didn't make them sick."

Her eyes were glittering with rage. "No, but someone did. And I'm sorry, Waters, but I don't for one moment think this is a coincidence. Too many disasters are striking all at once and all since shit-for-brains came down here."

Waters went to her side, gathered her into his arms, and sat in the desk chair. "Baby, relax. He's unlikely to sabotage his own film. Why would he do that? It doesn't make sense considering the amount of money he'd lose, and if you'd calm down, you'd see that for yourself."

"The film is insured. He'd recoup his investment if it went down. Wouldn't be the first time a producer tanked a production to get his money back. You seriously don't think this is all too convenient?"

Waters brushed stray hairs behind her ears, then drew the backs of his fingers down her cheek. "I think it's too early to make accusations." His eyes held hers tightly while he emphasized the final three words.

But, yeah, baby. I think these missing items and sick

crew are way too convenient. Just can't have you attacking Big Bird.

"Look," he continued. "You can still film. You know how to use the camera, right?" She nodded. "Then let's grab your list of contingencies and see what we can film off of that until your crew can get back on set."

Kubrick threw her arms around Waters' neck and hugged him tight. "So fucking perfect," she whispered in his ear. "I was so busy throwing a shit fit I didn't think of that. Thank you."

He smiled as he hugged her tightly. Damn, he loved this woman. Lilac scent, Dodgers gear, swear words, passionate highs and lows, and all. "I've got you, baby. I've always got you."

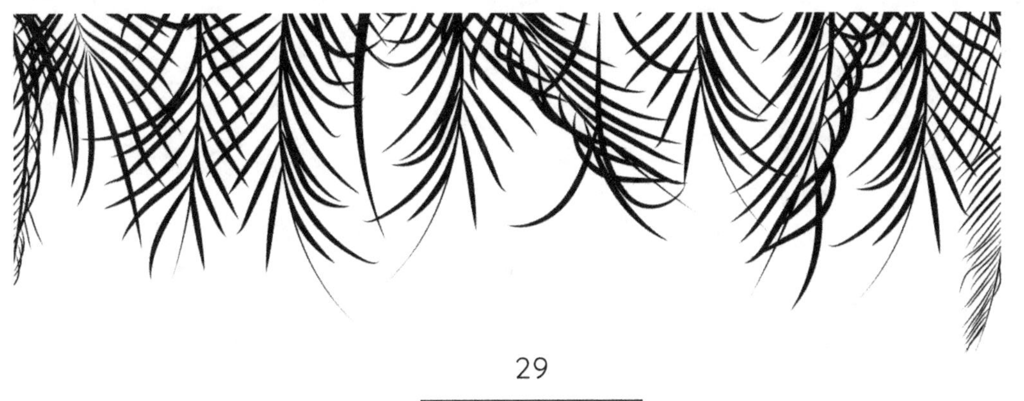

29

———————

MARCH 27TH

Kai

THE CREW WAS BACK ON SET. LUCKILY, ALL RETURNED as healthy as they had been before they were struck down by the food poisoning. Kai had managed to keep filming for three days until they were back to full strength, but now they had little room for any more major disasters. She somehow couldn't help but feel that more would come.

A third of the way through filming. Can we hold it together another twenty-eight days?

Waters was doing practice run-throughs of the upcoming fight sequence to be filmed. She never got enough of watching him work. His intensity and focus were the two qualities she loved most about him. It didn't matter if he was working out, rehearsing a scene with the actors, planning a fight sequence, or simply having a conversation. Whatever he did had all of his attention without question.

And when he's focused on me, then his intensity is at its

absolute peak. It's enough to make a woman want more.

Kai looked away from the group, going through a slow-motion pass of the scene, and shook her head in disgust with herself. It was imaginings like that, of wanting more with Waters, that would be the early ruin of what they currently had. He had been open with her that this was all he could give. A few weeks of pleasure between takes, so to speak. When the filming was done, so were they. He'd go back to his "projects" with Tribe, and she'd carry on with editing the film, then move on to the very first film, all hers from top to bottom. The time they spent together would be nothing but fond memories.

Would he look back on them fondly? Or would she be just another woman in the promenade of his past?

Her personal lack of experience with men in terms of romance, combined with her refusal to lie to herself, caused her to believe it would be the latter. She also knew that no matter what she told him about understanding their affair was on a time limit, that she was okay with that, she knew she was anything but okay with it. She had well and truly lost her heart to the former SEAL in a very short span of time. And while she didn't regret her choice to let him into her life beyond the film contract, she knew that her heart would be broken when it came time to say goodbye. When that time came, somehow, she would have to be convincing that she was fine with everything ending.

And I won't be okay.

Turning her attention back to the fight rehearsal, she noticed they were now running through the sequence at half speed. Once that run was complete, they would run it at full speed. Waters would debrief them on anything he saw, make corrections, and possibly repeat the triplicate rehearsal sequence if a significant enough move needed to be made, and only when he was convinced they had it solid would he give the go-ahead to begin the sequence in film mode.

A sigh of frustration came from off to her right. Her eyes closed for a moment as she took a deep breath, held it for a three count, and then slowly exhaled. "What's wrong, Craig?"

"This is taking too long. You should be filming. I thought all of this was worked out in your weeks of training?" She could hear his sneer in the final word.

"The scene was choreographed in those weeks, yes. And they have practiced it, again and again, to make it the strongest it can be. But that doesn't mean they don't need to continue to practice."

"Overkill. Wastes time," he grunted.

She turned in her chair to look over her shoulder. "This is a standard fight choreography practice, Craig. Anytime you're going to run a fight sequence, you run it three times. First time is in slow motion. Second time is at half speed. Third time is at full speed. We're not doing anything any other film wouldn't be doing. And on top of that, it's not a waste of time or money if it prevents someone from getting hurt. That would cost us more time and money than we have budgeted. You, of all people, should be able to approve of those considerations."

"I've been making movies for almost twenty years, Serrano. I think I know what standard operating procedures are. I hardly need a lesson from you, a director who has made eleven small-budget films."

"Don't build yourself up, assfuck. You don't make movies; you finance them. But let's say you do have some sort of knowledge regarding actual filmmaking. If you're so aware, why are you busting my chops over this? Safety first and always. You know that. Or are you so desperate for me to fail that you're hoping to goad me into making a mistake?"

Big Bird advanced two steps toward her, so his height towered over her. Arms folded across his chest, his smile was near reptilian. "There's no need to hope for a mistake. It's inevitable."

His words were smug. She knew he was attempting to intimidate her, but while she disliked the man intensely, he did not frighten her. He never had. Nothing frightened her. She stared him straight in the eye without blinking, determination burning in her narrowed eyes and her jaw set firmly.

Then she turned her back on him.

It was probably a mistake to do that, but she knew it would annoy him more if she ignored his attempts to provoke her. "Go away, Stapleton," she droned. "I have too much work to do to spend time arguing with you regarding things that are pointless to discuss."

She waited him out. Despite the sounds of grunts and dialogue from the fight sequence in front of her, as well as the crew's general hum of business surrounding them, she could hear his ragged breathing. A sure sign that he was pissed.

Good. I'm glad he's pissed.

It was over a minute before he spoke again. "We're not finished, Serrano."

"Yes. We are finished, Craig."

"I still don't have the full audit on your work so far. Tonight. Nine o'clock." With that, he turned on his heel and stalked toward the trailer area.

Only when she could no longer hear his footfalls did she let loose a ragged sigh. She felt her entire body deflate, although the tension still radiated throughout her body.

A pair of hands fell gently on her shoulders. A warm breath of air blew on the shell of her ear. "More molting?" the voice asked lowly.

Kai shook her head. "No. Just shaking tail feathers. It was actually quite calm. But he wants a full audit of work so far at 9 p.m. tonight. Good thing I do reports daily, without fail; otherwise, there's no way I'd be ready. Pretty sure that's what he's hoping for. What a clusterfuck," she grumbled.

His thumbs brushed a few soft passes back and forth along the base of her neck. Then she felt a subtle kiss pressed to the back of her head through her ball cap. Allowing herself just a moment to lean back against the canvas of her director's chair and, by extension, his chest as he stood directly behind her, she let him know she appreciated his comforting gesture.

"We'll be ready for him. Apparently, it was worth it waiting up late for you to come to bed every night."

She wasn't so sure of that. Instead, perhaps it would have been in her best interest to spend more time in bed with him than filling out rehearsal reports.

Time to get your shit together, woman.

Despite how comfortable it would have been to turn into him, she pushed aside the desire and sat up straight, resettling her Dodgers cap over her eyes to shade the sun. "Are they ready?"

"Whenever you are," he replied.

Kai nodded, putting her director's face on. She slid out of the chair and strode toward the group of actors. After briefly reviewing what she wanted to make sure she saw in the wide shots, she stepped back behind the camera and watched perfection at work. All worry about Big Bird's douchebaggery, or Waters and his place in her life, now or later, was lost in her focus on the job at hand.

30

MARCH 27TH

Waters

AND THIS IS WHY SOME SPECIES EAT THEIR YOUNG.

Waters had seen and dealt with many assholes in his thirty-four years, but Big Bird was in a class all his own. Granted, he was keeping the worst of his comments to himself right now, probably concerned that Waters would make good on his earlier threats. He clearly wasn't pleased with doing his audit in the kitchen since he'd been banned from the War Room. But his attitude, nonverbals, and facial expressions were almost as bad as what would have come out of his mouth.

There was a knock at the door, and then Demon entered the back door leading into the kitchen. "Sorry to bother you, Waters." He was dressed in his undercover gear —short-sleeved, button-down shirt, khakis, and deck shoes. His dark hair was slicked back, and he had glasses perched on the end of his nose. "I've got that medical report you asked for." A pointed look passed from the man to his superior as Demon passed him a folder with his finger in between some pages.

Kubrick looked up with a start. Her eyes were frozen on his. "Medical report?"

Waters waved her off as he took the folder, slipping a finger into the same slot that Demon provided. "Not a big deal, Kubrick. I just asked him to throw something together since you were meeting with Stapleton. Cataloging visits to the medic, etc."

He opened the folder and squinted at it. He glanced at the page, then looked up at Demon. A quirked eyebrow was all he communicated, but to cover the moment, he said, "Is the stuntman accounted for?"

Demon shrugged. "He was less than communicative at first, but finally, he gave us the story. A fall. Shoulder was dislocated, but he actually put it back into the socket on his own. Shouldn't be any lost time, although he was advised to lay low for a bit."

Waters slipped a look at Big Bird from under his eyelashes. The man grunted and went back to the papers in front of him. Waters slid a quick look at Kubrick, who was looking at him with her own squinting, assessing gaze. Turning his back on the room, he laid the open folder on the counter that he had been leaning on. Very smoothly, he slipped the memo sheet into his shirt pocket, then pretended to peruse the documents in front of him. When he turned back to the room, the folder now closed, he handed it to Kubrick. "Everything looks fine. A few bumps and bruises, but other than the food poisoning cases, nothing major."

Her expression let him know she was not as obtuse as Big Bird. She looked at Demon, then back to Waters. Just to let Waters know she was not amused at her discovery of one of his men on site and that she knew the report was not about one of her stuntmen, she flashed a flirtatious grin at Demon. "Thanks, Doc. Glad to hear it. Cup of coffee? I didn't realize we had such a good-looking doctor on our set. I've been remiss."

Demon's expression was inscrutable, but his mouth tipped up on one side. "Don't mind if I do, Kubrick. Right?"

"Yes. But you can call me Kai if you like."

A soft snort came from the blond consultant off to his right. Waters saw Demon sneak a look at his boss before he sat at the far end of the kitchen table next to Kubrick. "I'll stick to set protocols. I wouldn't want anyone to think I was getting special privileges," he said with a smirk. "But, thanks, Kubrick."

She stood, grabbed a mug, poured Demon a cup of coffee, and then returned to her seat. Waters was back to his leaning position against the far counter, gazing pointedly at Demon.

After a cursory look at what was an honest but bogus report, she slid it over to Big Bird. He glared at her. "This should have been with the daily reports."

Prick. You're just pissed she had everything lined up for you, and you couldn't dress her down for not being ready.

"The daily visits are on the daily reports, Craig," she reminded him. "Waters was just efficient enough to give you a compiled listing. I'm sure you'll see everything matches up exactly."

Big Bird grunted and went back to reading, and damned if the asshole didn't go down the list, line by line, to match up each infirmary visit to each day, looking for something, anything, to nail her for.

Demon and Kubrick made small talk about filming on

some of her previous projects while Waters watched the producer like a hawk. The man was up to something. The only thing he knew could go sideways were the invoices that originally matched up with the inventory, but would the man catch the fact that the original tallies no longer matched the current inventory? Since the original inventory aligned, Kubrick could hardly be blamed for supplies that went missing under someone else's guard at a warehouse over ten miles away. And yet he knew Big Bird would find a way to make it her fault if he found the discrepancy.

Demon stood up from his seat. "Thanks for the coffee, Kubrick. See you at dinner tomorrow." He flashed a quick look at Waters, his smirk a little larger than before, and exited the kitchen.

Waters had been so focused on Big Bird that he hadn't heard Kubrick extend the dinner invitation to the man. He could feel his teeth grinding.

"Serrano!" Big Bird called her name, sounding like there was an "A-ha!" behind her name, distracting her from watching the doctor leave.

"Yes, Craig?"

"What's with these invoices for additional supplies?"

Well, shit. So much for missing the orders.

Kubrick shrugged. "We needed to order some additional effects and batteries. Hardly out of the ordinary."

"It is for you. Most of the time, you end up returning inventory on your projects."

Time to wade in.

"Those orders were at my suggestion. We loosely discussed adding some additional effects sequences. I checked the budget, and we have the room, so I thought it would be better to have the items on hand if needed, knowing they could always be put into backstock for another production if we ended up not needing them. No sense having to sit and wait for supplies to arrive if we ran out. Wasted production time if we have to sit, which means spending more money than purchasing extra supplies."

His gaze never faltered from Big Bird, but he could feel Kubrick's narrowed gaze. He had a sneaking suspicion that he was in for an argument for stepping in but damned if he would let her take the hit on this.

"I wasn't speaking to you."

"I know you weren't. But since the call was mine, I answered."

"If those rounds aren't used, or the picture goes over budget, then it comes out of your consulting fee."

Waters knew the producer was spouting crap, so he just returned the man's stare. Arms crossed over his pecs, hands in his armpits, legs crossed as he leaned on the counter, he gave all the impression of being nonplussed by the feather-shaking. Inside, he was seething at the constant attacks on his woman, but he kept it in check for her.

"All right, gentlemen. Stand down," Kubrick ordered as she stood up. "Craig, you've been at this for over two hours. I have digital copies of my reports. If you want to keep at this, be my guest, but I've got an early morning tomorrow, and I'm going to bed." Pushing her chair in, she left the kitchen without a backward glance.

There was a beat of silence before Waters spoke. "I don't know what you're up to, Stapleton, but I'm not stupid."

Big Bird smirked. "I doubt that, boy."

Not showing the disgust he felt, Waters turned to follow Kubrick.

"That's right, grunt. Follow after her like a puppy dog."

Waters wanted to continue down the hall without

dignifying the man with a response, but his body had a will of its own and turned back to stalk into the kitchen to get right in Big Bird's face. "Make no mistake, Stapleton. I would follow that woman to Hell if necessary, and she wouldn't even need to ask. She'd be worth every tortuous moment of it. You aren't fit to be her judge, let alone her boss. Leave. Her. Alone." With that, he turned on his heel and went after Kubrick.

And following her to Hell is exactly what I'm doing. Sweet Christ, I'm just going to admit it. I'm fucked. She's mine, and that's all there is to it, damned be the consequences.

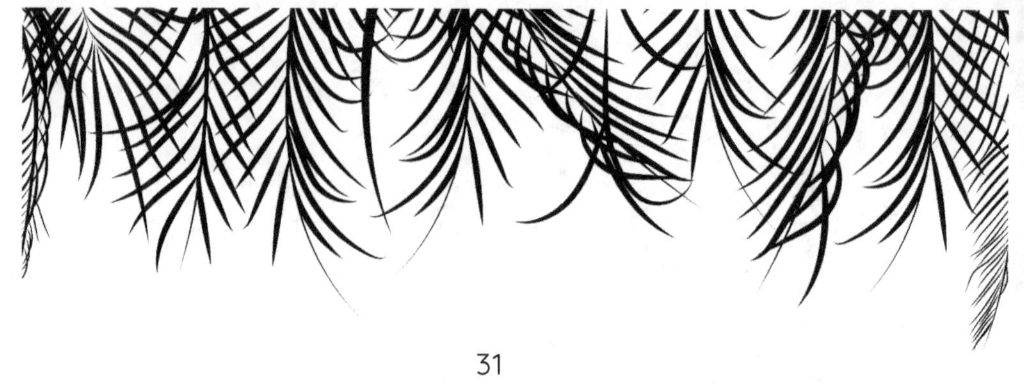

31

———

MARCH 27TH-28TH

Kai

SHE HEARD WATERS ENTER THE WAR ROOM, CLOSING and locking the door behind him. He went no farther, just stood there, hands at his sides, looking across the room at her. It felt like her head was on fire, and her heart was going to explode.

Men are such assholes!

She was going through the desk, looking for something. She had no idea what for, but the loud thuds of objects hitting hard surfaces and the banging of opening and shutting drawers, along with the muttering under her breath, complete with various creative expletives coming through, made her feel better.

She looked up. "What the fuck was that?"

He didn't answer.

"Goddamnit, Waters, you don't answer for me. Ever. That was the agreement. You said you knew that I could

280

take care of myself. That you would stay out of it unless he crossed a more serious line. Then you go in and put yourself in his crosshairs, protecting my ass on something I don't need protection on."

He still said nothing.

"Your motives are good. I get it. Protector mode and all that fucking horseshit. But now he's going to be worse than ever. It'll be a never-ending litany of how I need a man to speak up for me. That I can't be trusted and am letting my consultant make my decisions for me."

Still nothing.

"To top it all off, I discover you've got one of your team here, hiding out as our set doctor. I feel like a fucking idiot. Did it ever occur to you that this information might be important for me to know? Or even just general fucking courtesy? Fuck me, Waters. What the hell is going on?"

He shrugged. "SOP."

"You bastard! Don't give me that 'standard operating procedure' bullshit. This is a simple consulting job. The real project is out there finding my dumbass brother and getting him out of whatever stupidity he's gotten himself into. Jesus! Just like when we were kids. Always in trouble and getting by with the skin of his teeth. Now he's involving me in his dumbassery." She rounded the desk and grabbed her backpack, pulling everything out of it and slamming the contents down on the worktable as she vented her rage on it. "Your guy should be out there helping look for Ka-Bar, not here." She huffed out a frustrated breath, then looked him in the eye. "How many more?" she asked.

"'How many more what?'"

"Don't play that game with me, Waters. You know exactly what I mean."

He put his hands in his pockets, looking for all the

world like he could care less that she was angry with him. "Does it matter? If I say one operative or I say one hundred operatives, you're going to be pissed either way."

"Yes, you're right. I'm pissed, Waters! Pissed as fuck!" She pointed her finger at him. "You do not get to make decisions for me! You do not get to decide what I need and what I don't. I'm not the one missing!" She had picked up a throw pillow from the couch during her temper tantrum and made it into a missile that she projected at his head with stunning accuracy.

His hands raised just in time to catch the pillow from hitting his face. He underhanded it back to her. "Missed. Care to try again?" he taunted her.

She gave a guttural scream in frustration and threw it at him again, still amazingly accurate for how mad she was.

He began stalking toward her, throwing the pillow back onto the couch as he passed. It was foolish of her, she knew, but she felt herself get more indignant with each step he took. She could feel and smell the smoke coming from the gears grinding inside her head.

"Finished?"

"Not even close," she hissed.

She picked up another pillow and fired it at him, which he simply batted away as it reached him.

Then he was standing inches in front of her, and if she could have, she would have shot fire out of her eye sockets. "Okay, babe, you've had your hissy fit. Are you done?"

"I am not having a hissy fit, and don't call me 'babe.'"

His eyes went dark at her second hissed comment. "Oh, yeah, 'babe,'" he emphasized the final word. "You're having a hissy fit. My job, Kubrick, is to help you do your job. That means not only do I advise you on aspects of the film, but it also means I have your back. Always. I've warned you that

Big Bird is an asswipe, and he is not to be trusted. I've told you repeatedly that I will decide when he has crossed certain lines and that I will deal with him accordingly.

"What I just did was not meant to make you feel incapable or vulnerable or whatever other shit you're imagining in your head right now. Get that through your stubborn skull right now. I know you can take care of yourself. I have allowed you, again and again, to deal with the shitweasel, watching you take hit after hit, whether it's about your cast, your crew, me, or, more importantly to me, you. But there are moments where I need to step in because I will not allow him to make you feel small.

"Tonight was one of those times. You knew you couldn't hide those purchases from him forever, so I just headed off whatever venom he was going to project at you. Better me than you. He means nothing to me."

He took one more step so that his lips were centimeters from hers.

"So I ask again. Are. You. Done?"

She glared at him. "No."

She saw something change in his eyes, and for a moment, she felt herself tremble with something that was more thrill than fear.

"Good. Let's put your righteous anger to effective use. You have three seconds to turn that wicked ass around and get into our bedroom before I put you over my shoulder and take you there myself. And I don't plan to let you up for hours."

He did not just say that. Oh, hell no!

Kai's eyes opened wide, and her mouth gasped. "You asshole!"

"Time's up." He bent down, picked her up, threw her over his shoulder, and proceeded to smack her ass as he strode to their bedroom. She gave a shriek of indignation, but it had less power behind it than her tantrum originally had. "Keep squawking like that, and I'll spank you again, brat."

"You wouldn't dare!"

He threw her down on the bed, then turned to close and lock the double doors. As he strode back to her, she scrambled to find purchase on the sheets but only ended up getting tangled in them since she refused to make the bed.

Well, fuck. Screwed now.

He pulled his shirt off over his head from behind, something that never failed to melt her to goo, and stood over her as he folded it. "Strip." She swallowed hard. "I'm not going to ask again."

"You didn't ask, G.I. Joe," she snarked.

He set his shirt on the dresser. "You're right. I didn't."

And then he was on her.

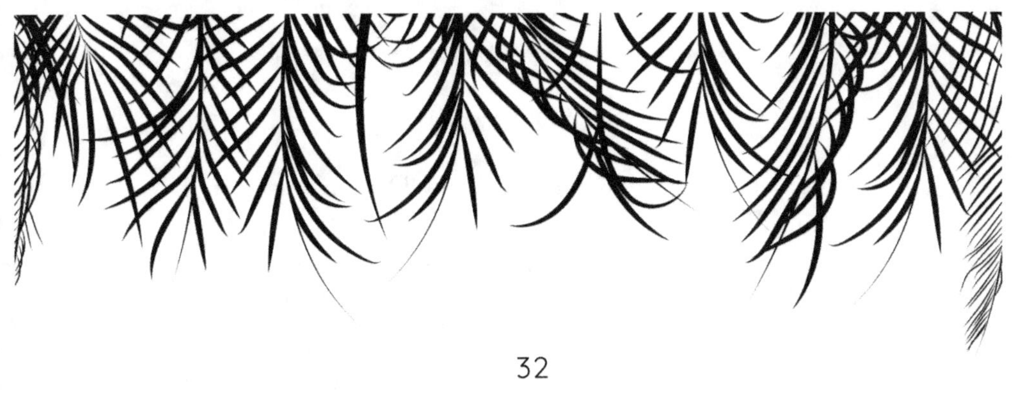

32

———————

MARCH 28TH

Waters

His thumb made slow circles on the soft skin of her arm as he held her close. She was curled up into his side, head on his chest, her leg thrown over his, and her hand over his sternum, his other hand holding it there. He turned his head to kiss the crown of her head.

"Better?" he rumbled.

"Much," she replied. "I should still be pissed at you."

"You weren't really pissed, you know."

"No. I wasn't," she admitted. "How did you know?"

"Because I've never seen you afraid." His eyes were glued to the ceiling. "But when Demon handed me that report, there was a moment where your eyes dilated as if you knew he was bringing me news that couldn't wait. And it was a look I've never seen on your face before."

"It was about Ka-Bar, wasn't it?"

285

He deflected. "How did you know Demon was part of my team?"

She snorted. "No deal, Waters. What did the report say? Something about a dislocated shoulder? None of our stuntmen dislocated anything." He lay in silence. She picked her head up, resting her chin on his pectoral. "Don't keep secrets from me," she begged.

He squeezed her hand. "Some things are need-to-know."

"And if it's about my brother, I do need to know. Please."

He considered for a moment before relenting.

I've already broken rule number one. Might as well break another one.

"You know my teammate, Steel, was headed to Egypt."

She nodded.

"He found where your brother was initially hiding. The ambassador, his friend, Jacques, at the embassy did some questionable things, so we followed up. It looks like he managed to meet up with your brother, possibly with an exit contact. Ka-Bar left a breadcrumb, which is what we're trained to do. Steel was following the lead and ran into some trouble. He was injured."

"The dislocated shoulder."

"Yup. But the fact that he ran into that trouble makes it clear that he's on the right track and that Ka-Bar is still out there somewhere."

"Why not ask Jacques where he is?"

Waters sighed. "We can't. He was in a car crash."

She picked her head up, and he looked her in the eye. "Jacques is dead?"

Waters brought her hand up to his mouth, kissing the

back of it. "Yeah. It looks like a truck ran through an intersection by accident, but... unlikely. Too coincidental."

"What happened to Steel?"

"While he was looking into a warehouse we figured that Ka-Bar was hiding out in, a small explosion went off. More of a deterrent message than a large-scale destruction situation. Luckily for Steel, he was at the periphery. Sent him flying into a brick wall. He's incredibly lucky he got away with only a dislocated shoulder and a concussion."

They lay in the quiet. A minute or so later, she asked softly, "Your guy, Demon. He's not here to give you medical reports."

He closed his eyes and kissed the top of her head again. "No, baby, he's not."

"You have others here?"

"Yes. Two more."

"Where are they? Are they on the crew?"

"No. They're on overwatch. You'll never see them."

"Are they good at what they do?" She gave a short laugh. "Stupid question, I guess. I can't see you working with less than good."

He rolled her over onto her back, settling into her side, raising himself on one elbow over her. He brushed her hair back from her forehead, trying to reassure her with his steady gaze.

"Nope. I only work with the best. When Steel's former teammate comes calling needing a favor, he gets what he needs, no questions asked. He's Tribe by default since they served together."

"I get that someone thinks I have something. But they could just steal it, like they tried to at my trailer and here. There'd be no need to protect me. So what's with the bodyguards?" she asked.

"Babe," he started, then stopped. "I need you not to panic."

She grunted. "When have I ever gone into panic mode?"

"This is a little different than a Big Bird molting." He exhaled. "Ka-Bar is either hiding well, or they have him, and he's not giving up information. They know you have this 'package' or at least believe you know where it is."

"I'm in danger." It wasn't a question. "You think they're coming for me, either to use me as leverage to get Ka-Bar to talk or get the information out of me."

He refused to lie. "We think so." He brought his lips to hers, brushing them softly. "I won't let anyone hurt you, Kubrick."

"I know." She smiled gently at his serious face, caressing his cheek. Then she closed her eyes, her hand flopping back to her side on the bed. She sighed. "Fuckin' Ka-Bar. I am so going to kick his ass."

He grinned. "Get into trouble often, did he?"

The snort she gave this time was less than ladylike. "You could say that. But it sounds like this time it might be the royal fuckup of all fuckups. Especially if someone might be coming after me for something I have no fuck-all clue about."

Waters chuckled. "How many times can you use 'fuck' in a sentence, woman?"

"Don't know. Never counted."

"Mmm." He kissed her again, then nuzzled her nose with his. "Such a lady."

"Fuck that noise," she teased. "I am many things, but I have never professed to being a lady."

His mouth traveled down to her jaw, then to the hollow

of her throat, the tip of his tongue barely brushing there. "Fuckin' noise is correct. You're loud."

"I am not."

"Umm... why do you think I kiss you when you orgasm? I'd much rather watch you, but you're so freaking loud, I'm worried you'll wake up Coxen Hole from here."

She smacked his shoulder. "Bullshit."

"Babe. I watched Lazarus hand Dawg a pair of earplugs."

"Liar!"

"Who the hell do you think he got the earplugs from? I had a pair for everyone."

This time, she punched him. "You fuckwitch!"

Laughing hard, he rolled over her, slid his knee between her legs, and settled his body between them. Propping his upper half up with his elbows but making sure their hips lined up, he kissed down her chest, between her breasts, then slid further down the bed and raised up on his knees as he got to her belly button. Suddenly, his hands were under her ass, lifting them to rest on his thighs. "Yes or no, babe?"

"You've ruined me, you know."

"How so?" he asked, stroking his hands up and down the insides of her thighs.

"I was never really all that interested in sex. Now I'm a freaking horny mess."

He smiled lazily. "So, does that mean 'yes'?"

"Yes. Always yes."

He leaned over to the nightstand beside the bed, opening the drawer to retrieve a condom. Making short work of putting it on, he quickly slid inside her channel and began a slow, steady rhythm. The angle he had allowed him to easily drag his cock across her G-spot, which caused deeper and deeper hitches of her breath with each pass. At the top of each stroke, he ground his hips just enough to stimulate her clit that caused little gasps of single-syllable words like "please" and "more."

Pulling himself completely upright to a kneeling position, he slid his arms around her body and pulled her up to rest against his chest, her ass directly on his thighs. "Take it, Kubrick."

Arms wrapped around his neck, she rose and fell on his lap, grinding every part of her body against him that she could. "Waters," she warned.

"Go, babe. I'm ready."

As soon as the word "go" was out of his mouth, she clamped her teeth tight to prevent herself from screaming. She locked tight, her walls squeezing his dick like a vice, head thrown back, the ends of her long hair barely touching his thighs. He groaned as she wrung him dry.

As the last of the shudders passed through her body and he'd stopped pulsing inside her, she sat up straight, her arms wrapped around him in a near stranglehold.

Nothing. Nothing better than this.

He buried his face in her neck, chest heaving both with the rampant heartbeat from his body's release and the realization that he couldn't let her go. He'd already claimed her inside his head, but now he knew beyond a shadow of a doubt that though they might part ways in a few weeks, there wouldn't be anyone else for him. This had been inevitable.

Kubrick ran her hands over the close-cropped hair at the back of his head, placing her lips against his brow. "Waters. I'm in trouble."

"I know, Kubrick. So am I."

Both squeezed each other tight.

At just before 4 a.m., Waters' watch beeped. He tried to stretch, but he was tangled in Kai's limbs. Smiling, he kissed her temple. She muttered in her sleep and rolled over, allowing him to easily extract himself from her. Sitting on the edge of the bed, he searched for his pants. Kai had basically ripped them off him when he'd cave-manned her into the bedroom after her snit, and now he couldn't find them. That brought on a bigger smile. His woman was pure fire. She burned him, leaving an indelible scar to go with the rest of those on his body. He'd known she would be trouble. But right now, it felt like the best kind of trouble.

Finally, he found them half under the bed. Slipping them on, along with a T-shirt, he padded out to the War Room and stood before the television. He tapped out a code on his watch, and a few moments later, the screen changed from black to Midas.

"Good morning, Bossman. How's my sassy girl?"

He shook his head. "She's fine. Asleep. But she'll be waking up soon, so get moving. I saw Demon's report. What do we know?"

"Steel is back up and running. Before he nearly got blown sky-high, he found Ka-Bar's trident. He was definitely there at some point."

"Any leads on where he went from there?"

"Still working on that. The trident was stuck through the corner of a piece of paper. Just a corner of it. Looked like some kind of advertisement, like what you'd find on a public notice board. I'm working on trying to match it up with others I can see on public cameras, but it's slow going. Steel is looking around on foot, trying to see if he can find something as well, but he's hampered a bit by the fact that it's clear someone knows we're poking around."

"Okay. Keep looking. Any word on Jacques' accident?"

Midas rolled his eyes. "Accident, my ass. No truck barrels through a major intersection in midafternoon without trying to hit the brakes unless the driver is in some sort of distress. I broke into the interrogation feed at the local police station. He claims his brakes failed, and the police wrote it off as a terrible tragedy and let the fucker go. Now he's in the wind, but Steel is on the lookout for him, too. Somebody had to pay the guy off."

"Other casualties?"

"A warehouse maintenance guy was caught in the blast. Jacques' car exploded on impact. The blast from that took out two other vehicles and their occupants. Some bystander injuries."

"What about Jacques' family?"

"Here's where it gets interesting, Boss. They're missing, too. Shortly before Jacques went into the safe, they were escorted out of the main residence and put into a car. That car was found about six miles out of Cairo on a deserted road. Looked like it caught on fire, but not like it had been run off the road. I'm thinking it was torched purposefully, and they caught another ride.

"Or they were taken," Midas grumbled. "No bodies or remains found, and nothing to suggest struggle, though, so the first assessment is probably accurate. And finding what ride they caught is pretty unlikely. There are no cameras out that way, as it's a relatively unused highway. No way to know if the car they switched to came from the same direction. I'm looking, but I've only got so many monitors I can watch at a time. Which route do you want me to take?"

Waters pulled at his bottom lip as he considered. "Follow the trident. While I hate the thought of that family being in the wind, it's doubtful that they know anything about Ka-Bar. We've got to stick with what we know. Keep facial recognition running and all other SOP for them, though."

"Copy that." Midas was already clacking at keys to pull up camera footage. "I've also got facial recognition working on all transportation cameras I can that exit off that highway, but it's a longshot."

"Understood."

"Also, both your tablet and Kubrick's laptop are dead ends. They flared to life briefly, then went deader than dead. I'm guessing someone destroyed them."

"Why take them if you're just going to destroy them?"

"No idea. Maybe they realized they could be tracked through them?"

"Doesn't make any sense," Waters pondered.

"So..." Midas started, clearing his throat. "You get everything worked out with the missus? No more pillow bombs?" He tried to keep from laughing but failed miserably. "She's got good aim."

"Erase that footage," Waters threatened.

"Too late. God was online at the same time. Priceless."

"I'm serious. Erase it."

"Fuck that. It's going on the BTS of the DVD from your original meeting with Kubrick."

"I'm warning you, if that doesn't get erased, I'll set TB on your ass, and I will look the other way when he whales on it."

Midas looked at Waters through the screen. "I was only teasing. No worries, Boss. It's already scrubbed."

"Thank you."

"Doesn't mean you're not going to continue to get shit about it."

"That's fine. I don't want to take the chance that she learns this room is under constant surveillance. Don't want her to be self-conscious."

"Got it. Beep you when I've got something." With that, Midas signed off, and the screen went back to black.

Waters sighed, putting both hands behind his neck and lacing the fingers together.

What a fucked-up mess.

His eyes went to the door of Kubrick's room, and he couldn't help but smile. A quick glance at his watch showed it was quarter after four. Just enough time to wake her up and enjoy the process.

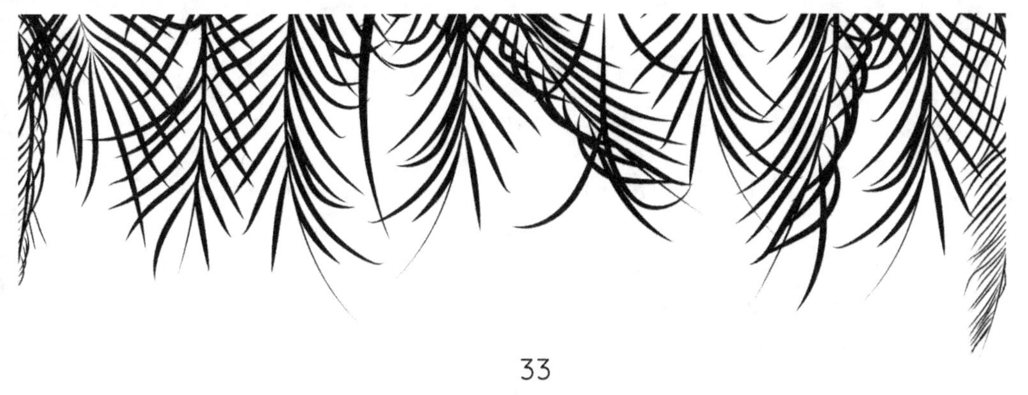

33

———————

APRIL 8TH

Kai

TEMPLES POUNDING, KAI LEANED BACK IN HER SEAT. She had been working in the War Room answering emails. At least Big Bird had brought her a brand-new computer with his unwanted arrival. This kind of work was murder on her eyes and painful mentally to do on a phone. Which also needed replacing from the day she pitched it across the room and caused the screen to crack and shatter. It still worked, but it was impossible to read through the spider webbing without suffering a severe migraine.

She had just checked on some more replacement supplies as additional items had gone missing over the last ten days. And, of course, since Big Bird was down here now, there was no way to hide it from him. It was almost like he knew they were gone and was just waiting for her to report it so he could pounce. She was beginning to suspect more and more that he was behind the sabotage going on.

In addition, a stuntman had gotten injured two days earlier, for real this time. He had personally checked his rig and placed his pitons for the cliff rappel scene, but somehow, the piton had come loose, and he'd fallen twenty feet. It could have been much worse. He suffered a broken ankle and collarbone, but Kai was spooked. Originally, Jumper was supposed to do his own stunt, but given all the weird occurrences going on, Waters thought it might be better for the stunt crew to take on a little more than first intended. She shuddered at what could have happened if it had been Jumper instead of the stuntman.

As she was about to sort her supply invoice from her most recent purchase into the appropriate folder, her eye caught an error. Or she thought it was an error until she remembered that her supplier used European dates since he was based out of Paris, and he used military time on orders to make sure it was clear when they came in. Her face scrunched up into a frown of concentration. Something was tickling the back of her brain.

Her eyes opened wide, and a hand went over her mouth.

Oh. Fuck. Me.

"Stupid, Kai. You're so fucking stupid." She scrambled out of her seat and ran into the bathroom where Waters was finishing his shower. "Waters!"

Ho.Ly. Fuck. I can die happy now.

He stood in the claw-footed tub, gloriously naked, toweling his almost non-existent hair as he looked at her. Every mouth-watering inch of him was open for viewing. She couldn't help staring. It was impossible not to. The man was fucking perfect, scars and all.

He raised an eyebrow at her. "See something you want, babe?" he teased.

"Umm…"

"Words, babe. I need words." He stepped out of the tub and walked nonchalantly over to her in the doorway, holding the towel in his hands but not covering himself up.

"Words. Right. Why the hell did I come in here?"

"Dunno. Not sad you did, though." He threw the towel on the pedestal sink and gathered her close to him, immediately swooping in to gently suck on her rapid pulse point. "I thought you were working on invoices."

"Shit! Right. Can your computer guy find old emails? Even deleted forever ones from another computer? One that's not here with me?"

Pulling back from her neck, he grinned at her. "Did you seriously just ask me that question? And why are you asking me that when I'm naked?"

She huffed. "Don't fuck around right now."

Waters reached for the towel he'd just abandoned, then wrapped it around his waist. "If he knows exactly where the computer in question is, and it's plugged in, he can access it remotely. If it's off or unplugged, not sure. Probably. What is it?" He grabbed her shoulders. "Kubrick. You're hyperventilating. What is it?"

"I think I had the key to Ka-Bar's 'package' all along. The problem is that it's in my personal email, and I only ever access it on my personal laptop, which is at home on my desk. It's a Gmail address, but I deleted it almost immediately after I got it, and I delete forever old emails religiously the first of every month."

"So pulling it up on your work computer or your phone is a no-go. Okay. Let me get dressed, and we'll call Midas."

Two minutes later, Waters was in front of the telescreen in the War Room, tapping in his code. Midas appeared on the screen. "What's up, Boss?"

Waters ignored the stunned look on Kai's face as she saw the computer hacker's face on the television as well. "Midas, I need you to remote access Kubrick's laptop at her home."

"Two seconds." Keys clacked, then suddenly, he was also pictured in the upper left corner of her new laptop. "Hello, Kubrick." He grinned. "Nice to finally meet you."

She sat down in front of the screen. "Hi," was all she could muster.

"No worries, beautiful. I have that effect on a lot of women." He winked. "Hey, Waters." He acknowledged his boss, who had pulled up a chair behind the desk next to her. "Shall I patch everyone through?"

"Yeah, go ahead."

"Okay. Gimme a moment." More keys clacked, and within ten seconds, several faces popped on like the Brady Bunch grid. A blank square appeared as well. "Hail, hail, the gang's all here."

"Kubrick, this is my team. God and Demon, you already know. Midas, our computer guru, you just met. The others are Steel, he's the teammate your brother called his favor in to; TB, who's here on overwatch; Nemo, Midas' brother, who's also here on overwatch." Each of the men gave a wave of greeting or head nod as they were introduced, except for God, who was still invisible. "Guys, Kubrick has something."

"Well, I'm not s-sure," she stuttered.

How did I miss it? If he dies, it will be all my fault.

"Kubrick?" Midas was watching her with a look of concern over the computer screen.

"I had a sudden epiphany when going through some invoices, and it triggered a memory about the last email I got from Kent. I mean, Ka-Bar. Can you pull up my emails from

Ka-Bar even though I completely deleted them over thirty days ago?"

"Does the Pope wear a funny hat? Nothing's ever truly deleted."

The emails were already appearing on the left-hand side of her screen. She scanned the top several communications, which were actually her trying to contact him after he had disappeared. She clicked open the sixth file, which was his second last email to her.

12-13-22 7:41 a.m.
Hey, Kai.
Sorry, but I'm gonna need to trade on some of my big brother cred here. I'm an idiot and left a package behind at the embassy in Cairo. I meant to send it home before I left, but then I got called out and didn't get to it. I assume you're heading home from Budapest in a day or two. I know it's a lot to ask, but I also know you won't mind visiting Amal, so I'll owe ya. When you get to the embassy, ask for Jonathan Carter. He'll make sure you get what you need. Thanks, sis. I always know I can count on you. Make sure you check the date on your calendar, and I'll owe you one bottle of sake and dinner at that place south of Hayato's. Sorry this is all so back asswards. Love you.

"You said the package wasn't there, though," Waters reminded her.

"No, I said no one knew anything about a package and

that the official I spoke to said Carter wasn't at the embassy, and he didn't arrive before I left."

"So?" Midas asked.

Waters frowned. "What are you thinking, babe?"

"I think that package was way more important than Ka-Bar let on." She bowed her head in frustration. "Fuck, I'm so stupid. It wouldn't be difficult to hack into my emails, see that, then think I had that package at my trailer or even with me."

The black box's wavelength popped up and God's voice came over the speakers. "But Waters just said you didn't get a package."

"No, I didn't. But I missed a key piece of his message. That's where I really fucked up. Look at the date on the email."

They watched as Midas squinted at the screen. "December 13th, 2022, at 7:14 a.m."

"Now look at the email." He scanned the communication, his lips moving and no sound coming out of his mouth. "Why put a date on an email when the program automatically puts one on it in the inbox?"

The minute he saw it, she knew. "Your brother is fucking brilliant. Where, Kubrick?"

"Hayato's is on the 1300th block of 7th Street. Go one block south, there'll be a shipping store of some kind. You'll need to get to box 417. The combination will be 22-31-21."

"I know you just got back, but get your ass on it, Steel," God barked.

"On my way." His box closed.

"Waters," she started. "I fucked up."

He shook his head. "Steel's got it. You saw it now, that's what's important. It was clever, Kubrick. Maybe too clever. Whatever it is he needed you to collect must be really important for him to hide it that well. How did you figure it out?"

"I was filing invoices from my email. The rappelling company I purchased pitons from is French. They use a European date format. And military timing. All of a sudden, I realized there was something weird about the numbers in Ka-Bar's email. Then I thought about some of the other information he gave me. It just didn't make sense. At the end he apologized for everything being back asswards. He meant everything was backward from what he was really saying. I should have realized, in particular, because of the mention of Amal. He was the first... you know." She blushed as she looked at Waters. "He's married now, and I would never disrespect his wife that way by showing up to visit. But I was in such a hurry that it didn't register. Ka-Bar would have known I would feel that way, so he was saying DON'T go to Cairo. Ugh."

"What about the agent?" God asked.

"That's even dumber of me. I love science fiction, and I went through a huge comic book phase as a kid. There is no Jonathan Carter. He's a fictional character from a comic book by Edgar Rice Burroughs. A soldier who ended up traveling to Mars. I think my brother may have used it as one of his aliases when he needed an exit strategy several years ago. He probably used it as the name to rent the shipping box."

Plastic wrapping could be heard crinkling. "And when you went to the embassy and asked for this agent, either the flunky you talked to got tipped off that Ka-Bar was either in trouble or it was a red flag to someone in the know to hack into your correspondence." God hmphed and began crunching his sucker.

"Enter Jacques' surreptitious flight from the embassy,"

Waters interjected. "Also, could be a predetermined code of some kind. The flunky might have played dumb for Kubrick but then reported to Jacques about someone asking for an agent that didn't exist. The ambassador would then understand that Ka-Bar was in trouble."

"And whatever I was supposed to 'bring home' was already out of the country and in that shipping box. Look. He tells me one bottle, or one block because of the letter 'B' at that place south of Hayato's. Then he tells me to check my calendar. Not save a date, but to check the calendar."

"The date the email was sent doesn't match the date on the actual email," Midas affirmed.

"No, but the numbers are so close that even if someone looked at them both, they probably wouldn't see it right away. Our brains autocorrect a lot of errors for us. Plus, if all of his information is backward, that means the numbers will be as well."

"Box 417. The combination will be 22-31-21 to get inside."

"Yes. But what the hell could he send me that was so important that he's basically erased, and now I'm in danger?"

"I guess we'll find out soon enough." Waters redirected his attention to Midas on the computer screen. "Midas, can you use your voodoo to figure out where Ka-Bar was when he sent that email?"

"Does the Pope's funny hat have a cross on it? Why do people keep asking me if I can do things that a child could do?"

"Cheeky," warned Waters. "If nothing else, that could give us another point of origin to try and locate him."

"I already did it while you were talking. He didn't even try to hide the IP address. He was at a coffee bar in Cairo, just down the street from the Museum of Egyptian Antiquities. He actually used his credit card to pay for the internet time at the cafe. He wanted us to know where he was."

Midas acknowledged, "There was the first breadcrumb, which is why we had such trouble finding one initially."

Kai turned to Waters. "He knew he was in trouble, and we'd need to come find him," she whispered. "Oh my God, Waters, it's been almost four months." Her face dropped into her hands. "I've killed him."

Waters slipped out of his chair and kneeled beside her. "Kubrick. Stop it right now. We don't know what kind of trouble he was in. He could be in hiding. All we know is that he walked out of that embassy to this cafe, sent you this message, and then disappeared. There are far too many options of what could have happened after that to assume anything."

His hands reached up to take hers away from her face. "Kubrick. Baby, look at me." Tears were running down her cheeks, and the devastation in her eyes was breaking his heart. "Your brother is one of the best at what he does. Men like us, we've got exit contacts all over the globe we can reach out to, and for him, Cairo would be a perfect choice since you lived there at one time, plus he was stationed there. He would have had money stashed where he could get to it. Weapons. Burner phones. Supplies. Possibly even passports under fake I.D.s that could at least pass muster to get him through border checkpoints and even smaller airports if he couldn't get to his initial contact. And even if he can't access those things, he would have additional contacts like Jacques who could help him. If he struck out there, he would have contingencies. He didn't get to be the best without those things. If we're really lucky, he's hiding out in a bolt-hole he's got somewhere."

"Logically, I know you're right, but it's still terrifying that somehow he got caught, or killed, or—"

"Kubrick! You cannot let panic take over. It won't help him or us. All it's going to do is raise your blood pressure. Breathe. We will find him. It might not be today, but I sincerely doubt he's dead. Whatever he sent you is too important to them to do that. They won't dare do that until they know they have it because he's the only person one hundred percent sure where he hid it. If they kill him, it's possible their only source of information disappears, and with it, the hope of recovering what they're looking for. Trust me, okay?"

"I've always trusted you."

"And that's the greatest thing in the world to me," he admitted with a smile. "Steel is going to collect whatever he sent you. He won't let anyone get to it. We will protect it so that no one can. Then we'll find Ka-Bar and bring him home."

Kai threw her arms around Waters' neck, clutching at him like a woman drowning. "I love you," she sobbed.

34

———————

APRIL 8TH

Waters

HE FLINCHED AS IF A BULLET HAD STRUCK HIM through body armor. He couldn't help it.

Did she say what I think she said?

His hands were on her forearms, pulling her stranglehold from him. Out of the corner of her eye, he registered that her computer screen had gone completely dark. Midas heard her admission and was politely cutting everyone else from the moment.

I owe that man a lot of tequila.

Her arms went limp, her eyes on the floor. She was too embarrassed to face him.

Both of his hands reached up to Kubrick's face. It felt like there was a slight tremor in them as they brushed stray hairs back behind her ears. The silence was deafening as they continued to caress her face, his fingers tracing the lines of her furrowed forehead, the cheekbones flushed red

305

with her admission, the tense lines of her jaw as she ground her teeth in embarrassment, and the seam in the frown of her lips. The same hands framed her face between the palms, his thumbs brushing away the tears falling from her eyes. "Kubrick," he exhaled. "Kubrick, look at me."

She closed her eyes and turned her head.

His hands turned her face back to him, but she refused to open her eyes. "Kubrick, please," he begged.

Her tears came harder, afraid to hear his protests to her confession. And her tears were his undoing. He'd only seen Kubrick this defeated once before, and it twisted his insides today as much as it had that day before they left for Roatán. No, worse this time, because these tears she was shedding were over him and something he'd said at one time and no longer meant.

No, the truth is I never meant them. I used them like a shield to keep my heart from breaking if something were to happen to her. And it no longer matters what God thinks. I can't stop this, even if I tried. Even if I wanted to. Come what may.

He had to stop her tears. Make her understand. But even more than that, he needed to believe what she'd said.

In a fluid motion, he stood, swept her up into his arms, then gathered her close on his lap in the chair she'd just been removed from. One hand curled around the back of her head. "Kubrick. Look at me right now. Please. I need you to look at me."

Reluctantly, she opened her eyes.

His voice, when it came, was desperate. "Say it again."

She inhaled. "Wh-what?"

He brushed away more tears. "Please. Say it again. I need to make sure I heard you right. So say it again."

She searched his face. She must have seen that he was serious instead of angry. "I love you," she whispered.

His forehead bent to hers, his lips a breath away from hers. "Again." He stopped breathing.

"I love you. I'm sorry," she apologized. "I know I wasn't supposed to—"

A finger touched her lips, keeping her from apologizing further. He withdrew his finger and used that arm to curl around her waist. He pulled her tight, his face buried in her neck beneath her ear. Only when she was as tight to his body as he could get her did he breathe. "Again, Kubrick. Say it again," was his muffled plea.

She clutched him tightly. "I love you, Waters."

A ragged sigh escaped him as if he was holding back tears of his own.

His watch beeped.

Waters pulled back, and his hands framed her face again, his thumbs swiping away more tears. "This isn't finished. Right now, I need you to dry your eyes, baby. Midas has something for us."

She inhaled deeply and nodded her head that she was ready to hear what Midas had.

"Go ahead, Midas," Waters called out, but his eyes never left hers.

The screen came back live, and Midas appeared. TB, Demon, and Nemo were gone from the screen, but God's square remained. "Sorry, you two. My timing is shit, but there was no package at the shipping store in that box. There was just an envelope."

"Did Steel open it?"

"Negative. Wanted Kubrick's permission first."

"You've got it, Midas. Open it," she ordered.

Eyes still on each other, foreheads touching, Waters'

thumbs stroking her jawline, he heard the sound of ripping paper and something sliding out of it. A low whistle came from Midas at whatever he was looking at. "Umm, Kubrick?"

She sniffled, shaking herself free of Waters' gaze, wiping her cheeks with the back of her hands. "What is it, Midas?" she asked, turning to face the screen.

Waters directed his attention to the screen as well, one arm sliding down her back to rest around her waist, the other crossing her lap and gripping her opposite thigh. He had a sneaking suspicion she was going to need physical support in addition to mental.

"Who is this?" Midas turned the single sheet of paper in his hand to face the screen. It was a five-by-seven photograph of an Egyptian woman standing in the middle of the open plaza before an Egyptian tourist site.

Kubrick leaned forward to get a better look. The woman wore a white gauze dress and a sunhat. Her face was turned in profile and lit up with a beautiful smile, eyes shining. She shrugged and shook her head. "I don't know. She's beautiful."

Waters squinted, looking more at the background than the woman. "That's the Temple of Philae."

She looked closer. "You're right. But I don't understand." Her face depicted true puzzlement over the picture.

Midas pulled the photo back, scanned it, and it popped up on their screen in the lower right corner. "Look at the bottom of the frame."

A shadow showed at the bottom of the photo, the outline of a person holding a cell phone to take a picture. Kubrick leaned in further to the screen, her frown deepening. "Midas, can you blow the photo up?"

"Again, with the silly questions. Any particular portion you want enlarged?"

"Her eyes."

Midas zoomed in tight on the eyes of the girl. They were a golden-brown, lighter than normal for an Egyptian woman.

"No," Kubrick whispered. "It can't be."

"You know her now?" Waters asked.

"She's older, obviously. But I think that's Zahra Kader."

Midas' keys were clacking in the background, and another photo popped up on the screen. It was a casual, large group photo of mostly adults who were laughing and toasting the camera. Some were clearly Egyptian dignitaries, but others were clearly civilians, including Kubrick's adoptive parents.

Waters couldn't help the grin that spread across his face. There was his woman perched piggyback on an older teen, her index and middle finger in a "V" shape over his head. The adopted siblings appeared to be in the Egyptian embassy's courtyard. Her signature blonde ponytail was in a braid that was wound around her head like a hairband, blue ribbons waving in the breeze, but the edge strands were just as flyaway then as they were now. And the smile was full of absolute joy. She had always been beautiful. And it was also clear from the laughing face of Ka-Bar trying to look backward at her that he adored his adopted sister.

"Well, aren't you just as cute as a button," Midas chided.

"Zoom in on the girl two over on Ka-Bar's left," Waters ordered.

"Your wish is my command," he quipped. Instantly, the picture enlarged to a young Egyptian girl's face, her eyes focused on something to her right. Then, he put the two photos side-by-side on the screen.

"It is Zahra," she whispered.

"Who's Zahra, baby?" Waters asked.

"She's... well, she was... my brother's girlfriend. I think. I was ten in this picture, so as far as I was concerned, she was. I caught them kissing once." She smiled at the memory. "I thought Ka-Bar was mad at me when I teased him about it. He actually shook me until my teeth rattled. Made me promise never to breathe a word to another soul. He made it sound like he'd be killed if anyone knew. So dramatic." Her smile faded. "But my ten-year-old heart couldn't bear the thought of losing my beloved big brother, especially after all I'd already lost. So I kept my promise." She shook herself out of the bad memories. "We left the embassy shortly after that picture was taken. James, our adopted dad, was sent back to New York, and that was the end of our stay in Egypt until Ka-Bar's home base became Cairo."

A low whistle came from over the monitor. "Bossman, we've got potential problems."

Waters frowned. "What is it, Midas?"

The photographs disappeared and were replaced with a newspaper article. The story was in Egyptian, approximately six months old, but the photo was Zahra in an olive hijab and a fashionable yet modest matching robed dress of the same color with gold accents. "The article is about her being missing. And that's not all." Another picture appeared on the screen.

Kubrick inhaled.

Waters swore.

Zahra appeared in a photograph holding her very pregnant belly.

God spoke up. "We found the package, gentlemen."

FOUR HOURS LATER, WATERS WAS STILL ONLINE WITH his team, coordinating all efforts. Kubrick had nearly collapsed from the adrenaline rush and shock. Demon had realized it was coming, so he left his post in the medic trailer and brought over a sedative to give her. Once it had been administered, Waters lay with her until she was asleep. When he returned to the War Room, it was to see that TB and Nemo had shown up.

"How long until everyone comes back to the house?" TB asked.

"The actors are out with the second unit director doing some distance shots. We have a couple of hours, maybe. Sunset tops."

"We lost Big Bird in all the excitement. Do we have any idea where he is?" Nemo asked.

"Not our concern right now," God barked. "Focus."

Waters was gazing intently at the screen, but he didn't appear to be looking at anything in particular. "Something's wrong."

"What do you mean?" God asked.

"If Zahra and the baby are the package, then why did someone break into Kubrick's trailer and then the house here?"

"Maybe they wanted the picture," Nemo suggested.

"Doubtful. Wouldn't whoever is looking for them know the package was a person and whom they were looking for? We're missing something. We've got to be." Waters blew out his frustration with a loud exhale. "And how do Big

Bird and all the film stuff fit into this? Nothing makes sense."

"I don't know that we're going to get any answers on any of this until we locate Ka-Bar," God admitted. "Finding Zahra and Ka-Bar are the primary objectives now. The only objectives. It's time to regroup."

Waters looked at the television screen and God's black box with suspicion. "What do you mean 'only'?"

"Exactly what I said. We need to regroup. Reassess. The objectives have changed. It seems to me that Ka-Bar wanted us in Kubrick's life to help her get to this package. Now that we know what the package is, the course of our work has changed. I want you back on a plane and at the office in twenty-four hours."

Waters' skin went cold, and he felt like his heart had both stopped and pounded with a deadly tattoo at the same time. "No," he whispered.

"Don't fuck with me, Waters. Get your ass in gear and get back here. The more people on this now, the better."

"We can't just leave Kubrick here by herself with that shitweasel."

"While I appreciate that you're concerned over your lady director, she is no longer the center of our work. She's a strong woman. Before she knew you, she was dealing with fuck-alls like him and doing just fine." God paused briefly. "Get back here. That's a direct order."

God disconnected from the video chat. Everyone in the room stood in silence, looking to Waters with concern and for direction. Even Midas on the screen was unsure how to proceed.

And this is why you told her not to become involved. That this was only temporary. You couldn't even follow your own directive. Instead, you followed your dick. Dumbass.

"Jesus Christ," someone whispered.

"Boss..." He wasn't sure which man tried to address him, but he had to shut it down quickly.

They all saw this as some sort of fantasy. You let them suck you into it. You knew better. You knew this was coming. You just thought you had more time.

Grinding his molars and tensing his body, Waters barked out orders, "Pack. We leave at first light."

There was an inhaled gasp.

Waters went to the corner where he stored his gear and began repacking. The men stood stock still, looking between themselves, not wanting to believe this was happening. Without looking up, Waters barked, "What are you waiting for? You heard the man. Get your asses in gear."

With a final look at each other, the men began to file out of the office in silence. Demon was the last to the door.

Jesus, I actually fell in love with her. This hurts worse than any physical wound I've ever had. There's no way I can leave her unprotected.

"Demon."

The Irishman stopped and turned to look at his boss. He said nothing. No expression on his face. Just waiting. Waters still didn't look up. "You're staying."

Demon's green cat eyes were solemn. "Copy that."

35

—————

APRIL 9TH

Kai

HER EYES FELT GRITTY AND HER MOUTH LIKE ASH.

What the...

Then it all came flooding back.

The email.

The envelope.

Zahra.

Telling Waters she loved him.

Him not saying it back.

Truth be told, his reaction was confusing. He had seemed happy, yet not. Her stomach was rolling. She had a bad feeling inside about what was going on.

She lay on her side, staring out the window into the moonlit yard.

What a colossal fuckup I am.

"Why's that, babe?" a voice asked from behind her.

She turned her head to look over her shoulder to see

314

Waters propping himself up on his elbow and looking over at her.

"I didn't say anything."

"Yes, you did. You said, 'What a colossal fuckup I am.' Why are you a colossal fuckup?"

"I really have to learn to filter my mouth."

"I like your lack of filter. Told you that the second time we met. It's probably my favorite feature of yours."

"That's your favorite?" she questioned unbelievingly.

"Well, maybe one of my favorites."

He lay back down behind her, gathering her back tight to his front. "Go back to sleep, baby. You've had a rough day. You need your rest for tomorrow. You've got a busy day. Big rescue scene to film."

His word choice didn't escape her.

"You" have. Not "we" have.

"You're leaving."

He didn't answer.

"I guess I should have figured you'd all be taking off to go look for Ka-Bar and Zahra."

He squeezed her as a form of response, then groaned. "I want nothing more than to make love to you right now, and I can't. You're still under the influence of that sedative Demon gave you, and I won't take you while you're foggy." He left unsaid what he knew would be even more difficult. He hugged her again. "Sleep, baby."

"Will I see you again?"

Silence.

"Stupid question. Forget I asked. Go. Find Ka-Bar. Find Zahra. I need my brother back. That's what matters."

Kai continued to stare out the window. Tears filled her eyes, but she refused to let them fall.

He warned you.

Wary of saying too much, of begging him not to leave, of screaming at the unfairness of it all, Kai closed her eyes and attempted the greatest acting job of her life. Pretending to sleep. She concentrated on slowing and evening out her breathing. It must have worked because after a while, she heard the quietest of apologies, followed by a lingering, tender kiss to her shoulder. Then the bed shifted as Waters slid from it. A moment later, she heard the snick of the door closing.

He was gone.

And then the tears came.

36

APRIL 9TH

Kai

IT'S A DAMN DOOR, SERRANO. FUCKING GO THROUGH IT.

She'd been unable to make herself go to the War Room before now, just past midnight. She'd even been so much of a coward that earlier, she'd had Lazarus go in and get her computer and backpack and bring it to her out in the makeup trailer.

Her hand reached out to the doorknob but didn't quite make it to touch it. Her brain was telling her fingers to grip the knob, but they wouldn't follow through, as if they couldn't bear to commit to the action, knowing he wouldn't be there.

He'd never be in that room with her again.

Instead, she found herself stepping up to the doors, placing both hands on the side-by-side panels at shoulder height, and leaning her head against the wood.

317

A shuddering sigh went through her entire body from top to bottom. "Fuck."

Sucking up as much air as she could, she felt her psyche begin to batten down its shutters to keep the pain inside and hidden away. Her hands slid down to the knobs, and on the exhale, she twisted and pushed the doors open violently.

As she crossed the threshold and stepped through, she noticed immediately that his gear that he left in the far corner was gone. She crossed the damp room to stand before her desk, arms crossed and grabbing her biceps. She simply stared at the empty surface.

She felt empty. Cold. Dead.

She heard the snick of the door. Without looking up from the desktop, she said, "I figured he'd leave you behind."

The Irish accent swept low through the room. "He would never leave you unprotected."

She gave a single nod. "I could fire you."

"But you won't."

His soft Irish lilt was somehow comforting.

"I should."

"Even if you do, I'd stay."

Crap! How did he get behind me so quickly and quietly? They're all freaking ninjas.

"No," she whispered, "I won't." Then she doubled over, sobbing as if she had just heard Waters had died. Demon came around to the side of her, reached down, and raised her to standing, then pulled her tight to his chest. Gently, he stroked her hair and kissed the top of her head as he held her. "Do me a favor. Never tell him I held you while you cried. And if you tell him I kissed your head, he'll go apeshit. He knows a feck-ton of ways to kill me so that no one will be able to tell how I died. Of course, that would mean someone would have to be able to find my body when he was done with it."

A bark of laughter issued from Kai at his attempt at a joke, which probably really wasn't a joke. "Do any of those ways involve a napkin?"

Demon chuckled. "Probably the most dangerous of the ways he knows."

She pulled back from his chest, looking up at him. "I won't see him again. He didn't have to say it. But I'm glad he left you behind, Demon."

He wiped the tear tracks from her face and slid his hands down to rest on her shoulders. He gave them a gentle squeeze. "Go get some sleep, Kubrick. I'll be out here to keep away the angry bird."

She stood on tiptoe and kissed his cheek, then drew away and went to her bedroom. When she reached the door, she stopped and turned her head over her shoulder. "I love him. I thought I could avoid it."

"He knows you do. And nothing's ever FUBAR, Kubrick. There's always a way. You need to look for it, and then you have to be willing to make it happen at all costs."

She sighed. "I wish I could believe that. Tribe is his life. And I get that. I love that for him. I wouldn't want him any other way. But he'll always have to choose between it and anything else. And Tribe always wins," she admitted, echoing his words. Then she continued into her room and shut herself in.

37

———

APRIL 10TH

Waters

IN THE DARK OF HIS OFFICE, HE SAT STARING OUT THE windows to the buildings across the way, but he wasn't seeing anything. All his brain could see was Kubrick as he slunk out of her bed and left without saying goodbye. Or telling her, "I love you."

It's not like you had a choice. And telling her that would have made it worse.

His watch dinged with a text notification. Four a.m. He'd been sitting here for hours, mentally paralyzed. Reaching for his phone, he swiped the screen, entered his passcode, and pulled up the text. It was a photo of Kubrick leaning her head against the War Room doors. He could read the pain in her posture.

She'll get over you.

Three bubbles started popping up, but after a minute, they disappeared and never returned. Appar-

320

ently, Demon thought better of whatever he was going to say.

She deserves better than you.

When they'd arrived back at Tribe, Waters didn't even look at anyone. He had just headed straight back to his office. When Midas tried to call out a question, he heard a whispered, "Leave it," from TB. He didn't need to see TB to know that he was probably flashing a warning with his eyes as he continued down the opposite hall to where they would strip down and stow their gear.

Once inside his office, he hadn't even bothered to turn on the lights. He threw his gear in the corner, then threw himself into his desk chair, and swiveled around to look out the windows. He'd been sitting there for hours.

His watch beeped, this time with a call notification.

Great. I so do not want to deal with this right now.

Knowing it was useless to pretend he didn't hear it or that he wasn't here still, Waters swore under his breath and booted up his computer. After running through the security protocols, he clicked the audio chat feed open that connected him with his boss.

"Yeah?"

"Where the fuck is Demon?"

"Don't have a shit hemorrhage. Demon's with Kubrick."

"We need him here."

"You never specified you wanted everyone here," Waters explained. "You ordered me here. So, I'm here. But I need him there, and right now that trumps whatever you fucking want, so that's the trade-off. Let it go." The last three words were quiet and put an end to any further discussion. It was deathly silent on the other end of the link. "If that's all, I'm really tired, and I'm—"

"No, that's not all, fuckwitch," God grumbled. Waters

couldn't help the sad smile at the invective. Kubrick had infected them all with her creative swear words. "Of all of you goons, I thought you were the smart one."

"Well, I've proven you wrong on that one. Twice now. Should I make sure my beneficiaries are up to date? Oh, wait. Dead men don't have any."

"This is part of why I originally didn't want you all attaching yourself to people. It gets messy. It creates problems. I don't like messy or problems."

"I'm sure you're safe from a bad Yelp review. Don't worry."

"Save me from idiots," God mumbled. "I have no words for this situation."

"And yet you keep talking."

There was muttering on the other end of the phone. Normally, that would have amused Waters, but now all he wanted to do was get off this call and drink until he forgot his own name. Not that he would, but that's what he wanted. And he also knew it wouldn't work. He might forget his own name but nothing else.

"Sarah is still fucking you over, even now, two years later."

"She has nothing to do with this."

"She has everything to do with it, Taylor. Don't forget. I know you. I know what you're thinking before you do. She's always been a part of the equation. She always will be. Your body is covered with that equation. It's time to let that shit go."

"Your rule was in place long before Sarah."

"I'm not talking about my goddamned rule!" There was a pause. God's voice came back calmer and quieter. "I'm talking about leaving people vulnerable. You're doing it again, just in a different way."

"I'm dead, right? I don't exist; therefore, I'm not vulnerable. Demon's there protecting her to keep her from being vulnerable. We can work without him right now. One more body won't make a difference. There was no way in hell I was leaving her there unprotected from dickwad. End. Of. Story." There was silence. "Look, this conversation will just go in circles and piss us both off. Can we please focus on the bigger picture, which is Ka-Bar?"

"We are not done with this conversation by a long shot."

Yes, we are most certainly done, but that's beside the point.

Waters ignored him. "I'll talk to Steel. We move forward from there. I want to be in Cairo, or wherever we need to be, by the end of next week at the absolute latest and get this shit done and off of our books. Then it won't matter anymore, and things will go back to normal."

There was a snort on the other end of the link. "They'll never be normal again." Then, there was a click, and the link was severed.

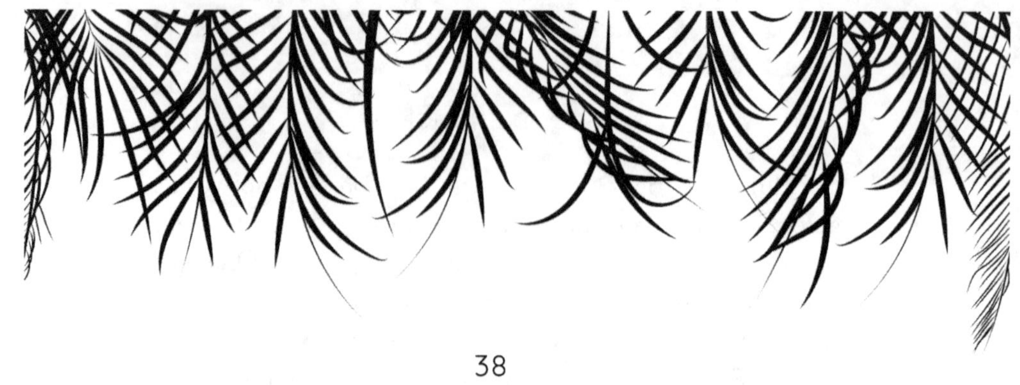

38

———————

MAY 1ST-2ND

Kai

As she finished packing her Backpack of Death, a knock sounded at the War Room door before it opened, and Demon walked in. When he was opposite her over the desk, he shared the news. "Halfway to success."

It was all he said, but it was enough to cause Kai's legs to go out from underneath her. Luckily, the desk chair was directly behind her to catch her fall. "Zahra or Ka-Bar?"

"Zahra. Jacques' family was picked up on facial recognition at a private airfield in Nicosia, in Cyprus. The passport names didn't match, but it was clearly them. And guess who was part of the family."

"Zahra."

"Zahra and... a newborn. A boy."

"They're okay?"

"We were able to intercept them there. The entire group has been moved to a safe house for now."

Closing her eyes and exhaling in relief, Kai put her hands flat on the desktop. She wanted to cry in relief. "Did she say what happened?"

Demon perched on the edge of the desk, arms folded across his chest. "Apparently, when Ka-Bar was reassigned to Cairo, he went and looked Zahra up. She was more than just a kissing partner. They were in love, but her father didn't approve. The two began seeing each other in secret, one thing led to another..."

"The boy is Ka-Bar's."

He confirmed her suspicion. "Dad was not happy that his baby girl got pregnant by a man not of his choosing, let alone not Egyptian, so rather than get locked away, she ran."

"And let me guess. Ka-Bar was trying to send her to me."

"Figured once she was in the States, she'd be able to be better protected."

"He figured wrong."

"At least she's no longer in the wind."

"Can I see her?"

"Not yet. Until we find Ka-Bar, God's keeping the whole group locked up in a safe house. Steel is babysitting them until replacements arrive from the company, but while we snoop around yet for your brother, God doesn't want them or their location compromised. They're in good hands. We won't let anything happen to them."

Kai nodded. "Thank you, Demon. Ka-Bar will be forever grateful, as am I." She looked to her left and out the window. "Is... is everyone safe?" She knew that the operator would understand whom she was really asking about.

"Yeah. He's safe."

Sucking in her lower lip, her gaze traveled down to her lap. "What happens now?"

"I escort you back to L.A."

"And?"

He shifted slightly. "I report back to Tribe. We keep looking for Ka-Bar."

Exhaling, Kai tipped her head back against the desk chair. "Thank you."

"No need to thank us, Kubrick."

"There's every need. You're giving me back at least part of my family. A part I didn't even know I had. And if worse should come to worst, a piece of my brother."

"Don't give up hope. If whoever has him doesn't know that we have Zahra, then the chance he's still alive is high. They won't do anything to him until they know he's not useful to them in terms of information on where she is."

Kai stood up and continued to pack her backpack. "I'll be ready to go within the hour."

He unfolded from his position on the desk and turned to look at her head-on. "Kubrick," he began, "he's hurting as badly as you."

"Don't!" She held up a hand to stop his words. "I can't deal with this right now, Demon. I'm still too raw. It's like it all happened minutes ago, not weeks. I don't know if I'll ever recover, but I know I can't if you give me any sort of platitudes or even honest hope that things can be different. They can't. I know it. He knows it. And deep down, you know it. It's just the reality of it. I'm a big girl. I'll be okay. Eventually."

"It's a stupid rule."

"Stupid or not, it's how it is." A tear escaped, despite how hard she tried to stop it. "The rule that matters is the one that says Tribe always wins," she whispered.

Arriving back in L.A. the next day, Kai was exhausted. She had been unable to sleep on the plane, but it was also too painful to talk to Demon, so they flew back in silence. And really, what was there to say?

Demon grabbed his and Kai's bags off the carousel, then walked her out to his Jeep in the parking structure. Someone had obviously dropped it off in short-term parking for him that morning. After that, it was a short distance to Kai's house. He walked her to the door, but before she could cross over the threshold, he laid a hand on her forearm. Turning, she saw a cell phone in his hand, a cheap plastic pay-as-you-go version of no-frills service.

She looked up at him with questioning eyes. "I bought it at the airport, plus a matching one. The numbers are programmed into each other. My work line will be dead to you once I leave you here. All the lines you had access to will be also."

She understood what he was saying. All communication with Tribe was being severed. Permanently. None of the numbers would work.

"But if you need anything... this will go to me. Not Tribe. Use it if you need it, Kubrick. For anything at all. I mean it."

Once again, Kai's eyes filled with tears, but this time, she let them fall as she clutched the man to her. "Thank you," she whispered. "For everything."

He hugged her tightly. "It was my pleasure. I just wish..."

She put a hand over his mouth and shook her head. When he stepped back to let her go, Kai walked through her door without looking back, then shut it.

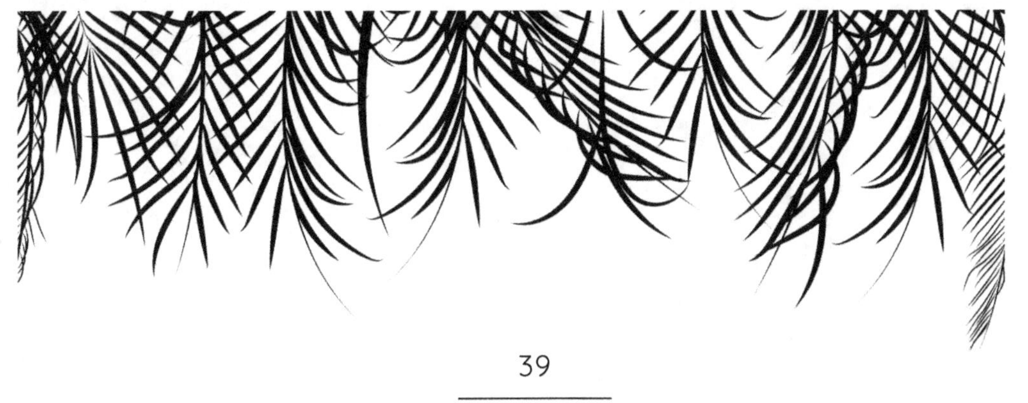

39

———

MAY 2ND

Waters

WHILE SITTING AT THE TABLE IN HIS OFFICE, PAPERS spread out all around him, pen in hand, computer open, Waters heard Demon return before he saw him. The man bellowed, "Where the feck is he?" to which Cherry murmured something, and then Waters could almost feel the heavy footsteps stomping in his direction. When Demon arrived, he didn't even bother to knock, he just threw open the door and glared.

"You're a fecking arsehole!"

"Welcome home."

"That woman is dying inside. Fix it!"

"God wants a debriefing in thirty minutes." He turned his attention back to the paperwork in chaos before him.

"Don't fecking ignore me, you twat. You can't tell me it's not eating you up inside." Waters continued to ignore him.

"Fecking Christ, Waters, letting her go will destroy you. Fall on the sword if you have to. Don't do this."

"It's done, Demon. Let it go." Even to Waters, his quiet response sounded defeated.

Demon muttered under his breath in Gaelic, and none of it sounded complimentary. He stomped to the door, and when he got there, he wheeled around. Waters was pretty sure he had intended to let loose on him, but something stopped him. Instead, in a voice of chastisement, Demon told him, "Feck the stupid rule. Feck God for making you think you have to follow it. And feck you for being the dumbest man on the planet by holding yourself to it. You better think long and hard about what a fool you're being. And how you're going to fecking fix it."

The door slammed in Demon's wake. The echo of the slam rang in the air.

"He's not wrong, Boss," Midas' voice gently added through the speakers of Waters' laptop. The two men had been going over surveillance maps when Demon had burst through the door, not realizing he'd been on a conference call.

"Don't you start, too, Midas. I'm getting it from every direction. Don't you all think it's difficult enough?"

"Maybe that should tell you something."

"Aren't you all forgetting that we have a bigger boss that we answer to?"

"Oh, I'm not forgetting. But even God makes mistakes, Waters, and this is definitely a mistake. A big one that was made in a time of extreme grief. You know it. We know it. And I'm betting the guy upstairs does, too, but he'll never admit it." Midas looked at him intently through the computer screen. "I'm just having a really difficult time understanding why you're not fighting for her. Do you honestly believe she's not worth it? We all know you love her. But here you are, refusing to go to her."

Waters shook his head. "I can't, Midas."

"Why ever not? Christ, you really are an idiot, aren't you? You can do whatever the hell you want. We've got your back as far as God's concerned. Our loyalty is to you, not him. He just signs our checks. And if it's her that's holding you back, grow a set. You may have to grovel a bit to get her back, but Jesus, do it, for fuck's sake."

"I would in a heartbeat, Midas, but God has made it very clear where he stands."

"Has he? Has he really? I wonder. I wasn't aware he'd even once said anything about how he feels about you and Kubrick." Midas shook his head. "I need a break." Waters' screen went blank as Midas cut the feed on his end.

Fuck. Was Midas right?

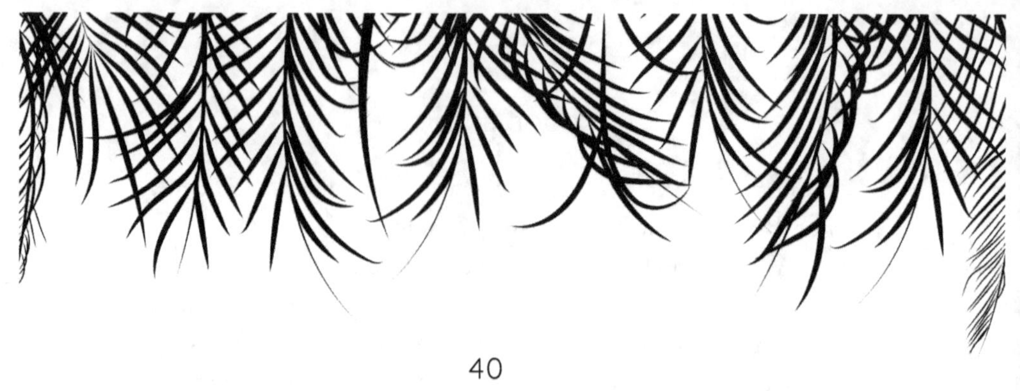

40

———

MAY 20TH

Kai

Kai breezed through Big Bird's door, threw her Backpack of Death on the floor, and then intercepted his administrative assistant from closing the door.

"Leave it open, please, Felicity. I would prefer at least one witness to our final conversation."

"Close the damn door. This is a private conversation."

"Leave it open, Felicity, or I walk and call a meeting of the board members."

The producer began to grind his teeth but waved off his assistant with the command of, "Hold my calls."

Not until the man sat behind his desk did Kai sit in one of the uncomfortable chairs in front of Big Bird's desk.

Another fucking power play. Uncomfortable chairs mean uncomfortable people who will be distracted and agree to things quickly to get out of this office. I wonder how many

332

people have gotten screwed out of millions because of these goddamned chairs.

"The final edits are done. All paperwork has been filed. The picture is officially finished."

Big Bird grunted. "Unfortunately, it is unlikely to get to the theaters."

Kai's gaze narrowed. "And just why would that be, Craig?"

"Because the picture is not good quality. It's been a waste of money from the minute you were hired."

Crossing her legs, Kai picked imaginary lint off of her black leggings as she counted to ten in her head. She needed to go all the way to twenty-two before she was able to speak without yelling. "Bullshit. And even if that were the case, the blame would be with you as you hired me."

"I didn't want you. Kowalski convinced the rest of the board that you were the best choice. I tried to explain to him why that wasn't the case." Big Bird leaned back in his expensive, ergonomic chair. "An eight-to-one vote meant I had to hire you."

"Fine. So explain to me why the film is not good quality."

"I screened the film after you left last night. The acting is subpar, particularly that Sookie Carter, plus she's too fat. Your cinematographer can't frame for shit, the stunts are less than riveting, and the script is a disaster. And don't get me started on the military connections. I've made my opinion known on that from day one, so there's no need to address it again."

She pursed her lips, then sucked them back to her teeth. "You are full of shit, Stapleton. Each and every actor cast had the board's approval. Sookie is absolutely perfect, according to every man I've ever seen or talked to. Every frame of film was given to you each day for viewing, so if you had concerns about anything with filming, you would have said immediately. Yes, the script was shit, but we fixed it, and that only happened because Tribe headed off the mess before we left for training. This all goes without saying that you picked the film in the first place, and allegedly, you have golden vision and can see a hit even with your eyes closed."

"Well, apparently, when I was outvoted for the choice of director, I've now achieved my first failure." He picked up a copy of the contract binder and threw it across his desk at her. "And after going through the final audit, I see I was correct to voice my displeasure. Weeks of unnecessary training at an exorbitant price, then your consultant up and left with no notice. At least that's one budget line I won't have to pay out since he violated the contract by leaving before finishing the job he was hired for." He smiled. "His leaving must have broken your heart, Serrano. Got bored, did he? In all honesty, I'm surprised he stuck around as long as he did. Or was it so bad it wasn't even worth the seven-digit fee?"

Kai stared at him with no expression on her face.

His false tirade continued. "Then let's add to it the missing inventory. Overspending by replacing items that are 'missing' and attempts to cover up said missing inventory. And now, I hold here in my hand"—he lifted a manilla folder about a quarter of an inch thick—"sworn affidavits from several locals in Coxen Hole who identify you as the individual who approached them with an opportunity to sell said missing inventory on the local black market for cash." He threw the folder across the desk at her as well.

"Finally, crew members were compromised by a food poisoning outbreak, and a stuntman could have died due to improperly verified safety procedures. All situations perpetrated by you to slow down production and allow you a cut of the insurance check when the film had to be scrapped." Two more folders filled with papers landed on the pile. "Well, you're going to get your wish on that last one, aren't you? The losses will be heavy, but I think the studio will agree with my recommendation after they've seen the evidence I've compiled. We can't put this piece of shit out there and ruin the reputation of the company."

He steepled his fingers in front of his face. "All of this, of course, can be kept out of the press for now if you leave quietly and forfeit your fees. If you want a reference of any kind or a desire to work in this industry again, I suggest you leave this office right now without another word, clean out your shit, and be off the lot within an hour."

"Bribed or threatened?"

"Excuse me?"

"Were they bribed or threatened? People in Roatán live in pretty much abject poverty. It wouldn't take much to get them to say anything you wanted if it meant they could ensure food and shelter for their families. Also, wouldn't take much to scare them into doing or saying what you wanted for the same reasons. And as far as the crew and the stuntman, unfortunately, there are plenty of weak and vulnerable people in the film industry who can be manipulated just as easily when it comes to staying employed or when given promises for the future. And I'm guessing those opportunities will never come despite those promises."

"No bribes or threats needed when it's the truth."

"So. You're threatening me with these lies?"

"Oh, it's not a threat, Serrano. What I said is exactly what will happen if you don't leave my office as I just described." His smile became predatory. "I almost hope you try to fight me. I will love watching you and your career go down in flames. But I should warn you, if you do fight me, all of this evidence will go to the police, and your career will be over."

This was that final battle Kai had worried about. The one where all the small lost skirmishes led to. She could feel rage bubbling from her feet, up through her body, to her brain. "You are so lucky I don't have a gun on me," she hissed. "I'd shoot you right here where you sit and not blink an eye."

"Tsk, tsk, tsk. So violent. Who's threatening who now, Serrano? You always were such a hothead. Never could keep that mouth of yours shut. Always spouting some sort of vitriol. And you were dumb enough to have Felicity leave the door open so everyone could hear your threat."

He was twisting all of their battles to suit his narrative.

So that was the game all along. But why?

"Fuck off, Stapleton. There's probably a long line of people out there waiting behind me to have the opportunity to put a bullet in you. Most of them work directly for you in this goddamned office."

Kai stood directly in front of his desk, hands flat on the surface as she leaned over. "Now you listen to me, you arrogant, misogynist prick. I'm willing to bet every penny of every film I've ever made, as well as my reputation, that all of your so-called evidence against me is really evidence against you. You have been nothing but a burr on my ass from the moment I accepted this job. Everything was always wrong. No decision I made was acceptable. No choice was right. And based on what? You kept spouting budget concerns, but the truth is, it's you who was the real problem. I know you're the one behind the sabotage of the film. The fantastic film we still managed to make, finish on time, and come in under budget. I'm willing to bet the board hasn't even seen the final cut yet. And when they do, I think they'd agree with me."

Suddenly, in her head, she heard Waters. As painful as that sound was, she grasped it like a lifeline.

"You can only take so much punishment before eventually, the damage will become too great to rally. When that day comes, you'll need to lean on those people when those moments come. You have an army you aren't even aware of. They'll heal the wounds you suffer, and they'll do it gladly, without question."

She stood up straight. "You haven't counted on one thing, Stapleton. And that is that I have a tribe. Everyone I work with will know that everything you spill out of your mouth is a lie. Every piece of so-called evidence you have is trumped up. It won't matter how solid it appears because I've spent years building my tribe up around me. They know me. They would do anything for me because they know I've protected them from cocksuckers like you who think because you hold the combination to the money vault, you're untouchable. That you can do whatever you want, say whatever you want, and have whatever you want.

"Each and every one of those people will have my back, no matter how miserable you aim to make me or my life. Somehow, I must have known I would need every one of them one day. Today is that day."

She picked up her backpack, swung it over her shoulder, and made for the door. When she got there, she turned to face him. "Do your worst. I promise you that I will rain down fire on whatever you put out there, and then I will crush you like a bug under my boot. You don't scare me. You've never scared me. And men like you never will."

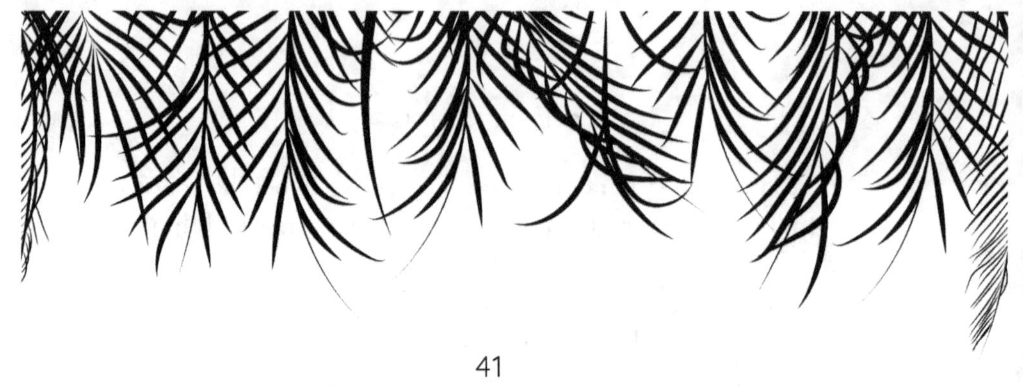

41

———

MAY 20TH

Waters

THE BAR WAS A DIVE. THEY'D BEEN COMING HERE FOR years, mostly because it wasn't somewhere guys like them would hang out. There was a pool room that never seemed to get used except by them, so it became their place to hang out when things were slow at the office. Mostly older, blue-collar workers hung out here drinking beer, watching sports, and paying no attention to anyone around them. It was perfect for hiding in plain sight. No women. No fights. No bands or gimmick nights. No food. Just blissful anonymity.

What the hell am I doing here?

The team had dragged him out at lunch. He didn't want to be here. He wanted to be at the office. He had work to do.

No. That was a lie. He wanted to be with Kubrick. But that wasn't going to happen.

And whose fault is that, dipshit?

As soon as someone came in the door, the sun sliced

338

through the dimness of the main room. The only other place there seemed to be light was here in the side room with the one lone pool table and the three bar-height round tables, each with a couple of stools that had seen better days. The room was rimmed by high-set windows above a row of mirrored beer signs. The late afternoon sun was shining in through the grime and dust.

He chalked his cue stick and went to the upper left corner of the table, bent over, ready to sink the striped seven ball into the lower left pocket, then run the rest of the table and clean Nemo out of his paycheck. Just before he took his shot, his eyes registered movement in the doorway, so he looked straight up to find Kubrick standing in the doorway.

If this were one of her movies, there would have been an electric fritz and a loud crackling noise. Waters felt like all of the oxygen left the room as his eyes met hers. He didn't blink. He didn't move. All sound was gone.

He registered the missing baseball cap, the hair that was half out of the ponytail, and more flyaway than usual. Eyes wide as they surveyed the room around him, her hands clenching and unclenching, then crossing over her stomach, gripping her elbows as if she were cold. Or in pain. She shifted from foot to foot, her expression skittish, like a deer poised to flee from a hunter. When she almost immediately let go of herself, he noticed what looked like red blotches on her crisp white blouse, and it appeared that one sleeve was ripped, possibly a button or two missing.

What the fuck? Kubrick?

Like an internal monologue moment in a film, every-thing was in slow motion. Waters took the shot. Sunk it. And without ever checking the ball went in, never removing his eyes from hers, he stood up behind his cue, his left hand cupping the top of the stick, his right fist cupping the left fist, his weight evenly distributed on both feet, falsely relaxed as his eyes stayed on her.

Oh, sweetheart, what the hell happened to you?

He felt a pang in his gut but resisted the urge to rub it in commiseration.

Just.

Suddenly, it was like the movie reel sped up to put them back in real time. Waters swore he could feel the pressure change as time began to move at its normal pace again.

Wordlessly and without glancing over, he handed his cue stick to Nemo, then walked over to her. He stayed on his side of the threshold as if there were a glass wall separating them.

He couldn't help but be truly concerned. This was not his woman. Something was terribly wrong.

She's lost weight since I saw her last. There are dark shadows under her eyes, and she looks pale as a ghost. Most definitely freaked the fuck out about something. And it's bad if she somehow managed to hunt me down.

He realized that there was only one way that could have happened.

Demon.

Time would tell if he was going to thank or kill the motherfucker.

The pink tip of her tongue darted out to wet the pink flesh of her lips, and her teeth worried the bottom one. He desperately wanted to cover her mouth with his, plunge his hands into her hair, and pull her in tight.

"Waters." Her voice came out raspy. "I'm... um, I'm sorry to bother you," she tried again.

He dragged his eyes back up to her gaze. "What's wrong, Kubrick?" He tried to project nonchalance, but he wasn't sure if he actually was.

Her eyes flicked from guy to guy in the pool room behind him, resting on one in particular for a moment longer, then back to his hazel gaze that had never strayed.

He moved his head to look at the left side of her face. His anger ratcheted up as he grabbed her chin and turned that side of her face to see it in better light. She winced at his grip, so he relaxed just enough to allow her face to slip back to frightened rather than frightened and in pain. "Who did this to you, babe?"

"I have a... a situation."

It was not lost on him that she didn't answer the question. Up close, those red blotches were clearly blood, and she had more bruises on her arms and hands. He removed his shirtjack and coaxed her arms into it. He had a feeling that blood needed to be out of sight. She also had a bump to the head above the bruise forming on the left side of her face. He stared into her eyes for a few moments, his expression never changing and weighing her words, her body tightness, and her vocal inflections. Then he nodded to her, gesturing for her to lead the way. She turned on her heel and headed to the exit.

He turned to look at Demon, and the two men shared a look of anger. "Someone hit her. Did she tell you what's wrong?"

Demon shook his head to the negative. "Just said she had trouble and didn't know who else to call."

Waters gave an extra beat in his glance to Demon, who gave Waters a chin lift, then stepped to the back of the pool room and went for his phone. Waters felt them all tensing, ready to take an order. Even they felt her aura was off.

"Be at the ready," he told them.

Waters followed Kubrick, watching her stiffened posture, and the clenching and unclenching of her fists continued. Once outside, Waters pulled out his aviators from the inner left pocket and put them on against the setting sun. She was standing motionless, as if clueless about whether to go left or right.

Yeah, something is seriously wrong.

He came up along her right side, a hand to her mid-back. "Kubrick?"

She flinched slightly at his use of her nickname and his touch. "I took an Uber." He heard a sense of confusion and lostness in her voice. Now, he was getting nervous.

Gently, he took her left elbow in hand and directed her to his truck. Without thought, he scanned the streets, looking for anything out of place, including any people who shouldn't be where they were. He clicked open the truck door and handed her up into the passenger seat, then closed her in and jogged around the front of the truck, hopping up into the driver's seat.

He started the truck. "Where to?"

"My house." It was nearly a whisper.

"Seat belt," he intoned as he slid his phone into the dashboard clip, hit a small blue button next to the GPS, and pulled out into traffic.

She made no move to put on her seat belt, so he reached across her, grabbed the belt, and buckled her in. It brought back a silly memory of them before. Her struggling with the belt. Him buckling her in. Her over-the-top flirtatious bimbo impression. Now, she was a shell of that woman. Not quite an automaton, but definitely not a self-assured individual right now.

The drive was silent. He watched her out of the corner of his eye, trying to get a read on her. She was looking out the front window, a blank stare and a ramrod spine, those straight white teeth were now worrying her right thumbnail.

Yeah, not good.

He pulled up in front of her house, turned off the truck, put his left forearm on the steering wheel, and angled his body to watch the house itself, waiting for her to speak.

When her voice came, it was just above a whisper. "I watched the final cut last night. Had breakfast on the lot. Met with Stapleton on the final audits. That was a total shitstorm of apocalyptic proportions." She was laughing, but it was more incredulous with a touch of hysteria thrown in. "When I got home from that meeting and got to the top step, something felt off." She stopped.

He shifted his head to look at her instead of the house. She was still looking straight ahead. Not out the window at the house. Not at him. Just staring straight out the windshield.

"Kubrick?" he encouraged softly.

She put a hand up to her nose and pinched the bridge. "I know I should have called the police, but... I couldn't. I've fucked up big time, and I'm scared." She looked down at her hands, twisting them in her lap.

Waters wanted to put a hand on top of her twisting fingers. Instead, he just said, "Stay here." He got out of the truck, but before closing her inside, he hesitated a moment and then offered, "There's a Glock under your seat. Remember what I taught you."

"Oh, I remember," she murmured sarcastically.

He frowned.

"Did you lock everything back up?"

"No. I don't know. I just... after..." There was a slight hitch in her breath with the unfinished thought.

Okay, so expect the unexpected.

With that, he shut the truck door, locked the truck from his fob, and began moving up the sidewalk. Attempting to look casual, he pocketed his aviators and jogged up the sidewalk and five steps, kept his keys out as if they were keys to the doors, and pushed open the screened-in porch door.

He was about to go for his lock picks when he saw the gap between the door and the frame. A slight nudge with his elbow allowed the inner door to swing open. Waters reached behind to pull his second Glock out of the holster beneath the Henley he wore.

What was that saying Kubrick used? Holy hell, horse-shoes, and hand grenades!

He was not prepared for what met his eyes, but someone watching him wouldn't have known it by the way he stepped through the door and began to clear the main floor.

Living room.

Clear.

Closet.

Clear.

Upstairs.

Quick scan up the stairs. Pass momentarily.

Kitchen.

Clear.

Basement.

Wait for that. Too much to clear on my own and way too many questions that need answering.

Waters shot his left arm free of his sleeve and spoke into his watch face. "E.T. Call home." The face lit up with a neon green outline.

The watch beeped twice, and then God's bark came over the speaker. "Just talked to Demon."

"Kubrick's house. Need a cleaning crew. Big Bird got canceled. Heat is out, but I'm not sure how long it's been."

"Already on their way. ETA six minutes. Do we still have eyes?"

"I'm not sure if Midas removed them when he knew she was coming home."

"Ask him when he gets there. He'll have to remote access if Cyclopes is up but dormant."

Waters stepped through to the porch, closing the door behind him by pulling the lip of the door up top as far as he could. He forced himself to walk slowly and deliberately back to the truck, like he didn't have a care in the world. In reality, his eyes were canvassing everything around him.

Based on what he just saw, Kubrick was clearly in a whole heap of trouble that looked really, really fucking bad. He snorted.

I knew she was in trouble, and I followed God's orders anyway, leaving her on her own and vulnerable once she came back home. Fuck me.

She was still staring straight ahead, but he could tell she wasn't seeing anything. If she was retreating into herself, that meant it was even worse than he thought it was. She flinched as he unlocked the passenger door. Grabbing her knees, he swung her ninety degrees in the seat to face him. Her eyes were wide, and pupils dilated in fear and panic. To her credit, she wasn't shrieking or crying, but he wouldn't have blamed her if she had been. Seeing she was not in a good headspace, he gently pushed her knees apart, and he settled in as close as he could to her, his palms gently bracketing her face as he gazed into her eyes. He tilted her face to him and ducked down to meet her eyes. "Kubrick, look at me." Her eyes looked up into his. "We'll get through this. The guys are on their way."

"You're not going to call the police?"

"Hell no. There's a dead body in your living room."

She gave one quick nod of her head. Finally, she broke down. In less than the time it took to inhale her lilac scent, her knees involuntarily squeezed tight at his hips, she burrowed into his chest, face first, and wrapped her arms around his middle, the hands clawing at his Henley. Inwardly, he groaned in pain and pleasure.

His arms went around her shoulders, and he gripped her firmly in his arms, creating a shield with as much of himself as he could. Then he closed his eyes and tried to exhale with control. Soothingly, he stroked her hair. "Babe? What did you do with the gun?"

He felt her breath catch, and the exhale didn't come.

"Exhale," he softly ordered. "I'm going to help you, but you have to tell me what you did with it."

"I panicked." Her muffled reply came from his shirt front.

"Where?"

"Silas' Pond. About a mile back on the dirt road."

She began sobbing quietly. Briefly, he thought about untangling from her since the guys would be there any second. But he didn't. Her fear and tears were breaking his heart. His strong woman was hurting. She was frightened. He couldn't leave her without his arms protecting her, comforting her, reassuring her, no matter who was showing up. More than that, he didn't want to. He had wanted the two of them wrapped around each other again just like this since they'd parted ways six weeks ago. No way was he strong enough, or willing, to let go again. While the timing and situation sucked, he had gotten the second chance he'd been hoping for.

This time, I'm Never. Ever. Letting. Go.

Two minutes later, Demon's doorless Jeep pulled up behind his truck. Demon hopped out with his kit and an emergency ice pack already crushed and primed, which he placed against the side of her face. The medic did a quick check of her eyes with his penlight, totally ignoring that she was still physically wrapped around his boss. He said nothing to either of them, but his glance was guarded. Waters knew that Demon was still unhappy with him, whether Kubrick was currently in his arms or not.

TB's Hummer pulled up in front of Waters' truck. Steel slipped out the passenger side and went to find a spot for Overwatch. TB exited his vehicle and came up curbside of the Ford, grabbing the open doorframe. "Midas and Nemo had to go back to the office to grab Midas' laptop. Should be here in a couple of minutes." He tipped his head in Kubrick's direction. "She okay?"

Demon snorted and walked back to his kit, which he had dropped on the hood of the pickup when he arrived.

These men. Such loyalty for my woman. What the hell was the matter with me?

Waters shook his head lightly. "I cleared the first floor, but not well. Yellow entry."

A Bronco cruised up the street toward them and parked on the opposite side of the F-150. When he exited the truck, Midas had a laptop under his arm, which he quickly set on top of Waters' truck and began typing on. Nemo stood at the back end of the truck, watching the street for pedestrians, but the road was quiet.

He never took Cyclopes down for a nap. Owe him more tequila for that.

Waters focused on Kubrick. "We need to go in and look around. Do you want me to have Demon stay with you here at the truck?"

"I..."

His thumb caressed her pale, unbruised cheek. "You don't have to go in."

He watched the mask slide down her face and body as she schooled her expression and straightened her spine. Her legs eased from around his hips, and he was both proud of her resolve and sorry she was retreating. "I can go inside. It would be better if I did, right? You need your team members with you rather than babysitting my paranoid ass out here."

Waters caught the smirk on TB's face before he turned it away as if he were scanning the area for hidden assailants. "Having you close, where I know you're safe, and Demon there helping to clear the house is preferable, yes. But I would understand if you can't go inside."

Indecision and a touch of fear sparked in her eyes again as Kubrick bit her bottom lip and ducked her head. But a moment later, when she raised her face to Waters', her voice was solid, like it had always been on the set. "Okay."

Waters' eyes lit up, and he smiled for the first time that day. Probably in six weeks. "There's my girl. Knew she was in there somewhere." He smoothed the hair back. "Okay. Nemo, I've got her six, you lead."

She slid out of the truck, and reluctantly, he let go of her only for her hand to reach back for his as they walked.

Well, fuck.

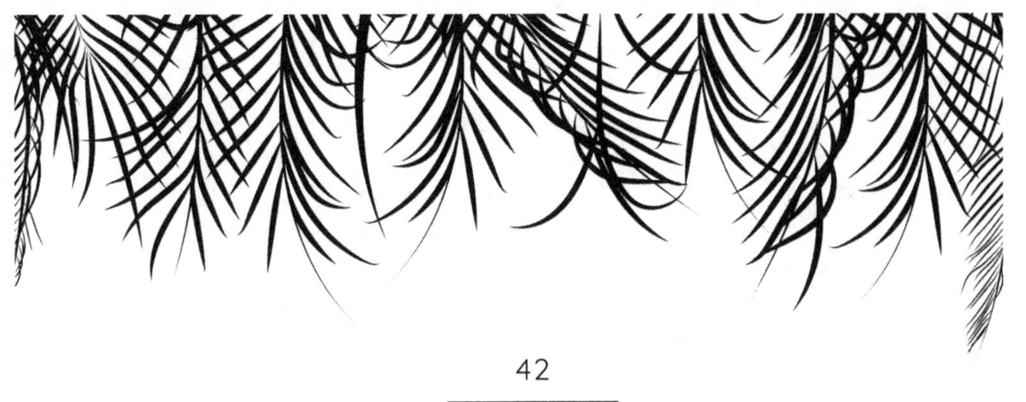

42

———

MAY 20TH

Kai

She was pacing the length of the conference room. It didn't matter that she knew someone was watching her through the hidden cameras. She couldn't sit. She couldn't stand still. This whole situation was freaking her out, and no one was talking to her. Not that she really wanted them to talk to her. Whatever they had to say wasn't going to be good.

Despite holding her hand as they went back inside her house, Waters had not said anything else to her other than an occasional direction of where to stand or where to go.

Demon had given her face another quick once over, focusing particularly on her eyes. He'd asked a couple of quick, cursory questions, probably checking for a concussion, then he'd moved on to the body in the middle of the floor. When he was done, he'd looked up to see her staring at it, then pulled a quilt from off the edge of the sofa and

349

used it to at least take the face out of her sight. He offered her a small nod, then disappeared to whatever his next task was.

While the men had gone through the entire house, none of them had spoken to her, nor had they appeared to be looking at her. But she knew without a shadow of a doubt they were aware of everything to do with her.

The door of the conference room opened, and she whipped around to see Waters come into the room, followed by the rest of his team. He placed the starfish in the center of the table and engaged the security protocols. The windows shielded, the lighting muted to the red emergency tones, and everyone was seated around the table except for her, clutching the back of the chair in front of her.

"Sit, Kubrick." Waters' voice was soft, but it was clearly a command.

"I..."

"Please," he added.

She nodded and nervously sat in the chair she'd been standing behind.

This is not going to go well.

God's disembodied voice chided, "We don't usually see clients once a job is completed."

Kai sneered at the starfish. "I wasn't aware the job you'd been hired for had been completed. You abandoned me mid-consultation and when I was still in danger, despite our not knowing that it had nothing to do with Ka-Bar. And speaking of my brother, he's still swinging out there, so you're not even close to finished with this 'job.'" Someone in the room coughed. She hung her head, eyes closed.

All right, shut that shit down right now. You are in a

fucking mess, and vocalizing your panic is not going to help your cause.

Inhale. Exhale. Eyes opened. "What do you need from me?" she asked.

"Top to bottom, what happened," Waters encouraged her.

She expelled a deep breath before speaking to the group. "Like I told Waters, I spent the night at the studio. I watched the final cut of the film. I went to breakfast. Then I went to a meeting with Big Bird."

"Was it a scheduled meeting?"

"Yes. 9 a.m."

"His request or yours."

"His. Ish. It was the final audit of the budget. He always requires an exit meeting when everything is complete."

"Was anyone else there?"

She spared a glance at Waters before answering. "No. It was just me." His face didn't change, but she swore she saw a tic in his cheek. "His secretary was out front the entire time, though."

"Was the meeting ugly?" Waters asked.

"What meeting with that shitweasel wasn't?" She rubbed her forehead with a sigh. "This one was worse than all the others, though. He started making accusations. Accusing me of stealing the stuff that had disappeared. About me trying to sabotage the film with the accidents. Said I was looking for personal publicity. That I wanted the film shut down so I could collect the insurance money and my fees."

She began shaking again. Demon appeared silently and kneeled next to her chair, putting his jacket around her shoulders. "She needs rest. Not that anyone's going to listen to me." Demon flashed a cranky glance into Waters' eyes.

He snapped his fingers off to his side, and someone put a small bottle of water into his hands. He unscrewed the top and put the bottle and the top on the table in front of her. "Drink," he ordered her. Then he grunted and turned to give an angry look at Waters.

"Thank you, Demon." Placing her hand on top of one of his on the table, she drew his eyes to hers. She tried to reassure him with her gaze, then took a long drink of water. She continued, "By the end of the meeting, my filter had turned off completely. I said some pretty awful things, most of which I don't really remember. It was like this red haze came down over me. Next thing I remember, I was storming out of his office and back to my trailer."

"Would the secretary have heard all that was said?"

"Stapleton and I were both pretty loud from moment one. And I didn't close the door when I went in so that there were potential witnesses. She probably sold tickets to the entire staff like it was the finale before the apocalypse."

Someone snickered quietly.

"Okay, so you went to your trailer. Then what?"

"I called Kowalski. Warned him what Big Bird was planning to do. He said he was hanging up and calling a meeting with the board members. I packed up some things I had there. A few changes of clothes. Some toiletries. Notebooks, that kind of thing. Threw them in my 'vette and drove home."

"What time?"

"I guess around eleven?"

"So you get home, and he's inside the house," Waters growled.

Suddenly, Kai was transferred back in time to those moments earlier today that changed everything.

Dragging what felt like a ten-ton emotional weight, Kai approached her front door. Could things be any worse? Big Bird was molting worse than ever.

Suddenly, she stopped. Something was wrong.

Someone's here.

She wasn't sure how she knew that, but the hair was standing up on her arms. Reaching for the door to get inside quickly, she noticed that the door wasn't completely closed, and the wood around the lock had slivers sticking out like someone had taken a screwdriver to it.

What the hell?

Without thought, Kai pushed the door open and looked around from the doorway. Nothing seemed disturbed. She entered the room and closed the door behind her as silently as possible. The house was as quiet as a tomb. It was unnerving, and she still felt like there were eyes on her.

I need a weapon.

So, instead of turning and walking out the door, then calling the police, she made a move toward the fireplace and the ornamental tools. Before she got more than two steps, someone grabbed her from behind. Immediately, her hands went up to try and pry the arm from around her neck. Whoever had her in their grip was crushing her windpipe. Their arm was covered by a long-sleeved dress shirt, so her teeth and nails were ineffectual in biting or scratching the skin to try and cause pain. And now, the inability to get any air was ramping up her panic, and the edges of her vision were closing to pinpoints surrounded by blackness and stars.

Her brain suddenly flew back to Roatán and her fight training with Waters and the cast.

Go for the testicles, the instep, the eyes, and the nose to inflict the most immediate damage to try and escape.

With the last of the energy she possessed, Kai raised her booted foot and stamped down, grinding her heel viciously into her assailant's instep. The intruder let out a pained yelp, his hold weakening on Kai, then threw her down on the floor. Her head hit the exposed wood arm of the antique couch as she spun out of his reach, bringing a wave of stars and nausea. Still gasping for air from her bruised neck, she tried to scramble away from the man, but she didn't make it more than a foot before he was back on her by grabbing her hair at the scalp and pulling her head back hard.

The pain was excruciating as he used his hold to swing her head back toward the arm of the couch. A second hit, this one directly to her temple, caused Kai to black out.

What was probably only seconds later, she reopened her eyes, trying to shake the edges of unconsciousness free. Everything was blurry, including her first look at who had attacked her. Blurry or not, it was very clear who it was.

Stapleton!

"Craig?" she asked incredulously. Her fear ratcheted up exponentially as she watched him pull a gun from his pocket and aim it in her direction.

"Why couldn't you just be like any other female director, Serrano? Any other woman I could have charmed into paying no attention to anything other than my dick. But not you. You were immune to everything I threw your way, making me resort to having to be clever."

Pissed off now, her filter turned off completely. "If all of your actions were clever, you need to look up the word in the dictionary. I don't think you understand what it means." Her stomach began to roll.

"Shut the fuck up!" he snarled at her, recentering the gun's aim at her face. "I figured, fine, I couldn't get to you. Plan B is always the assistant. They always want to curry favors so that they can make their way up the ladder. Ambition is a heartless bitch. But even there, you screwed everything up. Not only were you immune, but you refused to hire a personal assistant. Nothing like a director with a God complex."

"I don't have a God complex," Kai rasped. She could feel stomach bile trying to creep up her throat.

This is not good. What an understatement.

"Oh, yes, you do. You need to retain all control over all aspects of your project. It was annoying as hell, especially since you were meticulous with your files and records, making my life much harder when it came to hiding what I was doing. You made everything so fucking difficult. Why couldn't you be just as clueless as any other director? Too overwhelmed to pay attention to what was happening around you that wasn't actual filming." He sneered at her. "Then you went and brought in Captain America, and everything became ten times harder because he was just like you. Always watching. Always noticing things."

"I knew it. You were stealing from the production. You bastard. For what? To make it look like I did it? What the hell is it about me that you hate so much you'd rather have a production fail than make you a shit-ton of money?" The ache in her head grew worse, and the room began to swim.

He sneered at her. "It has nothing to do with you, bitch. Although it was about money. A lot of money. Down in those third-world nations, a crate of weapons, even fake ones, goes for more cash than you could possibly imagine. The average person wouldn't know a fake gun from a real one. Imagine how easy it is to intimidate people with weapons in hand. It was perfect. Everything had been going so well until the board insisted on hiring you. I knew I wouldn't be able to control you. Your reputation of being locked down and focused is almost legendary. So I was forced to resort to grander tricks to try and distract you so I could finish out my retrieval of supplies for my buyers."

"You arranged the break-ins to try and scare me. The food poisoning and the injured stuntman to derail filming." Her ears were still ringing, and she felt like she was going to vomit everywhere, but Kai fought to stay conscious, always looking for an opportunity to exploit so that she could try and flee.

"I needed to find a way to scare you. When that didn't work, I had to cast doubt on you. I couldn't run the risk of you completing the final audit on the film with the board. So much for that. But, if an accident were to happen and shut down filming temporarily, the distraction would give me time to doctor the books. Those idiots don't even know how to read their own spreadsheets. But no, you figure out a way to keep filming.

"So, how to get rid of you? I figure home invasions are so tragic, don't you think? Nice and dramatic for our beloved director. And it will be so moving when I give the official statement about the terrible loss to the Hollywood community, especially since you've directed what will surely be the biggest box office smash of the summer. Even if the film were awful, your death would cause people to flock to the theaters to see your last work. Luckily, the filming is brilliant, so it's going to make way more money than even I imagined."

"I thought you said it was worthless," she snapped.

"I would never have admitted to you, even if only Felicity overheard, that what you put together was any good. But now? You won't be there to counter any story I put forth. Don't worry, though. I'll make sure there's an opening dedication in your memory. I sure as hell won't lose any sleep over saying all kinds of wonderful things, remembering you fondly, even hinting at how attracted I was to you, and the loss I now feel that I never had a chance to tell you how I felt about you. Because inside, it will give me indescribable joy that I'm going to be the one to put you down."

Make him mad. Maybe he'll make a mistake. You're going to have to move fast if he gives you an opening.

"There's only one problem, Craig. Kowalski. He knows what you said to me today. I called him as soon as I got to my trailer. He's probably already rounded up the board members by now. Even if you manage to pull off your little home invasion scenario, they'll look at you first, considering the meeting we had earlier."

And then the opening came, as she had hoped. Her confession that she'd actually told someone what had happened forced his hand. He took a step closer to her, straddling her calves and bringing the gun within point-blank range of her head.

"Say goodbye, bitch."

Before he had the wherewithal to pull the trigger, Kai raised her leg up with lightning speed, hitting him full force in his balls, then swiped his feet out from underneath him with the same leg. He went down like a stone, the gun flying out of his hands and coming to rest under the couch.

Kai scrambled to the side, trying to avoid his falling figure and reach the gun, but she wasn't quite fast enough.

Despite the incredible pain he must have been in, he reached for her, managing to wrap both hands around her throat, choking her. She had a split-second choice. Try to get his hands from around her neck or try to reach the gun. Knowing that he might actually strangle her in his rage, Kai chose to go for the gun. Blindly reaching with her fingertips, she struggled to keep conscious. If she gave up for even a second, it would all be over.

All of a sudden, Kai felt something cold and hard under her fingertips. Unfortunately, Stapleton realized she had managed to get herself within range of picking up the weapon. Without letting go of her throat with one hand, his other reached out and wrapped around the wrist of the hand, grasping at the weapon. He slammed her wrist down on the floor hard to try and get her to drop the gun. Between the pain in her head, in her hand, the nausea, and the oxygen deprivation sweeping over her, there was a bang as everything started to go black. Over her, Stapleton stilled in surprise, then fell on top of her. His unmoving weight was crushing her, but his fingers had relaxed from around her throat and wrist, and her fear of being asphyxiated by his body made her push with every ounce of strength she could muster until she rolled him over and off of her.

Like a crab, Kai scrambled sideways to clear Stapleton's body. It was clear he was dead. If the pool of blood forming quickly underneath him wasn't enough proof, the wide-eyed, lifeless stare in his eyes was. She whimpered, clutching the weapon tightly in both hands.

Oh my fucking God, what have I done?

Had she been thinking clearly, she would have rationalized that it was him or her. That he had tried to stage a home invasion to cover his tracks. That he had meant to kill her. But at the moment, she was far from rational. What the hell was she going to do now?

SHE GULPED DOWN THE LAST OF HER WATER, squeezing the bottle so tight it collapsed.

Waters pried the bottle from her hands. "Why did you end up in an Uber, Kubrick?"

"Honestly, I've no idea. Probably because of the gun. I knew I needed to get rid of it, so I fled out the back door and straight to the pond. I threw it in, and the next thing I knew, I was out on the back road. I called Demon on the number he gave me, and then I caught an Uber when I got down to the main drag. Then you took me back to the house, the rest of you showed up, and that's it."

There was silence.

"Ka-Bar is temporarily on the back burner. We have a fuck of a disaster to clean up, gentlemen. Let's get to it.

"Midas, double-check all communications between Kubrick and Tribe to make sure they have been destroyed. Next, find that Uber driver and erase all traces of her digitally. We can't do anything about her being there physically, but it's hard to go beyond he-said-she-said when there's no record of a fare. Then get scrubbing cameras everywhere from the bar, to the studio, to her house, especially any security cameras in the neighborhood that show footage relating to us. Do the same for Stapleton to her home. Erase that shit so it looks like nothing has happened other than Kubrick's normal traffic. Make sure to pull all cameras from her home.

"TB, make that shitfuck disappear."

"Demon. Get to the pond. Find that gun and destroy it.

"Nemo and Steel, start on housecleaning.

"Waters... get her locked down.

"Steel and Demon will have the first shift of babysitting the happy couple at whatever bolt-hole he chooses, then TB and Nemo will take over. I want a twelve-hour rotation until we clean up this goddamn mess.

Then God clicked off the line.

The men got up and scattered their different ways, which left Kai in the conference room with Waters. He got up, pulled a couple of water bottles out of the refrigerator under the side table, and returned to his seat next to her. He twisted off the cap and set it in front of her next to the empty one from Demon. "Drink."

On autopilot, she did as she was told. She felt so numb. Almost like she was watching events unfold instead of taking part in them. "I don't understand why you're helping me."

"You're in some serious shit. You think we're gonna let you swing when Big Bird tried to kill you?"

"You left me." She hated how whiny that sounded. Like a spineless teenager.

"Yes. I did. I didn't have a choice."

"Maybe. But you didn't have to leave the way you did."

"Possibly. But I can't change it now."

She sighed. "No, you can't. I'm sorry things went as they did. I wish..." She shook her head. "It doesn't matter what I wish." She paused. "He hates me."

And there's the whiplash.

"Who does?"

"God. I've made a mess, and now he feels like he has to get me out of it because I'm Ka-Bar's sister."

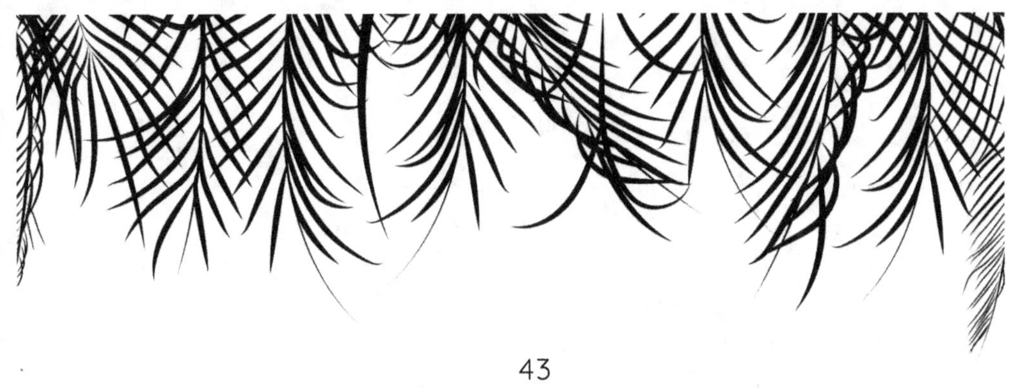

43

———

MAY 20TH

Waters

WATERS PUT HIS WATER BOTTLE DOWN AND LEANED ON his forearms folded in front of him on the table. "What if he does? I've never known you to be concerned with whether or not someone hates you. I'll set aside that part of your psyche for right now because I know you're scared."

He raised a hand to her mouth as it opened up to deny it.

"Don't even try," he warned.

Kubrick closed her mouth and looked down at the tabletop.

Oh, hell no, woman. Don't you dare pull inside yourself.

He reached across the table and, with one finger, tipped her chin back up so that she'd look him in the eye. "Now, putting aside the 'why' question, where the hell do you get that he hates you?"

"You know, I had to triple the rate I originally offered to

361

get him to agree to actually consult. Now he's really going to charge me out the ass for getting you all involved in my mess. Especially since he isn't calling the police."

"You are correct. From the get-go, he hated taking this job, but he did it because he knew you were in danger. In order to make it look on the up-and-up, he made it as painful as possible for the studio pricks. If it hadn't been for Ka-Bar calling in Steel's marker, he wouldn't have even met with you. But he did, so that got you in the door. We're not exactly in the straight and narrow kind of business. When he thought this was somehow connected to your brother, there was no chance in hell he wasn't going to take the job, but he had to make it look good. In all honesty, he doesn't like anyone. Even us."

Don't even think that last part is a lie.

Waters cleared his throat. "We just had two separate things going on at once and got blindsided into believing they were connected. That should never have happened. Unfortunately, there were some extenuating circumstances."

He watched as Kubrick chose to ignore that uncomfortable conversation.

"Well, his dickishness didn't stop when he signed on the dotted line," she argued. "Whatever test you seem to think I passed, I obviously didn't. So, what other evidence do I have? One, the nickname. Two, the barking at me. Three, he talked about me like I wasn't even in the room today. Four, he makes unreasonable demands that compromise everything about me, my job, and my situation by telling you to lock me down. And last but not least, he makes me feel like I'm just another Hollywood princess in an ivory tower who needs rescuing by one of his stud castle guards."

Knowing an actual grin would get him a kick to the solar

plexus, and from experience with her during training, those hurt like a sonofabitch, Waters was grinning from ear to ear. On the inside.

Stud castle guard, am I? Good to know.

"Okay, stop. You are so far from living in an ivory tower and requiring protection, it's ridiculous."

"Really? Could have fooled me."

"Since you're dying to overanalyze this clusterfuck, let's clear up some things."

Her face looked down at the tabletop again.

"Hey! Look at me," he whispered. This time, he gently grabbed her chin and turned her face up to his. Instead of letting go completely, he cradled the unbruised side of her face with his hand. "That was not a cut at you. I'm trying to explain some things to you so that your head's in the right space."

His thumb stroked the curve of her cheek. "One, all our clients get nicknames so that sensitive information doesn't get into anyone's hands who might manage to listen in. We use codewords for all kinds of things, and your practices with your filming philosophies played nicely into that. Why he chose that moniker is on him, so I can't give you the whys and wherefores.

"Two, he barks at absolutely everyone, me included. He's a big junkyard dog that's used to puffing up and making a lot of noise to get people to jump to his bidding. Tongue lashing is part of the gig, and it hurts worse than any flaying of skin. The average person hates yelling. They will do almost anything to avoid conflict, so they try to pussyfoot around things. Yelling implies conflict, so God yells to cut through the bullshit and get done what needs to be done.

"Three, he knows you're in the room. Everyone on the team does. It's hard not to know you're there. Trust me on that one. Whole fuckin' useless group of them are half in love with you." He tucked the last part under his breath, but she must have heard him because she scrunched her eyebrows together in confusion.

So clueless for someone so smart.

"He's treating you like an inanimate target so that he doesn't lose it over what this pathetic shitfucker did to you. God talks around you to create a disconnect, which allows him to think clearly about an assignment.

"Four, he makes 'unreasonable demands'—and let me just add that I'm hurt that having to stay with me seems 'unreasonable' to you—that compromise your everyday life because this situation is that fucking serious, baby. You ignore just one of his orders, and it could be the difference between you being able to go back to living your life the way it was before and being locked up. The police won't look much further than the obvious, and then your ass really will be in jail, at least until someone with a brain cell sees it was clearly self-defense.

"And, last but not least, God is in charge of every life that touches him. If we get all *Knights of the Round Table* on you, it's because your safety is important to us.

"Babe, you put yourself in my hands for help and protection, and I would still take a bullet for you. I would die to protect you. By extension, that means my tribe would do the same, including God, whether you want them to or not. And that comes complete with a castle guard.

"However, make no mistake, Kubrick, you are not a 'Hollywood Princess.' God's way of disconnecting, maybe, but you're one of the strongest, most capable, kick-ass women we know."

"Yeah, real kick-ass. Broke down like a teenage girl over what happened at my place. Sorry about that."

He covered her clenched hands sitting on the tabletop. "In case I need to remind you, baby, there was a fucking dead body in your living room. Someone attacked you intending to end your life, for fuck's sake. And you defended yourself with equal force. Of course you fell apart a little. Taking a life, intentionally or unintentionally, has a cost that comes with it. And later on? There was absolutely, positively no reason to go back into that house, but you did. You did not need to deal with that shit a second time. The fact that you had to deal with it for the first time has made me want to breathe fire."

"Pisses me off that now I have a blood stain on my antique wood flooring. That's never going to come out, and I'm going to have to remember that fucktard every time I go in my living room." She snorted. "That is if I don't go to prison."

Waters grinned and leaned back in his seat.

There she is. She's back.

"You're not going to prison. The team is taking care of your house, Midas is going to make it so there's no record of him going anywhere near the direction of your house. Demon went diving for the gun. He'll probably have it by the time I get you home."

Her face blanched. "God told TB to make Big Bird disappear."

"Don't worry about the details. I promise. No one will know. We have a lot of skills that you're better off not knowing about."

"You're covering up a murder."

"No, it's not a murder. You defended yourself. But we're not exactly a regular channel kind of group. We're not 'good guys,' Kubrick. We're hired to do sketchy things all of the time. Even knowing that, your brother sent you to us because we get shit done."

"I'm scared, Waters. Beyond scared."

He brushed her hair back behind her ear. "I know. But we've got you now."

"But—"

"Stop. Now, I'm going to take you back to my house in the hills, and we'll hang out there for a few days while everything sorts itself out. Did you have any meetings or projects in the next few days?"

"No. I was scheduled to go out of town. I usually take some time right after a film closes up shop."

"Perfect. That's still going to happen, just not how you planned." He stood up and reached out for her hand. "C'mon, babe. Let's go. We've got a drive in front of us."

WATERS' HOUSE WAS JUST UNDER TWO HOURS FROM the heart of L.A. in the rolling hills of Escondido. The ride was silent, with Kubrick staring out the passenger side window the entire way. When they arrived at the A-frame luxury cabin, she simply stared out the front window at it. Waters watched her process what she was seeing.

"Wait for me to open your door." He hopped out of his truck and then walked around to her side of the vehicle. "C'mon. Let's get you inside."

He put her just in front of him as they walked to the door. When they got onto the porch, he made sure to cover the entire back of her with his body as he disarmed the security system.

When he ushered her through the door, he watched her take in her surroundings, trying to see the house from her perspective. Vaulted ceiling. Pine floors that gleamed. Log walls that matched the outside, although there was insulation between the inside wall and the outside wall. A kitchen with stainless steel appliances and a kitchen island breaking it apart from the living room. A stone fireplace. Floor-to-ceiling windows showed that there was a second-floor deck, both windows and deck giving a spectacular view of the orchards on the side of the mountain that spread down into the valley. A staircase that went upstairs to the open bridge hallway connecting the two sides of the gallery formed the bottom of the U-shape to bedrooms on the left and right side of the structure. On the left was a closed-off room. On the right was a loft guest room the kids had shared with each other or friends when the family vacationed there. Or the occasional other guests that Tribe housed there.

Her eyes and nose scrunched up again.

So fucking cute.

"Not what I pictured for you."

He pocketed his keys and reset the security system. "What did you picture?"

"Honestly? A bunker."

"I read so military that you imagine me living underground like a doomsday prepper?"

She shrugged and hugged herself. "I guess I never thought about where you lived. Everything with us was always so right-here-right-now that it wasn't something that existed in my head."

He left that commentary alone. He was on dangerous ground here and didn't want it all to go sideways by saying the wrong thing. "You tired?"

"No. Amped, actually."

"The crash will come."

"I don't have anything with me. How long will I be here?"

"Cherry went out to grab you some things from the stores. The guys will bring them up later."

She whirled around. "God said they'd be babysitting?"

"They'll be so invisible, you'll forget they're even out there. As for a timeline, probably a week. Maybe two." He shoved his hands in his pockets. "Why don't you have a seat?"

She moved to the leather couch, and he watched her consider sitting down. Reading her right now was painfully easy. He could almost see the wheels turning, envisioning the leather couch in the War Room. He swallowed hard and tried to bury his own memories of that couch.

She jerked suddenly ninety degrees and instead sat on the edge of the matching leather chair, her hands underneath her thighs. "Thank you," she said so softly he almost missed it.

"Thank you for what, babe?"

"Finding Zahra and the baby. Finding Jacques' family. Taking care of them and making sure they're safe."

"No need to thank me." He sat on the edge of the coffee table in front of her, elbows on his knees, leaning toward her. "I'm just sorry we're still hunting for your brother. His gifts, which are so valuable to the military, are the very reason we're struggling to find him. But we will find him. It's just going to take time and patience."

Weakly, Kubrick smiled at him. "And we know how good I am at being patient."

"Don't sell yourself short. You're patient when it comes to a lot of things."

"Not so much when it comes to self-control."

"Self-control is overrated."

She slouched. "Ka-Bar could have used some, and he wouldn't have been in this situation. And neither would I, or you and your team."

"While it is true that, in hindsight, it would have been much better for him to have just brought her to the embassy for sanctuary, we have no idea why he didn't. He might have had a damn good reason. Then again, sometimes love blinds people to the obvious, and they make decisions that later are defined as 'What the fuck was I thinking?' moments. No one is immune to those, even the most brilliant of us."

They both knew that Waters wasn't just referring to Ka-Bar at that moment.

He continued, "In his defense, I think sanctuary was the initial plan. But something must have told him that it wasn't a viable option. When I spoke to her, Zahra said that he couldn't get her out of her father's compound without creating an international incident. Then he got a visit from one of her father's security team who threatened him to find out where Zahra was. That was when she took matters into her own hands and disappeared without telling anyone, trying to protect Ka-Bar. Both sides thought the other was responsible for her vanishing act when neither knew she was on her own."

Kubrick shook her head, murmuring, "Fuckin' Kent."

"Hardly surprising how it all went down. If it had just been about Zahra, seventh child of seven, and the third daughter, her family probably would have been pissed but just written her off. Some of the most traditional families in any culture don't have much use for daughters. Especially ones that have fallen in love with 'the infidel.' But three of the brothers have died in military action, and the baby is a boy, so..." His voice trailed off.

She nodded in agreement. "A possible heir to the family name."

"She's Ka-Bar's wife—"

"So she's tribe. I know."

"Exactly."

Fuck. Here goes nothing.

"Kubrick?" He expelled a pent-up breath of nerves. "I need to apologize to you."

Kubrick's posture became ramrod straight; what little color she'd had was now leaking from her face, jaw clenching, and eyes going blank.

"You were right. The way I left. I should have waited. I wasn't thinking clearly. God ordered us out immediately, and I was angry. Unfortunately, you were the one who suffered for it, and it shouldn't have been that way."

"It's okay, Waters."

"No, it's not, Kubrick, and you shouldn't be accepting of it. I could have at least waited for you to wake up, to be clearheaded. To explain what was going on. Instead, I fell into old habits even when I knew it wasn't how you deserved to find out what was happening. It was easier for me to leave like I did, but I should have worried about was what was easier or better for you. I have no excuse. I've been making decisions based on a fucked-up paradigm for so long that when I needed to make a really important decision and do it right, I totally screwed it up."

He both felt and saw her armor go up before she turned her eyes onto him. "It's okay, Waters. It's not like we didn't know that we would be separating eventually. It just happened before we thought it would. And you needed to go. If you hadn't, things might have gone much worse for Zahra and her son. I'm not angry."

He reached over and brushed the unruly strand of blonde hair that had fallen forward and settled it back behind her ear. "Maybe not. But I hurt you, and that was the last thing I wanted to do. I should have listened to the team. I should have ignored God." He reached for her hands, prying them out from under her legs, and held them, brushing his thumbs over her knuckles. "I should have stayed."

"But to what end?"

"Baby, you were left alone and vulnerable. You had Demon to be a buffer for you for the last three weeks on set, sure. But now, here at home, you were left off even more vulnerable, and the situation could have ended up so much worse. I'm absolutely sick thinking what could have been if you weren't so amazingly you."

"Don't, Waters. I'm fine. Besides, the end result would have been the same for us. And unfortunately, now I'm just going to have to go through all that pain again." She pulled her hands back from his to cover her face. Her shoulders started to tremble. "I'm so fucking weak. I've never needed anyone, and for the past few months, I've been dependent on you or Demon to get me through."

Waters felt his molars grinding a bit at the thought of Demon helping her with anything, but he'd done that himself. His watch pinged. He stood. "Speak of the devil."

I'm going to fucking kill him. His timing is shit.

He crossed to the door and flipped up a hidden panel. On the security camera screen, Demon and Steel appeared in the Yukon, turning at the mile marker to the cabin.

Waters sent back a quick text and then deactivated the system so he could open the door when they arrived and let them in. He looked over at Kubrick, who hadn't moved an inch since she sat down.

"Look, why don't you go upstairs and lie down. Try to take a nap. The adrenaline crash is coming. Take a shower, and then you're going to need to eat. And I'll need whatever clothes you have on right now."

"Why?"

"Bloodstains. Part of the cleanup process."

She looked down at her lap and nodded. "Right." Stiffly, she got up from the chair and went up the staircase. Once she was out of sight, he let out the breath he didn't realize he'd been holding.

How the hell do I fix this?

STEEL HAD PARKED THE YUKON IN THE CAMOUFLAGE carport about a half mile down the road, and they walked in. Demon didn't bother to come up onto the porch, but he pierced Waters with a hard stare as he stood at the bottom of the cabin's steps.

The chance to get your shit together and fix it has been dropped into your lap. Don't be a douchebag.

Message received.

Waters gave him a single nod, and Demon grunted as he went around the side of the cabin to find a position to watch from.

Steel stepped up to one stair from the top of the porch and handed him a duffle bag. "You might want to open that first before giving it to her. Cherry threw some party favors in there. Might not be good if she saw that first."

"Shit," Waters muttered. "Can't you people stay out of this?"

"Nope," his friend said with a slight grin. Then Steel jumped to the ground and went in the opposite direction of Demon to find another overwatch position.

Waters took the duffle bag inside, locked the door, and rearmed the system. He placed the duffle bag on the counter. Opening it, he removed the extra package from the top of the bag with the sticky note on it that said, "Remind her!" and then a smiley face that was winking at him. "Good grief. Sex doesn't solve all problems," he murmured.

He stopped in mid-zipping of the bag. What the fuck? Since when did he spout shit like that, even just to himself? Perhaps his Navy buddies had been right with his name. Way too sensitive for a guy.

Putting the bag at the foot of the stairs, then throwing the box in the downstairs bathroom in the back of a drawer, he headed to the kitchen.

Five steps out the door, he turned around and came back to open the box and tore three condoms off the strip, placing them in his cargo pocket.

Power of positive thinking? Obsessive Planning Tendencies for contingencies, right?

He shook his head. Time to go see what food was around so he could make Kai dinner.

Kai. Not Kubrick.

She's not a client, and she hasn't been for a long time.

He had taken the duffle bag upstairs and found her asleep in the open-air guest room. He would have preferred her to have picked the primary bedroom since it could be closed off, but somehow, he knew that she had found that too uncomfortable, given how things had ended between them. After placing the bag on the dresser where she'd be sure to see it, he took the quilt from the rocking chair in the corner and unfurled it, laying it over her sleeping figure. Gently, so as not to wake her, he brushed his lips to her temple, then left as silently as he had arrived.

He stood for a long while at the living room windows, looking out over the valley at the orange groves. While this upcoming conversation with Kai about their relationship was littered with minefields, he would navigate it as best he could. In all honesty, he had no idea how she was going to respond, but he did know that if she shut him down, he wasn't going to give up. She was worth the fight. How it would all work out between her job, his job, and God was the bigger issue. The team treated the whole situation like he was making way more of the situation than it was, but Waters wasn't so sure that was true.

The sun had set by the time he heard Kai moving around and then the running water of the shower. Waters had just finished taking the baked chicken and oven-roasted potatoes out of the oven when he heard the creaky stair he'd learned to avoid as a teen when he or Sarah were sneaking out. He turned around to see her two steps from the bottom, with damp hair and clean clothes. Cherry had packed the duffle filled with Kai's go-to wardrobe—leggings and baggy shirts—including the oversized, long-sleeved Dodgers T-shirt she was currently wearing. He couldn't help but grin. "Well, that should make you feel a little more comfortable."

Kai gave a small smile. "Something smells good."

"I'm no master chef, but it's comfort food. Come, sit down."

He watched her sit down at the table, clearly noticing he had put the two settings next to each other on a corner instead of across from one another. He put the baking dish on the table and went to the refrigerator for water while she helped herself. "It's filtered water," he said as he set down the pitcher.

"I'm not that much of a snob that I won't drink tap water," she joked.

"Ewww. But I am. Yuck." That got a laugh out of her. "Sleep okay?"

She nodded. "Yes, I feel a little better. I don't even remember lying down, actually. You were right about the crash."

He nodded. "Some of the best sleep I ever had was in the Navy after missions went to hell."

They ate in silence for a while. He could tell she was trying to figure out how to have the conversation she wanted to have with him, so he let her grind her gears to figure it out. He knew from their time together that she needed the processing time.

Weird how much alike we are that way.

Uncomfortably, she cleared her throat and put her fork down. It reminded him of the day in the diner when she first let on that she thought she wasn't on his level.

Think it's more the other way around. I don't deserve her. Then again, I don't have her again. Yet. Hopefully.

"So, who showed up?"

He wiped his mouth with his napkin and took a sip of his water. "Demon and Steel." He caught the slight grimace. "Something wrong?"

"I'm just surprised Demon agreed to be here. He's not the happiest with you."

"He's not doing it for me. He's doing it for you."

"I didn't sleep with him!"

He reached for her hand and held it beneath his on the tabletop. "Relax, I know you didn't. I didn't mean it that way. I'm not sure how much of his trust I've lost or if I can ever gain it back. He's angry at me for leaving. Can't say I blame him. I'm angry at myself, too. However, that's neither here nor there now."

"So, what happens now?"

"We lock down here until God gives me the all-clear for you to return to your life."

Her eyes bore into his, searching for something. For the first time with her, he wasn't sure what. Normally, she was an open book, but this was uncharted territory for him, and he had no clue where she was headed.

"So, I go my way, live my life; you go yours, live your life." Firmly, she pulled her hand from under his and stood up. "Noted. I'll do my best to stay out of your way until he gives the all-clear."

Fuck. So much for trying to be subtle. When did that ever work with her, dumbass?

She began to move with purpose toward the stairs. He slid out from the table, following her and catching her at the foot of the stairs. He grabbed her elbow, spun her around to face him, and leaned her up against the wall.

"Don't, Kai. Don't run away or shut down on me." His grip on her arms gentled but still denied her the ability to continue to run away. "I fucked up, okay? Multiple times. I get it. I'm always so sure of everything, but you come along, and that all gets shot to shit. Now I'm floundering, saying the wrong things, or not saying things I should, doing the exact opposite of what I should be doing. I'm all sorts of fucked up when the last thing I want to do is drive you further away."

Her chest was heaving, and her eyes were glassy. No tears, but it probably wouldn't take much for some to fall. He stepped as close to her as he could, pressing his forehead to hers. "Please don't run again."

"I didn't run the first time."

"No, you didn't. But you started to just now, and that is not going to happen. I'll keep chasing you until I catch you because I know you don't really want to go."

"What choice do I have? Your team knows how I feel about you, including your boss. I know the rule. The rule hasn't changed. And I can't come back into your life for another brief period of time only to have you leave me again."

"Fuck the rule," he growled.

I can't avoid this. I have to tell her. Maybe then she'll understand.

He stood up straight, dropped his hands from her, and took a step back. "Look, I have to tell you something. It's not going to be pretty. In fact, it's going to be fucking ugly. But I don't know how else to make you understand why I left without a fight."

He could almost feel the blood draining from his body. The one thing he guarded more than his name. The one thing he'd sworn he'd never talk about, and he was going to tell her.

He sat down hard on the stairs.

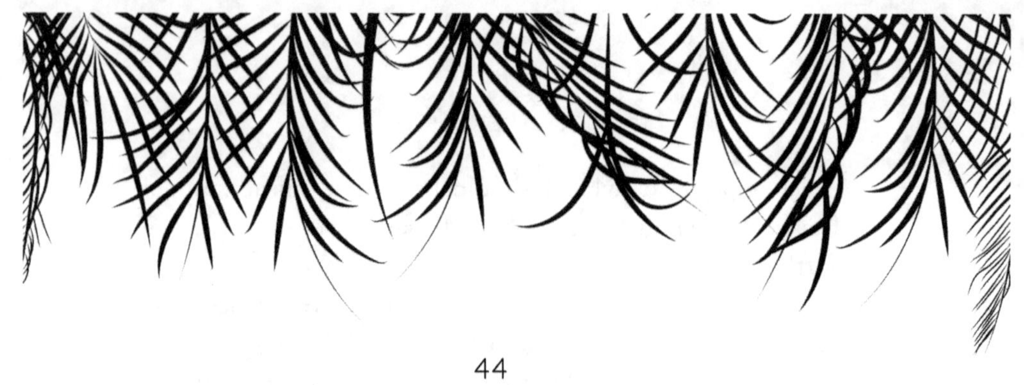

44

TWO YEARS EARLIER

Waters

CRACKS WHIPPING AGAINST HUMAN FLESH. SCREAMS echoing off of stone walls. Sobs falling like the dripping water from the stones. Pleas begging Waters to shut down his hearing and sight. Then suddenly... silence from the punished.

My fault, my fault, my fault.

He could hear voices in Arabic. Laughter at crude jokes. While he knew enough of Arabic languages to get the gist of what was being said, his brain refused to process the horrors that were about to be performed next.

There it was. A moan so quiet it was barely audible.

No, no, no, no, no, stay quiet, don't let them know you're awake, no, please, no, make it stop.

Ripping next, as if something was being torn from top to bottom, a sound louder than any clap of thunder he'd ever

378

heard. More laughter and the sound of a heavy table being dragged across the room. The rattling of keys and the click of shackles being opened and then closed again. More moans, a little louder than before. She was coming to.

No, no, no, no, no, no.

A clunk as her body hit the table. The harsh voices, the taunts to the woman who lay barely conscious on the table, more ripping, and an agonizing yelp of pain, the laughter and obvious joy of what was to come.

The irony that his face escaped any sort of beating was not lost on him. Broken noses, jaws, lost teeth, damaged eyes, cuts, and abrasions that took months to heal—those were the foundations of torture sessions for soldiers caught in enemy territory. But not for him. Oh no. His captor, the bastard, had wanted Waters to be able to see what he'd ordered done to her. His heart was breaking.

My fault, all my fault.

Someone crouched in front of him, holding a destroyed piece of material. Blue like the sea, silver zipper, a layered piece that had once been a kick pleat. His tormentor rubbed the remains of the filthy, bloodied garment in his face.

Waters refused to give him the satisfaction of looking up. More than that, he was afraid to. He was a coward. He couldn't bear what would happen now.

The men laughed, and his tormentor moved behind him, using the material like a noose to pull his head up and back. Waters kept his eyes closed. He would not look. How could he?

Using the other hand, his tormentor spread his fingers over the top of Waters' head and down to his eyes to pull back the lids to force Waters to see the scene unfold before him.

He forced himself to go inside his head. His eyes were open, but he refused to see what was going to happen. If he did, he'd never unsee it. It would drive him mad with grief, and he would not survive it. Not that he would want to, anyway.

And so it began. She screamed and screamed again to Waters to shut himself down. The more she yelled to him, the more the men laughed at her, taunted her, and egged each other on. He heard slaps and punches. Thumping as the table rocked with each grunt and groan that rose to a fever pitch, then stopped, then started up again but in different pitches than those that came before. Crescendo, halt, repeat. Over and over, he had no clue how many times. Eventually, the screams became muffled gurgling and gagging combined with even cruder taunts. And the other noises continued amidst the new ones, a sickening melody and harmony.

They'd been promised a reward, and in their eyes, they had certainly received it.

The man behind Waters lowered his head to Waters' ear and whispered horrific things to him, but he did not hear them. He'd managed to retreat so far back into his brain that it was all just static.

And then, suddenly, it was over. He was released from his tormentor's hold and the makeshift noose. Waters' head dropped forward, and his sight and hearing returned.

Even in this state of being beaten within an inch of death, he could actually hear a void in the room. Without asking, he knew she was gone. He hoped his own end would be brutal. He deserved it.

My fault, I caused this, all my fault.

The silence seemed to vibrate, which was odd. It was as if he could feel the ceiling shake, reverberating down through the hook in the ceiling, through the chains that held him upright on his knees, his ankles chained and shackled to bolts in the floor. Who knew that silence could be sensed through touch?

The vibrations increased, and dust from the ceiling sifted down onto him. An explosion. Rapid gunfire. Yelling in Arabic and English. Screams of surprise and pain went quickly silent with the thuds of his jailors hitting the ground.

As the dust settled, he heard fast, booted feet approaching the chamber and then a horror-filled whisper. "Jesuchristo!"

Steel.

The booted feet approached the table with the woman's body splayed upon it. Softly, the voice spoke into a throat mic, "Sarah Miller is here. She's deceased." Waters registered the slight crack in Steel's voice. "Demon, I need blankets. Sheets. Something." He walked over to Waters, blocked the view of her body with his, and lifted Waters' head. "I also have Waters. Massive trauma. TB, Demon, ándele, brothers."

Oh my god, just too late, just too late, just too late.

It didn't matter if they let him see her or not. His imagination created worse visuals than anything he would have actually seen.

Steel returned to the lifeless body of Sarah Miller. There was the clinking and clanking of chains being moved, followed shortly by running feet into the chamber. An abrupt stop. "Oh, feck!" Demon's whisper did nothing to hide the medic's agony at the sight.

"Keep it together," Steel whispered. "Give me the blanket. He can't see this. Go check on Waters." There was a rustling of materials that he knew Steel was using to cover Sarah's body.

Demon tore his gaze from the woman's body, rushed over to Waters, and began a quick examination just as TB's massive frame came through the chamber door. The terminator-sized giant grunted at the shrouded sight of Sarah Miller, then focused on Demon's examination of their teammate. The medic clicked into his Bluetooth. "Nemo, we need immediate assistance at the LZ. Shattered kneecaps; multiple broken ribs; bloodied chest; bloodied back; all open wounds look on the verge of infection; both shoulders dislocated. The lights are on, but nobody's home." He looked up at TB. "He's not walking out of here. Careful when you take him down."

Gently, TB and Demon freed his ankles from the floor bolts, then turned his body one hundred eighty degrees on the suspension hook, which burned like a sonofabitch. He'd gladly take the pain if only it meant Sarah was still alive. Now that she was dead, nothing mattered.

He felt the chains go slack, his wrists released, and someone had his body in their grasp, keeping it from falling completely to the floor. "This is gonna hurt, Boss." Waters felt himself get slung over TB's shoulders in a fireman's carry.

"Steel," Waters groaned. "He needs to—"

"Under control, Boss, he's got her. Close your eyes," TB ordered and began to carry him out of the chamber and to the waiting chopper.

As they exited, he heard a prayer being spoken in Spanish, which his brain translated.

"We beseech Thee, O Lord, in Thy mercy, to have pity on the soul of Thy handmaid; do Thou, Who hast freed her from the perils of this mortal life, restore to her the portion of everlasting salvation. Through Christ our Lord, Amen."

With that, Waters passed out.

THE SILENCE INSIDE THE CABIN WAS AS HOLLOW AS THE silence the day Sarah had died. He had no idea how long they sat there, but when he finally freed himself from the memories, the sky outside his windows was filled only with stars.

"When God recruited me for Tribe, I brought in my sister with me. Our parents had recently died. She had just graduated college. Fluent in over a dozen languages and had an eidetic memory. She was amazing. Between her skill set and mine, God had the perfect foundation for bringing in work. We set to recruit the field team.

"Two years in, we were hired to reclaim some children who had been captured by traffickers. They were set to be auctioned. We went in, broke the supply chain, and brought back fifteen girls and boys between the ages of seven and twelve, and six women in their late teens. We were careless. Thought we were untouchable and didn't clean up after ourselves. We left too many clues about who we were, and that organization somehow figured out how to find us. So they took Sarah.

"We had the intel to go get her, but God ordered us to stand down. Reminded me that I had advised a family some time earlier, in the exact same situation, that a rescue mission at that point in time would be futile. Used my own analysis against me. But it was my baby sister, so of course, it was different. I took off on my own. I convinced myself that I didn't need him or my team. That I could get Sarah back by myself.

"These assholes were notorious. Still are. There isn't a day that goes by that I don't think about her. About them. About what they did to her. And all because I pissed them off by intercepting a single shipment of kids and women. They used my sweet, innocent Sarah against me, and I was so angry. So blind. So stupid. The only thing that changed in the outcome was that I watched her die. I have no way of knowing if it would have been as horrifying and painful had I not been there. All I do know is that I bear the guilt of knowing that she definitely suffered because she was my sister, and I was there."

"The tattoo," Kubrick murmured. "The 'S' is for Sarah. The Kraken is the Titan, the monster who took her. And its tentacles are the pain that squeezes your heart where you hold her memory."

He nodded.

She knows me so well.

"When I woke up back home, I understood exactly why God made the rule that he did. I vowed it was fine with me. That I supported it." Then he looked at her for the first time, seeing the tears running down her face, the horror in her expression. "For two fucking years, I have lived that goddamned rule like it was the only way to breathe. She may have been my sister, but I extended that fear to any woman who came into my orbit. No attachments. I couldn't risk another innocent woman being taken because of her connection to me. If I could, I avoided being involved directly with women clients. Then I walked into that goddamn conference room and saw you, and it all went to hell.

"I tried so hard, baby, to resist you. I really did. Then, when that failed, I told myself that I could indulge short term because I knew your high-profile job and my need to be low profile kept me from being able to be more than a short-term affair. My job is dangerous enough for me, but feeling anything for you beyond sexual attraction would make you vulnerable. Someone figures out what you are to me, they can use you to get to me, just like they did with Sarah. So I held back as long as I could." He huffed out a breath. "We both know how that ended up.

"The guys have known from day one how far into my soul you are. Midas showed them the video of that meeting, and the razzing began. Then I doubled down on how gone I was the minute you wrapped yourself around me on camera in Roatán. And back here, when they showed up at your house and saw you and I wrapped around each other in my truck, any denial I would have tried to make would have been useless. How I feel about you is no secret.

"And for the past six weeks that we were apart, I spent most of my time distracted, wondering what you were doing, where you were. I couldn't stop thinking about you. I was miserable and took endless shit from the guys, pushing, taunting, begging me to go after what I wanted."

He reached his hands out to her, which she grasped tightly, and he pulled her down onto his lap, burying his head in the waterfall of her hair below her ear. "You want to know how much I wanted to be with you? I dialed your number to call you or text you, which had to be twenty times a day, but then I refused to hit the send button, convinced I was fooling myself that you would want to hear from me. How could you after the way I left?

"Then you plummeted back into my life today asking for my help, and I knew. The moment I saw you in that bar,

I was lost. And when you wrapped yourself around me in the cab of my truck, I told myself I was seriously fucked because then I had to make you mine, whether you wanted me or not. And I did not care how it happened. I swore I would find a way to be with you. To hell with high profile. To hell with God and his stupid rule.

"I love you, Kai. I should have said those words back in Roatán when you told me. I meant to. I was just so damn shocked, and then everything happened so fast after that. But I'm saying them now because I am not going to lose you again, Kai." Then he took her mouth with his, and the explosion hit.

Hell, she tastes even better than I remember.

When he came up for air, she dragged in a ragged breath, her eyes in a pleasure haze he had created there with his confession. She stroked the hair at his hairline, looking like she was memorizing every part of his face. "No takebacks, Taj."

He shivered a little at hearing his name whispered from her mouth. "No takebacks, Kai."

"No holding back, either. I want it all. I've wanted you since I met you, and when I got to have you in Roatán, my brain couldn't stop imagining all the things I wanted to do to you. With you."

He stopped breathing.

He blinked.

He felt like a captive tiger that had just been let out of his cage to roam the jungle.

And big, bad kitty wants to mark his territory.

His voice dropped again, and it sounded raw even to him. "I'm going to take you to my bed now, baby. Say no now if you're not ready. I'll wait to fuck you if today has been too much, but either way, that sweet body is next to mine tonight and every night going forward. I've had six weeks to create a whole list of things to do to you that could take days before I even think about sliding my cock into that pussy of yours."

Honestly? Could I go any more caveman on her? Fuck!

He grabbed her tightly by the hand and pulled her up the stairs to the main bedroom. Once inside, he kicked the door shut and leaned her up against it. One hand around her waist, his hips crushing hers to the door, he punched the code panel next to the door, and the locks engaged. The windows shuttered, and a blackout door slid over the bullet-proof sliding glass door to the deck. Another button created a soft glow from a small light on the mantle across from his bed. "Steel enforcements in the walls? Seriously? Your bedroom is a panic room?"

"We use the cabin as a safe house occasionally." Hands bruising her hips, he put his forehead to hers, eyes seeming to blur as they bored into hers. He growled again. "Say yes or no, baby. I need the word."

She opened her mouth to answer, but he cut her off before she could push anything out of her mouth. "Say yes, and I fuck you until your throat is raw from screaming my name. Say no, and we curl up in my bed, and I hold you until you fall asleep. Either way works for me because I know that we'll get to the first option another day. But know that if you say yes, there's no going back. You. Will. Be. Mine. Not just tonight but going forward. I will not hold back tonight or any night after. If you're in my bed, you will get whatever pleasure I can give you every night. And just know, I can give you sweet, but I will take you every way you can imagine and then some. Can you handle me?"

The irony was not lost on him that the question he

asked her was near the same question God had asked him three months ago.

"Bring it on, Taj."

Oh, hell, yeah. Mother. Fucking. Perfect.

Hitching her onto his hip and with a quick pivot, she was turned and beneath him on the bed as he replied with one of her catchphrases, "It's on like Donkey Kong."

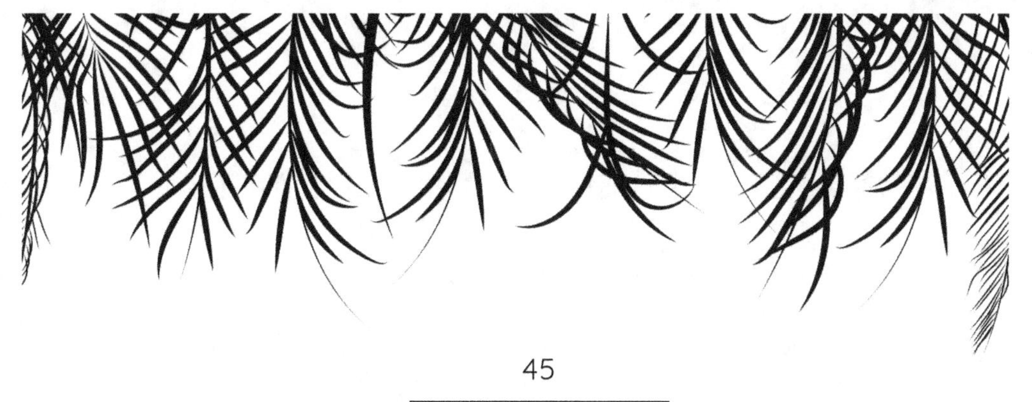

45

—————————

MAY 20TH-21ST

Kai

HO-LY *HELL, HORSESHOES, AND HAND GRENADES, HE'S not kidding!*

One hand was cradling her head, the other holding her leg tight to his hip, his weight pressing her down into the mattress, and his cock was making its presence clearly known. He made a noise that sounded like it might be a laugh.

"Oh, shit. I said something out loud again."

"You did. But I'm glad to know my dick has made a lasting impression on you." He bit her lower lip. "You compared me to the stud castle guard earlier. You just misunderstood, baby. I'm no guard. I'm the goddamn dragon."

And then he was on her again. She was so over-whelmed; his hands were everywhere, his mouth was everywhere, and she felt like she couldn't gather any air into her lungs.

"Taj!" she gasped. "Slow down." He reared his head back, and he started to let go of her as he began to move off of her, but she grabbed his wrist. She shook her head at him, her breath sawing in and out. "I didn't say 'stop.' I said, 'slow down.' I can't breathe."

His mouth turned up into a grin she'd seen only a few isolated times when they were working on the film. The one that made her blood boil. The one that made her feel like her skin was on fire. The one that made all her bodily fluids feel like they were rushing to her pussy because all other exits were blocked. "Slow down, hmmm?" He settled back into her body. His eyes locked onto hers. "I can totally do that," he murmured as his mouth came down onto hers, eyes open and holding her gaze. "Open for me, baby," he whispered against her lips.

Ever so gently, she felt the tip of his tongue. When she tried to curl her own around his, he retreated from her mouth, resorting to simply an openmouthed kiss. After a moment, he reattempted his entry and tender touch but retreated again when she tried to apply more pressure. He pulled back slightly, biting her bottom lip tenderly. "You said you wanted slow. So that's what you're getting. Be careful what you wish for." At her mewl of frustration, he trailed openmouthed kisses to the center of her throat, then down the front. His fingers worked agonizingly slow at sliding the long-sleeved tee up her body, gently exposing her breasts to him. The soft touch of the tip of his tongue along her centerline as he followed the path of her shirt, the tingling beginning between her thighs, and the rushing of her pulse all made Kai feel dizzy in a delicious way.

He smiled that carnal grin again and pressed a series of

soft kisses in the valley between her breasts. "Lift up, baby." She rose slightly off the bed, and he slid the material of her shirt over her shoulders and arms, leaving her upper half clad only in her bra, as he folded it ever so neatly and laid it on the bedside table.

Neat should be boring, not sexy. But wow, does it slow down the action and ratchet up the tension. Going to have to remember that for my next love scene.

Looking down at her, he complimented, "Very nice. Not pink, but very nice." With him tracing the tops of her mint and black plaid bra with a small charm at the center, she felt like the sexiest woman on the planet. So very much "good enough" for this gorgeous man.

He made her heart pound. She needed to get her hands on more of his skin. Yet, it was like her brain was misfiring because even though he was right there in her arms, she couldn't seem to do anything more than slide her hands under his Henley and hold onto his shoulders. He pulled the cups of her bra down, exposing her to the air, and when his tongue touched her flesh, it felt like it was curling around her entire nipple and managing to pull it further out from her body. Another gush of fluid felt as if it poured from inside of her with his latest tug at her breast, and she whimpered.

"Taj, please, I need to feel you against me." He removed his mouth from her nipple and sat up to pull his shirt off over his head. He folded it and laid it on top of her shirt. Then his mouth returned to her breast, where he blew on the tip. She shivered as her skin pebbled. The tip of his tongue dragged from the swell of her breast up past her clavicle, along the arch of her throat, and then pressed against the corner of hers. Resettling himself on top of her again, he absorbed the bulk of his weight by placing it on his forearms, his fingers brushing back stray hairs that clung to her flushed skin.

His forearms also served as leverage to grind and thrust his hips where she needed them. He lay his cheek next to hers, his lips right at the shell of her ear. "So perfect, baby. Gonna fuck you crazy."

She gasped, then whimpered, as his current thrust had his zipper grinding against her clit through the thin material of her leggings.

"I wanna feel those nails digging into my skin."

Kai's hands rose automatically to settle on his pecs, then curled in just enough so that as she dragged them down to his abs, he knew he'd see welts later. "Yes, baby," he groaned. "Just like that. Dig in. Just like you've marked my soul. So damn deep."

A moment later, he felt those same greedy hands working at his belt, undoing his buckle, unsnapping, unzipping, and diving into his pants. She stilled underneath his kisses, and her eyes went wide. "What's the matter, baby? Nothing you haven't seen or had inside you before."

"I think you've been feeding it way more than virgin sacrifices while you were away," she squeaked. "I need to see you."

"I'm right here, baby," he teased her as he pressed his mouth to her neck, biting slightly, then sucking her skin between his teeth.

"No, Taj, I mean, I want to see all of you."

He moved back from her neck and sat up and back on his heels on the bed, and she followed his movement, propping herself up on her elbows. Before she could sit up further, he put a hand out in a "stop" gesture. "Don't. Move." The order came low and with a hint of a growl. She stilled.

The caveman mentality was flooding back into his system. Slowly, he backed off the mattress, his eyes never breaking from hers as he finished undressing. "You want to see who's going to claim you?" Her eyes were still trapped in his gaze as his right boot went to the edge of the bed. Deliberately and efficiently, he undid the laces. "Wanna see who's going to fuck you until you scream his name?" Right boot to the floor, left boot to the edge of the bed, laces undone. Left boot removed as he put his foot down, then the right boot followed. He pulled off his socks, tucked them into his boots, then slowly put his hands on his opened belt. "I guess we better give baby what she wants." Next, he pulled the belt from the loops, coiling it around his hand, and gave it a light toss on top of his boots. "Brace, baby, because it's all for you." His hands went to the waist of his pants as he shucked them down his legs and stepped out of them to the edge of the bed. He folded them in half, then half again, and laid them on top of his belt.

Lying before him, her eyes were riveted on his cock that was standing straight up. She bit her lower lip, and her breathing sped up.

He smiled that wicked smile. "I guess you like what you see."

She nodded.

She sat up on the edge of the bed, her lips barely an inch away from his shaft. She placed her palms on the tops of his thighs, lightly sliding them upward over the cut of his hips, then up to his chest. "I love that you're bare. I wouldn't have thought a stud castle guard like you would be, all that male testosterone." She was trying to flirt, but it came out breathier and in awe. "You're beautiful. Like the statue of David." She blushed. "Well, not quite like David."

"Not quite," he agreed.

But while his skin was smooth all over, it had a definite texture. She re-traced and re-learned his scars. Some were only visual and did not change the landscape of his body. A couple of bullet hole pockmarks. Some shrapnel peppered on his shoulder that was mostly hidden by his Kraken tattoo. Others—the ones that had been deeper and more dangerous —were smooth, but they had ridges to them and, in some cases, an unnaturally smooth quality. Those were the more recent ones.

"Lie back, baby. I need to get back to you."

"But I..."

He gently nudged her shoulders back to the bed. "Plenty of time for me," he promised. He knelt on one knee on the edge of the bed and lifted her leg. "Slide up more, baby. I can feel the tension already. It's going to be a long night, and I can't have you getting cramps in these legs of yours." She pushed herself away from him on the bed as his hands grabbed her foot to remove her socks, and he startled. "Fuck me. They don't match."

"I wanted to see if I could get out of my head."

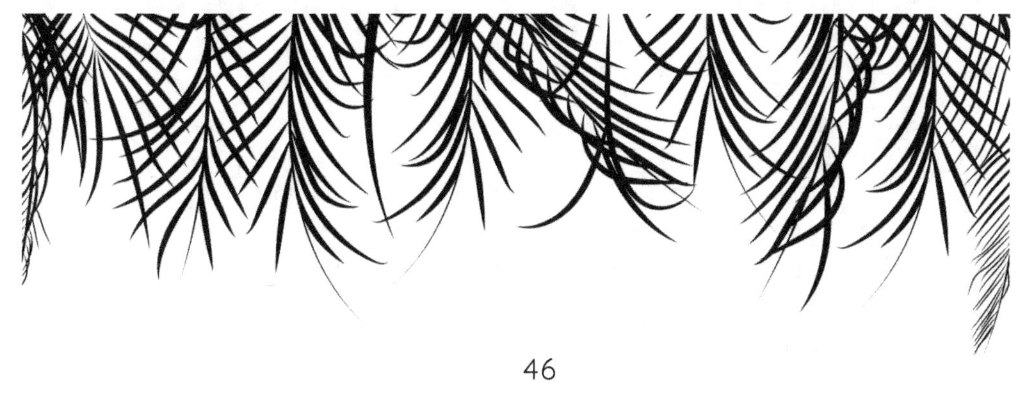

46

———

MAY 21ST

Waters

"Oh, baby," he whispered. "I can take care of that for you." He slid the sock from her foot and kissed the instep before placing her foot flat on his chest. His hands gently massaged her foot, then the calf, before gliding over and repeating the process with her other leg. "Miss those fucking boots. As soon as we can, you're wearing them, and we're leaving them on."

Kai giggled. "Then I guess you'll be fucking me from behind because you won't be able to get the leggings off if you don't take the boots off."

"Mmm. Now, there's a picture. Can just see you bent over my kitchen table. Leggings and panties bunched at the knees. Naked up top, my hands playing with your tits, sinking my teeth into your shoulder as I glide in and out of your pussy from behind." His eyes glittered. He lowered her leg, and his hands found the waist of her leggings. While

395

peeling them off her, his eyes were caught by her tattoo on the front of her right hip. A baby Kraken strangling a bleeding human heart being stabbed by a trident.

No. Fucking. Way.

"Babe." His voice was raw in his throat, the sound coming out graveled.

"I got it the day after we got home from Roatán. I hope you're not mad."

Hazel eyes looked up into hers. "It's..."

"I needed at least some small piece of you with me. On me."

He leaned down to kiss the tattoo as if it were sacred, then nuzzled it, eyes turning up to hers, burning with unshed tears. "This means everything to me, Kai. You are everything to me. You are so much more than good enough, Kai. In every way."

Pressing another kiss to the tribute, then trailing his finger across her bare pussy, his mouth watered at the scent of her arousal glistening there. "So wet already." He traced a finger along her seam and then brought it to his lips to suck her juices off it. A groan came forward. "Oh yeah, there's my sticky sweet." He drew his finger back and forth through her lips again, slow, teasing. "I think maybe... just maybe... instead of fucking that sweet pussy, I'll hold you up against the table with one arm, one fist full of a perfect tit, my other hand working this sweet pussy while my cock is claiming that sweet ass of yours."

Suddenly, she grabbed hold of his wrist and forced his hand down hard in place on her clit. He watched her eyes go glassy; she moaned, her back arched and her flesh pinked, and suddenly, his hand was flooded with more of Kai's honey. "Damn, woman. I barely touched you. Did you come just from me talking to you?" he whispered.

Kai closed her eyes and nodded, arching again as the final waves ebbed away.

Well, that's new.

"Has that happened before?"

She shook her head, eyes still closed. "Hell, no." She opened her eyes, the pupils blown out. "I had no clue dirty talk could be such a turn-on. It always seemed so fake when I'd hear people in movies try to do it. But when you do it? It makes me feel like everything inside is twisting in knots and bursting into flame. You've made it into an art form."

He felt something inside of him snap, and he kneeled on the floor at the edge of the bed, hooking both her legs under her thighs and putting them over his shoulders. "Gonna leave whisker burn on your thighs so that the friction leaves you with no chance to forget my mouth was on you. Gonna mark the insides of those thighs as mine. I'm going to eat this sweet pussy now. Gonna lick, suck, and nibble every inch. When you're good and worked up, I'm going to spear that cunt with my tongue and make you come in my mouth and all over my face. Want to hear you scream my name as you flood my mouth. Want you to soak my bed with your sweet honey, Kai. I want all of it."

"Jesus fucking Christ," she whispered, "do something, quick!"

He felt her tense again, so he quickly inserted two fingers inside her just in time for him to feel the squeezing of her walls. He felt the stranglehold her inner muscles had on him, felt her orgasm take over, and he crooked his fingers inside her. Instantly, her orgasm slicked his fingers and spread down his hand. His woman was something else.

"Open your eyes, sweetheart." She shook her head again.

This is going to be fun.

He removed his fingers and stood between her spread-open legs. "Open those eyes right now, Kai, or you're going to miss what I'm about to do."

Her eyes flew open. "You promised—"

His laugh was dark. "Eager now, aren't ya?" He pulled his soaked hand from inside her and brought it to his cock. He stroked her juices up and down, his eyes narrowing at the feel of his slickness. "So good. But I need more." His hand slid through her wetness again, gathering as much of it as he could, then bringing his wet hand back to his shaft, which had darkened almost red. "Had the best of intentions, babe. Wanted you to come all over my face, but that new trick of yours? I can't wait another minute to come. Gonna stroke myself off with your sweetness. You gonna watch me come?"

"Oh, God, yes!"

"You wanna know what I thought about all those nights I lay in this bed thinking of you and jerking off?"

Her breathing sped up again.

"Oh, yeah. My girl wants to hear. She wants to know that I'm picturing myself lying here, sleeping alone in my bed, naked except for the sheet.

"It's just past dawn, and the sun's starting to stream into my room. I wake up to your body sliding up mine until you're hovering over my cock. You're dressed in just one of your sexy long shirts, unbuttoned, bra, and no panties. Your boots with all those buckles are biting into my thighs as you straddle me. Then your warm, wet pussy slides down onto my cock.

"I come out of sleep all bleary to your hands with those short pink nails scoring my chest, using that grip to push yourself up and down, squeezing me tight. You're so slick and hot, it's like you have a fire burning inside you. And when you come, you throw your head back and let loose my name at the top of your lungs. All that sticky, sweet honey coats my cock and flows out onto my balls.

"That's what puts me over the edge, Kai," he groaned in both pain and pleasure. "I love that you can do that. That your honey just pours out of you. That I can make that happen." His breathing sped up, his voice becoming choppy as he neared orgasm. His eyes bored into hers. "Can't believe you're here in my bed. Never thought I'd get so lucky to claim you as mine." He gave a quick grunt. "I'm going to come on you, Kai. Do you want that?" His hand motions sped up as he gazed into her face. He could feel his release working its way from root to tip. "Here it comes, baby. Gonna paint you so pretty."

With the first rope of release that hit her skin, Kai's moan mingled with his. He watched her hand instinctively reach to her clit, and the heel pressed down while three of her fingers slid inside her already-soaked channel. He watched as her juices poured out of her again, as his hit her skin, particularly two of the trailing legs of her Kraken tattoo. The final jerks of his cock caused him to collapse onto his other arm, straight-locked at her hip, to keep him from falling down on her and crushing her.

When he finally managed to calm his breathing, he opened his eyes to the sight of one of Kai's wet fingers drawing patterns in his release on her belly, then slowly rising out of sight. His gaze snapped up to catch her sliding her soaked finger into her mouth.

She hummed with appreciation and closed her eyes in ecstasy. "Now I see why so many women love the combination of salt and sweet."

He growled, and his eyes narrowed in a predatory gaze. "You get three minutes."

Her eyes snapped open. "For what?"

His fingers, wet from his own release, painted her upper lip. "I'm going to go grab a warm washcloth, clean myself up, clean myself off of you, and then I'm going to do what I told you I was going to do before you distracted me." He shook his head in slow disbelief. "I just made you come four times, and I've barely touched you. You've exploded every time. I've never seen a woman go like that before. Good goddamn, woman, what's going to happen when I get my mouth on you or my dick inside you again?"

She gave him her own predatory smile, glancing down at his still-hard cock. "Make it two minutes, and after you get your dessert, I'll have mine."

He was back in one.

47

———

MAY 31ST

Kai

SHE WOKE TODAY THE WAY SHE'D WOKEN UP EVERY DAY for the last nine days. Waters moving over her, sliding between her legs and inside her body. Today was different, though. He didn't talk to her. He didn't watch her as he made love to her. This time, he had her gathered as close as he could get her, his face buried in her neck. She sensed something was bothering him, but she didn't want to distract him. She was afraid to ask.

Usually, he was all about multiple go-arounds, ramping her up, pulling her over the edge, then winding her back up over and over again until she passed out from exhaustion. But today, he was all about the slow and sweet. When he made her come, he was right behind her on the first wave. And he stopped. He turned onto his side, pulling her with him and grabbing her leg, keeping it over his hip, just laying with her, his head still buried in her neck. He didn't even

401

stroke her skin as he usually did. Instead, he held her tightly to him. Afraid to speak, she simply lay in his arms. He'd tell her what was wrong when he was ready and not before.

He sighed, and then she understood.

It's over. We're back to the real world.

It wasn't like she believed they were going to live out the rest of their lives like they had the last ten days. In fact, she should have known yesterday that this was coming. They were rarely apart longer than a few minutes at a time, but he had to take a phone call away from her, which he did upstairs behind the secured confines of the steel and bullet-proof glass, and he'd been quiet when he came downstairs almost an hour later.

"I love you, Kai." She smiled at his admission, even though she felt sad. The inflection of his voice was honest but painful. As if he was going to follow with something she wouldn't want to hear.

"I love you, too, Taj." She turned her head and kissed his hair. "When do we leave?"

He raised his head to look into her eyes. "We need to be on the road in half an hour."

She nodded and peeled herself from his body. Collecting her bag from the closet floor, she went into the bathroom and got into the shower. When she emerged from the bathroom fifteen minutes later, she saw that he was no longer in the room, and she could hear water running down the hall.

She glanced at the mussed bed. He truly was out of sorts. He never left the bed without making it, a holdover from his military days, even if he intended to have her back in it within the hour. Sadly, she smiled and left it unmade. A last piece of her for him when she didn't return because, despite his claims of the opposite, she didn't honestly believe a future for them was possible.

Downstairs, she gathered up the few personal items she had and stowed them in her bag, just in time to hear Taj come down the steps heavy-footed and buckling his watch.

Another oddity. He always moves like a cat, with no sound.

He pulled her into his arms, saying nothing, and just held her tight. They stayed like that until his text alert went off. Arms around his waist, she gazed up into his face as he smoothed back those stray hairs from her ponytail that he loved to try and tame into submission. Standing on tiptoe, she brushed her lips to his, nuzzled him with the tip of her nose, and then backed away to grab her bag.

He stood, watching her inscrutably, then turned to disarm the security system and open the door. TB was leaning on the hood of his truck. "G'day, boys and girls. Ready?"

"Morning, TB," Kai greeted him. "Ready." With that, she walked out the door toward Nemo, who held the rear passenger side door open for her into the back seat of the Humvee. Waters entered from the other side, Nemo hopped up into the front passenger seat, and TB took over behind the wheel.

Demon and Steel were getting into Steel's Avalanche and following behind.

Waters grabbed her hand, laced their fingers together, and placed it on his thigh.

No one said a word the entire drive to Tribe.

And what would anyone say anyway?

When they arrived in the underground parking garage of the office, TB and Nemo got out of the truck, closely followed into the elevator by Demon and Steel, but Waters made no move to get out. Kai looked at their fingers twined together, wishing she had something pithy to say, but nothing would come.

It was Waters who broke the silence. "He wants to see you."

Kai frowned. "Who?"

"God." His thumb stroked hers back and forth. "Yesterday, he said he wanted to see you first thing today when I brought you in."

"Why?"

Waters shrugged. "He didn't say."

"Okay. He's actually here? I thought he had a batcave somewhere or an Area 52."

Huffing a dark laugh, Waters shook his head. "No, he lives in the penthouse of the building."

"He's here? Then why the whole *Charlie's Angels* secrecy thing?"

He shrugged. "Don't know. We've learned not to ask questions."

It was then that Waters projected himself out of the back seat and came around to her side of the vehicle. She could see he was grinding his teeth, forcing whatever emotion he was feeling back down his throat. When they got to the elevator and she stepped inside, Waters did not get in with her. "Just be yourself, Kai." He lingeringly kissed her on the cheek, then stepped back and closed the elevator door on her.

The elevator moved almost immediately, smoothly, and quickly up toward the penthouse apartment. She placed a hand on her stomach, trying to quell her nerves.

As the car came to a stop, the voice coming from the speaker startled her. "No need to shake in your shoes, Kubrick. I don't bite."

Hand to her heart, she chided, "Please don't tell me I'm going to stand in this elevator to have this conversation with you. It's a bit like talking to the Wizard of Oz before Toto pulls back the curtain."

The elevator door opened onto a living space that was done in browns and golds, heavy on leather seating and cherry woods. She stood just inside the car, her head poking past the threshold.

"Hello?"

"I'm on the patio, Kubrick!" God called impatiently.

Tentatively, she stepped out of the car, the doors closing immediately behind her. When she turned to look, it was like the elevator doors didn't exist, they blended into the walls so seamlessly. Slowly, she walked through the living space, noticing that despite the dark furniture, the room appeared light. Parquet flooring and the gold accents on all the furniture reflected the sun pouring in through the large skylight over the living room. Continuing through the space, she approached an open sliding door that led out onto a large wooden patio framed in green plants. A hot tub was embedded in the far-left corner, which connected to another room in the penthouse. Framed by a pergola covered in ivy, the view to it was blocked to anyone who might be outside its walls.

Not that you could see anyone without being in a plane, anyway. Too freaking high for me!

"Thank you for joining me, Kubrick."

The voice came from her right, and she turned to an unexpected sight. Sitting in a dark brown high-backed wicker chair with gold cushions, a movie-star quality man in his mid-forties sat facing her, his forearms resting on the chair arms. A linen suit coat hung over the back of the chair. He wore a white dress shirt and sky-blue tie; his hair was dark blond, cut short, and parted over his left eye. His eyes were a lively green and while he wasn't smiling, one corner of his mouth ticked up in a sort of smirk, like he was enjoying her discomfort.

"Sit. Cherry is just bringing breakfast."

"Well, I'm really not—"

"I don't recall phrasing it as a question."

Wow. He's as bossy as before, but otherwise, totally not what I pictured.

Kai sat across from God, unfolding the linen napkin into her lap. Cherry appeared suddenly to her right, placing a plate in front of her. Three fluffy pancakes, chock full of chocolate chips, drizzled with chocolate sauce, real whipped cream, and raspberry garnished on top.

Kai looked at God, one eyebrow raised. "Someone's done their homework. Is this why Waters didn't feed me this morning?"

"Told him you were having breakfast with me and wanted to know what you actually ate. Some of what he told me was appalling. This seemed safest, but he said despite the crap content, the sexiest thing he's ever seen you do is eat."

"I'm not sure whether to be insulted or turned on that eating is my sexiest feature." She took her first bite of the pancakes, and her eyes rolled back in her head.

God stared. "I didn't believe him yesterday when I talked to him, but he was right.

Kai opened her eyes to dive into another bite. "Right about what?"

"That watching you eat is sexy as fuck." He snorted and shook his head.

Kai stopped mid-bite, the fork still in her mouth, lips wrapped around it.

These men are so weird.

She dragged the fork from between her lips, desperately working to keep from acting like a total heathen and licking the chocolate sauce left behind on the tines. She almost didn't succeed. "Dare I ask why?" she questioned after she was done chewing.

"We're in L.A., Kubrick. Women subsist on kale, water, and somehow air. I've rarely seen any of them eat. And when they do, it is not with the abandon and enjoyment that causes moaning. Food orgasms, indeed."

"I did not moan," she whispered.

"I'm afraid you did. He warned me you would. He also warned me about your filter that causes you to say things out loud that you shouldn't. No wonder he couldn't resist. I'm actually a little jealous."

"How embarrassing." She blushed and began to set her fork down.

"Don't you dare, Kubrick," God growled. "Eat. I prefer women who enjoy things. Then we need to talk."

Breakfast was quiet, but not nearly as scary as she had thought it would be. By the last bite, her bravado had reined in, and her curiosity was going full throttle.

"So," she began, "why am I really here? I know it truly wasn't to watch me eat."

God sat back in his chair, dabbing his face with the napkin to catch any stray food crumbs or chocolate sauce. "I wanted to let you know that your producer has gone missing. It was quite the mystery for three or four days." His inflection was deceptively light, like he had no clue himself what had happened. "Eventually, the authorities discovered that a large number of his personal items were missing, as well. And a Mr. Kowalski informed the police that a large amount of studio funds is also gone. A string of airline tickets, paid for in cash and under a variety of names, has led the local authorities to believe he has absconded with his embezzled funds to South America. Of course, they've been unable to catch him on any security cameras or other means.

"They'll continue to watch for a while, but eventually, something bigger will come along, and he'll be long forgotten," he reassured her. "Probably sooner rather than later. You know Hollywood and its scandals."

There was a pregnant pause as they studied each other.

"I owe you a thank you. For not turning me over to the police and for helping him escape, so to speak."

He waved her thanks aside. "He deserved worse. The guy was a total fuckwitch."

Kai smiled.

"However, more importantly than giving you that news, I wanted to see you up close and personal. I'm good, but despite my reputation, there are a few things that I can't tell through a computer screen. Normally, that's when Waters comes in handy, but he's not exactly unbiased in this instance. Besides, this is a little more personal."

"And what would that be?"

He waited, probably trying to make her squirm. When it didn't work, the napkin in his hand was laid down on the table, and he continued. Elbows on the table, fingers threaded together into a single fist on the table's surface, he declared, "I wanted to make sure that the woman who's causing me to lose my best operative is worth that loss. It puts me back immeasurably if it ends up being a mistake. He's already damaged goods after working with you, but I can't afford for him to become irreparably damaged to where he is no longer useful to me."

Kai stared into God's green cat eyes and stiffened her

spine. She could feel the anger pulling up from the soles of her feet to the top of her head. "Taj is not damaged," she spat at him. "He's worth more to you than any of the other men just by breathing. How much more will you ask him to give up to make your balance sheet come out in the positive? What is so fucking important to you about him?"

God glowered at her, and he leaned in, hands on the table. "Loyalty, Kubrick. Absolute loyalty. He is, in this world, the right hand of God. By declaring himself to you, his loyalty is now divided." He leaned back in his chair. "Fuck that, he's loyal to you first, which makes him compromised. If he is compromised, his team becomes compromised, which in turn means I'm compromised. Our tribe is everything, and I can't just let him throw that all away over Hollywood pussy."

"You bastard!" she hissed, shoving herself up and away from the table. "I am done dealing with men like you. Men like Stapleton who think just because they have a dick and deep pockets, they can bully people to do their bidding. Tired of being treated like I'm somebody's toy. Tired of having to defend every woman who comes into contact with men like you who think that two X chromosomes mean the bearer is weak and controlled by her estrogen levels.

"I didn't ask Waters to leave the field. If he chose to do that, then he did it without telling me or even discussing it, which is a conversation he and I will be having later when I have room to kick him in the solar plexus. That shit does not fly with me. That decision affects us both.

"And as for loyalty, Taj gives it in spades. His first thought is always to others. Where is *your* loyalty to *him*?"

God had watched her entire tirade impassively. He shifted in his seat, one forearm resting on the chair's arm, the opposite hand gripping the other arm of his chair. "Are you finished?"

She was so angry she didn't trust herself to say more.

"Sit down, Kubrick."

She glared at him. Despite wanting to storm away, she did.

"My loyalty, Ms. Serrano, is *always* to Taylor Miller. I could have left him for dead in Egypt two years ago. Has he told you what happened?"

"Yes. He told me while at the cabin." She'd been horrified at what had happened to Taj's sister. Despaired at the decision he'd had to make to go after her alone after God had denied him support. Appalled at what that decision had cost him, mentally and physically. He hadn't wanted to tell her, but he chose to do it so she would understand why he had let himself push her away rather than fight for her. And she couldn't blame him for it.

God continued, "I know you feel that my loyalty to Waters is hypocritical based on his sister's situation."

"How could you not support him? I'm trying not to judge because I only know a small piece of the puzzle."

"Understand this, Kubrick. I would do anything for the tribe except put them in a no-win situation. Sarah Miller was a no-win situation. Everyone, including Sarah herself, knew it.

"When she was taken, it was not to sell her into sexual slavery. She was a pawn to be sacrificed to get straight at Waters for interfering in these traffickers' pipeline. Yes, she was brutalized. Yes, she was raped. Yes, Waters was forced to endure it in person while it happened. But know this. She would have died that way, no matter what. No matter how long it would have taken, she would have been held in captivity until Waters was secured so that he could witness her death.

"So while it killed me to say no, I did because I knew that it would cause me to lose not just Sarah, but Waters and potentially the other five as well. Had Waters not gone off in a heated rush, she would have lived. Not happily, not comfortably, and maybe not safely. But she would have lived, and hopefully, we would have found a better route to get to her in the future." His voice changed to something broken with his next statement. "It was never my intention to leave her there permanently."

He looked off into the empty sky as he spoke. "Did you know that he advised another family whose daughter was taken in retribution for an act of theirs of the exact same thing? That's the cruel irony of the whole situation. He analyzed a similar situation, presented the scenario to the family, and denied the job. Said that it had less than a one percent chance of succeeding. That more information was needed. We wouldn't give up. We would watch and wait for a better opportunity. They should trust us to update them when it was a viable situation to go in for a rescue. It was not prudent, even for my ridiculously skilled team, to go running off to Egypt to rescue the girl *at that time.*"

"What happened?" Kai asked, although she was pretty sure she knew the answer.

"The family stormed out. Found another group of mercenaries who were willing to take the job. Waters even tried to warn the men off by handing over our intel. Not a professional courtesy, but because he was convinced that going after the girl then was suicide. Turned out he was one hundred percent accurate. The mercenaries were captured, they were killed, and they were returned home to their boss in a box. In very small pieces."

"And the girl?"

"No idea. Then Sarah was taken in retribution for a different reclamation assignment that Waters executed. Despite being the same intel he had gathered on the original girl, despite my direct orders not to do it, he went after Sarah anyway. If he hadn't had a tracker inside him, we would have had no idea where to look for him.

"So we plotted and planned. For two months. He suffered being tortured, watching her assaults, knowing no one was coming to get them, for two long, hopeless months. I knew that if I sent the team in to get them, the odds were zero that I would get all seven of them out of there alive. They thought that if they could free Sarah, whatever happened to the rest of them was fine. That Waters would feel the same. So, knowing it was a suicide mission, those five men he leads went after their boss and their teammate, but this time with my blessing."

"Does he know?"

"About the mercenaries and the girl? Now, yes." He turned his angry glare onto her, but somehow, she knew he wasn't angry at her. "I am so loyal to Waters that I am willing to let him change his paradigm with me. But I had to know that anyone he was willing to fight me for would also fight for him. Even if the odds were zero percent."

Kai stared at God. "The rule."

He nodded. "The rule."

Another fucking test.

"Yes, it is a test."

She grimaced.

"And there's the unintentional speaking." He grinned briefly. "It's for all of them. I'm not a monster, Kubrick. No one should go through life alone. But if they're going to get involved with someone, romantically or otherwise, the consequences can be astronomical for all of the team. Therefore, it had better be someone whom it's worth breaking the rule for. No one leaves the tribe. Because to be let go from the tribe means to be let go from this world. And not just digitally erased."

The weight of God's words lay heavily on her heart. "I'm not worth that."

"He feels differently. And the fact that every single one of his team would throw down for you and him should tell you that you *are* worth it. Especially Demon, whose damage goes so deep, I don't know that he can ever redeem himself. But mark my words, if any of them felt you were less than worth it, they would let him know. None of those men are shy about sharing their opinions."

"I don't want him to give up what he loves. He loves this job. If this is it, then he should do it."

"I'm losing the operative, Kubrick, not the man. He'll continue on as he has been this past year. He has a true talent for the work. He's a fantastic operative, but he's an even better analyst, which I knew he would be one day, and why I recruited him to begin with. He just needed time to mature from the hothead that he was. And now that he's found someone to stand beside him, he's an even better man. Or, at the very least, he's found someone to kick his ass to make sure he stays that way." He glared at her. "Take care of him, Kubrick."

Kai stood shakily from the table and began to cross to the elevator. It was when she got level with his office that she stopped flat-footed. On her way in, the partially open door had been in such a position that she couldn't see inside. Now, coming from the opposite direction, she could. Her curiosity got the better of her, so she walked to the threshold and gently eased the office door open further.

Without realizing she had done so, she stepped into the center of the room and turned three hundred and sixty degrees, finding herself closed in by walls covered in framed movie poster prints. *The Shining. A Clockwork Orange. Paths of Glory. Lolita.* More. They appeared to run completely around the room like a fence line.

When she was facing the doorway, it was to see him following her with the help of a wheelchair.

"I wondered why 'Kubrick' for my name. A bit of a fanboy?" she teased.

His gaze locked with hers, and she saw respect within. "Because from the very first, you reminded me of his story. You carry so many of his traits. Self-taught. No patterns to your work in terms of content. You allow your actors to create and be a part of the birthing and aging of the film. You plan meticulously, but you also are willing to recognize when something doesn't work, that the plan can be improvised upon successfully. But most important? You refuse to sacrifice art for art's sake."

"That's how you run your team."

"I allow them to run by themselves. Like you, I merely facilitate. Just like you do with your actors. You and I are not so different."

She bowed her head at him. "Thank you."

"For what?"

"For looking out for me. For rescuing my brother's wife and son. For continuing to look for my brother. For gifting me Taj."

"Thank you for recognizing that he is, in fact, a gift. But don't thank me until your brother is home, safe and sound, to be with his wife and child." He scowled. "Go to Taylor, Kai. Kick his ass for not discussing his choice with you, then kiss and make up. And tell him that I don't want to see him for at least four weeks."

With a grin, she replied, "You know he won't listen."

"No, he's stubborn. He's already planning to be back in two weeks. That is when I really want him back anyway. And then he'll say fuck it and stay out six weeks just to be an assclown." He winked. "I know how to work my people."

"Can I ask another question?"

"I believe you just did." She rolled her eyes and stuck her tongue out at him. His eyebrow arched. "I'd quote his rule six to you, but I'd run the risk of death for speaking about your tongue. What's your question?"

"Why do they call you God?"

"Ah." He gave a single nod of understanding, then shrugged. "Because I'm a faceless voice in the cloud. I rule all when it comes to Tribe, my creation. Because, unfortunately, sometimes I decide who lives and who dies."

She thought about the missing girl.

About Sarah.

About Waters.

About her.

"They've never seen you, have they?"

"Only Cherry."

"And now me."

"And now you."

"Why? Why me?"

"Every once in a while, there are certain people that I need to speak with instead of to. Like my namesake."

She nodded in return. "Thank you for not setting something on fire to do it," she joked. She leaned down and kissed his cheek. "Your secrets are safe with me. Always." And then she turned and left.

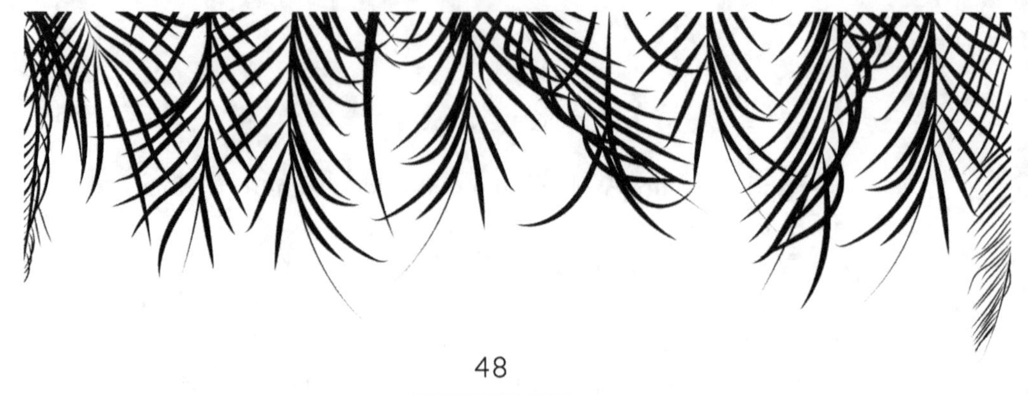

48

MAY 31ST

Waters

THE ENTIRE TEAM WAS HANGING OUT AROUND MIDAS' desk. The tension was nearly unbearable.

TB was throwing knives at a poster of Sheikh Ahmed Yassin.

Midas was running eight million coded programs on what felt like the same number of monitors and playing Tetris on an old Gameboy from the eighties.

Nemo was scrolling through his phone, blowing bubbles, and cracking his gum.

Steel was sitting next to him on the couch, leafing through the reports on Ka-Bar. Without looking at the man, Steel took his pencil and popped a particularly large bubble, causing it to splat all over Nemo's face.

Nemo nonchalantly pulled the gum off his face and put it back in his mouth.

Demon had his sunglasses on and was tipped back in his chair, feet up on the table, dead asleep.

Waters was standing in front of one of the wall monitors, staring at the screen, seeing nothing.

A soft knock came at the door, and then it opened to reveal Cherry, who ushered Kai into the room.

Everything in the room stopped, all eyes pinging between the couple, and nobody breathed.

Kai stopped five feet from the desk, put her hands to her hips, her gaze narrowing. "Is there something you forgot to tell me, Mister Miller?"

Nemo guffawed. "Dude, you are so busted."

Waters walked slowly to Kai until he came within inches of her mouth. "I'm sorry. It was the only condition he gave me for my proposal of non-operative status. And even then, he didn't say yes. It was dependent on his meeting with you." Waters put his hands on her hips and lowered his forehead to hers. "I've been sick to my stomach, no clue what he was going to say to you. Are you okay?" he whispered.

She smoothed her hands up his biceps and nodded, her forehead not breaking contact with his. "I'm fine. He shook the heavens a little, but I was myself, so I guess I'm in his good book." They both laughed at her analogy.

Nemo spoke up from behind Waters. "So, what does he look like? Spill it."

She looked at Cherry, who smiled at her from her place in the doorway. With a chin lift worthy of a Navy SEAL, the confirmation of a promise was sent via silent communication. Kai looked to Nemo and, with a completely deadpan expression, said, "Exactly what you think a deity looks like."

The men groaned.

Kai noticed the whiteboard behind Midas and shook her head with her own groan. "I'm glad I provided you all with so much amusement."

She swore she heard Waters murmur, "You have no fucking idea," but she wasn't quite sure.

Midas put his hand over his heart. "Aw, Kubrick, you made my life on a daily basis with your Kubrickisms. Our office hasn't been the same since."

She glanced at Waters. "Do they speak Kubrick now, too?"

He put his arms around her waist and pulled her close. "Not fluently. Just enough to get by."

"Mmm," was all she said, glancing at the full board, her swear words, and all the hash marks behind each one. Then, her focus went back to Taj. "God said he doesn't want to see you for four more weeks. Apparently, it's going to take you that long to recover from me kicking your ass over not including me in decisions."

Taj snorted. "I'll suffer the ass-kicking. Besides, he knows I would normally be back in half that. Just to fuck with him, I'm taking six."

Kubrick let out a full, loud laugh.

I don't know what's so damn funny, but I love it when she laughs.

He pulled her tight and kissed her crazy, right in front of everyone.

"Let's go home. I just realized I forgot to make the bed."

ACKNOWLEDGMENTS

This first time around will be long. I apologize! No one ever tells you how difficult it is to write a book. You know, loosely, that there will be writer's block. But there's also befuddlement when the characters begin improvising, panic when you can't figure out how to transition from one scene to the next, and bewilderment when you've typed "The End"... and have no idea where or what to do next. Then begins the house of horrors of the actual publishing process for the first time, and that can be paralyzing. Through all of that, there are endless people who assisted me in order to keep me inspired, motivated, and focused. These are those people.

Angela Knight – You are a goddess! Your "Burning Ink" class on Savvy Authors' website in 2020 was the genesis of this novel and all the chaos that has ensued since. I hardly noticed I was in the midst of a pandemic because I was so busy writing. This book does NOT exist without discovering the Mageverse and your course on writing romance.

Cabe McKinley – Thank you for saying "Yes" when I invited you to my Accountability Group. If it weren't for your butt-kicking shoes when I became too scared to move forward with publishing, I never would have sent that editing inquiry in and made this happen. (And thanks for the blurb help!) You are an amazing sprint buddy–always encouraging, whether I was stuck with a block or just plain stuck in my own head. I'm so thrilled to have you as a friend.

PJ Fiala, Kennedy L. Mitchell, Caitlyn O'Leary – Thank you for your generosity in giving up time to talk with me about author "things" and your overall encouragement. Your books have inspired me.

Dani M and Rachel H – You are the chaos to my mayhem. I "heart" you. (How many days left?) Thank you for a metaphorical place to jump up and down, squee-ing in celebration of all the moments.

Writers on the Storm – You made the summer of 2023 one of the most focused and productive of my life. Whether it was writing, editing, or other general administrative work, the fifty-on/ten-off timeframe gave me a structure I so desperately needed. (And those ten-minute offs were where I learned so much and laughed so hard.)

Mom & Dad – Did you ever think you'd see the day the Polish Princess would be an author? Thank you for everything you've done for me. Even the stuff I may not have liked or understood at the time. Thank you for forgiving my screw-ups, big and small, and for loving me anyway. Thank you for encouraging my reading when I was young, including endless trips to the library, and "Just five more minutes?" before lights out at bedtime to read a few more pages. And thank you for always pushing me to try harder, do better.

SJ Higgins, Stef White, Vanessa Esquibel, Kelly Finley, and Kat Wyeth – You took a petrified first-time author and built her into a confident hot mess, rather than an ordinary hot mess! You addressed my fears with sensitivity; you built my confidence by recognizing the things I loved most about my work without me having to tell you what they were; you were honest and forthright without being cruel. I never expected the encouragement I received, and it always felt genuine. I was warned it might take a while to find editors that were the right fit. I struck gold on the first try.

Mistress Mandy & Little Nate – The laughs. The tequila. The tropical storm. The birthday shenanigans: unicorns, and dinosaurs, and kittens, oh my! Your friendship. Never telling me to shut up when I'd give you all the info on this book. I love you both.

Nicole Craig's Tribe – Thank you for being a part of my reader group. We are small, but we are tribe.

My ARC Tribe – Thank you for taking some of your valuable time to read and review my novel. I know it's not an easy job. I appreciate your honest reviews.

To Anyone Who Reads This Book – Thank you. I hope you fall in love with Kai and Waters as much as I have.

Ebook ISBN: 979-8-9892144-0-2

Paperback ISBN: 979-8-9892144-1-9

ASIN: B0CJFSW6LZ

Developmental Editing by Sara-Jane Higgins (Kat's Literary Services)

Editing by Steph White (Kat's Literary Services)

Proofreading by Vanessa Esquibel (Kat's Literary Services)

Internal Formatting by Kelly Finley (Kat's Literary Services)

Cover Design by Deranged Doctor Design www.derangeddoctordesign.com

Nicole Craig

Visit my website at https://nicolecraigauthor.godaddysites.com/

Join my Reader's Group at https://www.facebook.com/groups/362438775117 0522

Printed in the United States of America

First Printing: January 2024

ABOUT THE AUTHOR

Nicole Craig lives in Southeastern Wisconsin with her husband and three furry children. She began writing in her teens in Creative Writing class and into her years at college, but it wasn't until the COVID-19 pandemic that she actually decided to get published. After taking an online class on how to write romance novels with Angela Knight, Nicole's personal Frankenstein monster was born.

Three-and-a-half years later, it's now on Amazon.

Please consider leaving a review on Amazon or GoodReads. It's one of the best ways to thank a writer (besides buying their books!) for the work they've done.

Check out her Facebook Reader Group or any of her social media links to get the latest updates on The Deadman's Tribe series or other upcoming projects.

Facebook Reader Group: Nicole Craig's Tribe

Website: https://nicolecraigauthor.godaddysites.com/

instagram.com/nicolecraigauthor

tiktok.com/@nicolecraigauthor

Interested in reading more about The Deadman's Tribe? Want to know if they're ever going to find Ka-Bar?

TB's story, **Bad Enough**, is up next on August 18th, 2024.

He's got NO clue what's coming for him–all 5'o nothing and sugar sweet. How the mighty will fall... Good Girl + Bad Boy = TROUBLE